MW00644106

LUCY
OF THE TRAIL
OF TEARS

Novels by James D. Yoder

The Yoder Outsiders

Sarah of the Border Wars

Barbara: Sarah's Legacy

Song in a Nazi Night

*(Published in hardback and large print as **Black Spider Over Tiegenhof**)*

Lucy of the Trail of Tears

A Branson Love

Simone: A Saint for Outsiders

Echoes Along the Sweetbrier

Mudball Sam

LUCY
OF THE TRAIL
OF TEARS

Survivor of the Trail -
Oklahoma Seminary girl,
and Andrew's Wichita Bride

James D. Yoder

Copyright © 1999, 2006 by James D. Yoder

All rights reserved. No part of this book shall be reproduced or transmitted in any form or by any means, electronic, mechanical, magnetic, photographic including photocopying, recording or by any information storage and retrieval system, without prior written permission of the publisher. No patent liability is assumed with respect to the use of the information contained herein. Although every precaution has been taken in the preparation of this book, the publisher and author assume no responsibility for errors or omissions. Neither is any liability assumed for damages resulting from the use of the information contained herein.

This is a work of fiction. Names, characters, places, and incidents either are the product of the author's imagination or are used fictitiously. Any resemblance to actual events or locales or persons, living or dead, is entirely coincidental.

ISBN 0-7414-3329-X

Library of Congress Number: 99-91894

Published by:

INFINITY
PUBLISHING.COM

1094 New DeHaven Street, Suite 100
West Conshohocken, PA 19428-2713
Info@buybooksontheweb.com
www.buybooksontheweb.com
Toll-free (877) BUY BOOK
Local Phone (610) 941-9999
Fax (610) 941-9959

Printed in the United States of America

Printed on Recycled Paper

Published May 2006

TO MY SECOND GRADE TEACHER AT CLEARFORK
SCHOOL IN MISSOURI, MISS LOIS HARTZLER.

A
NOTE FROM
THE AUTHOR

I am indebted to Jon Roe of the *Wichita Eagle* for his article featuring Cherokee Lucy Greenway, who came to Wichita, Kansas, in the 1860s. Jon's account directed me to Al Witherspoon, archivist at the First Presbyterian Church of Wichita, who shared materials regarding Lucy's early life in Wichita and when she was chosen to be one of the 13 charter members of the church in 1870.

In addition, Al gave me tours of Wichita's Old Town and showed me river sites as well as other locations necessary for settings in this story, including Lucy Greenway's grave site in the Highland Cemetery.

Major works providing background material included John Ehle's *Trail of Tears*, Doubleday: New York, 1988; Grant Foreman's *Indian Removal*, University of Oklahoma Press: Norman, 1980; Leon Fouquet's *Hurrah for My Free Country*, University of Oklahoma Press: Norman, 1990; Maggie C. Fry's *Cherokee Female Seminary Years*, Rogers College Press: Claremore, Oklahoma, 1988; Wilfred Knight's *Red Fox*, The Arthur H. Clark Company: Glendale, California, 1988; Wilma Mankiller's and Michael Wallis's *Mankiller*, St. Martin's Press: New York, 1993; Thomas E. Mails' *The Cherokee People*, Council Oak Books; Tulsa, Oklahoma, 1992; Devon Mihesuah's *Cultivating the Rosebuds*, University of Illinois Press: Urbana, 1993; Craig Miner's *Wichita: The Early Years*, University of Nebraska Press: Lincoln, 1982; and Ronald Wright's *Stolen Continents*, Houghton Mifflin Company: New York, 1992.

I am indebted to Delores Sumner, Assistant Professor of Library Science, Special Collection, Northeastern State University, Tahlequah, Oklahoma, for her and her staff's assistance during my research there.

Many other articles, old pamphlets, and unpublished papers also provided insight and background information. These are too numerous to mention.

In addition, I conducted research at the Cherokee National Historical Building near Tahlequah, the Wichita Public Library and the Wichita State University Library. My study included perusal of newspapers, such as the *Cherokee Advocate*, the *Vidette* and the *Beacon*, early newspapers in the Cherokee Nation, and in Wichita, Kansas.

Though many names appearing in my book are actual historical names, the story is fiction, built around the Trail of Tears experience of the Cherokee people.

Since Lucy Greenway was chosen to be a member of Wichita's First Presbyterian Church in 1870, it seemed to me she had to be not only a remarkable woman, but also an educated woman. Thus, I chose to begin the story with Lucy and her mother as emigrants on the Trail of Tears. Records indicate that Lucy married Wichita trader Andrew Greenway. Andrew operated a ferry on the Arkansas River. Later, a Wichita street was named after the Greenways.

I have tried to build the story on an accurate historical framework, bringing the family to the Indian Nation in Oklahoma in 1839. The Cherokee Nation built both male and female seminaries for their youth. Graduates returned to eastern colleges to complete their education. Discovering this, I was able to develop the story of Lucy as a seminary student who received classical education.

I hope my story captivates readers and is a fitting tribute to Lucy Greenway, whose desire to be a member of the church must have been very strong. I am convinced that Lucy's life was an inspiration to many, even though she was called upon to live in such heartbreaking times.

I give special thanks to my wife, Lonabelle, for the first reading of the manuscript, to Mary Rempel for copy editing, to artist Susan Bartel for the cover painting, and to my novelist friends, Bernell Baldwin and Orville Voth, who critiqued some of the chapters,

James D. Yoder

CHAPTER ONE

A bright-eyed child in a violet calico dress bounced over the threshold of the cabin door. "Father, Mother, the *Cherokee Phoenix,* fresh off the printing press." Eight-year-old Lucy Drake burst into the sunlit room filled with the aroma of her mother Abby's bean bread, baking on the hearth.

"Off the press so early?" Abby reached to take Lucy's school books and lay them on the edge of the hand-hewn oak table.

"And Mother, Mr. Boudinet said Father should read it right away." The dark-eyed child smiled.

Benjamin reached for the newspaper. It rustled as he shook it open to study the black headline: "Loss of Tribal Homelands," followed by the words: " . . .forced removal ordered by President Van Buren—to be carried out by General Winfield Scott and his soldiers . . . ."

Lucy stared at her father's face as he dropped the paper and sagged to a bentwood chair made by his own hands, eyes transfixed in shock and grief. He stood, dug his hands into his pockets to hide their trembling. "I'll have to race over to Spring Place and tell Mother Drake, and Aunt Rachel, Abby. General Scott's broom sweeps swift and clean like the great winds that shredded the hemlocks on the Hiwassee."

Abby, face drawn, straightened her shoulders and drew Lucy to her side. Her bosom lifted as she sucked in the mountain air laced with the smells of spring water and sweet balsam.

For a moment, Abby glanced through the window to the giant hemlocks and clustered cabins. Her eyes caught on the billowing clouds sweeping across the tops of the Great Smokies. Wispy tendrils drifted near the crowns of towering oaks. Her fine-boned face turned to her husband, Benjamin. "How can the government force us out after our braves saved President Jackson's life at Horseshoe Bend?" Her pokeberry-dyed homespun skirt swished as she stepped over to the hearth to stir the coals for the bread.

"They're like the weather in our mountains, Abby, ever-changing—from one week to the next. President Van Buren may enforce the treaty." Benjamin glanced up at their framed marriage certificate, and Abby's baptismal certificate issued by the Mission. His chin sank to his chest, betraying the ache gnawing his soul. "I signed the treaty for the sale of our homelands, Abby—the removal treaty." His voice dropped. "I thought that by doing so, it would save our lives."

Abby wiped her hands on her blue apron and stared into his dark brown eyes. "You followed your conscience, Benjamin. There are good arguments for taking the money and moving to the Oklahoma lands, though God knows when it will happen, or how many of The People will survive such a journey."

"May be I should have supported you, and Chief Ross. You admire him so. He made several trips to Washington pleading our cause."

"In our nation, husband, we're free to cast our votes without judgment. Your signature was honorable. You were weary of broken promises and—"

"Chief Hick's words still ring in my ears: ' . . .as long as the mountains and rivers shall last, or the sun shine.'" Benjamin stepped over to Abby and brushed her flour-stained cheek with a kiss. Then he vanished through the door on his way to Spring Place to warn Mother Drake and Aunt Rachel.

*　*　*

Already the sun had risen, the air hot and humid. How had it all happened so quickly? Abby struggled, her shoes rubbing blisters on her heels as they plodded on the hard-packed trail.

"Mother, the soldier said that a wagon would bring some of our belongings. Do you think they will put in our blue willow plates?" Lucy's hand swept back a fallen strand of hair.

"No, my child, we cannot hope for that. But we will need our winter wraps. The wind may blow cold in the new land. We must trust God." Trust God? How? Already they were weary and Gunter's Landing still a day's journey away. Abby could hear murmuring rising behind her—sounds similar to that of a frightened animal moaning for the comforting walls of a familiar cave.

Lucy reached for her mother's hot hand and held on. "Mother, they said there'd be a shelter tonight beside the Tennessee River. And boats, big boats to carry us all to the new lands." Lucy tried to steady her voice in spite of the grief twisting her heart over watching the government buildings in her beloved New Echota town go up in flames. "After all, Mother, the soldiers said the government would pay all of us for anything we had to leave behind."

That night Abby and Lucy slept fitfully on the ground inside the rude bark-and-plank shelter hastily thrown up by government recruits. They could hear the roar of the Tennessee River on the other side of the plank wall. Tomorrow, the head sergeant had told them, they would be routed out and forced at gunpoint up gangplanks onto the keelboats. The wail of a steamboat shredded their spirits. "We will endure, my child," Abby said, clasping Lucy's hand." In her mind, the words circled without ceasing. Benjamin, my loving husband. Where is Benjamin? He will surely join us at one of the landings on the Tennessee, won't he?

*   *   *

"Mother, will we ever see Father again?" Lucy echoed her mother's thoughts as she reached for a hold on the rail when the keelboat heaved in the boiling Tennessee River. Abby attempted to grab Lucy, but the keelboat rocked and she was thrown into the side of an old Cherokee in buckskins who closed his eyes and murmured ancient prayers.

"Brace yourselves," a soldier recruit yelled to the solemn horde of The People who were packed like lengths of cordwood.

Lucy clutched her mother's arm with one hand as she again grasped for the railing of the 130-foot keelboat with the other. Her worried eyes scanned the two-deck boat, last in the flotilla of six pulled by the steamer, *Maybelle*, as it whipped like the tail of a coachwhip snake. "For God's sake, hold on," the young soldier yelled, his back braced against the wall.

Lucy shivered. At the vortex of the whirlpool called The Suck, the angry waters heaved the keelboat against a rock as if it were a withered oak leaf and catapulted Lucy, her mother, and two others over the rail. Lucy landed on the edge of a plowed garden. Abby, though, had less good fortune. Her head struck the sharp edge of a rock. A trickle of blood coursed from her forehead down her classic face. Lucy, shaken and bewildered, tried to focus her eyes upon a small group of village women who dropped their milk buckets and lumbered toward them.

The woman in faded calico lifted Abby's head and held it in her lap, as a stout milkmaid in blue-dyed homespun reached for Lucy, whose wet, black hair hung on the sides of her face. "Oh, Jesus, save them. Are you all right, my child?" the woman cried as she stroked Lucy's forehead. When she recognized that she had suffered no serious harm, she dropped Lucy's arm and the silent child crawled toward her mother. Though her heart quaked, Lucy struggled to keep the fear in her breast and not allow it to show on her face. Her small fingers closed around her mother's limp hand.

The government appointed doctor, who'd managed to climb down the makeshift gangplank to the rocks, ambled over. "I'm Doctor Barnes. Move back," the lean man in the green-black coat announced. Lucy stared at his lined face as he kneeled to examine the comotose Abby.

"She'll come around. I find no broken bones." Doctor Barnes raised his craggy head from Abby's breast after he had checked her heartbeat. He opened his worn black bag and reached for a roll of cloth. His trembling hands wound the white bandage around Abby's smooth-skinned forehead. He then swept the wet strands out of Lucy's face, her wide eyes steady upon his grey ones, framed in wire-rimmed glasses below his bushy white eyebrows.

Though the woman in blue homespun had already inspected Lucy, Doctor Barnes held her thin arms and checked for broken bones. "You're a brave one, my child." His mouth sagged and his shoulders slumped. "So like my granddaughter, Claribelle, back in Chattanooga. Of course, darker, a full-blooded child," he whispered to the waiting women. Lucy stroked her mother's disheveled silky hair, her fingers attempting to straighten the violet collar of her dress as she waited, heart still knocking at her ribs.

An overall-clad, barefoot boy, jaw swollen by a wad of tobacco, hollered, "Stinking Indians." His cheeks flushed red at the excitement of a river accident. "Getting rid of the Indians at last." Anger flared and Dr. Barnes's cheeks flushed.

"You know nothing of these people." The doctor turned his grey-streaked head to the boy, his brow wrinkling. "Many of these people speak two and three languages. Their home, New Echota, had schools, courts, stores, and a printing press."

"Well, why they moving them out then, they so educated?" The boy's lips curled.

Doctor Barnes's sad eyes met the boy's own as he said, "We don't know what we're doing, boy. We don't know what we're doing. This woman lying here can probably write and spell better than your own schoolteacher. They tell me she speaks English, Cherokee and French, and is a baptized Christian."

The sweaty boy dug the earth with his toe.

"I'm told this little girl here," the doctor nodded toward Lucy, "can speak the same languages as her mother, and she's Christian, baptized at the Mission."

The boy lowered his eyes, hands digging into his pockets. "You don't say—"

"Leader of the group said this bright-eyed girl," Barnes's thumb pointed again to Lucy, "can play Brahms's minuets on the grand piano in Chief Ross's parlor. You ever seen a grand piano, my boy?"

"Why, no, don't reckon I ever heard of a grand pi-anna or that man you mention." The boy slunk toward the blacksmith shop.

With the raging Tennessee behind them, the murmuring voices of the rudely dislodged Cherokees and black slaves rose in the air as the orange ball slid behind the cloud bank in the western sky. Lucy still held her mother's hand as she asked, "Dear Lord, where is Father?"

CHAPTER TWO

Benjamin Drake leaped through the fragrant sumac along the dusty trail and up the incline to Spring Place village. *Great Above Being, let Abby and Lucy be there when I return.*

Ahead, a group of Cherokees, young and old, clothes whipping in the wind, stumbled toward the river as they tried to obey the shrill commands of the guards. Turban-bedecked heads bowed, they shuffled toward the newly constructed stockade, with its bark roof and open sides.

Benjamin's searching eyes fixed on his mother, Priscilla Drake, standing by her cabin door as the butt of a gun broke the glass of her kitchen window and a second soldier thrust his gun barrel at her.

"Off the porch. At once. I'm Sergeant Sedgwick. General Scott's orders," he said, face contorted as if he'd taken this job, believing the sooner the land was rid of Indians, the quicker the houses, gardens and fields could be grabbed by *real* Americans.

When Benjamin saw all the armed soldiers, he realized there was no exit, in spite of Chief Ross's unceasing efforts. He knew that the stockade on the riverbank below would soon bulge with silent Indians. His eyes betrayed what he knew in his gut, that the imprisonment was only a foretaste of the sorrow that lay hidden in the rivers, mountains, flatlands, swamps and treeless plains ahead.

Benjamin raced down the path to his mother's cabin. Even though his feet were encased in high-top leather boots, there was scarcely a sound. Before he could grab the recruit's rifle, three more ragtag guards shoved their guns around the corner.

"Halt it, Indian. Ain't no getting around it this time. You git." The rifle barrel pointed downhill toward the stockade.

Four armed guards surrounded him. Stumbling down the hill,

he recognized Black Wing and his wife, who clasped their new-born to her calico-clothed bosom. Benjamin knew her heart was breaking, but she did not cry out, but only murmured, "Hush, hush, my little Jumping Deer, Unelanohe watches over us. There will be another day."

To his left, he saw and heard the crash of rifle barrels thrust through old Eagle Wing's kitchen door. She was the beloved medicine woman in the valleys and hills of that part of the nation. Benjamin struggled to keep himself from racing up to the stripling soldier, shoving the barrel aside, and pitching him off the porch.

He knew that old Eagle Wing would pick up her basket. Her brown hand would reach out to follow their long accustomed chore and spread the golden corn for her chickens the last time. It would be all she could do. No turning. No crack in the wall. No door. Obedience to the Stripper From Homelands was all any of them could offer, if they willed to live.

They were caught, surrounded by hundreds of armed soldiers. A brave person endures what cannot be changed. A courageous person accepts the unthinkable, dispossession from his homeland, separation from his loved ones, until that day when Unelanohe gives him an opportunity to change such soul-rending reality.

It was evident that Major Ridge's treaty party had accomplished its goal. I signed the treaty. Benjamin groaned. Take the five million dollars and resettle beyond the Father of Waters. The day had come.

They hunched, Benjamin, his mother, Priscilla, and Aunt Rachel, in the sweltering heat of the stockade, pressed against hundreds of others, full-bloods, Cherokees of varying degrees of blood, a few whites who had married Cherokees, and a scattering of moaning black slaves. They waited for the morning commands, which would order the old to pack themselves into the wagons, and the rest to form lines to begin the 1000-mile march to Oklahoma Territory.

Will I ever see Abby and my beloved Lucy again? Benjamin's black eyes stared at the rippling waters of the Hiwassee flowing by the stockade wall.

CHAPTER THREE

"Thank you, thank you," Lucy said, her soul forced by the events to stretch beyond her age. She turned to look at the old black woman who had helped lay her injured mother on a torn piece of quilt on the lower quarter of the keelboat.

"What is your name?" Lucy asked.

"Why, child, on the plantation they called me Black Bee." She smiled from the gaps in her teeth. "Your mammy's comin' around," encouraged the old slave woman.

"I know you," said Lucy, staring straight into Black Bee's eyes. "You were the cook at Chief Ross's plantation, weren't you?"

Black Bee's stare told Lucy she should not probe too deeply. "That's right. Now old Black Bee has to make the journey same as you Indian folk. Ain't no difference. All of us going to fall off the edge of the world. You'll see when we get to that Mississippi River." Black Bee's eyes opened onto bottomless pits.

"She's waking up. Mother's waking up." Lucy realized she should restrain herself—her veins flowed with survival instincts. Though she'd slept little during the long night on the riverbank, she had since dozed off once or twice. Awakening, she thought of Brother Rabbit who used to dance his way out from prying wolves.

Encircled by voracious wolves ready to eat him, Rabbit used to ask them, "Wouldn't you like to see one of my new dances?"

The wolves, knowing that Rabbit was very good at dancing, replied, "Yes." After all, they had surrounded him and there was no escape. But Rabbit tricked and confused them, engaging them in a dance and song. By the fourth song, the wolves were having so much fun that they forgot about Rabbit as he danced right to the edge of the field, jumped through a gap between the circling wolves, and ran for his freedom.

The old legend comforted Lucy. She was aware that she was like Rabbit dancing with the wolves on this forced journey. The armed guards, the unfamiliar landscapes, the shuddering steamboat showering them with smoke, ashes, and sparks, frightening Long Man enough for him to open one of his holes where Uktena, the wild-eyed serpent demon, would yank them to the beneathworld of pitch.

Lucy remembered her father's words, "My child, there is always another day. Every hollow log has an opening at both ends." Where was Father, his warm, gleaming arms, smelling of walnut and hickory from his woodworking? And Grandmother and Auntie? And, my school friend, Todd? What terrors had swept down on Todd Wyeth and his family? A whole one-half of her soul walled itself within when Father Benjamin failed to return and they were corralled into the keelboat without him.

"Ain't you hungry, child? Try to chew on some of this cornpone." The giant black hand extended a morsel.

Since it came from the hand of one who had befriended her, Lucy opened her lips and tried to chew. She noticed, too, when the soldiers tried to distribute the evening allotment of a handful of cornmeal and a sliver of salt pork per person, only a few Real People even bothered to accept the food offered by the hand of the betrayer.

By the time the river mist shrouding the sun and the weeping willows on the banks had lifted, Abby raised her head and tried to focus her eyes in the confusion. Her cracked lips parted. "Water. My child, is there any water?"

Black Bee's worn hands reached out. "Here, Miss Abby, cool water. My, you done had a blow on the noggin, but your fine girl, Lucy, an' me are takin care of you."

Abby supped slowly. She closed her eyes, head still wrapped in the blood-stained white rag.

"My, Miss Abby, you had lots of doctoring last night. The

shaman danced and bent over you, lighting his little fire, throwing on his tobacco, seeing which way the spirits took the smoke." Black Bee's face spread in a smile. "But, I knew it was the Lord Jesus himself heard your prayer. Reverend Bushyhead prayed over you last night too."

It was evident to Lucy that Black Bee took comfort in the blessings of the Christian faith and solace in the spirits and the conjuring of the shamans as well.

By midmorning Lucy, watching her mother's every move, noticed her raise herself and steady her arm against a crate. Her mind seemed to clear. She understood that she was on the lower level inside the keelboat. Though the listing and bobbings of the boat added to everyone's misery, Abby strained to ask, "Does anyone know where we are?"

"Lawsy, Miss Abby, I don't know," Black Bee intoned. "I never been on this side of the Tennessee before, an I don't know but what you Indians are right about old Uktena getting ready to yank us under." Her bloodshot eyes rolled.

Lucy steadied herself as the boat rocked. She stared across dozens of heads, some covered with straw hats, some wound in Cherokee turbans, many bare. She surveyed her wrinkled calico dress as she thought, what if it rains, or the wind turns cold? She hadn't even had time to grab her coat.

Her eyes caught the face of a half-blood leaning his broad shoulders against the wall. He reminded her of her father, Benjamin, who, no doubt, was forced to plod the 1000 miles overland. Lucy did not allow herself to think otherwise. "Sir, do you know where we are?" Lucy asked.

"We're chugging towards Decatur, Alabama. The steamship's going to stop there tonight. Take on water, cordwood and supplies." The turbaned Cherokee smiled.

Lucy focused for a moment upon his wife, the lean woman in the pale-blue blouse, nursing a baby, watchful eye upon two toddlers playing with a yarn ball. The man's wife turned. "Anything we can do, child?"

Lucy recognized that the woman was from the Brainard Mission area, and like her mother, was educated. Maybe like Mother, thought Lucy, she wanted to see her children grow to learn their catechism and excel in their studies in their time. Or, like the Waties and Chief John Ross, go off to New England to complete their education. May be become lawyers or clergymen. Who knew but God above?

"Your mother's taken a severe blow. Going to require some watching for awhile. What's your name, child?"

"Lucy. Lucy Drake. We lived on a lot in New Echota near the Academy. Would you have a cloth so we could wash Mother's face with some cool water?"

"Just a minute, Lucy." Though it was obvious the woman's own heart was as heavy as a sack of rocks, she seemed to push the confusion and despair aside for the sake of her own family, and then now for another hurting one.

Shoving her breast back inside her dress, she handed the infant to her husband and gathered her muslin skirts about her, rose and picked her way through the murmuring pack. A small piece of flannel in her hand, she pushed herself to the rail, leaned over and dipped the cloth into the clear green water and wrung it out.

She wiped Abby Drake's swollen face tenderly. "There now. You just lie back. I'm going to fold this cloth and let you keep it on your forehead. Steady and cool. My name's Willa Bench. That's my husband, Herman, holding Buford and those are the twins, rolling the ball."

"Thank you. Oh, thank you." Abby closed her eyes and dozed off before she could ask her Indian sister to watch over Lucy.

But Lucy realized that among the Cherokees, she was every Indian mother's daughter or niece. Friendship, sense of family and love prevailed in their culture. She could see that her mother, too, took comfort in the watchful eye of Black Bee, the slave woman.

By noon, the heat was stiffing. A flock of cawing crows flew over the strange flotilla. The two-layered holds of the keelboat swarmed with the newborns, the old, the dying, the lusty young and the full-bloods who followed the old tribal ways, eyes steady and ferocious as they surveyed the goings on, waiting for a chance to bolt for freedom like Brother Rabbit from the wolves.

Lucy watched the six armed recruits' fingers never losing hold of their rifles as they turned their sun burnt faces, surveying the emigrants.

"Child," whispered Black Bee to Lucy, "them guards don't want to rile Captain Thomas's scorn. Ain't nothin we can do about them but obey." Her shiny eyes rolled.

"Over there, check it out," commanded one of the recruits, Corporal Bundy, as he pointed his rifle barrel toward the left stern.

Lucy stared at the corporal, uniform wrinkled and sweat-stained, as he made an attempt to step through the crowd without smashing a hand or wrenching a foot. He failed. Most of the victims of his boot heel or sole endured the crunched bones and pinched flesh in silence. "Hey, you redskinned Indian. That liquor you're swilling from that jug?" Bundy yelled.

Lucy, though she'd watched, hadn't fully understood the strange events at the wreck on the rocks the evening before, how the local moonshiners bartered and sold their liquor and women to those who could afford their inflated prices.

The cluster of young Cherokees in the circle by the stern rail smiled recklessly and tossed the jug to one another. "Have a swig, soldier" the tallest one said. "Going to ride on Old Long Man, might as well do it with fire in your belly." They howled as the firewater temporarily removed their terrors, their wrenching from lovers and families.

Corporal Bundy smashed his rifle butt against the head of the grinning Cherokee holding the jug. A slip of blood gleamed in the sunlight against the copper face as he fell backwards, his long hair tangling around the rail.

Bundy grabbed the jug only to find it empty. He tossed it overboard as hundreds of black eyes watched it bob and swirl before it sank. His longing eyes and licking tongue betrayed that he had wanted a swig, but he would now have to wait until they landed in Decatur and his relief took over for the night watch.

Lucy's stomach growled. Time for a morsel. No one wanted to heat the small cast-iron stove in each boxed-in enclosure or a 'berth,' in such August heat. Mothers offered breasts to sucklings if they could still provide. Helping hands extended a fistful of meal or a portion of a left-over corn dodger from the evening before. The allotment of salt pork, had any survived yesterday's supper, reeked in rottenness. A wrinkled old Indian called out, "Keep it, we'll use it for fish bait tonight when we stop." They would have to scrape and improvise for line and hook.

Lucy worried about her mother's lack of food. Liquid. A few spoonfuls of sassafras tea, the Cherokee woman, Willa Bench's cold water. Lucy knew Abby needed some nurturing broth. What could she do?

Black Bee dislodged her massive bulk from her portion of the floor. She sauntered forth, not to heist her skirts and relieve herself over the rail as many were forced to do, but to scavenge for food. Black Bee showed her confidence that it was not only Cherokee survival instinct that reigned on the flotilla, but black slave survival tactics too. She tromped hither and thither, ignoring the pleas of those smashed beneath her wide bare feet.

"Pardon me, Missie. Beg pardon, Sir. My, you a fine looking gentleman. Bet you sire a dozen sons." She nodded as she rocked over the planks of the keelboat where it seemed impossible to plant a single foot.

"Pardon, Ma'am. Yes, Ma'am, you are thirsty, ain't you. My, my." And her stealthy fingers and silent feet gleaned here and there, a piece of unwatched corn bread, a strip of dried fish, unwrapped while its owner searched for a slice of bread, a carrot saved for a later nibble.

Whoosh sank her massive body as she settled in the dead air, reeking of sweat and foul breath of the sick, the excrement of the infants and the old and helpless, languishing in the heat. "Here you are, Miss Abby. Old Black Bee's got lunch for you. Now you

just open them lips and chew." Her coarse fingers lifted small fragments of pilfered cornbread, softened in the cup of stale tea. "Lucy
needs you, now you just close your lips and swallow."

Abby obeyed the soothing voice, heavy as molasses. In spite of
her afflictions, Abby's face reflected that her spirit was anchored in
God and, no doubt, whispering, "Forgive us our trespasses as we
forgive those who trespass against us."

* * *

The steamer wailed as if it were looking for an opening to hell as it
approached the loading docks at Decatur, Alabama, a land where
the songs of slaves floated up to God through the Spanish moss on
the everlasting oaks. God of the dispossessed.

"Time to gather your belongings," a slump-shouldered guard
called. But who on this trip, thought Lucy, had any belongings to
speak of? She knew that those who had managed to pack a valise, a
box or a small trunk, now discovered that it had disappeared in
the ungainly pile, guarded by soldiers. "You'll receive your property upon arrival at your new home," the snickering guards ad-
vised them.

Two-thirds of the emigrants had already straggled down the
gang plank of the rocking keelboat when old Black Bee commanded,
"Now's our time. Miss Abby, you're gonna lean on me. That's
right, Miss Lucy, you grab my things."

Lucy bent and quickly scooped up Black Bee's rag bundle.
Their murmuring rose in the twilight as the river yowl and frogs
echoed in the evening mist.

"Mama, where are you?" a child wailed.

"Another step, Mother, and we'll be there," comforted a slender Cherokee maiden struggling to keep her mother, doubled by
stomach cramps, from falling.

"Captains, set up your circles and posts. Rations'll be distrib-
uted promptly. You're responsible for your group," a tall guard
commanded. The weary emigrants searched for their own family
members, and for any friend's warm embrace.

Others scattered, seeking bushes or trees for privacy to relieve the pressures of the bladder and bowel.

Lucy was no longer shocked when four grunting soldiers half-dragged the corpse of old Grandfather Wyeth from back at Spring Place, whose spirit, sometime in the afternoon, had parted from his body. Lucy asked, "Where is his grandson, Todd?"

"Back. Get back," growled the soldiers, jerking the corpse ahead of two wailing women and a bent-backed middle-aged man, blue kerchief tied on his head. Four other corpses lay on the edge of the riverbank, awaiting early morning burial.

Then Lucy, who had seated herself in the circle near Willa and Herman Bench and their children, noticed a small boy, contours softened by the evening light. The boy shuffled forlornly. When his bare feet reached the dusty edge of Lucy's circle where Black Bee was attempting to supervise the supper, he stopped.

Abby raised her bandaged head from her seat on a wooden crate. "Lucy, don't we know that little boy standing there?"

Lucy turned as Black Bee worked to strike a flint to light the fire under the pot. "Why, Mother, that's Todd, from Brainerd school. "Todd Wyeth, come here." She stretched her arm to the nine-year-old, who turned his silent face toward her. His black eyes pierced the gloom, seeking recognition of the voice that called him.

Lucy had tried to forget how Todd's father had been critically wounded and thrown in a stockade back at Gunter's Landing. Todd must have been separated from him at bayonet-point, then grabbed in a fleeting moment by his grandfather, who had died that day. Todd now was an orphan.

Lucy wanted to rush to her school friend's side, and embrace him. But following her Cherokee manners, she smiled instead. "Todd, you must travel with Mother and me."

Black Bee poured a gritty meal from her grey sack into the boiling pot. Her broad face turned to the ragged boy. "Child, you come and have supper with us. We may not know just quite where we're going, but we going to travel together. Preacher Bushyhead'll bury your Grandpap in the morning along with them others."

Lucy guessed they were blessed with at least a dozen preachers, in addition to the holy men, whose murmurs had already commenced, trying to ward off the sicknesses. Some hunched around little fires to begin conjuring, to try to discover which witches were responsible for the illnesses and the deaths among them.

Who to pray to on such a journey as this? The great being above called Unelanohe or to Ni ta we he u? To Ta ka tsi? Lucy pondered. Never had the shamans seemed to be so confused. When Father joins us, Lucy decided, she would ask him. She stared into the star-studded sky.

CHAPTER FOUR

Still numb from being jerked from the smoky mountains and the green valleys of his homeland, Benjamin trudged up the rocky hill, following the 34 lurching wagons packed with silent Cherokees. They creaked toward the threatening Cumberlands, wagons pulled by straining oxen or teams of horses and mules.

Baby cries rose above the groaning wheels while mothers nursed and rocked their babies. Benjamin watched two young mothers, Awadee and Misheeta, bend their backs and heave up the hill as if they had vowed to plod to the end of the earth with their babies strapped to their backs, rather than accept any help from the betrayers of their homelands.

"Back there, in line. In line." Sergeant Sedgwick cracked his blacksnake whip. "You turbaned Indian, stay in line with your group." Brown juice flew from his tobacco-stained lip.

Benjamin, appointed as captain of his group of 50, wrestled with red-hot fury boiling in his breast. Anger turned to near hatred. Bewilderment. Confusion and, lurking there also, the creeping fingers of self-doubt and the passivity known only to prisoners and slaves. Nevertheless, he struggled to set a proper example for his comrades. *If I can remain calm, endure the humiliation and fatigue, the ravages of changing weather, maybe we can save ourselves.* Too much to think of, all the lonely miles ahead. Only a portion of his spirit knew that time must pass before his body and mind absorbed the gratings of the trek. This step, this 100 yards, this half-mile. Who could comprehend a journey's end, 900 miles ahead? Who could ever get used to Sergeant Sedgwick's contentious commands?

Sergeant Sedgwick seemed glad the Indians were compliant so

far, though it was obvious he couldn't stand the women, wailing at
the hasty burials on the riverbanks. His face reflected his thoughts.
Why carry on so? Better to have the savages all on the other side of
the Mississippi where they can strip and run naked and do whatever heathenish things they do.

Benjamin watched as Mother Drake plodded silently. He saw
the numbing sorrow in her eyes from parting from her home. The
same with 70 year-old Aunt Rachel. Both faithful Christians, members of the Baptist church. Singers of hymns in both Cherokee and
English. Bible readers as well. Could their faith sustain them?
Benjamin's five-foot-seven frame leaned forward, as his booted legs
set a pace Mother Drake and Aunt Rachel could manage to follow.
Only three had died in the confinement in the stockade by the
river due to the heat, the dampness and the fears. Thank God.

Benjamin wondered. What God? Do I believe in God? Is it
possible that the Three Above Ones, who perpetually commune
in loving voices with each other, know of the sufferings of The
People below? Where is the compassionate Jesus of the Baptists,
the Presbyterians, the Moravians, the Methodists?

As he planted one foot ahead of another to the tune of cursing
wagonmasters and the groaning wheels, he wondered if they had
tossed aside their own sacred ways only to keep up with the white
people. Were their sins any different?

His thoughts whirled like the circle of buzzards above who
had already sensed death enshrouding their train. *Where is my
beloved Abby? Can Lucy survive such a trip as this?* He could see
Lucy's bright-eyed face. It was as if she were before him, her love,
her voice, "Papa, Papa . . . ." Would they ever again gather on a
vine-covered porch, sip sweet jasmine tea together and listen to
mockingbirds and the sigh of the wind in the giant chestnuts?

He hoped Abby and Lucy were among those who, according
to messages coming through the grapevine, were on riverboats,
heading up the Father of Waters. Their journey would take only a
third of the time this overland trek would take.

"Take the name of Jesus with you, child of sorrow and of woe;

It will joy and comfort give you . . ." sang his mother in time with her plodding feet. Aunt Rachel joined in singing the hymn. Determination etched on her face gave evidence that she could endure her aching legs and her blistered heels until evening. Benjamin hoped they could have a small fire in a grove of trees, or a cleared space along the road, a space to gather, sing and pray. That would be important for Mother and Aunt Rachel. He hoped the guards would allow it.

And he? Benjamin? He had not joined the church, though he usually sat in the services with Abby and Lucy. Someday, maybe. No problem with Jesus. No problem at all. His thoughts circled. A faith in Jesus, a help to any man. The way Jesus loved the people, even his enemies. The way he trusted the Great Father of all. The way he died, asking for forgiveness for those who crucified him, and the way he rose on the third day from the dead. Someday, when they had resettled in Oklahoma, Abby, Lucy, and he, maybe then he would join his church.

"Fifteen minutes for lunch and rest. Turn out in the clearing ahead," Sergeant Sedgwick's command echoed down the caravan from captain to captain.

"Lunch," scoffed Grey Wolf, a short Cherokee farmer. "Lunch, and we had no time to gather up any meal or flour, dried fish or . . . ."

"Rest? Rest?" The very word seemed ludicrous, Benjamin thought. Marching 16 hours a day and 15 minutes in the blazing sun, called rest? Murmuring rose up, but the migrants had by now been slowly beaten into submission.

Benjamin knew that if there were any recalcitrant young bucks who planned to make trouble and bolt, they would discover that the guards' fiery rifle bullets would drop them in their tracks.

Benjamin had learned by now. A scoop of ditch water with a dirty hand lifted hastily to parched lips while trying not to fall. A morsel of an edible sour dock, provided he could find it in this drought, snatched while not breaking rank. Benjamin sank wearily, his feet ached.

Mercifully, the locust grove provided partial shade for some. Those who were still standing in the roadway sought shade under or on the side of their wagons. Hordes sat bareheaded in the blazing sun, waiting as slaves wait for their master's commands. The shrouds of submission slowly enfolded their spirits.

No relief trench until evening, when captains were commanded to help dig slit trenches where those who had managed to hold their bowels could at last release them.

Benjamin's broadcloth shirt was salty with sweat under his arms and stuck to his back. Blisters broke open on the bottoms of his feet from the unmerciful tramping.

Maybe he had better try it barefooted, carry his boots for the rocky places. There was no distribution of food. He knew that would come when they staggered and fell at nightfall, if God were merciful enough to allow it.

Then, the stinking rations, barely enough to tilt the nose of a sniffing mongrel, would be shoved into the hands of the captains. He could smell the revolting salt pork now. Already, the entire snaking caravan emitted its own smells of sickness, unwashed flesh and excrement.

Various containers and water bags passed from person to person. Mothers opened their dresses to sucklings. Oxen moaned and lowed. Horses swatted stinging flies, stamped and neighed, awaiting a morsel of oats from the hand of a soldier, a sip of water from a leather bag or bucket.

Aunt Rachel and Mother Drake chewed a few grains of yellow corn and shared a water bottle, faces showing their thankfulness for the wetness, though it was only tepid ditch water, lifted from a brackish pool which the dry winds had not yet evaporated.

Benjamin's mind circled over the confusion. Abby and her Principal Chief, Little John Ross. Where was he now? What would he say of us now? Such faith she had in him. So many supporters he had, too. Benjamin remembered that rumor had it that John Ross was looking after himself. Petitioning the government for permission for his family to gather their carriages, their opulent possessions, their safely secured bank-notes, their slaves and servants, to purchase their own wagons and supplies and make their own journey to Oklahoma Territory. Couldn't they see that it had been a losing battle from the start?

Benjamin's mind hung on the sorry events. They had been proud of the white people's praise of them, civilized Cherokees. Academies, language and alphabets, newspapers and churches. Young Indian scholars in schools in New England. Former chiefs and Indian dignitaries in regal garb visiting English courts of kings and queens. Portraits of famous chiefs done in oils by noted artists, now hanging in the capitol, museums, governors' mansions, and galleries. Behind the praise were the soul-wrenching words: "They must go."

Chief Ridge's words still echoed in his mind, "Red Bull," as President Jackson had called him. Square-jawed, muscular, powerful in physique and temperament, beguiling with his tongue.

"I know we love the graves of our fathers, who have gone before to the happy hunting grounds of the Great Spirit—the eternal land, where the deer, the turkey and the buffalo will never give out. There is but one path of safety, one road to future existence as a Nation. That path is open before you . . .Give up these lands and go over beyond the great Father of Waters."

Benjamin reached unconsciously for a dry twig on the side of the road, the weight of Chief Ross's words hit him. *It is a Cherokee unwritten blood law which we will keep. Those who contrive to sell our lands beneath us must die.*

The confusing imprisonment and brutalities of the journey had kept the words from his consciousness. Benjamin allowed them to surface now. He had signed that treaty that forwarded the five-million dollars for the purchase of their homeland. Did that mean that he too would, somewhere, someplace, may be at the end of the trek, be singled out for death by Ross's executioners? It was the Cherokee blood law. Or, Benjamin thought, could the executioners be on this very stinking, migrant train?

CHAPTER FIVE

Doctor Barnes kneeled before Abby, who was propped against a discarded apple-crate. He soaked the blood-stained bandage until he could begin tearing it away from the ragged wound on Abby's forehead.

"Ah, it's coming, child," he spoke to Lucy, leaning to survey his every move.

"Your mother's going to have a shiny scar on her forehead for the rest of her life. Yep. There." The filthy bandage dropped away from her face revealing the three-inch jagged gash, now healing over.

"We've got to keep it from getting infected. Mercy. We need baths, soap and water." But, the doctor knew he might as well petition the wind that blew the fetid odors of rotting fish and stagnant waters over them.

"Child." He surveyed Lucy, straight as an elm sapling, dress sagging and wrinkled from days of travel, her hands folded behind her, face unyielding to despair, as she awaited instructions that would aid her mother. "It's up to you to keep the bandage clean as possible. In another day, take it off. May have to wash it and put it back on. Try to keep it clean." The rumblings of the awakening hordes in the morning sunlight on the river-wharf startled a flock of blackbirds from their perches in the willows and river oaks. They circled in sweeping spirals against the pink and yellow thrusts of the morning light.

A few emigrants tried to build fires to boil water for willow bark tea, or to bake a spill of corn batter upon a heated stone for a hoecake, if they had any corn left over from the night before.

"Mrs. Drake." The doctor snapped his fingers before her eyes.

He could see that she was weak from lack of proper nourishment, but another concern raked his mind. "How many fingers do you see in front of you, Mrs. Drake?"

Abby cleared her dry throat, lifted her head, and tried to focus her eyes in the light. "Oh, if I could only wash my hair. Why doctor, it's, it's . . . ." Her soft voice faltered. "Why, doctor, is it three? Two? It's your whole hand, isn't it?"

"What I feared. Concussion caused her brain to swell," he said to Black Bee. "This woman needs rest and as little movement as possible. Who launched this dastardly journey anyway? In time, her vision will clear. Too bad, they have to be moved again, folks like her."

*   *   *

Lucy had noticed that the lad, Todd, overcome by both fatigue and the death of his grandfather, mercifully slept by Black Bee's fire most of the night. He and Lucy turned toward the voice calling from a ledge above, where elderberries leaned, heavy with purple fruit. Preacher Jesse Bushyhead stood in the morning breeze, his shirt sleeves billowing, Bible in his hand. "Dear people, the burial's up here. Not much time. The guards say we have 10 minutes."

Lucy and Todd joined the crowd, which straggled forward and gathered around his lean form, as he stood at the end of the first of the five graves in the raw, red earth. Herman Bench and another captain had already placed the canvas-wrapped corpses in the graves, earth crumbling down on them.

"Near the cross I'll watch and wait, Hoping, trusting ever . . ."

Slaves of fate and faith lifted their voices, gaining comfort from the hymn. Lucy joined the singers with her clear, soft voice.

Preacher Bushyhead noticed Lucy and Todd. His eyes reflected his questions and pain. His people afflicted on this cross. His words caught in the wind and drifted over the river. The song continued, "Till I reach the golden strand, just beyond the river."

Lucy looked over her shoulder at the wide river. She knew of rivers. The beautiful Coosa, the murmuring Hiwassee, the raging Tennessee with its Suck and Boiling Pot. She had heard of the

threatening turbulence of the mighty Mississippi, which they
would soon know.

"The Lord is my shepherd . . . .," Preacher Bushyhead's into-
nations rose and fell, punctuated by sighs and grunts; he was like
an old warrior chief, conveying, "What else can one say? What
human words could possibly soothe the ragged minds and bleeding hearts of the mourners?"

Women began to gnash their teeth and wail. The mother, bury-
ing her newborn, rocked and lifted her hands in her grief.

In spite of the fact that she was a girl, Lucy reached out and
held Todd's grimy hand as he watched the clods drop on his
grandfather's cold body, his face a mask of unfeeling.

"You'll have to hurry, preacher, got to load up and get to the
trains," hollered Corporal Bundy, his voice ill-tempered from his
revelings during the night.

*   *   *

Bleary-eyed Black Bee helped load Abby Drake in one of the trans-
port wagons before it was overloaded. She, Abby, and Todd paced
along as the cloppings of the horses' hooves led them to the railroad station. A weird wail trembled and subsided and then began
again. Lucy shuddered. "What was it?" Todd's eyes widened.

"That's the train. The lo-co-mo-tive, children. Sounds like the
very devil, don't it?" Black Bee straightened her face as if to control
her fears.

Billows of stinking smoke rose above a long, shingled roof ahead.
Corporal Bundy's lips turned down in a scowl as if he hated the
misery of it all. The beggarly savages, leaning in to the unknown.

As they rounded the bend, Todd and Lucy laid eyes upon the
very devil himself astraddle the long, shiny rails. They leaned back.
Lucy grabbed Black Bee's massive hand and held on. The steam
engine wailed yet again, and to make matters worse, a second engine let loose an even more piercing wail. The Cherokees shuddered, clapped their hands over their ears, stopped in their tracks.

"Pshaw. Ain't nothin but two old iron lo-co-mo-tives that's
gonna take us on them rails over to Tuscumbia where we get back

on the Tennessee again. You children ain't just wanting to ride on keelboats all the way, are you? This old bag-o-bones is gonna climb up in one of them cars ahead and rest my corns awhile." Bee smiled as if to disguise that she too was afraid of the belching monsters.

*   *   *

Hand on Black Bee's shoulder, Abby Drake raised her fine-turned ankle, foot mercifully still in a shoe, as she lifted her body up the steps and into one of the 32 cars drawn by two devilish engines pouring the stinking smoke and sparks upon them. Her stomach heaved. Her head swirled. She dared not focus too long at the blurred confusion before her. She leaned, packed against Lucy and Black Bee, while Todd stood in the cramped aisle, rocking, lurching, his canvas pants torn at the bottoms, his calloused feet, bare and blistered. His eyes, staring with bewilderment.

"Oh, look out. I'm going to heave." A tall full-blood woman tried to rise and reach a window. Failing, her vomit cascaded over her bosom and splashed on the crush of people around her.

Abby knew that it was the spoilt foods poked down, the draughts of strange swill, the inroads of pestilence and the unceasing swaying of the railroad cars that caused scores of stomachs to heave as her comrades turned green.

She tried to hide the thought that scores were gravely ill from cheap liquors pawned off on them last night at inflated prices, leaving them bloated, some near death at daybreak.

Abby remembered Lucy's question. "What makes Black Bee's breath smell like that? And why were her eyes so glassy and her headache so bad this morning?" She realized that Lucy guessed it was because Black Bee was old and this journey was enough to kill a young person, let alone a huge, old black woman.

Abby Drake forced her splitting head and pressured brains to ponder. Where were Major Ridge, his son John and Elias Boudinot now? Had they secured themselves in Arkansas for awhile? Had they moved on to the wilderness of Oklahoma, they and the others who had put their names on that treaty, ratified by the United States Senate by only one vote?

Did this treaty party betray a sacred trust? And, didn't this dastardly wrenching from their homeland show what this country thought of the Indians? Had the Above Being abandoned them?

* * *

Wooded hills against the skyline indicated that the Tennessee River was just beyond. The mountains and hills with their interposed valleys, created by the Great Condor long ago, sent out to see if the floods had receded from the earth. The flapping of his giant outstretched wings had swept down to make the valleys and rising up, the hills.

A church steeple rose in the haze, announcing the town of Tuscumbia ahead and the river steamers and keelboats awaiting their arrival.

Abby Drake awakened from her fitful sleep. She'd been dreaming of the day Lucy was born, a bright October day by the Coosa River at Spring Place. Beautiful, sweet woods. Dogwood leaves blushing red. Mockingbirds singing. Cardinal calling "sweet cheer, sweet cheer, cheer, cheer, cheer."

There'd been hardly any pain at all, as the Cherokee woman healer bent over her with grunts and encouragement and the girl child burst into the world with her cry. She and the baby both had the blessings of the shaman's prayers and supervision as they immersed themselves in the cleansing Coosa waters.

"That's why Cherokees love baptism so much," said Preacher Bushyhead. "The waters have been for generations for our cleansing, both outwardly and inwardly."

* * *

"Only for those who can't walk," hollered a recruit, responsible for the small convoy of oxcarts waiting to roll over the hard bricks to the Tennessee River wharf three blocks below. A motley crowd of both country and town Tennesseans crowded the wooden sidewalk by the Tuscumbia station to feast their eyes on the sights of a lifetime, an entire nation shoved out of its homeland, leaving the land for the 'real settlers',who had pounced upon their holdings and houses even before emigrant feet hit the exile trail or the wide planks of the keelboats.

"Well, it's about time we had a president like Van Buren making sense about the Indians," confided a redneck farmer to his portly wife with straggly hair. She clasped her basket of eggs.

"Don't they stink? Maw, I told you Indians stunk," shouted a straw-headed boy as he picked his nose.

"Oh, God above, have mercy," whispered a black-bonneted Brethren woman, whose eyes filled with tears and pity at the afflicted ones. She turned to her bearded husband. "Eli, put those apples back in the wagon and take them down by the wharf and hand them out to these people."

Abby Drake lurched in the ox cart along with the others, who were too ill or feeble to walk, but it would have been better had she walked with sober-faced Lucy, the dusty boy, Todd, and lumbering, barefooted old Black Bee who chewed tobacco she'd garnered somewhere on the way.

Down by the riverbank, rats scurried, waiting to infect vagabonds and unwelcome travelers with their dreaded diseases.

CHAPTER SIX

Back on the overland trail, Benjamin knew Aunt Rachel was in trouble when he saw her gasping for breath. He could hear the rattling in her chest and then the cough that shook her thin body. When the captain ordered a halt, Benjamin leaped to her side. He held her, easing her body to the ground, as her frame shook with chills and her eyes glazed with the burning fever. "God. Abby's God, touch this loving woman and lead her into your presence." Benjamin choked back the tears at memories of Aunt Rachel making special bean bread for him when he was a child. "A wagon." His pleading eyes sought Sergeant Sedgwick's surly ones. "Allow me to lift her in a wagon."

"Can't you see there's no room?" Sedgwick growled.

Captain Jesse Bradley's caravan joined theirs at Golconda, Kentucky, adding hundreds more waifs and refugees. The shamans murmured more prayers, tossed tobacco into small fires and sought the sources of evil besetting them. Now, a starving, death-enshrouded caravan of over 1,200 Cherokees shuddered as they awaited the crossing of the broad Ohio River.

Benjamin was glad Aunt Rachel had died before they crossed the river ahead. Here, still in sight of the beloved wooded hills behind them. Here, where the gentle winds still carried the sweetness of home. Only God knew what awaited them across the turbulent waters of the Ohio. Benjamin attempted to block out any thought of the Mississippi, hundreds of miles ahead. Whipping winds and cold pellets of rain descended, chilling his shoulders.

* * *

"Get 'em buried, get 'em buried, Captain Pollit commanded. "Sun come out tomorrow and cholera'll break."

"Sedgwick, you're in command of the burials," Captain Pollit barked at Sergeant. Sedgwick turned his head to spit tobacco juice. "Have my way about it, no burials. No wasting time and energy, throw 'em in a ditch and burn 'em." Sedgwick's voice caught in the wind. Only 12 years back, there in Georgia, his own grandpap, a squatter, he and a gaggle of cronies drove the Indians out. Shot a few savages, too—was it three?

Anyway, a revenging party of Cherokee from around the Hiwassee River descended upon his grandpap's settlement and burned his cabin. Left three dead and scalped. Those Indians believed in and eye for an eye and a tooth for a tooth. Hardened by the hard task and suffering hordes, the bitter sweetness of revenge seeped into Sedgwick's consciousness. "You there, Drake. Whatever your name. You a captain, ain't you? You and a crew of your woods Indians, bend your backs and get some holes dug. Don't worry about goin too deep either, we ain't got that kind of time." He wiped stains from his mouth with the back of his hand.

* * *

How many times had he dug holes like this? Benjamin lost count of the burials. Funerals? Who could call them funerals?

Shamans sprouting up everywhere, betrayed their anguish that they had lost control of ancient powers. What was the matter with their formulas, their prayers? Who were the witches among them? The shamans stamped their blistered feet. They stooped over and wailed their laments and prayers into the air.

And The People. Recalcitrant, more passive each day from slow starvation and grief. Benjamin had heard a shaman sputter that if he could only herd the pneumonia-stricken ones down into the waters of Long Man for a cold, purifying immersion, they would emerge with visions of hope, bodies renewed as in the old days. Preachers giving advice. On this caravan, free-wheeling revival-type Methodists. Serious-faced Presbyterians. Hymn-singing Baptists. A few quiet and passive Brethren. Which? Who? Benjamin could scarcely remember who held which service.

Just then, Monroe Bates, who had moved to New Echota from

North Carolina years back, slid in beside Benjamin and sank a shovel into the wet earth.

Benjamin observed Monroe, a silent Indian, slow in expressing feeling or thought.

"Sorrowful task," Monroe murmured, hunching his shoulders beside Benjamin.

"Yes," Benjamin replied, turning to look at Monroe, blue handkerchief bound around his head, long hair in two braids hanging by his shoulders and a clean-cut face that women would find appealing. "Will it ever end?" Benjamin's voice ached with weariness and doubt.

"It'll end. You'll see, Benjamin Drake. We'll reach the new territory. Our numbers drop each day, still, left alone, our nation will grow again. You'll see." Monroe heaved the wet earth.

Fragments of comfort seeped into openings in Benjamin's soul, comfort from a fellow traveler in pain and sorrow. Comfort from a friend. Back in New Echota, Monroe had gone on a hunt with him only two or three times. "I hope it'll be so." Doubts weighed on his chest, mingling with grief over his loss of Aunt Rachel.

"When we bury our dead, side by side, we are comrades," Monroe said, stopping for a moment to stare into Benjamin's eyes. "Comrades in grief and pain."

Benjamin was surprised at this Cherokee's sensitivity, his kindly words. There'd been so little time for comradeship with the endless struggling, enduring the offenses of the weather, and the violations of the white people. Monroe's helping hands and human words comforted him.

Benjamin was too absorbed with digging a grave for Aunt Rachel and the indescribable burdens to remember that Monroe Bates was an ardent Chief John Ross supporter—quite against selling the land. More so, even than Abby. But no time to think of commitments to blood oaths now. Get Aunt Rachel and the others buried in God's blessed earth.

Benjamin's back ached. Blisters on his hands matched the ones on the bottoms of his bare feet in the rocky soil. He pitched red earth. He dug for Aunt Rachel, her sweetness. Her cooing to him when he was a lad with the first bow and arrow of his own. The rabbit he had brought to her. The stew she had made to celebrate. The sweetness of the towering walnut trees around her cabin.

Benjamin pushed back the thought: When will I be doing this for Mother?

Seven shallow graves and only two more to go. Benjamin hadn't realized how weak he was. Perspiration broke out on his forehead. Muscle cramps tortured his back as the earth resisted the pick ax and shovel, earth that had its own spicy sweetness, drifting up the nostrils in contrast to the stench above.

"It's done. Step back, Benjamin Drake. The preacher wants to begin." Monroe stared at Benjamin as he leaned on the handle of his shovel.

Too weary to talk, Benjamin stepped back, bare feet buried in the muddy earth. He leaned on his pick ax.

They sang a hymn. Their ears opened to the prayer from minister Going Walk's lips. Benjamin noticed the waver and hesitancy in the reverend's voice, which betrayed his worry over whether or not he still possessed any faith. "Though I walk through the valley and the shadow of death, Thou art with me."

Who? Where? Benjamin vowed not to discredit Abby and Lucy's faith because of his present doubts. Straighten my back. Clear my throat. Shut down the choking sob. Ignore the fact that my clothing is soiled and torn, my body unwashed. Breathe the prayer. But Benjamin could not sing as Mother Drake began: "This robe of flesh I'll drop, and rise / To seize the everlasting prize . . . ."

It was puzzling to Benjamin that they could still sing. Faintly at first, then those of Christian faith, gathered at the shallow slits in the earth, lifted their voices to share their faith, or as in his case, the shreds thereof.

What prize awaited them on this earth? How everlasting? For a moment only, Benjamin could have vowed that it was little eight-year-old Lucy's face that stared straight at him from behind the golden willow ahead.

CHAPTER SEVEN

The *Smelter*, 50 feet longer than the stern-wheeler, *Maybelle*, chugged down the Mississippi waters, boiling with silt from recent rains. Lucy, Abby, Black Bee and Todd hunched tightly in one of the berths of the heaving keelboat like captives in the hold of a slave ship.

Torrents of cold rain whipped the fragile craft as, the captain jerked the massive pilot wheel to avoid ramroding trees dislodged from the riverbanks. Refugee cries rose in the wind, "Deliver us from the jaws of Long Man."

"Lord, Lord, have mercy . . . ." Black Bee's eyes glazed, her tongue stuck to the roof of her mouth, her heart pounded. Her powerful fingers trembled as she searched her pockets and her knapsack. An empty flask. Tremors raced up her spine. She searched for her medicine, stashed whenever she could worm a coin from a secret pocket or an unraveled dress hem. Voices of the river-merchants rang in her ears, "Get them hooked on likker an we got income long as these government migrations last."

Though most of the passengers were silent, who could speak above the howling wind, the rolling of the waters? Yet, the murmuring circled in the wind, "Oh Lord, my head, my head." Unfortunates emerging from an intoxicating state, vomited and heaved, including Black Bee, her huge body sprawled in disarray.

"You mustn't condemn her," Abby whispered to Lucy, who leaned onto her arm. Abby, able now to sit up at intervals without the dizziness and splitting pain, reached out and enveloped Lucy's hand with her own. "She's a brave woman. Braver even than I," Abby said. "She's given me strength to live, caring for me."

Abby knew that without Black Bee and Lucy, her body would

be lying miles behind in a shallow grave on the riverbanks along with scores of others. Who kept count?

"She was a slave before in Louisiana, Black Bee was. She told me she had seven children, all sold to different masters. Chief Ross purchased her over 20 years ago for his kitchen." Abby cleared her throat to hold back tears.

They rocked in silence. Abby shoved back thoughts of their New Echota lands. Gone like the soil crumbling from the riverbank and dissolving in the water—swept on to the delta below.

Abby pondered. That's what's happening to us. Crumbling, falling, swept along—a people, not a people. Confusion. Swept to Oklahoma Territory. If they ever arrived, could they take hold and build new homes? Was there any hope left?

*   *   *

Todd, awakened from a fitful slumber, his legs cramped from the crowding, noticed the growing darkness and heard his stomach growl. He was hungry, but he would wait. Wait, in spite of the gnawing, until Abby, Lucy, or Black Bee opened their small sacks to allow some measly cornmeal to slip into their hands. An Indian waited. Only weak, self-centered people gave in to hunger. This, he knew. A brave on a hunt never ate until it was over. He remembered the last words of Black Wing, his father, and the glimmer of hope in his dark eyes: "Whatever happens, my son, remember that we are survivors."

Todd wondered about the new land ahead, Oklahoma. Some folks said the soil there was red like it was in Georgia. Was that true? He wondered if he would have to go to school there, now that his father was no longer alive and his grandfather buried on a river bank. Todd held back the tears that crowded the corners of his eyes. Though she wasn't a boy, it helped having a Cherokee friend to travel with, Lucy Drake. And, he thought, that old slave woman, Black Bee, tells hair-raising stories. He concluded he was thankful for old Black Bee's help, same as Lucy and Abby Drake's.

*   *   *

Ahead, Captain Donnell struggled with his wheel, commanded

his crew, spat tobacco juice and prayed, "God, get us to a safe haven." He had planned to make it to Portageville by dark. Though going downstream, the river raged against him with its ever-changing current. He realized they wouldn't make it and he would be forced to pilot in darkness, torrential rain and unpredictable waters.

*   *   *

Before she had awakened from her doze, Lucy had dreamed she was back at the mission school, back where the giant trees whispered eternally in love and sweetness. Her thin fingers held her chalk as she wrote endearing words to her father, who smelled of sweet hickory and walnut.

Dearest Father. Her fingers stopped as she realized she could never say within the confines of her small slate what she wanted to, or ask all the questions that flooded her mind.

Dear Father, I love you. Dear Father, are you well? I believe you are alive. Wouldn't I know it if God had taken you from this earth? Mother would know it. I would know it in my heart.

Somewhere, you too, dear Father, think of us. I know you must know Mother is ill. You feel it in your own heart of pain. Where are you imprisoned? I hear most of our people are forced to travel overland. I cannot even think of it, dear Father. A 1000 miles?

Grandmother Drake. Is she with you? Aunt Rachel? I smell her cornmeal and bean balls wrapped in corn husks, baking on her hearth. My heart tells me that Aunt Rachel is not with us anymore.

Do you weep, dear Father? Cherokee men do weep. I've seen them. Chief White Head. Chief Walking Horse. They wept for their people. They weep when our people's hearts bleed.

*   *   *

The keelboats wrenched as the steamboat shrieked in the wind, warning any other half-crazed pilot caught on these waters of their presence.

Corporal Bundy knew his instructions well. "Keep the Indians, the niggers, and the white-trash from revolt."

And, for Corporal Bundy, this meant splitting a few Cherokee heads with the butt of his rifle if the slightest sign of lack of cooperation called for it. He hated this lurching, life-threatening ride. "Too dangerous on a night like this. Is the captain crazy?" he muttered, as the rain pelted his lopsided face. Though he had put on his oiled slicker, the wind-driven rain and the thundering waves sent shivers down his chilled skin. His slicker flopped around him like wings of a stricken buzzard. His bones ached. He longed for nights on shore with a golden saloon light, and girls in red dresses smelling of perfume, rubbing the chests and shoulders of chilled government soldiers, such as he.

Positioned precariously on his small, wooden rise, he scowled at the silent Cherokee men, holding their aching heads, stomachs revolting from half-cured liquor. As they came out of their stupor, Bundy expected trouble. He was prepared. Hard to take aim, or butt heads when the boat lurched so. Strange too, he thought, how passive savages are when captured, herded together like this. And how those bucks changed when the liquor inflamed their brains. No, Injuns can't handle liquor.

Bundy knew they wouldn't make it to Portageville for at least another hour. "Captain's probably having himself a conniption fit over this mess, river out of control, rolling up at us like it is." Bundy poked the shoulder of a drenched recruit, who was attempting to shove shreds of tobacco into his jaw.

* * *

The *Smelter* wailed and orange sparks caught in the wind and drifted back in the cold rain. The steamboat wallowed as the Captain struggled to turn the ship aside when the tangle of tree roots loomed in front of him. Enough, he knew, to send them to the bottom to be buried in the silt along with De Soto of old. "Oh, Lord, save us." His breath raked through his lungs.

Too late. He grasped the wheel with gnarled fingers, attempt-

ing a turn as he gave weight with his portly body. The wheel caught
as his windshield shattered and black roots of the giant sycamore
shot into his cabin.

Captain Donnell yanked the rope and the boat's lamentation
rose in the rain and wind. He cursed. He prayed. The boat trembled
beneath his soaked feet, then listed to the right. Limbs of the
ancient sycamore wrestled the pilot wheel from his hands as its
spreading branches, each one larger than an ordinary tree, caught
in the main current, then slowly let go of the shattered deck, bobbing and nodding onward in the raging waters like a tugboat, lost
on the high seas.

"Merciful Mary, Mother of God," the Captain pleaded, trying
to find his sea legs, "we're aground on a sandbar in the dark. Ain't
no one else crazy enough to be out on this river, raging like this."

The emigrants, huddled on their keelboats, clutching rails,
walls and each other, rocked amidst the overlapping waves, praying that the Lord Jesus Christ himself come and take them. Lucy
Drake, foremost among them.

CHAPTER EIGHT

Back on the overland trail, Colonel Pollit's wide buttocks chafed from the saddle jolting. His soul chafed at the sorry state of affairs. He had overlooked the excessively long stretches between the government depots set up to supply the train with provisions.

Snaking in the last one at New Hamburg, Illinois, the whole herd of emigrants, officers and supervisors stood staring at their supply station, like London waifs in the rain before a bleak orphanage. The wind howling through the cracks and knotholes of the grey boards announced, "Empty, empty. More unfulfilled promises."

"Blast the Indians. Why didn't someone tell me they'd drag them along like starving cattle behind an empty wagon? Blast the suppliers. What happened?" Colonel Pollit's mind hit a stump in its wanderings. But he recognized that the suppliers were only ordinary farmers hired by the government to provide corn and oats.

And the emigrants? Day upon day of rugged terrain, shreds for moccasins or shoes, most with no shoes at all and the temperature now dipping into the thirties at night.

"God above." He turned, sighing at the spiraling human train behind him, the bowed black heads, the swaying bodies tied to their spirit by the strength of minuscule faith. Those who lost the last fragment of hope died quickly by the wayside.

"Only one blanket per family," ordered Sergeant Sedgwick, as the shocking realization flooded everyone's mind—winter will be here and we don't have enough blankets.

Benjamin and other full-bloods lumbered on, stony faced, wills beyond their own pushing their skinny shanks and torn feet. "Don't accept clothes or food from the betrayers," they whispered to each other. "Remember, blankets were once handed to our people by the hands of the white men, smiles on their faces. Embedded in them were the seeds of small pox."

"We'll have to butcher the last of the steers," hollered Colonel Pollit, sagging as he realized he was reduced to such a pitiful state.

Benjamin's plodding slowed. His shanks had human limits. Ten, 12 miles of marching every day. Rain, wind. Blasting sun. Fever. Chills. Mother, behind, struggling, praying every step.

Benjamin turned to look at Mother Drake, crooked stick in a hand, which looked more like an eagle's claw. Her swaying body bent almost to the ground, yet her feet, bare on the cold, cracked road, found purchase. Her spirit led her skeletal body as her pariah's rags flapped here and there over exposed flesh.

"Is there a Lord Jesus? How can he allow such a pure-hearted soul as Mother to suffer like this? What keeps her going?" Bitterness had not overcome his heart as it had with others, who had given in to the whiskeys pawned off on them by beguilers and betrayers. He knew Mother Drake prayed for him. Her little Red Wing of the forest. How she had smiled at his tiny first bow and arrow. The light in his eyes by the Hiwassee as she showed him how to catch a trout on a spring day. Memories. Blessings. A child's laugh, a child's eyes. These sustained her. She had prayed for her little Red Wing, now a man.

A man? Shoving one blistered, scratched bare foot ahead of another? She would have laughed, had it not been the naked reality, at his tattered shreds. Who could call them pants, tearing in the wind as he struggled? A man? Head captain of a gaggle of 20 at mealtime?

What a bitter cry that was. Yes, Benjamin concluded. A man. He had not yet yielded to the darkness. He lent his shoulder to the pick and the ax in the daily grave diggings. His shoulder, cut by the splintered edge of a ditched wagon, joined others to heave it back on the tracks with red shoulders, red flesh, red spirit.

Sloping hills rose ahead. "Oh, Above Beings, how many miles? Uphill again?" Shamans stared at the brassy sky for any portent—

an unusual cloud, a sudden whirling wind, a dust dervish—anything to break the spell of not knowing.

"Heave there." Commands to bellowing oxen.

"You stupid mules, haw, haw," drivers cried, cracking blacksnake whips.

Women, whose babes and children were buried in shallow graves in a land they would never see again, wailed in the wind. They wept for the ancient white-crowned ones who stepped off the earth when their hearts could pump their blood no more.

A wagon, breaking an axle on the last climb, delayed them for awhile. A wide valley stretched before them.

Benjamin realized that in other times, in other places, they would have stopped to share the impact of the scene before them. The meandering river. Oaks and cottonwoods stirring in the afternoon wind against white clouds. Grasses, touched with amber and gold of approaching autumn, rustled as the blackbirds rose and circled above their heads.

"Hold. Hold!" cried trailmasters and wagon drivers. "Hold." They yanked the long reins with their callused hands. Horses, mules, oxen, smelling the water ahead, neighed, bellowed and strained.

"Who knows the name of this river?" Monroe Bates called. Whatever its name, Benjamin could see it had neither ferry nor bridge. Colonel Pollit had personally ordered this change of direction. "Saves at least 20 miles," he'd shouted.

Colonels, trailmasters, and captains took counsel. They'd survived the miseries of the four-day crossing of the Ohio. "Who would have believed it?" They still asked each other. "Stupid Indians afraid of the wide river. Huddled and mumbling heathenish prayers."

Now another river and no bridge, no ferry. The river rolled ahead as they descended the last slope, drivers holding back their reins, the thirsty hordes trying not to overrun the livestock in their rush to get to the water.

"It don't take a fool to see it's too deep and wide to cross. Steep banks, have to dig inclines down the banks to even get the wagons to the water," yelled a driver. Cursing circled in the wind, which now changed to the east.

Prayers and blessings mingled as the wanderers found nicks and crevasses down to the water. Benjamin realized Long Man may be a source of fear, but he was also a blessing for their dry throats and empty bellies. Too hungry, fatigued and thirsty, the travelers did not even try to worry, "How will we get across the river?"

Besides, Benjamin knew they had to dig in and bury the dead before cholera broke out.

CHAPTER NINE

Benjamin's caravan dug in for four days along the willow-lined river. A scattering of families, with sick children and infirm elderly, huddled under the small canvas tents pitched by the swearing recruits, aided by Benjamin and fellow-plodders.

"Ain't it a wonder, how they don't fight for them?" Quartermaster Wolcott stared at the near-silent horde. Benjamin knew that Wolcott's brains couldn't comprehend that the Cherokee were a giving and loving people. Who were they to jerk a canvas from a brother or sister?

The wind blew cold draughts down their necks. Small groups built fires. Some clustered under wagons or beneath the giant maples and hazelnut bushes for shelter. Waiting. Waiting. The eternal waiting.

Benjamin lifted his head when a cluster of women began the hymn, "Thro' many dangers, toils and snares, I have already come . . . ."

Preachers bowed heads to pray, or intone, "Though I walk through the valley and the shadow of death . . ."

Shamans, not to be outdone and to assume their full responsibilities, took out shreds of tobacco and flints to light fires and observe which way the smoke drifted in the wind to discover the sources of sicknesses, the deaths, or a portent for tomorrow.

"Bridge is quicker. Remember the Ohio? Takes too long to secure cables for a ferry. Then, too slow. Hurry 'em over an improvised bridge," Colonel Pollit shouted. Pollit fussed at the constant delays. "Before we know it, November snow and ice on the rivers ahead." Benjamin knew he meant the threatening Mississippi ahead, but it was too overwhelming to consider just now.

*   *   *

Time weighed and autumn winds hinted of approaching cold. It had taken four days to secure loads of rocks and heavy boards, bolts, nails, and extra-duty chains from the lumberyards at Deer Village, where the grinning hardware merchants quarreled for the privilege of cheating them.

"Two thousand dollars? Yi, yi, yi," Colonel Pollit howled. Benjamin knew Pollit would have to petition the government for more funds.

By the seventh day the construction crew, aided by drafted Indians, Benjamin and Monroe included, managed to lay rock pilings that rose above the water.

"Now drag that board over here," commanded Oliver Leets, supervising the building. His hat blew into the water, and his bushy red hair leaped in the wind. "You Indians there, another board, an don't take all week."

Benjamin heaved and grunted, ignoring the bleeding cuts on his feet from the sharp rock edges and his empty stomach rubbing against his backbone. He knew there was no use mentioning extra cornmeal as the supply was depleted. Colonel Pollit had been reduced now to buying wagon loads of ear corn from the locals. Exorbitant prices and all. Benjamin thought of how he had sat on the supply wagon as the locals hooted and slapped each other's backs at their brilliance of unloading last year's weevil-infested nubbins on the ignorant savages. "Let 'em shell it off the cob. Corn can be et without grinding it," Sergeant Sedgwick announced, as if his fury rose at the thought that now it would be after Christmas before he could bed down in some heel-kicking territory town and frolic.

Benjamin struggled when he attempted to raise the heavy plank end to the piling ahead.

"Give you a hand. There. Better with two on planks like these." Monroe Bates's fine, long-fingered hands grabbed the rough board, relieving Benjamin of burdening awkwardness.

"Thanks, Monroe." Benjamin surprised himself that he could

still grunt thanks for offered help. "How long do you think it'll take?"

"If the weather stays like it is today, I'd say we'll have her done in about a week. Don't you think, Benjamin?"

Warmth crept through Benjamin's breast at the sound of a familiar voice. Though he and Monroe had little in common back in New Echota, Monroe's offered help reminded him of how life could be. He had almost forgotten human kindness still existed. How was Monroe's family enduring the trek?

Benjamin noticed how Monroe's wife, White Birch, also known in the English tongue as Felicia, marched along, head lifted in her attempt to rise above the humiliations. Her doeskin dress had not succumbed to the elements as had the muslin and calico garments of so many of the others.

"Now, let's both push and we'll have a walk-way across to the third piling," Monroe said, his face ruddy, shining in a shaft of sunlight.

A rivulet of uneasiness trickled across Benjamin's heart. He recognized his discomfort when he thought of White Birch or Monroe, and especially, their 14 year-old son, Jacob, a smiling, white-toothed lad, winsome and athletic. And the discomfort that had lodged there for 14 years.

"Another plank, Benjamin, and we'll reach the fourth piling. Heave." Monroe's broad shoulders swung and heaved along with Bejanmin's lifting and shoving.

The Above Being, throwing us all together like this . . . Benjamin tried to focus his brains on bridge building, the boards, the water below, and not let old regrets distract him. Yet, they crowded his mind. Especially, when Monroe's arm brushed his or their hands touched when they clasped the heavy planks.

Did Monroe know? Was it true?

Benjamin recalled how Abby occasionally mentioned to him, "Monroe and White Birch's son, Jacob, looks like he could fit right into our family, doesn't he, Benjamin?"

Benjamin thought of long ago, back in the hemlock and chestnut woods by the clear waters of the Coosa. "Don't let my mind wander to those days, I'll topple into the river," he murmured to himself. Focus on Abby, Abby, where is Abby?

"If you're out of corn or meal, come, sit tonight by our fire. White Birch managed to save a little extra. Jacob vowed to catch a rabbit. Wouldn't a hot stew boost a fellow? May be a couple of frog legs thrown in, that is if Jacob can still find them, late as it is," Monroe smiled.

The friendly words were too much. Benjamin cleared his throat as the trickle across his heart burst into a rivulet, a flood of old memories—wondering and the secrets of yesteryears.

Benjamin had cast a long, steady look at the lithe, bronzed Jacob, seven years older than Lucy. Oh, God. Where is Lucy? Only the Above One knew.

"Father, Jacob Monroe is like a brother to me, sometimes." How could he forget Lucy's words?

Eighteen then, and he had taken a hind-quarter of deer meat to White Birch's father's stick-and-wattle cabin, according to rules and customs.

White Birch, delighted, had murmured, laughed, stretched her long legs and led him to the Coosa where they spent the languid afternoon under willow fronds. How she had kissed him.

"Benjamin. Another plank." Monroe studied the bent shoulders of the man on the piling with him as if he noticed how the trek took its toll on Benjamin. "No, White Birch cannot marry you, Benjamin," her mother, Bending Hazel, had announced. You know White Birch and you are of the same Blue Clan." That was it. Outdone by old clan rules—old rules now left behind. Today, he could marry within his clan. Not then. Not at 18.

Should we have run away together? But he realized at that age he'd not been strong enough to buck the clan rules. While families whispered and palavered behind his back, he'd tried not to notice, besides, he was too busy nursing his wounded feelings. He tried to ignore it when White Birch attempted to soothe his wounded feelings, while at the same time, turned her affections upon Monroe Bates.

The child, Jacob, was born eight months later.

What did Monroe know? Why was he smothering him now with his help and friendship? Benjamin stared into the face women considered appealing, the men, brave, but at times as expressionless as the tops of white toadstools.

"Benjamin, you were one of the 20 who signed the New Echota Treaty along with Chief John Ridge, weren't you?" Monroe cleared his throat, dropped his plank and stared into Benjamin's black eyes, surveying his reaction.

Of course, Monroe Bates was wise enough to know that it was a loaded topic, enough to startle one, enough to rip open an old scab and let festering pus spew. Benjamin shifted a plank. The Coosa of long ago, the willow fronds and White Birch's sensuous laughter vanished in the October wind at Monroe's words.

He stared Monroe Bates straight in the eyes and said, "Yes, Monroe, you have always known I signed the Removal Treaty. That's why we're moving to our new lands. You know that. We're obeying the laws of Georgia and the laws of the United States of America." If the nervousness within his breast surfaced in any of his words, they were not yet apparent to Monroe.

"The reaty of tears. The treaty of backs turned against our people, the treaty of . . . ." Monroe held his tongue as if he remembered that he had invited Benjamin Drake to his fire, come evening, along with his aged mother. "Hold this plank, Benjamin, while I shove a brace against the piling."

Monroe smiled at Benjamin. Benjamin, face lean from deprivation, shifted a bare foot to keep his balance on the rocks and wondered: What is the meaning of this friendship?

CHAPTER TEN

Back on the Mississippi, the torrential rains lasted 36 hours. Raging, debris-ridden waters swirled around the sandbar-lodged *Smelter* with its two keelboats bobbing like corks in a whirlpool. Captain Donnell groaned and searched for his own whiskey jug.

On the keelboat hooked next to the stern of the sandbar-locked steamboat, Lucy Drake, drenched and shivering, stretched out her arms, balancing herself to keep from being pitched into the laps of those around her. Ignoring her hunger, she glanced back at Todd at her mother's side.

"I'll try to find something for her to drink." Lucy knew that without some form of nourishment, besides the rain and river water, her mother's life was in peril.

"Everybody's hungry, child. What you expect to find?" murmured a rain-soaked woman of indecipherable age, head wrapped in a soggy purple cloth. "Ain't no one going to save us, child. All we can do is to pray to the Lord Jesus himself to come down an take us. Don't you have that slave woman doing for you and your mother and that boy back there?"

"Black Bee's over there." Lucy pointed, tottering as the boat shifted. She pointed toward the left stern to the pile of the young and old, who had sought to drown their troubles with corn liquor and were now oblivious to external troubles.

Lucy cast her black eyes here and there. Huddled in wet clusters, many were asleep. She noticed sleep did not erase the groans of the unconscious ones caught in both the death-threatening outer nightmares and soul-terrifying inner ones.

Corporal Bundy no longer stood on his platform, supervising the wretched crowd. Instead, he hunched over with his shoulders braced against the rail, his pinched face a yellow-green, tobacco-stained-teeth chattering in the cold wind.

Lucy gave him some credit. Corporal Bundy had taken pity upon a sick Cherokee boy. Stripping off his ragged slicker, he handed it to the weeping mother, who, in spite of her feelings about officers and the government, covered her only son with it just before he died.

"We're doomed. Ain't no way we going to survive this." At first Bundy cursed, but the mocking elements and the raging river drowned his tongue.

Lucy remembered how Bundy shook from fear when yesterday, both their keelboats heaved from an unexpected swell and were overswept by a maverick wave. How many were swept overboard? They had long since ceased trying to keep an accurate record. Lucy glanced through the fog-draped trees on the eastern shore, then looked down at the suffering people at her feet. The trees shuddered in a cold wind and fog like ghouls trembling with foreboding.

* * *

Corporal Bundy, drab clothes plastered to his shivering thighs, reared his chin and muttered, "Another uprising of drunken young bucks back there come dark and I'll be overpowered." He realized his rifle and ammunition were useless.

"Can use it as a club. Done it before." This thought comforted him. However, Bundy was encouraged, by something else he had observed.

Among those young bucks at the stern of the keelboat, he had spied three who, in spite of their drunken stupor, still had flasks of blood-warming liquor hidden in their filthy garments, or underneath their shivering bodies. Guarding them like a mother-lode of gold.

Just as these thoughts surfaced in his brain, a small hand tugged on his flapping shirttail.

"Officer. Officer. Please, Officer . . ."

A child's voice, surprising too, rising above this wind and roar.

Bundy turned his lopsided face shadowed with stubble to Lucy, weaving before him, trying not to plant a foot on a prostrate body, or corpse, a foot still in a shoe, though a squishy one.

"Sir, do you have any medicine we could mix with water? Anything to make some broth? My mother back there . . ." Lucy pointed backwards as the boat pitched and she tumbled into his wet legs.

Bundy surprised himself. It wasn't the first time he'd touched an Indian, but he had hoped it would be one a little older than this wisp-of-a-girl before him. He had been whispering to himself, "Give me time, give me time."

Ain't a fellow got enough trouble without having an Indian stripling, girl at that, tugging at his shirttail?

"Sir, do you..," but her words were lost in the ruckus. Though the rain had stopped, the clouds still hovered like pea soup, making vision difficult. Evening must be nearing.

"Thief! Thief! Thief! Guards, help. Thief, thief . . ."

Bundy and the ragtag child, who was holding on to keep from falling, turned toward the sudden upheaval. Before them, on the lower aft deck, where the waters lapped over their feet, stood three male figures, rags flapping around their emaciated bodies, arms upraised.

"It's mine, you thief! Guard! Thievery going on and us asleep too," a bent-shouldered Cherokee of middle-age in a dark green shirt shouted. Upon awakening, he'd searched for his bottle only to find it clasped in the hand of a bare-torso Cherokee, younger than he, brown dungarees bagging at his buttocks.

Bodies tangled. The fight was on.

Curses ascended. Glass broke when the bottle hit the rail, shattered and fragments and liquid spread in the wind.

"Fool. Look what you've done," yelled the man in green, livid with rage.

Bundy smiled sickly. What I've been waiting for. Cussed Injuns warm their guts—why can't I? Now's my chance to take custody of the liquor, now that it's surfaced.

He surprised himself at how lightly he sprang to his feet in spite of sore muscles and cold joints. "Command, I must take command," he muttered to himself, attempting an official posture.

"Halt! Halt! You there." He lifted his rifle and pointed it at the small circle of tottering men, arms down, now up, shuffling for a half-filled liquor bottle.

"Let go, that's mine. Let go, I say . . ."

"Thud," went Bundy's rifle butt against the head of the Indian in the brown dungarees. Without a yelp, the Cherokee slumped into the laps of others arising from their stupor.

"You there in the green shirt, give me that bottle!" Bundy's gun barrel shot to the side as he reached upward for the amber bottle, which slipped and tilted in the struggling hands.

* * *

Corporal Bundy's shrieking commands awakened Black Bee from her snoring. "My bottle. Empty. Nothing to get me through another dark night . . .Merciful God."

"Black Bee, Black Bee," shouted the waif-of-a-child, 20 feet behind. "Oh, Black Bee, you're awake, Mother needs . . ." but her words were lost in the wind as Black Bee lurched upwards. Finding her sea legs, her broad, bare feet flattened hands and calves caught beneath. Her battering-ram-arm shot forward. "Gimmie that. You gimmie that." Her red eyes wide, fixed on the line on the bottle marking the depth of the liquid inside. She trembled and heaved.

It was obvious that Bundy hadn't counted on this. Old nigger woman heaving upwards like a submerged hippopotamus lunging to the surface.

His rifle butt thudded on the side of her powerful temple. Blood spurted and streamed down her shiny black face. She groaned, but she didn't go down.

Where is the bottle? The blessed bottle? There, in the hands of the fool in the baggy dungarees. But, no. The stupid corporal, beating the man unmercifully with his rifle butt, had the treasure in his hands. Then Black Bee understood. Bundy himself wanted the bottle.

Black Bee roared, her alcoholic tremors were threatening her again. She was driven to do what she had to do. Larger than two men, she heaved up her ponderous weight.

Her eyes glistened like black onyx, as her weight crushed against Bundy and the dungaree-clad Cherokee. "Thank you, thank you, I've got it, I've . . ." She and Bundy scrapped and fought.

The keelboat rocked with the added stirrings on the lower deck and dipped treacherously. With Black Bee's speedy thrust and her massive weight, Corporal Bundy and old Black Bee both crashed through the flimsy rail and sailed out into the gloom and the sucking whirlpools of the Mississippi, a river not known for its respect of one person over another. Not at all.

Bundy let out a blasphemous cry that rose above the slush of waves, the surge of angry waters and the groans of the water soaked beggars.

Silence reigned for a moment. Then someone called out. "Child, this, are you looking for this? We know that old woman was your mama's nigger."

A trembling arm of a woman, who had lost both husband and only child, hair matted and hanging to symbolize her grief, held up old Black Bee's dirty muslin sack. "May be some medicine or grain in there to help your mama." The woman sagged back on the water soaked boards. Lucy, tottering with Black Bee's soggy sack, shivered as her cold fingers tugged at the string.

CHAPTER ELEVEN

Back by the river in Illinois, Jacob Bates didn't catch a frog for his mother's stew pot; White Birch, however, was glad that he'd found a land turtle digging its hole for the approaching winter. The savory white meat in the boiling water, with a handful of shelled, corn and wild onions jerked from along the riverbank, made the stew actually appetizing and nourishing.

Thunder rumbled over westward behind cloud banks.

A few late-summer frogs croaked.

"Don't need any rain. Troubles enough with the crossing without the river rising," Monroe Bates said, sipping from a dented tin cup held in both callused hands.

"You're right. Any rise of the river would mean disaster for our bridge," Benjamin replied, thankful that he and his beloved mother were included for the meal.

A trace of a smile touched Mother Drake's lips, though her thin hands trembled as she shifted her tin cup to her mouth.

"Thank you, White Birch. Thank you. A bit of home, isn't it? People from New Echota, the wind, the trees . . . ." Benjamin knew she thought of how God leads, or that her mind was searching for the verse the reverend read in the evening devotions. "When thou passeth through the waters, I will be with thee; and through the rivers, they shall not overflow thee . . . ."

Benjamin knew his mother was sustained by an abiding faith. What about mine? My faith? How bright the stars, beyond the cloud bank. Benjamin wondered if there would ever again be any stars shining in the darkness of his soul. Here I sit, uneasy by Monroe's fire, near starving, holding myself back for fear of bolting my soup, guilty that I hunch here eating a handout from a neighbor.

"There is enough for a half-cup more for each." Reaching for their bowls and cups, White Birch lifted the dipper.

"Give it to the lad, one serving enough for me." Benjamin refused to take food from the elderly and the young. He observed Jacob leaning against an elm, legs crossed before him, a handsome lad. Get him through the troubles of this migration, keep him in school, he surely would amount to something. Benjamin knew he must lower his eyes, as the lad stirred and turned to glance at him.

Too much, the heart-stirrings, the tumbling mixture of old regrets and guilt, the buried hurt and shame, the loss, the rising affection he felt when he looked at the boy. White Birch turned to Benjamin. "You will be with them in another month or so."

"Yes, it's hope that keeps us going," Benjamin said.

"How Abby and Lucy will welcome you. I'm sure they were among those fortunate enough to go on the river steamers. Why, that would be a real adventure, an excursion. Not the dirt and stink of this overland trek." Benjamin hoped the old hurt didn't show as White Birch tried to offer words of comfort. Instead of comfort, her words only saddened him even more.

Benjamin cleared his throat and shifted his position on the hard ground. "God knows. God knows." He surprised himself. Did it mean he still had a mustard seed of faith that preacher Going Wolf always talked about, the mustard seed that gave rise to a tree large enough for a flock of birds? White Birch's reassurance fell to the ashes of his heart, like dying embers falling from a burning log.

"Your wife, Abby, was always a Chief John Ross supporter, wasn't she?" Monroe stared at Benjamin, rearranging his leg and foot.

Here it came again. Enough internal turmoil and feelings without the added goading about the factious parties back home.

"Yes, Monroe. Abby and I talked about it a lot. Seems as if it did little good, doesn't it?" Though a Cherokee tried to avoid staring at a fellow brother, he dared to look Monroe straight in his black, wide eyes.

"And strangely, Monroe, our political differences didn't seem to divide us. We both knew we struggled with forces beyond the control of our own wills. You know that, Monroe. You know the encroachments of white settlers and the arm of the United States government were forces too great for our people." Benjamin feared he had been too testy, here as a supper guest, too. Monroe cleared his throat and stood. Benjamin knew it was a Cherokee custom to dialogue and parley, often in drawn out and elaborate styles, Chero-kee politics. That was the old way of the Chiefs. He felt a pressure in his throat. Anger? Was the discussion leading to anger?

Monroe seemed to struggle to control his tongue. Benjamin acknowledged that the matter of land and its sale wasn't settled yet. It would be deliberated with zealous give-and-take in the new country ahead—new council, new houses of the government, though nothing like New Echota. Still, wouldn't they be 'a people' sovereign, holding lands in their own rights and freedom? But the old blood law. The sacredness of our land, stolen from us . . . . Benjamin's thoughts tangled as a roll of thunder startled the oxen and horses. Neighing and lowing rose in the wind, which sud-denly had turned cold.

Monroe dared another comment. "Sacred laws have their own built-in enforcement." He then seemed to realize he needed Benjamin's strength to complete the bridge and that tomorrow they would make the crossing. They both knew the calls and com-mands would start early in the morning.

* * *

Campfires dimmed. The bone-weary bridge builders, scavengers for food, the passive waiting ones, the sick and the infirm, praying to God for death, gave their bodies to the earth for a few hours of rest, some trusting their souls to the God of Abraham, others to the gods of their forefathers.

Lightning flashed. A sudden shower commenced and then a piercing cry from some mother the edge of the camp. "God above. Mercy. Mercy. Oh, my child, my child." A mother, whose strength had not completely ebbed from her skeletal body, rocked the blotched corpse of the child who had been racked by coughing and fever the entire day. Another child gathered into the bosom of the Above Beings.

Shrieks of grief now failed to move the multitude. Saturated hearts could only take so much pain. Roll the dead boy in a ragged shroud till morning. Benjamin, hearing the wailing, realized that he and the other grave diggers would again scoop dirt to make shallow graves. Reverend Going Wolf will stand like a stricken scarecrow and murmur prayers and verses they all now knew by heart. Death, life, up, down? Who had energy left to deal with such forces?

In spite of the soul's torpor, mothers threw back ragged blankets to check their children. Easy to ignore the death-grip of pestilence while trying to keep body from parting with soul.

More shrieks and moaning rose in the cold wind, now whipping the canvas tents, rattling the hazel bushes.

"Oh, oh, oh, husband, look. My child. Blotches. Blotches. Fever, chills. What coughing."

Here and there, fires were revived and shamans, ever vigilant to ward off the witches, the encroachments of shadowy spirits smiting the people with unknown pestilence, rose on knobby knees, searched for their knapsacks with their potions and rattles.

*   *   *

Old Doctor Reiff, vowing if ever he survived this trek, he would never practice medicine again, scrambled for his glasses, buttoned his pants and heaved his portly body. He headed for the stinking blankets. He'd known it the livelong day. He was silent only because there was nothing he could do about it. Measles, outbreak of measles among the children.

Lone Wolf and Grey Hawk, the most recognized of the shamans, tossed tobacco into their fires. They murmured prayers to ancient gods, their glazed eyes surveying every drift of smoke to ascertain the source of the pestilence choking the children.

Though they acted as bewildered by the upheavals and misfortunes of The People and the blighting from white man's abra-

CHAPTER TWELVE

"Did you believe we would ever get off that rocking keelboat, mother?" Lucy led her mother by one hand while holding Black Bee's dirty bag in the other. Todd swung another odd-shaped bundle containing scraps of left-over corn dodgers and three arrow heads his father had given him back on the Hiwassee.

"Well, child, at times I wondered if we could hope much longer." Abby looked beyond the wharf to the towering Fort Smith she had been told was built to halt the warring Osage at the head-waters of the Arkansas. Her vision yet a problem, she must watch her step, for unexpectedly everything she saw could blur and double. Her legs trembled but did not fold beneath her.

"Twenty-one days from the Ohio River down the Mississippi and up the Arkansas. Thank God for a landing at last." A raised, red scar slashed down from her hairline to just above her eye brow.

"Speed it up, you aren't the only ones, another ship'll be landing soon." Irritation dripped from the officer's raspy voice as he swatted gnats and mosquitoes.

Several hundred emigrants in various states of disarray, tatters, fatigue and illness, crowded around Lucy and Abby. Lucy turned to look at Abby as she struggled not to show on her face the terrible smells of their bodies that nauseated her.

"Old serpent Uktena nearly yanked us under back there on that Mississippi," shouted a tall half-blood woman named Cristy Mulberry, smiling and showing gratitude that she had at last been able to plant her feet on solid ground.

"Stuck there, water-logged and starving in the cold for three days before those two steamboats were able to rescue us," mumbled a middle-aged Cherokee man named Charley Wolf. His bewildered, sick mother leaned on him.

"God above answered our prayers," the feeble old woman murmured. "The waters did not overwhelm us."

"She's right. The waters did not overwhelm us. Almost. Our faith was tested," replied Abby, while she searched for a place to sit down. Then Abby realized that she hadn't taken full account of how weak she was.

"Over here, over here," commanded the supervisor, pointing to water-troughs, where, mercifully, the "dirty savages" could wash off some of the lice and filth.

"Slit-trenches behind that warehouse. Too many of you for us to build out-houses. Watch your step. Copperheads and water moccasins in them trenches," yelled a guard who wiped his forehead with a dirty rag.

*   *   *

An orange sun, monstrous when viewed through the hazy atmosphere, slid behind a mauve cloud in the west. Hills? Mountains? Were there mountains rising up over westward? Lucy Drake's black eyes scanned the scenery. "Mother, it looks a little like land by the Coosa and the Hiwassee, doesn't it?"

"Why, yes, my child. Tomorrow on the boat up-river we'll see more of it. Arkansas, it's called, and beyond, Oklahoma, where our people settled a few years back." She passed her hand over her face when the dizziness struck again. She thought of the treaty group, who'd gone on ahead a decade ago. Would they greet them? Wouldn't it be a blessing to see folks from back home?

Abby struggled to halt the threats of homelessness and poverty. Nothing but a few scraps. Where will we begin? How will we live? Where was Benjamin? Oh, surely, if they were marching overland, Mother Drake and Aunt Rachel wouldn't survive. A lump like soured bean dough weighed on her heart.

They finished splashing water on their arms and faces just as another official commanded, "Over here. Your new supplies, over here by the wagons."

While recruits and family members struggled to drag the corpses from the Arkansas riverboat, *Scioto*, anchored below, the wanderers surged toward the supply wagons.

"Mother, can you make it?" Lucy asked.

"You and Todd go on over. Tell them that there are three of us. I'll try to totter over if he requires it, or perhaps someone will bring our supplies over here by this big oak tree."

But there was no need for someone else. The two children had no difficulties at all carrying the pitiful bag of cornmeal and chunk of green-rind salt pork.

As the shadows lengthened, families circled here and there in small groups. Smoke ascended from fires. Voices caught in the evening air. "Water, son, run to the trough for water so I can mix this cornmeal. A flat stone? Quickest way is to toss the cornmeal mixture on a hot rock."

Folks scrambled, all bellies empty, gnawing against backbones.

"I'll strike a flint to light our fire," Todd shouted, voice reflecting the assurance in his skills in outdoor living.

"Here's a flat rock to cook on. Get it hot, Todd," Lucy said.

"Mother we'll have hoe cakes for you in a moment. Any more tea leaves in Black Bee's sack?" Abby looked up as if to say, that is another matter, Black Bee's sack. "Let me check it again." Abby fingered through the contents, a crooked ginger root, an old blue handkerchief still folded and stinking of tobacco, an empty whiskey-flask which they could use to drink from, a snaggle-toothed wooden comb, and the weird voodoo doll.

"Here it is, a small bag of tea. I have only my tin cup, but we can all share from it." Abby decided they would talk about the wretched-looking doll in Black Bee's bag later. Should have dropped it into the mighty Mississippi along with the remains of that man, De Soto.

Acrid smoke rose behind the warehouse by the slit-trenches. "They're burning the blankets of the dead," murmured a nearby Cherokee, stirring his cornmeal for his hoe cakes. "Keeps the cholera from spreading. And here at Fort Smith, the stationmaster decided to be generous. That soldier's stacking blankets over there," the stoop-shouldered Cherokee announced.

"Private Greenway over here. I'll be handing out these army blankets soon's I turn this wagon around and open the tailgate."

A few river village citizens emerged from houses that had sprung up around Fort Smith, like tilting toadstools. They parted the saplings and bushes to gawk at the savages shipped all the way from the woods of Tennessee and Georgia, making a journey far longer than any they would ever take. Many of the 'savages' more educated than they would ever be in their lifetimes, someone had told them.

Whippoorwills called, their cries seeming endless, interrupted only by the piercing call of a night hawk. Somewhere down river in the evening mist, a steamboat moaned, an appropriate sound to announce its load of slaves and the dispossessed.

Lucy lifted the first hoe cake from the flat sand rock with a small stick, sweet smell of baked cornmeal goading her own hunger. "Here, Mother. The first one's for you."

Abby knew there would be no refusing the child. "Why, thank you, Lucy and Todd. I'm certain it'll be very tasty."

"Blow on it first, Mrs. Drake. Blow on it first, it's very hot." The boy smiled, caught in his efforts to help the woman who had suffered such a blow to her head.

The water steamed. Lucy tossed in a few leaves. A spicy aroma spread in the air. Stars appeared overhead.

As they took their turns sipping from the cup, they each blew on the edge to cool it. They broke portions of steaming hoe cake, chewing slowly to savor the taste. The chunk of salt pork lay untouched.

* * *

Weariness enveloped the travelers like buzzards circling and settling silently in a locust tree. But before they succumbed, one more order broke the air.

"Over here. New blankets over here. Private Greenway, here,

will distribute the blankets," a supervisor called. "Remember, now, only one per family."

Todd and Lucy raced forward, bare feet pounding the dust. Already, there were dozens ahead of them. But not all of the Cherokees would take the blankets. Lucy already knew that, deprived as they were, some were unable to accept anything from the hands of the country that stole their homeland and forced them to this strange land.

"Name," asked a recruit, assisting Private Greenway.

"John Hogshooter," replied the tall Cherokee, leaning on a stick of driftwood. "Wife and three children in our family." Hogshooter received his one blanket for his family.

"Next. Hurry, gotta get this done before it's pitch dark. Name?" Five minutes. Ten minutes. Water fowl quacked and honked from the river below. "What did she say her name was? 'Laughing Girl?' We'll give her something to laugh about. Next."

Their turn. Lucy tried to hide her apprehension.

"My name is Lucy Drake. I'm with my mother who's sitting over there by that tree. She's too sick to come to the wagon." Lucy reached up at recruit Greenway, who leaned down and placed the folded army blanket into her open arms.

Greenway smiled. "There you are, little girl. How many in your family?"

"Three," hollered Todd. "Three."

There was no time for Lucy to straighten out that Todd actually wasn't a family member. But the way circumstances were, she concluded it was a small matter.

Private Greenway's grey-green eyes followed the children as they bounced back to their fire to Abby Drake.

"Sleep well. I'll see you in the morning. Great trip ahead of us in the morning," Andrew Greenway called. He smiled at Lucy as if she reminded him of a little sister back home in Kentucky.

Tomorrow, the journey up the Arkansas River on the *Velocipede*, keelboats in tow. Easy journey and, according to the reports, the riverbanks were crowded with stands of oaks and maples.

Hickory and ash loomed behind, the ash already tinged with the yellow of autumn. "Why, in no time at all you'll be at Fort Gibson where you'll be reimbursed for your lands and possessions left back in New Echota." The military officer tried to be encouraging, pity for the ragged emigrants reflected on his face.

Though bone-weary, Lucy couldn't drop off to sleep. It was not the hard ground beneath the blanket. The soul needed time to review the meanings of the incomprehensible events they'd lived through, so far. "Are you all right, now, Mother?" Lucy asked.

"Yes, Lucy, I'm doing better. Tomorrow I'll be stronger. You'll see."

"Don't you miss Black Bee, Mother? I do." Lucy shifted her body to be closer to her mother.

"I do miss Black Bee, Lucy, but she doesn't have to worry anymore about the cares of this world." Tears wet Abby's cheeks as she recalled the tender ministrations from Black Bee's giant hands.

"Mother, do you think she is in heaven?"

"Yes, Lucy. God loves people like Black Bee. God is loving."

"But Mother, Black Bee drank whiskey. She was drunk a lot, and oh, mother, how she died."

Abbey realized that her daughter needed comfort and reassurance. How brave she's been with my injury and helplessness. The child has lost her home. Where are her classmates? Where is her father, her beloved aunt and grandmother?

"Black Bee was a slave woman who suffered much in her life, yet she was brave in her own way. We mustn't judge her. I'm sure God looked down upon all the love in Black Bee's heart, all the good things she did."

"Then we will see Black Bee in heaven?"

"Yes, my child. Remember the words of Jesus, 'Come unto me all ye who labor and are heavy laden.'"

"But Mother, Black Bee had that heathen doll. You looked at it in the sack, didn't you, Mother?"

Abby could not evade the question. "Yes, Lucy. I saw the doll. It's still in the sack."

"Look at it, mother. I looked at it while you were sick and sleeping. It's got a long pin stuck through the head and the head looks like . . ."

Abby reached into Black Bee's dingy bag and lifted the voodoo doll so its face could be illumined by the fire. The greased, waxy face had been mauled and pinched by the old slave woman's strong fingers. "Trying to make it look like someone she knew, wasn't she?"

But Abby, who had noticed the likeness of the grotesque doll face, wondered why she hadn't gotten rid of it before it came to this. She wouldn't lie, not to this child who'd been so brave. "Yes. Lucy. It does look like someone." She cleared her throat.

"Mother, I think it looks just like that Corporal Bundy back on the Mississippi River steamer, the one butting folks' heads with his rifle. Don't you think so, too, Mother?"

Todd, still awake, listened and stared. Then his eyes focused on the wax head of Black Bee's doll. "Why, if that don't look just like that mean Corporal Bundy who knocked people's brains out with the butt of his gun."

Then, Abby Drake knew that she would slip the doll into the yellow Arkansas River in the morning.

"Well, I guess Black Bee had her ways," Abby said. She long ago ceased to criticize other folks' religion. "I believe the Lord saw the grain of mustard seed faith in Black Bee's heart, Lucy. I believe it."

"Yes, I think so too. Black Bee was good in her heart. So the Lord won't judge Black Bee too harshly?"

"No, my child. Try to get some rest now. Jesus is the one who pleads for us. Always remember that, Lucy. Try to go to sleep."

* * *

Abby Drake fell asleep on the Arkansas riverbank, a part of her, half-aware that she was dreaming.

Why it is Benjamin? She tried to lift her fatigue-ridden body and stretch her legs to run toward him, but she couldn't move.

Helplessness and grief fell on her soul like the waters of the Great River sweeping over their keelboat.

What is he doing? Abby strained, but it was hard to see in the fog enveloping him. Danger. Benjamin was walking on a narrow board, his feet, bare and cold—over a chasm, no, a river.

Why, he's building a bridge. Benjamin is building a bridge to come to me.

Love flooded her heart. Again Abby tried to rise, but could only lift her trembling arms out to him. She opened her mouth to voice the words, "Benjamin, Benjamin, oh, my love," but no sounds came out.

Icy fingers wrapped around her spirit. Abby realized there was something else. Danger. The river below his bleeding feet—but something else. Before she could sort it out, she tried to call "Benjamin, Benjamin," but, again, no words came. Abby Drake awakened and sat up in a cold sweat, too overcome with fear to pay attention to the wailing grandmother, 12 feet beyond, whose half-blood grandson, Little Smoke, had just died.

Benjamin. Benjamin. I know he's alive, but he's in danger. Abby decided not to tell Lucy.

CHAPTER THIRTEEN

A large flock of cawing crows in the locust trees, plus the squawking ducks fighting over minnows in the river below, awakened Lucy. Smoke from small cooking fires mingled with the river fog.

"Burials over there, Reverend Bushyhead holding the service," John Hogshooter called, massaging a muscle cramp in his leg. "Have to hurry, they want us on that river boat soon after sunrise." He limped toward the top of the rise where the wind whipped Reverend Bushyhead's shirttail. The preacher kept staring at Lucy Drake and the boy with her. John Hogshooter, along with Abby, Lucy, and Todd, was weary of the prodding, the shoving, the commands, "Hurry now. Shove off. Where do you think you're going? Over here, no time for that. Stop." Would the commands ever end?

Abby realized that they were becoming like sheep, barely baaing at the rude prodding. Succumbing to the put-downs and slurs from redneck recruits and the ragtag settlers hooting at them, making fun of the even more beggarly savages.

"Lucy, we won't have time to make a fire," Abby said, concerned about reloading on the keelboat. "We have enough hoe cake left over, Mother," Lucy answered. "Todd, take this tin cup and Black Bee's empty bottle and bring us some fresh water from the trough."

"I'm afraid I don't have strength to make it up to the burials this morning, children," Abby said. She'd tried to take a few steps, but decided she had better sit. "I can be with them in spirit here below. I can hum the hymns," Abby said, drawing the blanket around her shoulders. Only five burials this morning. Were things improving? By now, Abby and Lucy were used to funeral moaning and women with matted hair wailing, demonstrating their grief according to the customs.

The preacher's words drifted toward them in the morning wind. "I am the resurrection and the life . . . ." Stanzas of feeble high-pitched singing floated down from the throats of mourners choking with sorrow: "We shall meet on that beautiful shore . . .In the sweet . . ."

Reverend Bushyhead, tattered Bible in hand, slid down the riverbank following the burial. His eye focused on Lucy Drake. "Little Girl, the one there named Lucy . . ." He reached out a long arm.

Lucy turned to the tall minister with the sad, brown eyes. "I'm Lucy. Lucy Drake."

"Yes, I know. How old are you, Lucy?"

"I will be nine come November, Brother Bushyhead."

"Well, now. You from New Echota, too. Why, you remind me of my own little girl, Eliza. She left New Echota with a migration last year. I've been making the trips back and forth from Oklahoma. When you get to Oklahoma, Eliza could use a friend like you, about her age." The minister smiled warmly, obviously trying to give the girl comfort and encouragement.

"Why, yes, Reverend, when I get to Oklahoma I'll find Eliza. We'll study and play together. Does she play the piano, Reverend Bushyhead?" Lucy looked into the eyes of the tall man with the wild hair.

"I'm afraid not, Lucy. But you ought to hear her sing. She likes that new hymn the mission workers taught us: "O have you not heard of that beautiful stream / That flows through our Father's land? / Its waters gleam bright in the heavenly light, / And ripple o'er golden sand." Reverend Bushyhead's rich timbered voice caught in the wind.

"Well, I'll tell you one thing, Reverend Bushyhead, after that ride on the Mississippi, we all know what rivers are like. That 'Beautiful Stream' sounds more like the Coosa, or the Hiwassee back home." Lucy smiled.

"Yes, my child. Like the Coosa. Like Home." Sadness slid across his chiseled face when the steamboat wailed and the ragamuffin hordes shifted toward the gang plank.

* * *

A small sternwheeler, the *Velocipede*, rocked by the wharf where the waters roiled with carp and fighting ducks. "Get'em on board," muttered Captain Wattles. "We got two days yet to Fort Gibson." Hands in his hip pockets, he stared at the cloudless sky. "A rain'd help." His frown revealed the worry creeping at the edges of his mind. He brushed his grey mutton-chop whiskers with the back of his hand.

When Lucy heard the captain's words, she placed her hand on Abby's shoulder, trying to calm and comfort her.

The captain's words drifted. "This here Arkansas River treacherous under the best of conditions. Ain't had no rain come down now for a month. Them sand bars gonna be lifting their heads." He cleared his throat and checked his turnip-sized watch.

The *Velocipede*, smaller than the *Smelter*, pulled three keelboats, smaller too for the meandering Arkansas River which grew narrower as it snaked westward.

"Not so many of us anymore," Lucy said, Abby's arm hooked into the loop of her own. "You have our sack, Todd?"

By now, they no longer noticed the ever-present odors of unwashed bodies, the smells of sickness, vomit, excrement. It was evident that for some, at least, their noble efforts to remain decently human were wearing thin.

"No, children. We are a much smaller gathering now. How many do you think, Todd?" Abby lifted her splitting head, but her vision was too blurred to focus in the morning light.

"That soldier Greenway said there were 430 going upriver today," Todd said. His black eyes, shiny with anticipation, surveyed the other emigrants as they plodded onto the keelboats, selecting corners, nooks, and spaces, long used to the unhealthy crowding. "Same as on the Smelter, someone's hair in your face. Another's feet or legs shoving your back, or an elbow digging in your ribs," Lucy said, following Todd and allowing Abby to lean on her.

"Pack 'em in. Water's low. We oughta taken four keels. But we can get 'em all on three," the supervisor urged, scratching a boil on his neck with a dirty fingernail.

Fortunately, Lucy twisted through and selected a shady portion on the first deck where her mother wouldn't have to face the morning sun. "Here, Todd, and Mother, here." She stretched out her arms to save space as the full-blood family, the Hughes, plopped down. Todd and Abby slid to the deck before the space closed around them. They could still catch the sweet morning breeze blowing in over a cluster of wild asters nodding at the riverbank.

"Oh, it's you, the lady with the wound on her head. Drake, isn't it?" Elda Hughes turned, her hair hung loose and tangled, her arms heavy in her lap. She sighed as she sat back against the wall, staring outward with lusterless eyes.

"I'm afraid we're terribly crowded, here, Mrs. Hughes. Todd, Lucy, see if you can scoot over," Abby said.

"It doesn't matter," replied the full-blood Elda, tears in her eyes.

"I'm so very sorry about your baby, Elda. Your infant son, wasn't it? Back on the Mississippi in our terrible ordeal." Abby, in spite of her aching head, focused her eyes upon the sorrowing woman's face.

"We all have suffered. All of us grieve. I notice you have no man, is he gone too?"

Abby's hand moved over her breast as the pain clutched her heart. "I'm certain my husband, Benjamin, is traveling overland. Certain of it. If he were dead, I would know. I would know." Abby's voice faded at the remembrance of the dream where Benjamin seemed to be in danger. But weren't they all in danger?

The woman's husband, Three Killer Hughes, leaned forward, one of the few full-bloods traveling in native deerskin, hair braided in two long braids at the sides of his angular jaw. "Your man Benjamin Drake, isn't he?"

"Yes, Benjamin Drake, a farmer and carpenter back in New Echota." Abby made an effort to focus her eyes to see more clearly.

"I was at the Council when the Removal Treaty was signed. Your husband one of them, wasn't he?" Three Killer lifted his knees, encircling them with his lean arms.

"What do you mean, 'one of them'?" Stabs of pain shot through Abby's forehead and down her neck.

"That's why we're on this miserable journey, why we lost our homeland, those people who put their names on the treaty."

"You're right, Mr. Hughes, Benjamin signed along with the others. He believed it was the thing to do. He thought we would be overrun, shot, burned out, if we didn't take the treaty." Am I being singled out? Abby wondered. The *Velocipede* wailed, then the wheel began its laborious splashing. The keelboat jerked and rocked. Abby gripped her stomach, hoping she could manage her nausea.

"You agree with him, your husband?" The man persisted.

Abby shuddered in pain. "No. As a matter of fact, I signed a petition that Chief John Ross carried to Washington pleading that we be allowed to remain in New Echota with our government, schools, churches . . . ." Why am I getting tangled in this conversation? Abby gripped her head with both hands, wishing that she could lie down.

"We will see the day when we regret it. Even in Oklahoma. You'll see. It's not settled." Three Killer's black eyes stared sternly.

"Our situation would have been the same, though, treaty or no treaty, Mr. Hughes. Do you ever remember a treaty that the United States Government kept with our people?" Abby lowered a thin hand.

"The United States government kept no treaty, Mrs. Drake. One has to remember principle. What's right." Three Killer shifted his moccasined feet.

"I'm afraid, Mr. Hughes, that my injury prevents me from prolonging the discussion right now. If you will please excuse me . . ." Oh, for a sip of hot water mixed with crushed Red Cedar berries for this pounding in my head. Abby closed her eyes, leaning her head on the hard boards behind her.

"Here, Mother, let me push this blanket behind your head," Lucy said. Since she'd heard the conversation, her own worry reflected on her face. She lifted her eyes to Three Killer's stern face, but only for a moment while taking her mother's hand.

Abby allowed herself to disengage from the verbal encounter. Her mind focused on Benjamin. How serious had it been that he signed the Removal Treaty? Chief Hicks told everyone that there was no treaty that would stop the endless stream of settlers, cutting the timbers, burning their houses, turning them out. Chief Ridge and Stand Watie were certain of that. How many times before had she listened to the words?

And she herself, always standing up for Chief Ross. But then, who couldn't admire Chief Ross? Dropping in at school, smiling at Lucy laboring at her slate. Nodding and approving of Miss Blackburn's teaching. Dinner guest in our home. And Lucy, playing a Brahms minuet on the beautiful grand piano in his mansion.

"When we get to our new home in Oklahoma, all of us together, it'll all be over. We'll be settled. It won't matter anymore," Lucy said. Abby realized the child tried to reassure herself and comfort her.

*   *   *

By noon, the *Velocipede* chugged into a sheltered cove where the waters ran clear from a bubbling spring. The dogwood trees, leaves blood-red, contrasted with the careless splashing, here and there, of yellow goldenrod and purple asters.

While the keelboat rocked at the river's edge, Private Andrew J. Greenway, who had handed Lucy the blanket the evening before, smiled, showing his white teeth contrasting with his dark skin.

"Morning, Lucy and Todd. Top of the morning to you. Hope your mother's feeling better. Wonderful day for our journey upriver."

Lucy Drake smiled at Private Greenway. Her skirt flapped in the breeze and unraveled at the hem. Lucy had chosen to wedge herself in among those at the rails in order to study the towering sycamores and hardwoods behind, reds and yellows of autumn splashed here and there. Home. My Cherokee name means 'home.' Why, this land is just plain beautiful. And, I'm getting excited to see just where we will live. Then the sadness gripped her heart. Father. Dear father. Where is he? How shall we select a plot of land without Father? Who will help us?

"Hold that gangplank, Greenway," commanded Captain Wattles. "We gonna let 'em off the boat to relieve themselves an eat their lunches."

Those words again, eat their lunches, thought Lucy.

What lunches—how much eating?

"Come nightfall, we reach Turnball Point. Provender waiting us come evening." It was obvious the captain tried to be reassuring.

Those who could muster the energy and whose legs were not in spasms from cramping, staggered off the gangplank, Lucy and Todd included.

"If you see a ripe persimmon, child, bring me one or two." Abby attempted a weak smile, then closed her eyes as she adjusted her body in the shade cast by a tall honey locust with yellowing leaves that showered the deck with slivers of gold.

*   *   *

"Well, if it isn't my friend of last evening, Lucy Drake and her friend Todd." Private Andrew Greenway flashed that smile again, broke off a branch of the purple asters and handed them to Lucy. "Flowers for you, my little friend."

An offering. Friendship. Smiles. Lucy felt her heart warm, and the soldier didn't look old, either, like some of the others. She wondered how old he was, and she remembered her manners.

Then Lucy's curiosity got the best of her. "How old are you, Mr. Greenway?" she asked, her brown eyes focused on his handsome face.

*   *   *

Private Greenway's face spread in a wide smile, his thin, red lips parting over white, even teeth. "Well, I declare," he said. "Well, now that you ask, I have to tell you a secret. I'm still 17." He placed a long finger in front of his lips while staring at Lucy.

"Now keep it a secret. I wrote down '18' on the army enrolment form. With Pa and Ma Greenway struggling to grub out a living back in Kentucky, I had to do something."

"No, Mr. Greenway, Todd and I won't tell." Lucy guessed that with so many unknowns and mix-ups as on this journey, it mattered little if Andrew Greenway was 17 or 18.

"Decided to try my fortune in the army. Real adventure, steamboats, rivers, and moving you Cherokee to your new tribal lands. Why, Lucy and Todd, I wouldn't have met you if I hadn't put down that '18,' would I?"

"I guess not. Thank you for telling us. Thank you for the asters, sir." Lucy dipped her nose into the asters. After learning to expect only an ugly command, a kick, or a slap, Lucy recognized his kindness, but a part of her remained wary in spite of the flowers.

"Wouldn't go too far in the woods," Greenway called, seeing the children eyeing the forest beyond, the buck brush, the rising undergrowth of hazel, paw paw and lowland willow. Behind rose the wilderness of oak, ash, and hickory, climbing the hills and embracing the first layer of mountains.

"Bear and panthers in those woods. Get to Fort Gibson men'll all get back their weapons, guns, and blowpipes. Yep. Plenty of hunting. Finished with salt pork." He belched, as if relieving pressure from a hearty breakfast.

Lucy, who knew her trees, surveyed the undergrowth and tall walnuts. No persimmons. Just then, Andrew tromped toward her, three small, elongated objects in his hand. "Paw paws, my girl. Ripe too. One for Todd, one you, and one for your mother."

"I was looking for persimmons, but I see there are none. Thank you, Mr. Greenway. Mother'll be pleased with a ripe paw paw."

The *Velocipede*, having taken on water and wood, wailed. The People scrambled back on board, legs more eager, hopeful looks in their eyes. "Not so different, this country, from New Echota, is it?" Todd asked. Lucy felt her heart beat encouragingly above the layers of grief, loss, and pain.

Lucy held her paw paw and the one saved for Abby. Todd spit the large brown seeds over the railing, but she could tell he enjoyed the sweet meat of his paw paw, a real treat, considering their daily fare.

"Treaty land waiting for us. We own it in common, but each can select a plot. Plus the recompense fee each of us'll receive for making this trip, and payment on our property left behind . . .," Panther Foot, a half-blood from Tennessee, said. Lucy smiled, the fruit in her hand inspired hope. Hope still seemed to beat in the others' hearts too. They were more fortunate than the poor wanderers trudging overland. Why, back in Fort Smith hadn't they heard rumors about the overland plodders? Cholera. Many more deaths. Could it be?

*   *   *

Abby awakened from a doze as they chugged around a bend in the River. Three painted turtles plopped off a rotting sycamore log to her left.

"Mother, you're feeling better. A present, Mother, Mr. Greenway picked these himself." She handed her mother the olive-colored fruit with the heavy aroma and the branch of asters.

"A paw paw. Why, thank you, Lucy. Thank Mr. Greenway for me. I do like paw paws, and the flowers encourage me."

Ahead on the steamer, Captain Wattles pulled back the throttle. The steamboat rocked and dipped to a halt. The keelboats lurched and shuddered. The pool of water around the bend looked deep enough and certainly was wide enough for passage, however, Captain Wattles had been trapped on this river three times before.

"How deep?" His raspy voice floated out toward Hank Thinn who jabbed with his measuring pole. He leaned over the water from his platform. His jaw fell, and his eyes opened in obvious worry as he turned his stubby face toward Captain Wattles. "29 inches deep, sir. 29-inches."

The Captain, Hank Thinn, and Lucy who overheard, understood their predicament immediately.

Captain Wattle's mutton-jaw fell. He spit a brown streak over the rail, pulled his whistle chain and the *Velocipede* wailed their predicament.

"Need 36-inches for passage. Nine miles to Turnbull Point. Gonna have to edge her up toward the left bank. Greenway, get the gangplank ready. Indians gotta disembark. Hate to say it, but our river trip ends right here."

"Oh, no." Groans drifted in waves across the keelboats and faces fell.

"How many miles to Fort Gibson?"

"Are there trails and roads?"

"What about the elderly and the sick among us?"

"How can the children make it? Fifty, 60 miles through mountains and woods, you say? Swamps too?"

"Did I hear someone say swamps and woods full of timber rattlers and copperheads? Water moccasins?" But there were so many questions from The People that they didn't even notice the black cloud heaving upwards in the west like it was preparing to break the prolonged drought.

CHAPTER FOURTEEN

A sense of relief pushed at the edges of Benjamin's heart. That he'd been able to bury mother Drake on the eastern shore of the Mississippi River in a sheltered glen, under a buckeye tree, comforted him.

Seven days to throw up another bridge while The People grappled with the plague of measles that descended upon their children. Where was God? Benjamin's spirit wrestled to make sense of a life that seemed senseless. Captive. Bone weary, feet bleeding, shoulder, wrenched when a beam fell at the bridge, now throbbing. Chilling fog and rain engulfed them while the threads hanging on their skeletal bodies disintegrated hourly.

He'd known it would come. Mother wouldn't be able to survive the trek. Still, her face serene, her hope in God sustained each hour by the faith in her heart. She wore herself out, trying to nurse the sick children, most of whom died anyway.

What kind of faith was her Christian faith? Why was it that a touch of a smile seemed present on her face, despite the terrors, her body sinking into the earth? She kept mentioning the Apostle Paul's words, "He learned obedience through suffering . . . ." How? Why did not the bitterness fill her soul?

It was less lonely that way, Mother Priscilla buried on the eastern side of the Great River, nearer to her childhood home. Somehow, the river represented an insurmountable gulf.

When my time comes, I hope I can die with such yielding faith. Benjamin plodded in the heavy mud. He couldn't remember the song they'd sung, but the preacher's words still echoed in his ears: "I am the resurrection and the life."

Somehow, life and death are mysteriously linked in that man,

Jesus. When he again was reunited with Abby and Lucy, he vowed to find out more about this 'resurrection and life.' Could it be, all this suffering and agony is mysteriously connected with the loving God above? God? A suffering God?

Right now, the yard ahead, the quarter-mile, the half-mile demanded his attention as the oxen lowed, whips cracked and the wagons squeaked and wrenched. The People, silent.

When they approached the waters from the lowlands of Illinois by Green's Ferry, ducks and geese quacked and honked. They rose from the edges of the river, circling above their heads as if to caution that one must not take the Great River lightly.

"Oh, I never knew a river could be so wide," Jacob Bates cried.

"It is truly a wonder, this Mississippi," White Birch stared, amazement in her eyes.

"It is real Long Man. We've met him at last. Uktena now will pull us under. We're without hope," an old shaman murmured as he leaned on a stick. "Who would ever trust that floating chip they call a ferry?" another asked.

"That little thread swaging down, a cable? Look how the wind catches it," a trembling emigrant said.

"What keeps our people from turning back?" his wife asked, drawing her ragged shawl around her shoulders. "Surely the ones who went before didn't cross such Long Man," an old shaman said.

"Turn back. Can't we turn back?" others pled at the sounds of rushing and roaring of the waters. Fetid odors of mud, fish, and earthy waters engulfed noses. "Turn back."

Even though Long Man had his own sounds, the swirling, the rushing, the lapping underneath the overreaching leafy tree arms, The People ceased their speaking. Hearts palpitated in irregular rhythms, bones and flesh quaked.

"Begin the crossings first thing in the morning," Colonel Pollit commanded, anxious about such a venture. "Treacherous. Life-threatening. May be loss of life, animals as well as Indians. How long will it take?"

The threat of Long Man, ever gliding and rolling along in front of them, kept most of them awake. Benjamin, who had offered to assist Supervisor Leets, slept fitfully under a wagon, weary oxen resting nearby. Now and then, a cloud dispersed, allowing the full moon to brush waves and rivulets on the river with iridescent light. Beauty and terror intermingled and contrasted.

*   *   *

Colonel Pollit raged in fury next morning following his negotiations with the head ferryman, Wymer Morse, over the fees.

"Says right here in this government contract, two dollars and fifty cents per wagon, dollar extra for team, and one dollar for each Indian," Pollit pointed out, his contract wrinkled and stained by dust and rain.

"Well, now, that was some time back. Government papers don't mean that much out here. 'Sides, think we ain't got nothin to do with them savages pourin down on us like this, day after day? Starved people. Stinking ones at that. Busted wagons holding up our ferry. Mister, you take it or leave it. Cause if you don't take it, there'll be a thousand more redskins crowding the riverbank, stinking it up with puke and dung, come tomorrow." Wymer spat, hooking his thumbs in his galluses.

So Colonel Pollit had to shell out double the contract price on account of the 'change', and the situation of Indian removal, now out of control.

Four days, the crossing. Teams of wild-eyed mules, horses, and oxen trembled and staggered, led by recruits, Monroe Bates, and Benjamin Drake down the rutted incline that seemed to lead to perdition.

"Hold, halt, whoa there." They yelled to the terrified mules whose haunches trembled while froth dripped from their muzzles.

"We'll take four wagons and 50 people each crossing," Wymer Morse hollered, his baggy pants flapped loose from his boot tops.

The People descended upon the tiny platform called a 'ferry', dangling by two rods and two pulleys, which strained and creaked as the current swept and nudged.

"Shoot, it ain't nothin'," Wymer whined. "We've done put across 4,000-5,000 Injuns." Colonel Pollit knew, though, he failed to mention several capsized wagons, and scores of persons who drowned—the time the rod and pully failed, coming loose from the cable: two wagons rolled off when the ferry tipped, and eight or nine passengers spilled out into Long Man. Only two flailed back to the wood-chip-of-a-ferry. The rest, swept under by the treacherous currents.

On the fourth day, by mid-afternoon, a black cloud rolled up from the north and spread long tendrils eastward and southward. Colonel Pollit still had more than 400 of the sicker, weaker emigrants, camped on the eastern side, praying to muster strength and courage for the crossing.

Shaman chants mingled with the coughing of frail aged ones whose lungs were filling with fluid. A wrinkled old Cherokee preacher, named Tobias, stared at the approaching storm, lips moving: "He leadeth me beside the still waters . . .yea though I walk through the valley and the shadow . . . ."

Benjamin climbed to a wagon seat to steer the team of black horses, rumps covered with dust, down the steep incline. The horses neighed, betraying fear, their eyes wild as they saw the waters before them and the small bobbing raft beyond.

Benjamin yanked back on the reins. "Hold, hold, haw, haw." The horses stepped too far to the right. Acrid sweat steamed from animals and men. Clusters of aged Cherokees and seven children clutched wagon sides and each other in terror.

"Thud, thud, thud." The horses' feet hit the boards. Next, the wagon wheels. The ferry dipped to the right. Waters sloshed and heaved upward.

"Whoa, whoa," Benjamin yelled, skilled with nervous teams. While recruits attempted to calm the team, Benjamin returned for the next wagon and its four oxen, heads nodding, eyes glazed, their low bellowing lifting in the wind. A swarm of people followed, stunned in disbelief at what they were about to risk.

"All on. People and animals. Let 'er go." Wymer Morse ordered his underlings to lift and anchor the entry gate. "Pole, pole, pole, you fools, heavy load here. Get her out in the current." Wymer stomped and cursed.

Backs strained. Shoulders heaved. Long, stout poles dug into the waters. The ferry moved. The easy drift, the intoxicating wood-on-water floating, that can carry one away in a dream, under other circumstances, other times and places, where life and death did not hang so in the balance.

"We're moving—drifting out. Cable's holding. Look how it bulges!" a young mother said.

Young Jacob Bates held the reins, as a mare whinnied and pawed at the planks beneath her feet, a sound which thundered consternation and fear.

His father, Monroe, stood in the middle, holding the team of reddish mules, whose ears were drawn back in frustration and anger. They threatened to rear any moment. "You, there, stand back," Monroe cautioned, knowing that a blow from a hind leg could kill.

The raft-of-a-ferry twisted, slanting, front tilted down river as the powerful currents caught the right side. The shift of the waters rolled it along on the creaking cable toward the faraway Missouri shore.

"Wonders. A miracle," the emigrants whispered.

"Child, stand back. Lord, Lord, grab the child," yelled a slender mother who had lost her kerchief. Her skirts billowed around a belly that carried an unborn infant. She leaned over to grab her child who was on his knees trying to reach the muddy waters with his hand.

"You there, Buford, grab that pole and watch for logs coming down the river. Knock us to Kingdom-Come, hit us," Wymer Morse yelled, sweat dripping.

They rode. They floated. The cables groaned and creaked. The pulleys screamed. A flock of crows flew over, dipped down and cawed raucously, as if to deter them from any further progress. Waters roiled, boiled, and bubbled.

"Our Father who art in heaven," prayed Grandmother Yellow Root, her head shaking with palsy.

"Oh, Unelanohe, Maker of All Things," Shaman Trotting Wolf prayed, lifting first one foot, then another while shaking a gourd rattle.

Then it thundered. A reverberating, earth-jarring water-heaving thunder. The black northern cloud had spread, unnoticed by The People who were concentrating on the dreadful waters and the Missouri shore far, far across. Cold droplets of rain pelted like small hail. Lightning flashed, forked, and cracked.

Two of the motley-grey oxen by Monroe Bates lifted their tails, a sign of anger and vexation. Dung splattered. They shook their heavy heads, rolled their eyes, heaved, and pawed. "Hold it. Hold it. Halt, halt. Benjamin, give me a hand. They're going to push the wagon back and bust the end gate."

Benjamin rushed to aid Monroe with the wild-eyed oxen, necks heaving in their fright, trying to rid themselves of the yoke.

"Oooooh," The People cried, leaning back, but showing they had not yet lost faith.

Then the black, double-team of horses neighed, rose up and struck out with pounding hooves. The boat lurched downward enough for a foot of water to surge over the floorboards. Frightened, near pandemonium broke as wild-eyed mules, with lowered ears and slapping tails, mingled their braying with the neighs of horses too frightened to stand still any longer, let alone the double-team of oxen, lurching, humping, pouring their green dung on the backs of The People.

"Oh Lord God Above," old woman Snake Flower prayed.

Then the wind hit the northern right edges of the wagons—a sudden hurricane gust of wind descending from the black cloud. It howled and whined as it sucked up the cries of The People.

When the screaming winds hit the broad wagon side, it rocked, right wheels lifting off the ferry floor.

"Ooooohhhh," The People chorused.

"Nooooooo," they sighed.

The wagon, caught by a second, more forceful blast, teetered momentarily, then slid off the raft like a piece of pie sliding onto a plate. It splashed into Long Man and into the maw of Uktena below, horses screaming, dragged after. The sudden dip of the ferry pitched a cluster of Cherokees into the roiling water.

"I knew it. I could foretell it. Turn back, turn back." Shaman Trotting Wolf shook his terrapin rattles. His hair stood on end.

Groans rose in the circling wind as 11 emigrants floated out into the angry brown waters, bobbing, sinking, swirling. Some swam. All were silent.

Benjamin, barefooted, dove into the river, where now horses' heads bobbed up, then a side and wheel of the wagon, here and there a ballooning shirt, and just ahead, reaching up with one arm, a young Cherokee mother with her baby still clasped in the other.

Monroe Bates jerked off his boots and dove into the raging waters. Fourteen-year-old Jacob, one of the best swimmers on the Tennessee, made a flying leap to rescue one of the unfortunates.

Coughing. Spitting. Yelling.

"I have you, hold on to my back," Benjamin screamed to the terrified mother, who had not let go of the infant. The waters surged and tore down on his legs.

While shocked onlookers agonized and prayed, they slowly brought them in, the ones they could grab by a belt, an arm, a shoulder, a skirt, the hair. Tugging, wrestling against the terrible swirls and undertows of Long Man, as Uktena sought to do his work.

The young mother gasped and turned her infant upside down and patted its back. A young girl, who fought valiantly against the waters aided by Monroe Bates, finally surged back to the sliding ferry.

Jacob shoved a boy, not more than seven, into outstretched arms. Turning, he pushed out again. Too late for more than half of the capsized victims, yet, here and there, a black head, a bit of cloth ballooned up.

Soldier recruits who could swim, dove in, trying to help.

"Mother, Mother!" Jacob's shoulders ached from his exertions, lungs near bursting. "Mother, I'm coming, I'm coming."

Then, Benjamin, shoving an unconscious lad onto the ferry, turned to look. "Oh, God above, no."

The boy, Jacob, though weary, advanced rapidly in the waters, concentrating on reaching his mother. He could not see the half-submerged log with the long, angular limb, twisting and rolling.

Benjamin knew by the time the boy reached White Birch, the log would send them both to the bottom of Long Man. Benjamin stroked, one arm, then the other, again and again, while onlookers prayed and gasped.

Monroe Bates, seeing his son and his wife's distress, dove in again. Fatigue had taken its toll, how could any of them survive?

"Mother, stop struggling, I have you!" Jacob gasped for air.

The massive log surged upward. Jacob could see the piercing limb not more than six feet ahead. Surprised, more than terrified, his wide eyes stared in disbelief.

Before he could utter another word, Benjamin in a last frenzied effort, shoved the rolling log, deflecting it as it grazed past White Birch's streaming hair.

"You're safe. You're safe. Let me help. Jacob, I've got you now." Mercifully, Monroe reached for White Birch, getting a hold under one arm. "Save yourself, son. Save yourself."

The four struggled. "Too far out, never make it, groaned a cluster of The People. "We should never have planted our feet on this board." But Benjamin had an unyielding hold on the exhausted boy, while Monroe, heaving, gasping and kicking, brought White Birch nearer and nearer across the downstream current. The swim back was tortuous, lung-bursting, a swim by will power alone. Benjamin heaved the limp youth up on the ferry, his hands sliding down his naked chest, black hair streaming.

"We've got him. Hold on, Benjamin, hold on," The People urged.

On the rough boards, before Benjamin slipped into unconsciousness, the wind caught his words—the words King David murmured regarding Absalom: "My son, my son."

CHAPTER FIFTEEN

Back in the Oklahoma woods, Lucy listened to mixed commands. "Now it ain't so bad," Supervisor Haggler yelled, ordering the recruits and captains to pitch the few canvas tents, which would house less than one-third of The People.

"Plenty of nice shade, shelter in the underbrush fer the others," Haggler's mouth twisted. He spat.

One would have expected groans from The People, but this time, they remained silent.

"We sent recruits and an agent for oxen, horses and wagons. Government says you folks get to ride all the way, we gonna see to it, best we can." He fumbled for his last tobacco chaw and now was reduced to borrowing from someone else.

"We'll be all right, won't we Mother? Todd and I'll take care of you. That new soldier, Mr. Greenway, will help us." Lucy knew that childhood was something, for now at least, best left behind under the towering chestnut trees of New Echota, Georgia.

"They're giving the tents to the old folks and the sick," Three Killer Hughes called to Lucy, Todd, and Abby. "If we need to put up shelter, I'll help you cut poles and throw on some branches. Reasonable weather now, but it may change." Three Killer surveyed the sky through the white-branched sycamores and burr oaks, noting how the wind tossed their top branches.

"We'll rest peacefully here beneath this hickory. I love hickory trees, see how yellow the leaves are now? And, Lucy, Todd, scrape through the leaves, you may find a few fallen nuts." Abby leaned against the trunk of the hickory, but the shag bark hurt her back. I must hold on. One step. One more hour. The children, Lucy,

Todd. Oh, Benjamin, we're almost there. Her head fell forward on her breast.

The *Velocipede* hooted a parting wail as if it were ashamed of having dumped them on a forbidden shore. The captain thrust it into reverse, face betraying that he hoped he wouldn't have to back seven miles before he could manage to turn it around. Shamans actually smiled as they, bending and nodding, digging and searching, raked through the undergrowth and woods to replenish their herb and root supplies. Not far now, from the new land. At last, they could gain control over the mysterious forces of the bad times, cholera, smallpox, measles, and ague.

The People were at home with the trees, the blowing winds, the changing seasons. It was not these that chilled their hearts. It was the unknown. Soon they would be in their new homeland, receive their back payments, dig in to build homes. Traces of hope flamed upwards.

They sang. Preacher Bushyhead led an evening service.

"We've made a long journey. God has brought us nearly home." His hand, trembling perpetually from holding it over so many graves, clasped his worn Bible. "Soon, the voices of our people, the Old Settlers, those who went ahead three years ago, will greet us. We'll see the smiles on their faces. We'll enter the churches they've built and sing our hymns together."

The People smiled and nodded. "Amen. Amen," they whispered.

"We must greet them as brothers and sisters. We are one in faith. Like Ruth of old, let us say: 'Your people shall be my people.' We must put aside old differences that brought hostility and hurt, 'this party, or that party.' We are one people."

The People nodded and sang and prayed, as the evening winds turned chill and autumn leaves circled down from the trees and fell upon feet in shredded shoes, feet in torn moccasins and bare feet exposed to the elements.

Abby opened her eyes, trying to ignore her throbbing head. She noticed that Three Killer Hughes stood at the edge of the circle of worshipers, arms folded across his chest, staring, unsmiling, at preacher Bushyhead's remarks.

She watched The People nibbling on small hoe cakes. A few, half-green hickory nuts, cracked open with a hand-held rock. Water lifted by hand from a spring. Paw paws, but not enough for the crowd.

"Can't dig a slit-trench in this rocky ground with the underbrush, but plenty of trees and bushes when nature calls," Supervisor Haggler yelled. Faith still surged in their hearts.

"Meat. Supervisor Haggler said that the overseer at Fort Gibson is sending us some meat. See how God provides?" Smiles spread at such good news shared by Hog Killer.

One day. Two days. Grey clouds spread across the sky from west to east. Temperatures dropped. They plunged again. Heavy frost coated the bent grasses and curling leaves. Coughing rose up through the pall of smoke spreading in the fog. The People shivered and waited. Three days. Six aged ones passed silently into the future land of happiness, their lungs filled with fluid as their fatigued bodies refused to cast off the hold of pneumonia.

On the evening of the third day, the waiting hordes raised their weary heads to the approaching sounds.

"Wagon wheels," Todd Wyeth said, shaking Lucy, who had huddled under their blanket, trying to keep herself and her mother from the biting cold.

"I hear oxen lowing. God heard our prayers. They're coming," cried Preacher Bushyhead, struggling to hide his own pain from the rheumatism in his joints.

They lumbered through the woods and down the narrow, rutted trail; six wagons, three double-teams of mismatched lowing oxen, and three double-teams of mean-looking mules, ears lowered in defiance.

Supervisor Haggler's mouth turned down as he muttered to himself: "Robbed us. Them redneck settlers back there. Knew we had no other choice. Government allowed us two dollars for a wagon a day, charged us four. Government budgeted a dollar per horse or ox. Charged us three. And, with only six wagons, what we gonna do with these stinking Indians?" He spat away from the wind.

"Six wagons and over 400 people?" Three Killer, scowled, arms folded.

"Supervisor says more of The People are coming up river right on our tail. Push us off the path if we don't skedaddle," a young army recruit said, wiping his runny nose with his sleeve.

"You'd think we could kill some deer, some squirrels, even a bear. There's wild life aplenty in these parts," Timber Wolf said, eyes scanning a giant red oak for squirrels.

"Too many emigrants tromped this trail. Wild life aplenty, but they've scattered. Creek tribes moved through here, settled back beyond them hills. Migrations been going on now for years. Animals hightailed it outta here. Have to tighten our belts and wait for that meat from Fort Gibson. Blessing they have us in mind. We won't starve," Three Killer encouraged.

* * *

"Mother, when they stop the wagons again, I'll ask Mr. Greenway to help you in, you shouldn't try to walk anymore." Lucy leaned in to her emaciated mother, who sagged toward her. One step. Two steps. Again, another step. Her narrow foot, now bare and bleeding from cuts on the rocks, shredded shoes long disappeared.

"My child, I can endure it if I think it's a little journey of one step. One step at a time. With you holding me and by concentrating on where I put each foot, I don't even think about my headache."

"But Mother, you should climb into a wagon. You shouldn't be walking."

"Hush, child. The aged and the sick lie flat in the wagons. The infants and their sick mothers line the sides. No, child. It would be wrong for me to crowd them out."

Lucy walked silently, her heart near breaking.

"Look, children. Cast your eyes at the edges of the trail. See, we're in it, the earth, the beauty of it. Each step. We can make it a step at a time, if we concentrate on that yellow-orange persimmon bush, the red sumac on the left. Look at the pink tickle grass, the little sunflowers, the big sunflowers, the blue . . ." but her cough drowned out the rest of the sentence.

The temperature had not risen above 40 degrees the entire day, the cold wind lingered and the black cloud spread from horizon to horizon, casting a shadow over the countryside and the staggering emigrants, the lurching wagons pulled by decrepit mules and mismatched calves called oxen.

Allowing five minutes only for a rest stop, the supervisor commanded: "On your feet. Crack the whip, get them straggly oxen and obstinate mules moving again. We got a sizable creek, Bull River, ahead four miles. Get across it come nightfall, and we'll have provender arriving from Fort Gibson."

Lucy and Abby were not encouraged by the rest or by the anticipation of food by Bull River, come evening. Their feet were too weary, their minds too saturated with the mixture of evil and such a minuscule of good that they couldn't concentrate on it at all. Obey, obey. The role of the slave is obedience, they knew by now.

"March. Heeee, haw. Crack that whip. Captains, make sure you don't leave a woods Indian behind. Count your crew." The Supervisor scowled.

When the tops of the trees tossed and twisted together, The People knew. Rain would soon drench them.

"They'll let us stop if it storms," Todd said, as he picked up a fallen stick to aid his plodding feet.

Lightning cracked, flashing through three-quarters of a purple sky. Mules whinnied. Oxen lowed and dropped dung. They raised their tails and rolled their eyes in fear of the jagged streaks.

The rains pelted. Cold, miserable drops.

At first, the path beneath Lucy's unfeeling feet rose up slick and slimy. But in an hour, it no longer rose to meet a pounding heel, a bending toe. The heel and toe, foot and ankle sank into the squishy mud. Cold legs ached. Pull, plod. Pull, plod.

"Had we been able to snatch a jacket," Silver Wing said, "but the way it was, being dragged off to a stockade, I couldn't even bring a wrap."

Abby leaned forward, her shoulders nearly bare as her homesppun dress, rotted in the weather, caught in a blackberry bower miles back, tore off her shoulder and flapped in the cold wind.

"We'll plant our feet together, Mother. There, one, two, one, two." But, even brave Lucy was rapidly losing faith. What would she do if her mother slipped to the mud below?

They began to fall, the old ones at first, back 20 yards. There, up ahead. Grandmother, grandfather. An old man dragged his feet out of the ruts and collapsed before the wide trunk of a hackberry tree. Groaning, he opened what was left of his shirt, extended his palms outward, and stared ahead, waiting for one of the Above Beings to come for him.

Their gnashing caught in the wind, drifting, circling above their heads into the twisted treetops.

*   *   *

Up at Fort Gibson, Lieutenant Anderson, knowing that another emigrant train of Cherokee Indians was descending upon the Fort, and upon Tahlequah, dropped his ledger and commanded: "Recruits, those barrels of meat, salt pork we've been keeping in the cellar here at the Fort. Haven't been able to open them and feed the meat to the recruits. Roll 'em out."

Rusty hinges squeaked and large, oak barrels groaned and rumbled on the stones beneath them.

"Yes, those barrels. Been here now for four years. Government's gonna charge me for those barrels of good pork if we don't use them. Can't rightly feed them to the soldiers here, but the meat's good enough to sell to the Indians."

Recruits Stumpff and Billings heaved and shoved the barrels, rolling them outside the cellar to follow Anderson's orders.

"Open the barrels. Spread out the meat. You recruits take them scrapers there and scrape off the rot. Good meat underneath."

Strapped with such unwelcome task, Stumpff and Billings leaned over the table.

"Look here," recruit Stumpff said, "this meat's too slick to grab ahold of. Gotta have pincers to hold these slimy pieces." Then recruit Stumpff vomitted.

"Blow your head off, the smell." Billings gagged. "Probably poison us, too, breathing it in." He turned and raced to the door to empty his heaving stomach.

Finished with the grisly task, vowing never to eat meat the rest of their lives, they rolled the barrels up the board inclines to the wagonbed as the driver waited for the full load of the four-year-old pork.

"Giddayup. Hee." The driver cracked a whip as the recruits swung aboard, heading down the trail toward Bull River and the Indians, who, they'd been told, would just gobble up anything— anything at all. And Lieutenant Anderson here at the fort could match up the figures in his books, so he wouldn't have to fish in his pockets for the United States of America. Blessing, how things worked out. "Only thing," Billings murmured, shoulders rolling from the rough ride, "how on earth I ever gonna get the smell of rot and death from them slimy barrels off of my hands?"

*   *   *

One thing good about going to the Oklahoma settlement to hire teams and wagons, thought Supervisor Haggler, was a chance to get something to warm his chilling bones. He sneaked a drink from a whiskey flask he'd hidden in his pocket.

The People waited in clusters. Those without tents crawled back in the undergrowth to protect themselves from the wind and the rain.

Lucy, Todd, and Abby huddled under a stand of willows by Bull River, their soggy blanket draped around them.

"Well now, if that ain't a sight." Supervisor Haggler's cursings caught in the cold wind. "Them river banks too steep to get the wagons across. Gonna have to dig inclines down to the water and up again on the other side."

Silence. No groans. Just the sighing of the autumn, rain-laden wind. Shivering men waited for orders to begin digging, knowing they had little strength, but the digging might keep them from freezing.

"It'll warm us, pitch the dirt," Three Killer Hughes yelled. Abby, looking on, knew that it was anger and bitterness that kept him going, step after laborious step. Ignore the freezing feet. Ignore the pains in the gut. Ignore the ignorant commands of officers and supervisors, bewildered and lost themselves.

"Provender's coming. A messenger at the settlement where we got the wagons said a wagon load of meat and corn is on the way. Probably just around the bend yonder on the other side." The supervisor had hoped his words would encourage and calm, instead, they only added to the feelings of despair and abandonment.

Abby knew that if she was to reach Tahlequah alive, she must chew and swallow some food. Racked with chills, she turned to Todd. "Son, look in Black Bee's sack. Believe we have a nubbin of corn still there."

"Yes, but it's not ground, besides, I think weevils ate most of it long ago," Todd said, his trembling fingers fidgeting with the drawstring.

"We can eat it. We can," Lucy said. She took the five-inch nubbin of yellow pockmarked corn. Holding it in her right hand, she began to shell off the grains. In less than a minute, the pitiful grains lay in the lap of her dress. She counted. "Mother, here, 12 for you, 12 for Todd and 12 for me."

While the waters rushed by in Bull River and the willow fronds swayed, dropping their slivers of gold, they huddled, teeth grinding the hard grains, two or three at a time.

"Not so bad, is it, Mother? And, they say that meat and corn meal is coming." Abby realized Lucy was trying to encourage. She also knew that she had to keep hope alive within her own breast. She realized it would be easy to crawl over to the ancient oak, lean back in the blowing rain, face upturned, palms out and wait for

God to take her. I must not yield to such thoughts. "When I go through the waters, they shall not overwhelm me . . ." she prayed.

"Children, there will soon be a new home for us. Our people welcoming us. Money to build or rent a portion of a cabin or house. We'll have a fireplace, a kettle. I can roast a wild turkey. We can make a deer stew, and bean bread. Oh yes, and Lucy, your father is coming. I know he is coming." Her voice faded as a sob worked its way up her throat.

Darkness. Temperatures dropped. Ice gathered on the ends of branches as the wind howled. Smoke from trembling, half-hearted campfires stung the eye and caught in the throat.

Funeral wailing began again. Five infants and little ones, overcome by fevers and the chest-squeezing fingers of pneumonia, died before morning.

Shamans, busy trying to sort their newly gleaned herbs and roots, dropped them to again take up their chants and discern the source of the disaster. Like the long-faced Christian preachers, they seemed unwilling to give up hope.

Another day of waiting while those who still possessed a minuscule portion of strength shoveled and heaved the mud, making an incline for the oxen, horses and wagons down to the eastern bank and up on the other side. A day of silence. A day of huddling in smoke-layered fog and pestilence.

A half-day for crossing. Lurching wagons sloshed waters and mud. Infants and grandmothers buried on the riverbank—funeral moans prevailing more than the westerly winds.

By now, Todd and Lucy no longer noticed the corpses or the muddy holes where they were dropped. Their ears didn't even register the sounds of the grieving, shrieking mothers, the Shaman's rituals, the preacher's prayers and readings. It was all the same. Grey fog, grey flesh, icy cold, and bone-shattering chills.

On the western side of Bull River at last, the rain ceased and, blessedly, the sun peeped through the hazy clouds. Sounds of breaking bushes and cracking wheels indicated the wagons were coming.

"They're coming. They're here. Blankets. Food. The meat we were promised. Cornmeal. See how God provides." A few encouraged voices lifted in the cold air.

Abby knew that when folks are starving, the promise of food lightens the step and heartbeat. Light glistens in the eye. The sight of wagons, seemingly loaded with barrels of meat and sacks of meal, caused dry mouths and chilled tongues to drool.

"Stand back. Take turns. Enough meat for everybody," supervisor Haggler commanded. "Recruits, pry open them barrels. What? You didn't bring any corn or meal? Oh well, we'll be in Fort Gibson in no time at all. Open them barrels, I say."

The People in their eagerness did not notice that Supervisor Haggler stepped back a goodly distance from the barrels and took out his red handkerchief as if he needed to blow his nose. "Bring your cups, your vessels," Haggler ordered, trying to turn his head away from the grey-slick mass inside the barrel. Plunging in a long knife, he brought a portion of the scraped pork to the edge.

"OOOOOOOOOhhhhh," the ones first in line groaned as gut-wrenching smells of rot blasted their noses.

"Try it. Try it. Don't turn down the food. Probably better underneath," they encouraged one another.

But the unfortunate people could not even hold on to the slimy pieces of pork which seemed alive and leaped out of their hands like slippery eels.

Ruby Three-Killer threw a couple of slices of the grisly slabs into her pan of water and attempted to thrust the pan over the fire before she was overcome with vomiting.

"It's rotten and putrid. Don't eat it. We'll surely die. Oh, Above Beings, they surely don't want us to live."

And all the People wept.

CHAPTER SIXTEEN

Benjamin, staggered in the seemingly endless line as he rounded a bend in the trail near the shabby frontier village of Springfield, Missouri. Twenty-two days since we crossed the wide Mississippi, yet the terrors of the crossing still unnerve hearts and torture our minds as if it were only yesterday.

"I can't even see the end of the line," Benjamin said aloud, feet wrapped in rags discarded by some poor, now deceased straggler.

Like a giant snake, the train inched across the countryside. Benjamin knew that most of The People no longer knew or cared where the line began or where it ended. The horde was now bloated by hundreds more emigrants salvaged from other trains which had been devastated by cholera.

Benjamin knew that the captains and trailmasters had no certainty, either, regarding the bedraggled group. Who belonged to whom? When did it break down so? God Almighty. Why did General Scott agree to resettle the Indians? Why didn't he protest on behalf of the Indians? Why didn't the Indians wage an all-out war?

He pondered how Monroe Bates's wagon had been swallowed in the muddy waters of the crossing, dragged under by Uktena. He watched as Monroe, shoulders lurching to give force to his heaving calves, plodded along, steam rising from his nostrils and mouth. "Can't see the front, either." Benjamin's words faded in the chilling wind. Snow. Yesterday there'd been snow, then a melting, and now this hard, rutted earth which bruised the heel and froze flesh and soul.

* * *

White Birch straggled behind, leaning, moaning for the countless dead and at the catastrophic upheavals of life as a prisoner-emigrant. The sickness of it. The stink of it. The indescribable pain of it. Uktena had not pulled her under, but he had touched her mind forever.

"I thank God Uktena released his hold on me and on my son, Jacob." Her mind wandered, caught on fragments of the past. A vision of her three-room cabin. Her wrought-iron bedstead, covered with the quilted comforter made by her own long fingers. The hymnal from the Methodists, who'd sprinkled the waters of baptism upon her head as husband Monroe waited and watched. The Coosa River, 400-year-old chestnut trees.

But, no sooner had she thanked God, than a piercing wail erupted from her mouth, enough to curdle the snowflakes. "No, I don't believe in God. How can a God permit such sufferings?"

The Above Beings, the Christian God of Abraham and Moses, the Jesus of Nazareth and his compassion, no. No. No. "Faith, yes, it was my faith that disappeared in the maws of Uktena." White Birch wailed, her fine hair, no longer braided, matted and swirled in the cold winds. Bitterness filled her heart as hunger pains tightened their fingers around her stomach.

* * *

"You may have back your rifles, hatchets, knives and blowguns in order to supplement your government diet with fresh game," encouraged Colonel Pollit, no longer able to look at The People in the eyes.

Known as the most skilled blowgun hunter in all north-eastern Georgia, Monroe Bates examined his hollow reed with half-frozen fingers. He fingered his deerskin pouch dangling at his belt. He still had his walnut-root poison.

While more of The People stumbled and fell by the trail, awaiting the sweet peace from winter's icy fingers, Monroe searched and listened. He squatted on his quivering haunches. "Game? Game?" He spat. "Not even a rabbit." Only the north wind and stark-limbed trees raked the empty sky, their roots buried beneath the brown grasses which cringed in the elements.

His hunger twisted his innards as he admitted the obvious—

too many emigrant trains passing this way. All game, long fled miles away from the bow and spear of any hunter. He no longer paid any attention to the ugly little torn-earth mounds by the sides of the trail. Dead? How many? Even God would be confused by such human mortification.

Monroe stuffed his blowgun into the back of his trousers and staggered back through the stand of sassafras, not even wasting energy to think about chewing on the hard acorns in his pocket.

"When we get to our next depot, grain. May be vegetables and beef. Who knows? Government agreed to furnish provender. Only a half-day journey, now," the trailmaster rasped, finding his own faith faltering. Monroe knew that he hoped for a tavern so he could warm his chilled bones with a swig of bourbon.

*   *   *

The youth, Jacob, wobbled after his father, feet bound in burlap strips Monroe had twisted around his frost-bitten toes.

Jacob realized that a brave *Tsalagi* didn't complain. Father isn't complaining, he thought. I must follow father's example. One step. Another step. Then another. Heave. A fear curdled his heart as he heard his mother, White Birch, wail in the wind.

Icy droplets pelted his shoulder and neck. Jacob hoped his ears weren't freezing. He'd seen his Uncle Tall Corn's frozen ears once. They had flopped over, stretched like wilted cabbage leaves.

The pain. A brave didn't cry. Not even a youth at a ball game when the shaman combed his body, the quill-ends of the feathers set into a comb, pushed in and dragged down a player's arm. The bleeding. No crying out.

But could he endure the present hell in such spirit? This unceasing gnawing in his gut? This slobbering from the mouth as thoughts of squirrel stew obsessed him?

The smell of it. Mother cutting up the squirrels, two of them. The steaming sweet water. Dumplings. Rich dough tossed in the broth and meat, swelling out. Puffing. Eggs dropped in. Three or four of them. He nearly fainted. His foot jarred and bruised on a frozen clod.

Ahead a wagon wheel groaned, creaked and fell off, the left tail end of the wagon with its cargo of ancient ones and the dying, jarred to the earth. The jolting stirred not a sound among slaves, humiliated beyond understanding. Human flesh wracked by bone-shaking chills alternating with pulsing fevers. What matter, a jolt to the frozen ground, wrenching a shoulder and cracking brittle ribs?

* * *

Benjamin staggered ahead to see if he could help, knowing that delay from a broken wagon meant the postponement of food for tonight. What food? His teeth ground, as if attempting to flatten the weevil-scarred grains. Besides, more of The People will freeze to death.

"Halt, halt the train. You folks squat and get some rest," Sergeant Sedgwick ordered.

It was obvious Sedgwick wanted to sound in control, but such authoritative command had long since vanished, even before the crossing of the Great River. He no longer turned his head to look for the tail end of the train, lost beyond the bend in the road and the rise of the hill. Besides they wouldn't even hear his orders in the screaming wind.

Gloom descended, sweeping across the hilly Missouri landscape as black clouds in the west foretold a worsening storm. Snow, or sleet, this time. Too cold for rain. They had abandoned the broken wagon, regrouped the sick and ancient ones, mothers with infants near-dead from starvation and choking diseases.

Benjamin Drake grunted, forcing his shoulders forward, the once blue bandanna tied as a turban on his head, flapped in the increasing wind. May be he could endure a step at a time if he thought of Lucy and Abby.

Oh, yes. Lucy and Abby were in Tahlequah, Oklahoma, by now. In a town—a real town with streets, stores, houses, smoke ascending from chimneys, fireplaces with hearths where the bean bread baked, cranes that held the suspended iron kettle, bubbling with deer stew. Potatoes. Onions, wild-herb seasonings.

Benjamin was surprised that he drooled, considering he hadn't had a drink of water since morning. He could see them. In their own cabin? A rented portion of a kindly neighbor or friend? A goodly amount of money stashed away from the reparation payment. Thank God above, Abby's God and the blessed Jesus that they were able to go by riverboat, as rumor had passed it on. Safe in the new territory. Honoring the treaty that he himself had signed. Chief Ridge was right after all. The People would all be corpses strewn in the woods and fields of New Echota had they not extended their hands and put down their signatures and made room for the ever advancing "settlers". Hadn't he and the treaty signers "saved The People?"

The snow swirled around his head. Benjamin reached up with his cracked hand to tighten his turban.

But look at us now? As the snow flakes thickened and the wind howled up shredded shirt sleeves and torn skirts, announcing the dropping temperature. Benjamin Drake surprised himself with the question that most slaves, sooner or later, cease to ask. Why do we endure it? Why do we follow every command? Why have we become so servile and beggarly?

Wagons groaned and the oxen, shoulder-and hip-bones protruding, bellowed in hunger and pain as Indian slaves tottered through the upcoming village.

* * *

The frontier settlers peeped from small windows in rude cabins and makeshift houses along the way. "Would you look at that? Call them human beings?" the pointing settlers hooted from porch stoops.

"Lord, keep 'em going. Whatever would we do if they would stop?" a farmer's wife asked, scratching a fat hip. "Lice, betcha they're covered with lice."

"Ain't it a blessing they're going west? Where to? Oklahoma Territory? Lordy, Lordy, pray they keep moving," a solemn-faced matron said, who had left her spinning wheel momentarily to watch savages plod by her lean-to house. A few children threw rocks and frozen clods their shoe-toes dislodged from the ground.

"Set the dogs on 'em," a greasy-haired youth yelled, yellow teeth bared behind a hateful sneer, his false sense of "I'm better than you," reflecting on his pimply face.

But not all. Not all frontiersmen scorned the Indians.

One hobbling grandmother, grey shawl thrown over her round shoulders, rushed out with a whole pan full of rolls, freshly drawn from her oven. "Oh, blessed Jesus above." Tears streamed down her face at such skeletal human beings tottering in silence by her garden. "Oh, in the name of Jesus, please, please, take these."

Farther down the line Benjamin urged his will to make his legs keep on moving in spite of the numbing wind and his dazed mind.

The trailmaster cursed. "Thought we would be in Springfield. Be dark in half-an-hour." His lips turned down as if the bitter thoughts of his own career demise pierced his tired brain. Advance? Promotion? For honorable military career? Another merit badge for his lapel? At this? This humiliating, death-threatening trek?

He knew the darkness would enshroud them and they had no supper. Provisions were still five miles ahead. They would soon drop. What on earth would he do?

*　*　*

Questions circled in Benjamin Drake's mind. Questions that verified that after all, he was a human being. And, Benjamin thought. A human being can make a decision. A choice. Yes, that's what makes a man a human being.

Ahead, a narrow field stretched beyond the road behind the cluster of stark persimmon trees, thrust nakedly against the grey sky. A rutty lane led to a farmhouse, half-hidden by the scrub oak. Benjamin's glassy brown eyes noticed the pumpkins. Orange swelling pumpkins, bellying upwards toward the bitter skies. Pumpkins that would flatten to the ground as the freezing winds embraced them.

The People plodded on in silence. Wagon wheels groaned. A baby cried for a mother's milkless teat. "Death, death, chilling death," the wind wailed.

Still, the weary emigrants heaved themselves past the frost-glazed grasses by the edge of the pumpkin field. Then Benjamin Drake decided.

Only half-conscious, he leaned out from his place in the train, turned as his bleeding feet found purchase and heaved towards the unpainted house where the smoke billowed in the wind from its squat chimney.

Two yellow hounds howled and raced toward him, baring their teeth, nipping his ankles. Still, Benjamin, without a break in his step, heaved his near-prostate body toward the rude porch boards as the house door opened.

Benjamin didn't care as he glanced back to the trail that the trailmaster had commanded a halt. Halt, as one of the crazy people had wandered off the trail, a nervy one at that, pestering the rightful citizens of this county. Benjamin knew he risked scathing rebukes when he returned, thusly delaying the journey.

The farmer stepped forward and stared straight at Benjamin teetering on his porch, as if to say "What kind of a man is this? Such gall. May be I'd better get my gun, Indian approaching me, like this." He turned, calling, "Eunice, we got us an Indian come for supper, what you think of that?"

But, Benjamin Drake did not "come for supper." No, Benjamin Drake had made the decision to ask the question. And, it was a simple question. But, the simple question is often the best question. Benjamin Drake knew that. Knew it to the depth of his near-frozen bones. He lifted his stained face. His lips, so cold they could scarcely part for the words. But amazingly, they did part. And his tongue loosened in spite of no ditch water since morning. And his human eyes, with a soul behind them, looked into the grey eyes of the frontier farmer as Benjamin asked his question.

"Mister, I'm sorry, I don't know your name. You see those

people there?" His ragged sleeve stretched outward as his finger pointed to the bewildered hordes, looking like goblins in the swirling snow, 500 feet away.

"Those are my people and we are hungry." He'd said it. He'd announced before another human being a human state, an empty belly. Hunger. Thirst too. But, for now, the hunger.

"Mister, I saw all those pumpkins in your field, lying there. Be frozen and useless come morning in such a cold blast as we're getting this evening."

Eunice, short and heavy, motley dust cap stretched over her head, squinted her eyes in order to see this amazing Indian who dared to plant his feet on her porch.

"I would like to ask you, sir, if we, that is, The People, could eat some of your pumpkins for our supper?"

There. He'd said it. He'd asked it. Respectfully. In a civilized way. Saying, "sir." Saying, "could we", not coarsely demanding.

The old couple looked at each other as if the truth of "being human" touched their hearts.

"Why, yes. Why, yes. You can all eat in my pumpkin patch. Yes. Why, that's right. Them pumpkins be froze come morning and even the hogs won't eat them then."

And so a human agreement was made. An agreement, heavy with life-saving forces.

"I want to thank you, sir. I shall remember your kindness." Benjamin was amazed that his body and spirit had not parted. Surprised that from somewhere within, strength surged to enable one leg to wobble ahead in front of another, although his feet no longer felt the ground beneath.

"We can eat. This way," he waved a bony arm, copper flesh showing through the ragged sleeve. "We can eat. This way. Oh, mercy, this way."

The People, uncomprehending at first, used to harsh commands from trailmaster and sergeant, looked at each other with glazed eyes of long-jailed prisoners. Is he crazy? How could one of The People do such a thing?

But words have power. Benjamin's words had power. Even the trailmaster yielded to them. What better could he do?

And The People staggered and stumbled into the pumpkin patch, gathering in their small groups. At first, the silence. Then, here and there, one could, in spite of the howl of the wind, hear a prayer of thanks, "the blessing" as a Christian family partook of the food.

Yes, thought Benjamin, remembering the passage in the Gospel the reverend had read at Easter time. Yes, the blessed Jesus in the house on the Emmaus road, at eventide, took bread and broke it.

Here, there was no bread. Only odd-sized pumpkins, already half-frozen, yielding themselves as sustenance to quicken The People and keep their hearts beating one more day, their blood surging a few more hours.

CHAPTER SEVENTEEN

Clouds lifted by late afternoon. Against the grey late autumn backdrop, the wagon wheels creaked as the horses and oxen trudged down the road drawing their loads of the dispossessed: those who had survived the cholera back at the sloughs and the canebrakes, those who hadn't completely relinquished their spirits to despair, and those who still prayed, hoping for goodness somewhere yet attainable to human souls. Even Reverend Bushyhead, wild hair wrapped in an orange turban, leaned on a sycamore limb and murmured through his cracked lips as his fever-glazed eyes attempted to pierce the gloom with the words of Job: "What is my strength, that I should hope? and what is mine end, that I should prolong my life?"

Mired in the mud and slough for four days between two mid-sized rivers. Who would ever forget? Who could shut out the wails of the grief-stricken over the deaths of their loved ones? For how many years would their cries encircle the earth?

Old Chief Hicks, long ago when he became a Christian, said to The People: "It is good to model ourselves after this Jesus. Jesus steadfastly suffered the pains of his life, his crucifixion. It is good to model oneself after Jesus."

How had they endured their sufferings? Prayers were still heard as they whispered them above the cries of the crows in the morning cold. In spite of the closing in of the trail, the weather, the sickness and the unknowns, hope still flickered in hearts. The lamp of faith had dimmed in many hearts, yet endured, but would their bodies endure until their feet found purchase in their promised lands?

* * *

"We're almost there," Lucy called to Abby, as if she willed her mud-splotched, and chilled legs to keep plodding at the back of the wagon where Abby lay with the sick and dying.

Abby's bony knees shook, bone against bone, as the jolts of the wagon threw her wasted body. Only the pad of rags between her knees prevented further brusing. Each jolt a searing pain. Her head throbbed, red-hot, blinding. Pain, pushing the limits of endurance, caused her spirit to crawl to the edge of despair itself to ask, "What is the meaning of this? How can a mortal endure?"

To Abby Drake's surprise the affliction seemed suddenly transmuted. A part of her understood. God himself is a suffering God. God—present in brokenness, in darkness and prevailing gloom. Abby yielded herself, caught between God who is affliction and God who is bliss. Pain transmuted itself into light within her soul.

* * *

"I see the flag. Yes, it's a fort." Todd Wyeth, now more of a brother, having shared the pits of hell with Lucy, lifted his bare head, matted hair streaming behind. His soiled ticking pants, ripped in shreds, gave little comfort against the November cold.

"Home, you'll all be home in a couple of days. See. Fort Gibson rising yonder," a recruit yelled, thankfulness reflected in his voice that this miserable job of escorting Indians cast against the backdrop of the dearth of goods and supplies, failed support and broken government pledges, was nearly over.

"Get 'em in the compound. Open the gates yonder," Greenway commanded, as two uniformed soldiers ahead swung open the double gates of the stockade. Andrew Greenway looked back, grey-green eyes filled with pity at the skeletal refugees, clinging to life and the last vestiges of hope.

Fort Gibson, the western fort built to ward off the plains Indians and launch even further westerly caravans, spread three miles above the confluence of the Arkansas and the Grand. It was Colonel Matthew Arbuckle's power and command site. For the last five miles, Lucy kept her spirit from leaving her flesh by thinking of the Bible story of Ruth and Naomi. Ruth was a beggar in Boaz's fields, wasn't she? Who would be the kindly people who would let them glean in their fields? Who?

She and Todd called back and forth to each other as they heaved their aching legs. "Remember the day I could recite Sequoyah's alphabet all the way through? How easy, then it was to learn to read." Lucy still had hope for more schooling. But where were her books? Her red-bound arithmetic, her blue speller?

"I remember." Todd cleared the frog from his throat, trying not to think of bean bread. "You learned quicker than I. Miss Blackburn kept me in at recess because I wanted to run home and get my bow and arrow. I wanted to go squirrel hunting."

"We'll have a school, Todd. You and I will be in the same class. You'll see." She remembered her father Benjamin said that she was not exactly shy. She knew that was true. It was just that she couldn't hold back her mind from grasping so much of the world at once, then, surprised with what beckoned her, she had to hold herself back from blurting out her thoughts too quickly. Desire rising in heart and soul urged her spirit to latch on to the world of such good things. Father, Mother, school friends. Chief Ross and his beautiful wife, Quatie, and their piano. By closing her eyes, Lucy could imagine that the oak leaves, shuddering as she passed, were playing a Brahms minuet.

She had survived in spite of the odds, Mother Abby, on her back in the wagon load of sick, lumbering along over the last 17 miles.

"You'll make it, Mother, you'll make it." Her burning eyes gave their own life force to her mother. Lucy knew that without her, Abby Drake's spirit could not hold on to the edges of this world.

In the terrible swamp. The cold, black waters, the pitiful mud pad upon which they had huddled. The stinking, eye-stinging, lung-choking smoke from the pithy reeds. Mercifully, a shared muskrat which Todd had miraculously caught, was divided among three families and eaten half-raw. The howling wind. Cholera loom-

ing like a plague of Egypt swirling through the Israelites' streets in
the land of Goshen, caused The People to reel. Diarrhea. Stomach
heaving and gut-wrenching pains. Then, the fainting and indescribable fevers and weakness.

Even the shamans bent their heads earthward, hopeless. Like
an angel of mercy, old Doctor Barnes appeared before Abby, near
dead from fatigue himself. "Here, little mother, you must live.
You have this daughter. Take this."

He'd lifted his cracked fingers to pry open her lips for the
calomel and the oversized opium pill. "Swallow it, my woman.
Swallow it. God has need for you." Then, he drew away in pity.
The medicine, shoved between her lips, a futile token, was like the
bread of Christ, the blood of Christ. On the next morning, the
woman, Abby Drake, aroused and sat up.

One question tormented Lucy. Where to go in the stockade
ahead? Would the guards and soldiers imprison them again? Mother
couldn't possibly walk to the desk of the commander and seek the
promised money. Who would help her? The apprehensions circled
her heart and threatened the flickering life in her.

*　*　*

Two United States Dragoons, outfitted in their double-breasted,
dark-blue coats with two rows of gilt buttons, yellow cuffs and
collars, orange sashes, and hanging sabers, turned their lean faces
toward the advancing horde.

"Hold your nose, more stinking Indians," the tallest one with
a horsehair pompom on his infantryman's cap said. "Usher them
over there. Pitch tents on the parade ground. Captain wants to
keep them moving. Shove 'em out of here in the morning," the
second dragoon replied, lifting his white-gloved fingers to his aquiline nose to ward off the engulfing stench.

And the refugees rocked and staggered into the compound as
wide-eyed, solemn-faced Choctaws and Wichitas, legs in buckskins, shoulders covered with buffalo robes, stood back and stared
at the emigrant Cherokees, who looked as if they had just emerged
from the apertures of hell.

Wasn't it a miracle? As the wagons creaked and groaned into the enclosure, and The People, like beggarly ghouls, tatters flapping in the cold wind, hobbling afterwards, waiting, waiting, waiting. Blessedly, there came commands. Someone giving orders—sensible orders.

"A 100 tents stretched yonder by the block house, just behind the cannon," a Corporal yelled, waving his gloved hand to keep the ghouls moving. If they fall to the ground, let it be at the flap of a tent and not at the edge of his well-blackened boots.

*   *   *

And, The People obeyed. Obeyed as if they realized that there was some order in the world after all. Their dulled, prisoner minds awakened, as the odors of cornmeal gruel, real salt-pork thrown in, wafted in the wind.

Oh, no. Not inside the towering buildings, the dining room of the officers suited out in fine military cloth and accouterments. Not in the mess hall of the ordinary recruit, straw on the floor and tobacco juice flying. Here by the stockade wall. Cluster. Group in families. Families? The teeth-gnashing pain of the word. How it tore and wrenched the heart. At the mention of the word, memories of the gashes in the raw earth split their souls, but, amazingly, their lips did not part to emit the groans echoing in their hearts.

And so Lucy Drake and Todd Wyeth poked down their gruel, even though the salt pork was rancid. Heavenly. Could the tongue ever savor such bliss? And Abby Drake sat up, leaning against a foul blanket which supported her back.

"Mother, food. Food. Eat a few bites. You'll have more strength in the morning," urged Lucy.

It was almost beyond belief how a trembling hand that looked more like the claw of the morning hawk, could still lift the spoon. A spoon? How could it be that they were offered both bowl and spoon? Such luxuries were beyond comprehension.

*   *   *

In the morning, The People lined up early to follow the directions of the Chief Military Officer, who shrugged his shoulders to shake his opulent coat, epaulet fringes trembling as he attempted to shift it down over his massive belly. Glad, he was, that the matter had been reviewed before the pariah Indians staggered in. Colonel Arbuckle had cleared his throat and announced how it was in the flickering lamplight the evening before. Preparation ahead of time. Responsible, dutiful. Obedient.

"We are no longer honoring the agreements regarding reparations. Out of funds. Bank deposit depleted. We've written to the Government Indian Agency. You know how long that takes. No message from Washington. Besides, aren't you getting land? Good land."

So the Colonel gave the orders. "Don't allow them to dig out their papers or shove in here as families claiming payments for a lot or a log cabin left behind. We'll handle it with a general announcement. Better that way. Someone might get trampled in the rush, anyway." He cleared his throat as lamplight glittered off the brass buttons and medals studding his splendid chest.

The best way. Easiest way when the cupboard was bare. So Lieutenant Massey followed the orders and read the proclamation that reeked of subterfuge and dishonesty.

"Announcement regarding your papers and reparation payments." Massey coughed, and cleared his throat, wiping his purple lips with the back of his white-gloved hand.

The People clustered closer, ears more able to hear now with morning gruel and hot water in their bellies. Blood circulated again. Eyes flickered from dark sockets.

Lieutenant Massey lifted his paper, his eyes focused above the heads of The People. Why have eye meet eye at such news? Better the impersonal way, the flip-of-the-hand way, a dismissing, finished-with-you way.

"The United States government announces that there will be no reparations for this emigrant group. There are many reasons, including the cost of the migration, the fees for the riverboats, the extra cost for the food, and," Massy coughed, "Colonel Arbuckle reminds you all that the United States Government has given you land."

Groans began at the front edge of the circle of Cherokees, sweeping backwards to the swaying listeners, patiently waiting to receive what was rightfully theirs. Money. Cash. Payments for acres left far, far behind. The chest of drawers, the oak dining table and six chairs. The books. The clothing, woolen coats, shoes and stockings abandoned when they were corralled without notice or time to pack. The copper pots and Dutch ovens by the hearthsides.

Abby Drake's body slid sideways and would have fallen to the hard ground, had it not been for Andrew Greenway, who stepped up beside her, ears open for the news that would help Lucy, her mother, and Todd get settled somewhere near Tahlequah, someplace sheltered from the winter blasts.

* * *

This time, The People rode, rocking silently in the army wagons, drawn by fresh horses. Why murmur? Why lift the voice to spread such heartache?

The blessed numbing crept over their souls, in order that the life force within could flicker lowly, but not go out. By evening, they would be dumped in the streets of some village called Tahlequah. Indian Territory. New home. Named after the seat of their culture so long ago, beautiful Tellico.

A December wind howled, but bony fingers and quivering arms refused to even search for an edge of frayed cloth to draw over the flesh.

Andrew Greenway, holding back disgust and shame, rode a snorting roan mare by the side of the wagon where Lucy, Todd, and Abby Drake rocked toward "home."

CHAPTER EIGHTEEN

It would help if only the sun would shine. Lucy clutched the edge of the wagon, her thin shoulders shivering and swaying. Lucy was glad her mother's body was still warm. She leaned over as the wagon rocked up the rise, providing a view of the fertile valley and the oak-covered hills beyond.

"There it is. A town. Tahlequah." Todd Wyeth grabbed the edge of the wagon with his chapped red hands, his eyes wide open in his thin face.

Here and there smoke ascended from log cabins—substantial cabins. And, if Lucy looked carefully to where Todd pointed, interspersed between stands of cedars and oaks, she could see clapboard houses with brick chimneys. The red leaves of dogwood flashed here and there through the brown masses of oak. The black arms of the redbud lifted themselves in the undergrowth along the road, their yellow fallen leaves, a mat covering their roots.

"Lucy, yonder, look." Todd's shoulder-bone pushed the flesh through the top of his shirt where once a collar had been sewn. "A big house. Look at that!"

To the left and to the right on the plateau rising above the Illinois River valley, Lucy could see plantation homes. And The People stretched their scrawny necks in order to survey the promised land where they would soon be dumped.

"Why, this is very nearly like land back in Tennessee."

"I never expected to see that many farms and cabins."

"Well, I told you that Chief John Ridge and his group, the Treaty Party moved on ahead. Elias Boudinet and Reverend Worcester probably have their newspaper going again."

"That's good," said a half-blood young Cherokee. His pregnant wife lifted her head to him and smiled in hope.

"They'll greet us. All of those Old Settlers, they and the Ridges'll have it all organized, you'll see," a middle-aged woman, who still managed to hang on to a scrap of violet cloth tied around her head, encouraged.

"Don't count on it," said the full-blood who had inquired of Abby Drake regarding her political views back on the *Velocipede,* ferreting out her loyalties to the John Ross Party. "A lot of animosity festers between the factions. Lot of animosity, but we who held out, the Chief Ross ones, are the majority, aren't we?" He folded his arms across his bare chest, in spite of the winter wind, as he stared at the town of Tahlequah rising before him. When would Chief John Ross arrive? Just how would he save them? Lucy wondered. And, what ever happened to his grand piano?

*   *   *

The wagon train creaked into town along the rutted brush-lined road which bore the sorrowing emigrant trains last week, last month. Rounding a bend, the wagons snaked along the edges of Town Branch was rippled over rocks, edges gathering ice.

"Water. Like the Coosa. A blessing."

"And fields, gardens. Look, cabbages still in the garden and somebody planted turnips." Mouths watered as hope stirred above the layers of grief no years would ever erase.

Lucy Drake still wondered, Who will help us? Who will give directions? One friendly sign, the pointing of a finger to a lodge, a log house, a . . . When will Father arrive?

Another thought shoved out the former. How will we begin? No bed. No bed clothing. No clothing except these rags that cling to our bodies. Pots, pans? A fire?

*   *   *

Recruit Andrew Greenway stared ahead at the town square. Devoid of townsfolk, and a train of starving emigrants ready to dislodge. Where's the welcoming committee?

Greenway hated to admit it. But the truth was evident. The starving souls, who had miraculously held on through the months of their travels, bared their faces to an unwelcome square, and to a largely factious party of Cherokees, still torn by conflicts carried from back in New Echota. How could they, the Old Settlers and the Ridge Party, who had signed the treaty to save The People, deal with such descending hordes, most of whom had aligned themselves with Chief John Ross who caused such difficulties for them?

Does it come to their minds, the blood oath of the Cherokees? He who forfeits the land must surely die.

The villagers peeked from cabin windows. A shade drew down. A curtain closed. At the village store, those who saw the starving Indians staggering towards them down the road, lifted skirts, clutched their baskets and stepped quickly into the stores to commence their shopping.

Those caught on the streets, embarrassed by unresolved tensions between the tribal groups, dipped their faces toward the wooden planks of the sidewalk, steps quickening as they sought the protection of the hardware store and livery.

And The People slid, crawled and fell from the wagons. Those who had refused the ride and had walked all the way from Fort Gibson, turned glazed eyes, and starved faces toward the brick and stone stores, the hastily built little shops with rising rectangular fronts to enhance their prestige, and here and there, a sturdy red-brick Victorian house, complete with brass door-knobs and leaded glass windows, and now and then, the face of a black servant peeking out.

A Cherokee woman, who had risen to climb out of the wagon, wailed as she discovered the body of her aged mother lying breathless against her legs. "My God, My God, she endured for more than a 1000 miles and now, she died."

* * *

Abby Drake struggled. I must move one leg in front of another. Yes, I can still walk. The red-hot pain commenced again in her head as she leaned between Todd and Lucy.

"Children, do you see where we shall go? I must hold on. I mustn't faint now. Not now."

Slowly, like the unnoticed first melting of frost, the brown skirts of a tall Cherokee half-blooded woman emerged from behind a wall. Then, she stood in full view, a basket of bread in her hand.

Down the block at the little Baptist church, a small group of faithful members, faces still bearing the marks of their own sufferings, opened church doors, stoked the fire in the potbellied stove, then hastened up the road toward the refugees.

"This way. Shelter for the night. Oh, Lord Jesus, you poor travelers. We'll try to provide some bread and soup."

"Mission completed. Soldier recruits reassemble for our journey back to the fort," announced Officer Devon, who had supervised this emigration from Fort Gibson.

Andrew Greenway's feet hesitated in their muddy boots. He removed his wide-brimmed hat as he stood before Lucy Drake, her mother, and Todd.

"I'm afraid I have to obey orders. You see how it is." He cleared his throat, betraying a heavy lump in his throat at such naked incompleteness. These people? Stripped, weak, overcome with grief and unmentionable losses, now dumped in the middle of a muddy street while the winter wind howled around their dazed heads.

"Good-bye, Lucy. You were a brave traveler. You too, Todd. Remember, there are persimmons, nuts, and paw paws in the woods here. You'll find them. Though you'll have to wait until next fall for the paw paws and persimmons. But you can still find some hickory nuts and walnuts." Lucy surprised herself, yet Miss Blackburn had taught manners and etiquette back at the mission school. She stretched out her bony hand to give recruit Andrew Greenway, who had befriended them, a parting handshake. "Thank you, Mr. Greenway, for your kindness."

Todd, not to be outdone, dug his toe in the cold mud and stretched out a grimy hand. "Good bye, Mr. Greenway. You have a safe journey back to Fort Gibson. And, Mr. Greenway, I don't think I'm gonna stay in this new land. I'm goin' back to Tennessee."

In spite of her double vision and the red-hot fire in her head, Abby Drake clutched the rags which were trying to fall off her shoulder in the wind. "Mr. Greenway, I shall remember your kindness to us. God bless you. Will you be supervising another emigrant train?"

"No, Mrs. Drake. No. Colonel Arbuckle, back at the fort, issued orders. Soon as we get back, we're to organize a brigade to ride west. Trouble with the Cheyenne. Good-bye, Mrs. Drake."

And the young 17-year-old recruit, with the grey-green eyes and warm heart, turned back to the wagon and the snorting team as the mud sucked at his boots.

"Come, Mother, come. They're beckoning us to come down the hill to that little log church. Come, Todd." The forlorn trio struggled through the mud. They bent in the wind, penniless as *The Gleaners* in the Millet painting.

"Did you hear the news?" yelled a broad-shouldered half-blood in a buckskin coat, as he turned to a group of Cherokee young blades sauntering toward the livery. "Report from Fort Gibson that an overland train of our people got caught in a blizzard somewhere in Missouri, and over half of 'em froze to death."

That's when Abby Drake slipped to the cold mud beneath her.

CHAPTER NINETEEN

Lucy awakened from a fitful sleep where she'd seemed caught in a vortex of steamboat paddlewheels, splashing, turning, rivers overflowing the keelboats while crowded passengers stood immobilized. "What shall I do?" she'd called to a guard who turned his face from her and puffed on his pipe.

Then, before the whirlpool swallowed the keelboat, the sun split the sky and the waters receded. Next, Lucy's spirit was beset by the howling of a lonesome wolf. She couldn't see the wolf, but she knew it was an omen of bad luck. Just as the old shaman shook his rattle at her, she lifted her sweat-drenched head. Her ears picked up the sounds from home and field: a mantle clock ticking, chickens clucking and roosters crowing from the chicken yard.

Where was she? She opened her eyes, amazed to see herself heave back the comforter of stitched red-and-black squares. Snuggled in the cocoon of a soft flannel nightgown, she slid her ankles toward the edge of the bed. Her heels hit the braided rug by the bedside.

The recent events were more than she could yet believe. They'd clustered in the churches, Todd, Mother and she in the Baptist church, others in the Presbyterian and Methodist church down the valley. She remembered reaching out for the cornbread and a bowl of hot soup from Cherokee hands and smiling faces turned to her.

Then widow Esther Shining Star, who stood before them in her wine-colored coat, head bound in a grey scarf, said, "You must come with me, I have room for all three."

It was beyond human understanding. Lucy looked out the real glass windows. Beyond the sloping yard, she saw a walkway of sandstones set in the grass for human feet. A board-walk led to the village stores. Miraculous. How could it be?

* * *

Abby Drake opened her eyes and propped her bony body on an elbow. "I can't believe I rested my head all those hours on a pillow. Feather pillow—pillow sham, too."

"Yes, Mother, we're here in Tahlequah. Mrs. Shining Star brought us to her home last night. She bathed you with warm water and put you into this feather bed where we slept together. Todd's in the little room by the kitchen."

Todd was, that is. By now, he had both elbows on Esther Shining Star's table while he poked down cornbread and swilled hot cider from a tin cup.

Slowly they awakened to the new.

"Mother, I'll tell Mrs. Shining Star you're awake. No, don't get up. You're too sick and weak."

Lucy hesitated on the red-and-blue braided rug beneath her feet. It couldn't be true. A floor. A rug. Windows. Walls. Heat rising from the stone fireplace ahead. A crane, a black kettle. Skillets. The sizzle and overwhelming sweetness of the bacon, frying and splattering.

Esther Shining Star stepped into the bedroom doorway. "Oh, child, I thought may be your mother'd sleep till noon. Well, this boy, Todd, he's got the head start on you already. Threatening to go out and find him a limb and whittle a bow. Come, child, breakfast. Cornbread, grits with bacon. I'll break some fresh eggs. You probably heard my chickens out there." Widow Esther Shining Star smiled broadly.

Abby, bathed and resting, surveyed the bedroom walls of well-caulked logs, sturdy rafters above. A marriage certificate hung on the wall across from the window. Widow Shining Star fluffed the pillows and smoothed the sheets. "Now, you just lie there and rest yourself. You got a beautiful girl here and that nice laddie. They're going to be needing you. Why, in no time at all, I'll have you on your feet."

Abby was aware that Esther Shining Star was at her best. What deprivations and sufferings had she gone through on her own trek westward 10 years ago? Whatever she'd been through, she hadn't turned bitter. "Hard times, yes, my woman, hard times. But you'll see. Land enough here for everyone. Rich valleys. You ought to see the corn crops. And you can taste those winter turnips I didn't get around to dig yet," Esther said.

Esther parted and combed Abby's hair. Abby focused her eyes and lifted a finger to feel the rough scar on her forehead, aware that the pain was gone. Then the rich broth, the egg, and few bites of cornbread—more than she could comprehend. "How can we ever thank you . . .?" her voice faltered, tears clustered in her eyes.

"Give yourself time, Mrs. Abby Drake. Your turn will come to help the others still coming. Why, in a few weeks, your husband'll be here bursting his britches to get a log house started. Think of the fun of it, you picking out the spot. Me? I'd want a tall hackberry and some of those black-limbed redbud trees. Oh, yes, a few dogwood. Did I mention I have an extra spinning wheel?" Esther smoothed her blue calico bib-apron.

Abby turned her face towards Lucy whose eyes gleamed, hair in two braids. "Lucy, how beautiful you look. My, it's a fine blue-checked gingham." Abby smiled, as tears slid down her weathered cheeks.

Lucy hesitated with every move as if she thought, What if I dripped a spot of bacon grease on my dress? What if a stocking caught on a snag? A disaster if I scuffed the toe of these new black shoes. How could she live in such heavenly bliss and still be human?

Lucy pondered Esther's words to Abby, "He'll soon be here, your husband. He'll want to get started building . . ." A sorrowful weight bore down on her heart. Where was Father? Did she still have a Father? The words of the chilling night before still echoed in her ears. "Emigrant train of Cherokees got caught in a blizzard . . .half of them froze to death."

"Mother, you do believe Father'll come, don't you?" She stepped closer to Abby, the light from the window spread a yellow slash across the blue-flowered water pitcher and matching bowl on the oak stand.

"I pray each hour, Lucy. My heart still hopes. Yours too, Lucy. Oh, Lucy, could I but have spared you . . ."

"There'll be emigrant trains for months yet. Sixteen-thousand Cherokees moving to Indian territory? Why, reports come in every day about families. Folks surprising each other, finding each other. We'll check the posters on the square that list emigrant trains still coming," Esther said.

Esther Shining Star didn't mention the names not listed, or whisper the heartbreaking tales passed on about those who starved or froze to death, those who died of smallpox, dysentery, cholera, alcohol poisoning, murders, and drowning.

"I believe he'll come." Lucy stepped to the edge of the bed where her mother lay. She reached for her mother's hand. "I would know it in my heart if Father were dead," she said.

*   *   *

December. January. Ice-covered trees and dropping temperatures. The flow of the Illinois River slowed and froze over. Tree limbs cracked in the winter cold, the sap descended to their roots. Squirrels curled in the depths of hollow trees. Bears snored in caves. Deer pawed through the snow with sharp hooves to nibble the greenness beneath.

A gentle snow fell upon Widow Esther's dog-trot log house, a house common to these southern hills. Two log cabins, equal in size, facing each other, with the enclosed walkway between. Functional, homey. Blissful in the spring, with the wild dogwood nodding, blessing the steps.

Abby Drake, who could not yet see well enough to spin wool on the wheel, sat by the hearth, her arms encircled by a skein of yarn Esther Shining Star wound into a ball.

The fire crackled. The clock struck three. Todd whittled at a pine board, experimenting with the new penknife given to him by a friendly man, Reverend Worcester, a member of the Ridge Party,

who had settled up on the plateau called Park Ridge. Bible trans-
lator and missionary. Invited the hungry looking lad to services up
on the hill.

"Rich folks gonna be living up there." Todd coughed. "Lucy
and I took the trail up there last week. Mrs. Drake, you just oughta
see the houses they're building on that rise. Look like presidents'
houses."

The boy was correct. Chief John Ross and his entourage had
arrived. Traveled by carriages, train and river boats. Though Chief
Ross had to bury his wife, Quatie, an infant son, and his father
along the waysides on the journey westward.

*   *   *

Chief Ross had held out to the very last, selling his lands back east
for 20,000, couple of thousand for his livestock. Other money
safely forwarded to the banks. In spite of the seemingly eternal
sorrow, the powerful chief dug in. His men, his slaves, the best
contractors hired from Van Buren and Fayettville, Arkansas, heaved
and hammered as the new mansion, which he planned to call *Rose
Cottage*, lifted itself into the sky. Impressive. Prestigious, facing
Chief Ridge's mansion with the imposing white columns.

*   *   *

In the town of Tahlequah, the Old Settlers, ones who had migrated a decade before, looked southeastward to the rising village
of Park Hill. "Going to build a college there, a seminary," said
Little Terrapin to his squat, full-blood wife, Yellow Blossom.

"Going to crowd us out of our land, these folks. Not like us,
either. Besides, weren't those John Ross folks opposed to what Chief
Ridge, John Ridge, Elias Boudinot and those other treaty signers
did? The treaty signers saved the Nation, didn't they? Our people
would have been slaughtered if we'd followed Chief Ross, holding
out like he did. What good did it do?" She scoffed.

"Three groups now. One people and three groups." Little Terrapin drew his blanket tighter to keep out the winter wind.

"We're the Old Settlers. Know the land best. Laid out the
farms. 'Course, we'll share the land. Then there's the Chief Ridge

Treaty party. Don't know whether they did the right thing or not. Every Cherokee knows about the *blood law*. "He who sells his land without consent from the council must die."

"Thing worries me the most is that we Old Settlers and the Ridge Treaty group are outnumbered two to one by these new John Ross people. Have to sort it out in the council." Yellow Blossom stared at Little Turtle.

Little Turtle grunted, lifted his feet and headed for the General Store. Yellow Blossom plodded after him in the snow.

* * *

Buds swelled on the tips of maple branches in February. They pouted, reddish in early March, as a line of beggarly people zigzagged down the western hill toward Tahlequah.

There had been countless other migrations descending on the town, but, none like these grey ghouls, lifting skeletal shanks and bare feet from the freezing mud.

"A putrid smell drifts in the wind before them," Joseph Standing Turkey said to a cluster of folks on the sidewalk by the livery. They turned and hurried away, for what human had strength to deal with death and rotting flesh on bone as these, wobbling and groaning toward them?

Still, by some superhuman strength, the four hundred forty-two survivors bobbed and sagged toward the town. Each seemed to show that if he or she broke the rhythm of the lifting of gnarled knee to swing the foot, he or she would collapse to the ground, a corpse.

God above. No help for these. Fear clutched their guts at such death-reminders. The people scrambled from the frightening horde, where tatters and threads of once gingham dress, and ticking and cord trousers, lost the battle and parted from pariah flesh.

One broke loose from the ghastly line. Worse yet, dared to approach a sturdy Cherokee farmer. He tottered and teetered.

Nodding. Pointing. The wind caught the pariah's rags and the outward swing of the cloth sent him scuttling off the boardwalk. Yet, he didn't go down. Still he stood, inquiring.

It was obvious Tall Oak wanted to speed the conversation, to quicken his step to remove himself from such death talisman as that standing before him. If they stood there any longer, surely the buzzards would descend about him.

Tall Oak pointed a finger. He nodded. He turned as if turning away from the body of a three-day-old dead horse, bloated in the summer's heat.

And, mercifully, the skeleton with eyes burning like the eyes of Lone Wolf on the night of full moon, turned and lifted bones encased in skin, now one foot, now another. Like Lazarus wobbling from the tomb, he staggered down the hill.

A crowd turned to watch the ghostly figure. Man? Woman? Resurrected from what tomb? What recently earthquake-opened grave?

The cadaverous figure collapsed on the last stepping-stone on Widow Shining Star's porch. It must have been five minutes. Seven? The onlookers stood in silence, staring in icy horror.

And the ghoul, touched by some supernatural hope within, twitched and crawled upwards, onwards. Knee on wooden step. Bones of a paw on the split-plank floor until he'd reached the door. No strength left to rise. Bones and flesh and mind accomplishing a last task, a feeble knock with pure bone knuckles.

Five minutes more. The bones scraped the wood again. A mouth opened, attempting a cry, but weakness overwhelmed throat and lungs.

*   *   *

"I believe Tiger Cat's at the door. Go, Lucy, see if Tiger Cat came home, while I go get his bowl."

Lucy Drake put down the pillowcase she had been embroidering. She arose and stepped to the door to let Tiger Cat in. "Mother, Mrs. Shining Star, come. Oh, hurry, there's a dead man lying at our door." Then Lucy Drake's body sagged like a sack of meal to the wide floor boards below.

CHAPTER TWENTY

By the second week, Abby, hands trembling only slightly, carried the tray of steaming chicken soup and well-buttered chunk of cornbread into the sunlit bedroom where hollow-cheeked Benjamin lay, black eyes staring from their sockets.

"You're awake, Benjamin. After this tasty soup and mouthwatering cornbread, may be you'll be strong enough to visit. March wind's melting the ice. Green grass pushing through the snow."

Benjamin raised his skeletal body, propped by pillows and one elbow. Abby's quick eyes noticed the effort seemed easier than only yesterday. Abby knew, though, that his frostbitten feet must still throb painfully.

"Abby, Abby. How can I believe it? Together. Three of us. We'll make a home for Todd, too. Good sized log house, dogwood trees . . ." His trembling fingers reached for the spoon. Abby knew from her own experience how one had to hold back from gulping the food. The questions still loomed in her mind. Shouldn't one eat only a portion and save the rest? Would onlookers criticize if one bolted it at once? Would there be any for tomorrow, if I swilled the whole bowl of soup? Shouldn't one shove a portion of cornbread under the mattress?

Abby seated herself on the bentwood chair by Benjamin's bedside. She smiled when she saw his eyes focus upon her body, draped in the homespun woolen dress as she steadied the tray. The old questions circled in her head. Why did I take the opposing side, back in New Echota? Sure, Cherokee women are free to express themselves in council. Free even to go to battle, or become shamans. And, did Benjamin actually step up and sign that treaty? Scores signed it, didn't they? The ragged scar began to pulse.

"Benjamin, there's tension here in Indian Territory, and I, back in the old land, opposed *your* views."

Bejamin's trembling hand reached for her arm.

"My beautiful dove. Your God brought our family together. Who would have dreamed it? No, don't talk politics now. You were free to choose to stand with Chief Ross. That's one of the reasons I love you. You're an independent person. Besides, the Ross people, the Old Settlers, and the Ridge Treaty Party are all together now anyway." He lay back, exhausted. His lips formed the words again, "all together".

Abby stared through the bedroom door, glancing at Lucy in the kitchen, illuminated by the sunlight bouncing off the snow and beaming through the kitchen window. She watched as Lucy stirred a kettle of deer stew swinging on the crane. Warmth flooded her heart. A part of her told another part of herself that she shouldn't rush this newness of being together again. They needed time before all the pieces came together.

Abby knew, too, that her and Benjamin's positions worried Lucy. Didn't she have enough changes, without their political differences?

And Benjamin's skeletal body and haunted look from his abominable sufferings—the horrors etched on his face—screaming from his eyes. She realized she must give him time. In time, layer by layer, the pain and tragedies would surface. She would hear broken fragments of the incomprehensible story, the deaths of his mother and Aunt Rachel and where they were buried.

"Only one more thing, Benjamin, I know when you're on your feet you'll attend council. You need to know that within the ranks of our newly arrived John Ross people, there's bitterness toward your treaty group and the Ridges. Animosity against editor Elias Boudinot, too,—printing editorials favoring treaty signing back home." Relief settled on her heart like a butterfly nestling on a thistle blossom as she got the words out.

"We'll sort it out in the spring council, my love. Women are permitted to attend." Benjamin's lips trembled as he smiled at Abby.

"You needed to know, Benjamin, the council has been set for April. The People must deal with it—sort it out." Abby lifted her chin and composed her face as she attempted to hide the worry the situation caused her.

"You see it clearly, my dove. Clearly. That's what the council's for. Sort things out. Editor Elias made it safely. Translating the Bible into Cherokee, isn't he? Didn't he marry recently?" Benjamin bit a generous chunk of the buttered cornbread. "The Cherokee people have a way of working through their conflicts and I know, Abby, you and Lucy'll pray about it. Bushyhead too. Wasn't it a miracle Reverend Bushyhead survived? All the sickness, all the death, all those prayers and funerals . . . ." Benjamin's voice faded as if the memories were too overwhelming.

*   *   *

By the time the mayapples spread their waxy leaves and their white flowers burst open, Benjamin had staked off the portion of land overlooking the Illinois River. "We'll build on this rise, here. Water'll never reach this knoll, besides, look at these sturdy white oaks, that sycamore and the redbud, and dogwood on the east." Benjamin smiled, his body, more bent than before in New Echota, nevertheless, gained strength each day.

Abby delighted in the way his eyes took on new life and light. The spicy odors of the earth, the spring buddings elevated his spirit and helped him rise above the hell left behind. Abby gave thanks, too, that with Esther Shining Star's wholesome cooking, she'd gained weight and strength. The terrible headaches came only at infrequent intervals. She thanked God her vision had improved.

*   *   *

"Father, did you say four rooms? A log house with four rooms?" Lucy's voice reflected the surge of life inviting her beyond the prison-path and wreckage of the past year.

"Yes, Lucy. A bedroom for you, one for your mother and me.

A parlor for your mother, and a dining table in the kitchen, room in the loft for Todd."

Benjamin dug his boot-toe into the fertile loam that smelled like sweet aloes and clover. A few feet away a flock of quail scattered, the whirr of their wings blending with the stirring white oak leaves. "Stand here quietly for about 15 minutes, the deer slip from behind the gooseberry bushes along the ripples of the river."

*   *   *

Lucy lifted her arms from the keyboard for a moment, while sitting on the bench before Chief Ross's mahogany grand. She thought of the homesite her father had picked, the woods, the sparkling water, like the Coosa back home. No, trees not so gigantic and towering, nevertheless respectable walnuts, hickory, ash and white-barked sycamore. The dogwood and redbud evened things out, softening the forest with their graceful, curving trunks.

Lucy began to hum one of the Handel English Anthems she'd practiced last week here at Chief Ross's white-pillared mansion. His new mahogany grand—even longer than the one back in Georgia. Unbelievable, how things ended, after the . . . It seemed for a moment she heard angry sloshing of the Great River, cries of the dispossessed packed around her, and the lamentation of the surging steamboat. Who would believe it?

Sapphira, one of Chief Ross's black house slaves, dressed in sweeping new blue calico and matching head scarf, stepped into spacious room. She smiled, holding a tray with tea in a china teapot, and cups with pink oleanders on the sides and splashing across the saucers. Lucy rested her arms and hands for a moment at the spreading keyboard.

She found herself smiling now, more often. Just when she began to play the song again, reaching with her finger to include the ebony key for the sharp, a girl, Cherokee at that, slipped down the great hall, Sapphira's hand on her shoulder. The girl with hair that seemed to resist being parted, drawn back and plaited into two braids, stood politely, waiting until Lucy finished the music phrase.

"Now, Miss Lucy Drake, you got yourself a right nice playmate here in the preacher's daughter. This here is Eliza, Eliza Bushyhead." Then Sapphira slipped back down the hall, skirts rustling, to check the smoked ham roasting on the spit in the cavernous kitchen, the smells already causing Lucy's mouth to water.

Lucy saw that the girl, Eliza, slender, taller than she, in her violet chambray with the white sash tied in the back, had seated herself politely in the tapestry chair by the bay windows. The joy of, at last, a new friend in the strange land, one who, like herself and Todd, had the year before survived the wrenching of the trek and the threatening rivers. At the sight of smiling Eliza, joy flooded her soul like the light streaming through the great parlor windows.

Lucy turned on the bench, rose, straightened her brown velvet skirt. She felt her heart beat faster. Lifting her chin, she spoke, "Hello, Eliza. Your kind father, Reverend Bushyhead, told me so much about you. I'm pleased to meet you."

* * *

While Abby and her father strolled arm in arm along the sparkling waters of the Illinois, Lucy settled herself at the base of one of the sheltering walnuts. She bent her head forward and rested her chin on her hands, clasped across her knees. It seemed as if a portion of the warm sunshine spilling through the spicy walnut leaves, kissing her neck, reached inside and brushed her heart. A new life, a new nation. She wondered if she could have the patience to wait until she was old enough to attend that new female seminary the four crews of construction workers were building on Park Hill, up by the Mission.

CHAPTER
TWENTY-ONE

"Is it true, the reports of political dissension? his newly arrived loyalists asked as they stared Chief John Ross squarely in the eyes. Unusual behavior for Cherokees, but necessary, considering the dire times.

"No. We are ready to come under the Old Settler's government. We as newcomers were welcomed. But, anyway, let us hold a council." Chief Ross straightened his short frame. His legs braced in shiny boots, spread apart, broad shoulders holding his square head with the blue piercing eyes. His stance demonstrated belief in himself as a negotiator and a winner for his people. Let time tell. Wait until a council.

So the Old Settler chiefs, who had arrived in Tahlequah 10 years before, sent out announcements for the new council: "June the third, l839. Meet at Takotoka, not far from Tahlequah."

The June day seemed perfect. The sunshine, warm, the clouds highlighting the bachelor button blue sky. Spring sweetness lingered in the air as the winds blew through the sassafras and walnut. Sixty-thousand of The People descended upon the Takotoka grounds. Their brisk strides demonstrated how warm tribal blood coursed in their veins. Their faces reflected joy,—joy for the togetherness, after the indescribable agonies, losses and humiliations. They affirmed to each other: "We will not forget the many who died, their spirits, now with the Above Beings." Said John Ross, a great Chief now for 11 years. Where would it all lead?

John Brown, the first chief of the Old Settlers, those who had begun anew here from Tennessee and the Arkansas settlement and moved on to Tahlequah, stood up, arching his shoulders nobly. Light in his eyes betrayed his awareness of how lordly he looked in splendid new leather boots, expensive beaver hat and an orange sash tied around his double-breasted waistcoat. "We congratulate you, all you John Ross people, who survived the unmentionable journeying. The terrible ordeals are now behind you. We welcome all newcomers. The land is tribal land, and you have the freedom to select your portion. Only, you are responsible for your building upon it, and how you tend the land." Chief Brown grunted the end of his sentence to announce the weight of the statement. He lowered his eyes.

Council members deliberated. A wave of murmuring rolled from the front, over the thousands, to the back cluster. A few rose to second Chief Brown's words, adding their own affirmations. Splendid. Agreed. All newcomers will follow the national government set up by the Old Settlers. Wonderful how it worked out. Many smiled approvingly.

Then, to the surprise of all, Chief John Ross stood. Clearing his throat, his massive fist descended from his mouth. He stared straight at Chief Brown, then beyond to the hordes of people before him. No one so elegantly attired as he in his black serge frock coat and white broadcloth shirt, black tie, trimmed mustache and sideburns. Silence. Surprise erased the blankness from faces.

"I as the Principal Chief of the Eastern Cherokee ask, by what authority are we being received?" The voice, rich, booming, a voice of New England culture and poise. "I need to know upon what terms we new emigrants will be received."

More silence. Chief Brown realized that this was no time for bad manners, but, he must rise and at least ask for clarification of Chief Ross's puzzling statement.

"As I said, my honorable Chief Ross, you and your parties have been well received, and we heard you say that you were fully satisfied with the reception. I do not understand."

A sudden wind caught the redbud limbs at the edge of the clearing; the tiny flowers shattered to the ground.

Benjamin Drake shifted his feet in his scarred leather boots as he crossed his ankles. He picked up a fallen stick and toyed with it in his fingers. Why is Ross getting up? The Ross people were offered land, opportunities to run for election next council—didn't Chief Ross hear? May be the terrors of the trek had affected his brain. Benjamin scanned the eyes of other new settlers, eyes that seemed to say, "What is Chief Ross doing?"

Chief Ross seemed to ponder Chief Brown's words, then he turned. Wrinkles tightened in his forehead. His skin seemed darker than usual. "We need a more formal reception. You of the Old Settlers need to list specifically all the privileges to which we are entitled." He coughed, then stared at Chief Brown. The expectant Cherokees circled about him, shifted their bodies and looked at each other.

Wind rattled the early green leaves as Ross continued. Benjamin noted full-blood Monroe Bates and son, Jacob, two rows in front of him, both in deerskin shirts. Visions of a wagon swept off a ferry in the wide Mississippi, the boy, struggling, flashed before Benjamin's eyes, then warmth rose in his heart, knowing Jacob survived the ordeal. When Monroe Bates turned and focused his eyes upon Benjamin's, Bate's lips turned down. What did it mean?

Chief Ross cleared his throat and threw back his shoulders as he stood for his turn. "Your speech was a good speech, but it didn't offer enough. It is important for us newly arrived emigrants to remain as an organized body, with our own political force in order to settle our accounts with the United States government and secure the claims for all the losses . . ."

Ross seemed about to continue. But, when he surveyed the crowd, he realized that it was time to nod and defer. Then Chief Brown stood, struggling to hide his irritation. "Yes, agreed. For those purposes, keep your chiefs of the Eastern Cherokee and Judges and Sheriff, all with the name and style of the Eastern Cherokee Nation. Yes. For those purposes." Brown settled back as Ross again stood.

"Well, honorable Chief Brown, not to offend, but our eastern government is modeled after your own laws. They are the same. Let's meet at another council in October and draw up a new constitution." Again Chief Ross dipped his head toward Chief Brown, traces of a smile touched his thin lips.

Benjamin then saw the strategy. What was Ross doing? By making such a point, the Ross people, outnumbering all the others by two to one, will take over the government completely. The twig snapped in his hands. Monroe Bates turned back again, disapproval on his face.

Chief Brown again stood. Silent. Staring. The wind, picking up in the tops of the oaks and hackberries, sighed, sweeping a sudden chill over the necks of the waiting people. Benjamin pulled at his shirt collar. "We announce the council closed," The words fell like hard clods from Chief Brown's mouth. "Meeting adjourned." No grunts. No solemn sighs to emphasize the importance. Cold, cutting, slicing formality. Closed. Closed. The august chief turned to wend his way around the crowd.

And The People turned to look at one another, but only momentarily—to focus long upon another's eyes evidenced bad manners. They struggled to hide their shock and dismay. A new land, a new nation, but would they themselves fracture it before it had a sufficient beginning?

*   *   *

Three days later, Benjamin and his family gathered around Widow Shining Star's table. "I could hardly believe what I was hearing. I don't know why Chief Ross pushed the point, considering that Chief Brown had given him everything. Then, too, the next council would be open for new elections, come October." He glanced at Abby, who passed the ironstone bowl of steaming boiled potatoes. How was she taking all this?

"Father, since we are safe after our ordeals, can't we live in peace?" Lucy clasped the potato bowl, helping herself, she passed it on to Todd. Then she added. "I think we need to pray about it."

"Well," continued Benjamin, "Ross didn't want to accept that the meeting was adjourned. He pled for Chief Brown to continue deliberations so that your Ross people, Abby, could meet at once and draw up a new constitution. It only made Chief Brown angry. I think he was feeling used. Anyway, he said, 'No! meeting adjourned.' So all the Old Settlers left the meeting. I don't know where it'll lead." He mashed the boiled potatoes with his fork, looked up to see how Abby was taking it.

"You know what Chief Ross has been through. Eleven years, our chief. Always holding out for what was best for our people, at least what he thought was the best. He's lost his wife, a new son, a father . . . he's tired. Let's try to be patient. You're right, Lucy, a Christian ought to pray about it." Abby reached for a bowl of black-eyed peas. "Who would have expected such rivalries after what we've all been through," Abby said, lowering her eyes, her forehead creasing.

"Well, the Ross people wouldn't leave. They hung around and discussed the issues relating to the forced removal." Benjamin's eyes clouded in sadness.

The candle flickered as Esther Shining Star rose from her ladder-back chair to step to the pie safe for her cherry pie. "We'll work it out. Benjamin, you are on the council, you'll get it solved." Her smile seemed optimistic.

"But what worried me most," added Benjamin, was the way two of the full-bloods, Lying Fish and Rain Crow, sidled up to say: 'We saw Major Ridge, his son John, and the brothers, Elias Boudinot (Buck Watie), and Stand Watie, moving about in the crowd, talking privately with the Old Settler officers, trying to get them on their side.' May be that's why the Old Settlers didn't support Chief Brown more."

"Do you think they were plotting some kind of revenge?" Abby's eyes reflected worry.

"No," said Benjamin, "They're all Christians and interested in the welfare of The People. It's the resisters among them, the resentful ones still upset and nervous about the pains of the removal, the losses, the new land, all the strangeness. We need time. We should move slowly."

Esther Shining Star slid an oozing slice of pie on a saucer and set it before Benjamin. "And," continued Benjamin, "someone in the Ross band said, 'Let's take over the matter ourselves,' when they saw the Ridges and Boudinot Treaty People so involved. They didn't seem to notice matters were getting out of hand, or that they might have betrayers among them."

Benjamin's shoulders drooped. His dark eyes reflected sadness. "I wonder what they meant?" Could it possibly be that they meant to enforce the old blood laws? Executions, for signing our homeland over to the United States government?

Then Benjamin remembered the meeting with Major Ridge so long ago back in New Echota. When Chief Ridge spread out the treaty—how, after he'd signed his name, he said, sorrowfully, "Today, I've signed my own death warrant."

* * *

It was only three days later that Lying Fish whispered the secret to Benjamin of how three betrayers in Major Ridge's Old Settlers clan, which included Elias Boudinet (also known as Buck Watie), and his brother, Stand Watie, had met for judgment. Conclusion? Major Ridge and son, John, Elias and Stand—all must die first, since they were the first betrayers who'd signed the treaty.

Ignoring that the tribal law required the accused to be present, the dire circumstances and tribal tensions pushed them to hasty conclusions. "Guilty. Guilty. All who signed the treaty."

Benjamin suspected that they palavered, possibly threw numbers on paper into a hat, enough squared, numbered papers for all present. Whoever drew a paper with an "x" marked on it knew his immediate task. Enforce the blood law—an old and unbroken custom. These executioners knew clearly who their targets were: Chief John Ridge, known in the old land as Major Ridge, his son, John, and the Watie brothers, highly educated editor Elias Boudinet, and his brother, Stand Watie.

CHAPTER TWENTY-TWO

A slice of moon shone through the thorny locust branches as overland trail survivor, Monroe Bates, joined the night riders as they leaned over the heads of their mounts, shoulders lurching with the jolts. A horned owl hooted. Lights in the town of Tahlequah at last, turned out. The night was dark, foreboding.

The sounds of horses' hooves pounding the dirt road, betrayed their advance. Monroe, in his brooding heart, knew their sacred duties. They rode like ghouls released from a dungeon, hearts united in their common cause. Even the moon hid its face as if colluding with them.

Coattails extending in the wind like tails of night hawks, they descended upon the prestigious home of Major Ridge's son, John, his wife Sally, and their children. The Ridges were all asleep in the spacious bedrooms of their fine Georgian 11-room house.

Three of the nightriders dismounted. "Kick open the door," whispered the tallest one to Bates.

Racing into the room on the lower level, they found the awakening John Ridge and his wife. The squat, bandy-legged one shoved a pistol to John Ridge's head and fired. The pistol failed. Monroe waited in the shadows, his knife drawn.

"Get him outside," the tall Cherokee commanded.

Monroe Bates along with two others, grabbed the wide-shouldered chief and dragged him out into the flower-edged yard as morning light gilded the eastern hills. John Ridge was silent. Absolutely silent. Then he twisted his massive shoulders. He hunched and pushed with his powerful legs, fighting manfully.

Sally Ridge screamed, "Oh, my God. Don't kill your brother, don't . . ." Rude shoves sent her sprawling as the children on the stairwell watched, horror upon their faces.

Over and over descended the stabbing knife. A dozen times. Twenty times. Blood spurted. The body of the chief lay lifeless.

"Finish it. You know the rest," the tall nightrider sneered.

Next, the gloating executioners, bandannas over their faces, reached out with bloody hands, grabbed the body of the fallen young chief, signer of the New Echota Treaty, and tossed it high into the air. It descended with a "plop." Next, they jumped on the body of a man they considered a betrayer of his people. Then they slunk off in single file. Monroe Bates, the first to sling himself into his saddle.

*   *   *

The sun rose in late spring splendor over the eastern Ozarks. The song, "When Morning Guilds the Sky", a Christian hymn, circled in Editor Elias Boudinot's mind as he sauntered outside Reverend Worcester's Park Hill home.

How pleasant the path, how golden the light on the dewy grass. His steps quickened as he marched down the gravel path to the bending workmen, lifting rafters, hammering, nailing, sawing—his new home rising on the plateau by the mission. His heart surged with thankfulness and fullness. New bride. New home. New tasks. And, he was almost finished with translating the Bible into Cherokee.

In the deep leafy woods, 30 nightriders waited. Only the sawing and hammering, the laugh and pleasant "Good morning," of the workmen broke the air.

Four Cherokees in varied styles of attire emerged from the woods. They sauntered nonchalantly toward editor Boudinot who had printed the fateful editorials in the *Cherokee Phoenix.*

Startled, Boudinot noted the one in the blue ticking pants and rough boots stepped up, hand extended.

"Neighbor, we have sickness at our house, we need medicine, we . . ." Monroe Bates's imploring voice faded.

"Certainly. Certainly. Come back to Reverend Worcester's house where we keep the medicines. Can you tell me what kind of sickness?" The small party turned, ascended the gravel walk, edged by the white primroses, back toward the Worcester house. The path narrowed. It was obvious to Bates that it was logical that one should fall back, behind Boudinot. The long knife plunged between editor Elias's shoulders.

"Oh merciful God. Who will finish my task?" Elias cried as if the vision of his Bible and the new printing press flashed before him. "Our Father who art in heaven," he whispered, now prostrate on the rough path, his blood soaking into the gravel.

The second 'pleader for the sick' pulled a tomahawk from his waistband and split open his head. His brains spilled out. The new bride, Delight, now a widow. Bible translations halted.

But Delight Boudinot, seeing the indescribable horror before her, seemed to have an immediate knowing. "My pony. My pony," she yelled to one of the carpenters running up the hill. "I have to ride and warn his brother, Stand Watie."

*　*　*

The other cluster of night riding assassins now approached Van Buren, Arkansas, where old Major Ridge and his Negro assistant rode pleasantly along towards town. Before his mind had time to register surprise or review the interpretations of old threats and old laws, 12 shots rang out.

The great Major Ridge, Chief of the Eastern Cherokees, signer of the treaty to 'save the people' and provide them with new lands where they would not be overrun by settlers, heaved out of his saddle. Five bullets riddled his body.

When the blood-curdling news reached The People, hundreds of them hurried to surrounded Chief John Ross's stately Rose Cottage mansion.

"We must protect him from Stand Watie and hostile members of the treaty party. We must protect this great Chief," they chorused.

"I know nothing about it. Nothing at all," Chief Ross announced, over and over. "Send an appeal to General Arbuckle at Fort Gibson for protection," he commanded his subordinates. But there was no need. An army of the newly arrived Cherokees already surrounded him.

Only Monroe Bates knew that editor Elias Boudinot's brother, Stand Watie, in fear for his life, and somehow warned by Delight Boudinot of the riding assassins, had galloped off at breakneck speed with a party of supporters to the safety of Fort Gibson on the Grand River.

CHAPTER
TWENTY-THREE

A south breeze brushed Abby's cheek as she strolled arm in arm with Benjamin along the willow-lined Illinois River, a half-mile southeast of Tahlequah. She lifted the folds of her blue gingham with the puffed sleeves and gathered skirt as she planted a foot between the pink bush clover and the white heath asters which had sprung up in clumps in the bluegrass. Abby could not help but think: 'How bountiful are thy works, O Lord,' released as she was from the threats of the trail where they had nearly frozen to death or rotted in their rags.

With the sunshine slicing through the black-limbed ash, the stunning white-barked sycamores and the rippling sounds of the water to their left, Abby felt at peace—except. Except the dream that had repeated itself twice as she tossed last night.

Catching a glimpse of the grey blimp hanging on a high sycamore limb, she remembered. Wasps. Hornets. It was the sound of a hornet or bee, last night. She had awakened and automatically slapped at her neck, fearing an insect about to bite or sting. Then she awakened fully, realizing that it had been only a dream.

When she had awakened the second time, slapping at her neck, Benjamin stirred. "Lucy, what is it? You thrash about so."

"Only a dream, Benjamin." She remembered actually chuckling a little, for as children on the Hiwassee, they had sometimes taken long sticks and poked at the yellow jackets clustering underneath a rhododendron bush. Then, hightailing it in a fast gallop, they would laugh and hoot as they outran the yellow-and-brown zigzagging wasps.

The third repeat of the dream was different. When she awakened and propped herself up on the goose down pillow, she realized that it was Benjamin's neck. A determined wasp circled annoyingly around Benjamin's neck. She remembered chuckling to herself, then taking Benjamin's warm hand, nestled back against his body and lost herself in sleep. But, what was it? A portent? The shamans would say so. That she realized.

Should I say something to Benjamin? Abby, overcome by the beauty and charm of the day, decided to ignore what in other hours she would have considered an ominous portent.

Anyway, today Abby was glad that her strength had returned, her vision had cleared so that she could see individual leaves on the oak, and not a circular mass of green. The shooting pains in her head came only once in a while now. The smell of the spicy walnut trees, the fresh, sparkling river, the drift from the patch of clover, heightened her sense of well-being. "Isn't it something, Benjamin, a river here, this far west, named the Illinois?"

"A pleasant surprise, yes. I have to stop my mind from thinking about it, the trek through Illinois." He bent his head so that his lips could brush her hair which she'd combed back from her face and coiled loosely at the nape of her neck.

"It's the future that's important, Benjamin. Lucy, her education, our home. You, getting established in your carpentry. We can go on, can't we?" Abby squeezed Benjamin's warm hand.

"My dove, we'll go on. What was that verse Bushyhead always mentioned? 'The rivers, they shall not overflow thee'?"

"Yes, Benjamin. 'When thou passeth through the waters, I will be with thee; and through the rivers, they shall not overflow thee.'"

"From what Lucy told me, Abby, the rivers did overflow you on that keelboat on the Mississippi." Benjamin let loose of her fingers and shifted his hand to the small of her back.

"We were in the midst of death and the threats of death, Benjamin. You, also, on the trail overland. We have to go beyond the

agonies of it. God brought us through. Go on for Lucy, for ourselves, for the Nation." She looked up at his face and smiled.

"Sometimes, Abby, I doubted if we could ever put the pieces
together again, the pieces that make a home. Not just the wood
and stone, I mean being together again. Would our sufferings strip
us so that we would no longer care?"

"You survived, Benjamin. The love and care never left your
heart even though you could not feel it. I need you, Lucy needs
you. The Nation needs you. I believe that soon, you will be elected
to an office in the government. You'll see." Abby put her arm
around his back.

"You'd make a better officer than I, Abby. You have always
been interested in politics."

"When I'm an old woman, perhaps, Benjamin." Abby smiled
as they strolled together between two dark green cedars, boughs
heavy with the patina of blue berries. "I must tell you about Lucy,
Benjamin. Yesterday Chief Ross asked me to drop in at Rose Cottage when Lucy was practicing on his piano. I didn't tell you, but
he has hired a Miss Arlington from back east, a college, Mt.
Holyoke."

"Chief Ross always favored the eastern colleges, always insists
that our brightest youth should study in those schools." Benjamin
stepped around a patch of bright orange toadstools.

"Miss Arlington will help the Chief set up the educational
system here, Benjamin. She is also an accomplished pianist. Chief
Ross asked me if we would permit Miss Arlington to give piano
lessons to Lucy."

"You know, Abby, we have no money, only the tribal monthly
allotment. I will be earning, in time, but . . ."

"Benjamin, there is no fee required. The Nation pays Miss
Arlington for her services. She is glad to give Lucy lessons. She says
it would be a sin to deny a talented girl, like Lucy, such an opportunity."

"Then, Abby, I must say yes. For now at least. Someday in our
own home, perhaps on that knoll surrounded by dogwood and

ash facing the river, someday we will be able to buy a piano for
Lucy."

Benjamin noticed Abby's slowing steps and realized that it
was time for a rest. "Let's sit, Abby, here beneath this hazel bush
and pretend, as we look at the water rippling over the rapids, that
it is the Hiwassee back home."

Abby, glad for the suggestion, settled close to Benjamin, her
head on his chest. She reached to clasp his right hand with her
left. She could feel the warm, throbbing pulse and hear the regular
beating of his heart. Abby realized that it was life, life defying
death. Life pulsing, surging. They could go on. She smiled. We
can go on. Next week, Benjamin planned to begin their house.
Her health was slowly returning. Lucy already bursting with excitement over the new Female Seminary reaching skyward, and
her music lessons on the Chief's piano. Yes, thought Abby, God
and his Above Beings are good to us.

CHAPTER TWENTY-FOUR

"This is a good day. A good day," whispered Monroe Bates as he stroked his blowgun, thankful that it was one item he'd managed to save, in spite of White Birch's grumbling on the fated trek.

"Hunting today, father? Deer plentiful west of here in the valley of the Verdigris. Can I go with you?"

Monroe looked at his son, Jacob, stretching, shoulders widening in his deerskin shirt. Pride swelled in his heart.

"No, Jacob. Not this time." He turned, not wanting a prolonged discussion with anyone just now. He checked the small pouch at his waist. Poisoned arrows. Hatchet. Necessary supplies. His moccasined feet slipped through the low-hanging willow and buck brush, eastward, not toward the Verdigris, but toward the rippling Illinois.

*   *   *

Benjamin Drake smiled as he and Little Smoke, his closest neighbor on the Illinois, lifted the split oak log to fit it onto its notch in the cross log.

Stepping back, Benjamin wiped perspiration with his bandanna. "Last a 100 years, those white oak logs." He was glad, too, that his strength had returned and that he and Little Smoke were able to help each other build their houses.

Lucy will be pleased, bedroom with a window looking out on the dogwood trees and the river beyond. And, in time, we'll have real floor-boarding over the puncheon floor. Give us time.

While Little Smoke labored inside the cabin frame, hacking

with his hatchet to secure a proper fitting for the log, Benjamin
sauntered back to the log pile to retrieve another.

"Watch out for copperheads," Little Smoke called, "have to
send for the shaman, get bit by a copperhead." He pounded and
sliced with his hatchet. Smiling, he turned his face upward at the
spreading limb of the hackberry where a red squirrel fussed at
him.

"You'll get used to Real People living beneath you, little fellow, you'll see." He hacked some more.

The air was filled with the rap of the red-headed woodpecker,
the fussing chatter of the squirrel and the distant caw of a lone
crow. Little Smoke hammered and hacked at the white oak log.
Benjamin Drake stood to survey the woods and slant of land toward the river. Dreamily, he half-realized he could stand and lose
himself staring at the scenery.

*   *   *

A lone hunter, blowgun swinging on his back, moccasined feet
silent on the old deer trail, descended toward the river. Crouched
behind the grey-green hazel bushes, he waited. Poisoned arrow
inserted, he caught his breath, raised his blowgun and waited.

*   *   *

Benjamin loosened a log with his boot-toe, leaned to encircle the
rough end with his arms, trying to be careful and not get a nasty
splinter in the palm of his hand. He could smell the overpowering
sweetness of the freshly blossoming blackberry briars at his feet.

A sting in the neck? Mosquitoes? Not yet. Not mosquito time.
The log dropped. Before he had time to slap his neck with his
calloused hand, he realized his body was slumping in the clump of
mayapples and to the sweet earth. The descending hatchet split
open his head.

*   *   *

Little Smoke looked over toward the river where now only the
woodpecker rapped. He saw only the hazel bushes, the trunks of
the walnuts and the buckbrush.

*   *   *

The man with feet encased in the soft, beaded moccasins ascended the deer path behind the black-limbed walnut trees. No one saw him. He realized that he was not smiling and that a weight, greater than he'd ever felt, even during bridge building on the trail, now closed in upon his heart.

CHAPTER
TWENTY-FIVE

Abby insisted upon the spot, the rise on the west bank of the Illinois River, for Benjamin's grave. "It is a place Benjamin Drake would like. He always liked hickory trees, their brilliant yellow in the autumn."

So, Little Smoke and two comrades dug in the sweet red earth. They shoveled the crumbling soil which smelled of roots and bulbs, and growing things, and glistened with bits of gravel. The soil held its own promise.

"I liked the verse, Mother," said Lucy as she held her mother's hand. Eliza Bushyhead clasped Lucy's right hand as their feet split the bluegrass beneath their soles. Esther Shining Star and three shawl-draped Cherokee women followed behind the trio.

"Reverend Bushyhead's verses comforted our hearts. You must memorize them, Lucy. I learned them long ago at the mission when I was a young woman, 'But the mercy of the Lord is from everlasting to everlasting upon them that fear him, and his righteousness unto children's children'."

"I will repeat the psalm, Mother, every morning until I know it by heart. Eliza, do you know those verses?"

"Yes, Lucy. I'm glad I met your father before he died. He was kind and good. My father said, 'Did you notice what a fine voice Benjamin Drake has when he sings the hymns in service?'"

Lucy knew, though, that a part of Eliza, like herself and her mother, caught on the old snag of yesteryear where hung the bag of pain-filled memories of the Trail of Tears. Only their present hope, their present belief, the light in their souls at the moment could keep such a snag from ripping their souls, exposing memories too overwhelming for mortals to endure.

And at the mention of her father's singing voice, Lucy could not forget how Benjamin had learned to favor the new hymn she loved best: "O have you not heard of that beautiful stream / That flows through our Father's land? / Its waters gleam bright in the heavenly light, / And ripple o'er golden sand."

At the thought of the words, Lucy could not help seeing the rivers, the sweet water of the Coosa where she was born, the deep blue of the Hiwassee and its 300-old oaks encircled by purple violets, and the Tennessee with its terrible whirlpool that'd heaved both Abby and her onto the rocky shelf.

When she thought about it, Lucy could still feel the terrors of the broad Ohio, and the torments of the Mississippi. She could still smell the mixture of mud from the banks, and the blossoming locust trees as they leaned over the yellow Arkansas that'd narrowed and made them continue on foot.

Emerging from her reverie, Lucy asked her mother for permission to walk back to Tahlequah. "Look at the sunshine splitting the clouds and the meadowlarks on the rail fences. Already, there are lots of wildflowers, Mother."

"Yes, my child. Yes, and perhaps it will strengthen our spirits to walk the path home. Look, the wild roses ahead, they give hope, don't they, girls?"

Though Lucy's heart was heavy, the roses spoke to her in their own way as they leaned over the path, nodding in the warm breeze. Their pale pink petals and golden centers contrasted with the brilliance of their fringed leaves.

"Tomorrow, Lucy, I shall bring a bouquet of our hydrangea blossoms. We shall go and place fresh flowers on your father's grave." Eliza let go of Lucy's hand as they started down a yellow clay bank toward the road below.

When they reached the road, outlined by the rail-fence leading eastward into Tahlequah, Esther Shining Star walked side by side with Abby. "You must stay with me, Abby. I'd be so lonely without Lucy and you. You know the one-half of my house would echo with emptiness without you." Esther smiled at Lucy and Abby.

"At least, for now, Esther. At least for now." Abby turned her face with the shiny scar toward Esther and returned a smile, though her dark-circled eyes betrayed the grief weighing at her heart.

"Mother, I feel like it is our home. Besides," Lucy said, "the wisteria is blooming and makes me feel secure, the way it wraps around the porch."

Lucy hoped they could stay until they either moved to the new house by the Illinois, or until her mother sold it and they took something in town. May be across the street from Esther Shining Star's place. But Lucy realized that with all the changes she had endured, moving to a small house in town just for her mother and herself and may be Todd too, would be a change she could accept.

"For now, at least, until Lucy, Todd, and I get our bearings again, Esther. And," continued Abby, "I have to think of security for Lucy with school starting in September." Abby's high buttoned shoes swished through a patch of horsemint growing alongside the road.

"Chief Ross said that Miss Arlington could continue giving me piano lessons all summer, Mother. I'd like it. I love to play the Chopin on his piano." Lucy lifted her eyes to her mother's face seeking her approval. A mockingbird swished from one elm tree limb to another.

"Well, I'll talk to Chief Ross about it in another week. Take our time, child. We have had enough for now, this funeral, the awful events surrounding . . ." Abby wiped tears from her eyes.

"Your mother's right, Lucy. Don't make too many changes now. And, yes, if you could continue to take piano lessons at Chief Ross's mansion, I'd do it, if I were you." Eliza smiled encouragingly, as if she remembered humility is a virtue and that one must weep with those who weep as Saint Paul had said in his letters.

"Besides," added Eliza, "I never did get the hang of reading those notes like you do."

Todd, who'd straggled behind with three tribal boys, raced around his friends and now stood in line with Lucy and her mother. "Mrs. Drake, I want to tell you something that I've decided." He looked up, searching her face.

Abby looked into Todd's open brown eyes, as she lifted a hand to hold on to the edge of the straw bonnet Esther had loaned her. "What have you decided, Todd?"

"Now that Mr. Drake has been murdered and buried, I'm not gonna run away to Tennessee or Georgia. No. I'm gonna stay here in Tahlequah and take care of you." He smiled and straightened his back, sweat beads gleaming on his neck.

"You're a fine boy, and a courageous friend, Todd. Lucy and I love you and appreciate you." Again, Abby wiped tears.

"Tom Falcon Wing at the livery said he'd pay me five pennies each day, if I would come up and help him currycomb the horses. I like Tom Falcon Wing, Mrs. Drake. No, I don't think I'll run away, now." Todd dug his bare toe into the red dust of the road.

"Mother," said Lucy, looking up just as the wind caught the collar of her pink lawn dress with the white sash. "Mother, let's sing that song about the rivers. We ought to know about rivers, hadn't we?" She focused her hope-filled eyes upon her mother's grief-weighted face.

"A song about the rivers? Perhaps, a hymn would bless our hearts." Abby reached for Lucy's hand.

Then Lucy, in a clear voice that caught in the gentle wind, began to sing:

O seek that beautiful stream,
O seek that beautiful stream;
Its waters, so free,
Are flowing for thee,
O seek that beautiful stream.

Eliza clasped Lucy's other hand, lifted up her head with the troublesome hair and joined in. Her voice rang with faith and determination equal to that of her newly adopted friend, Lucy Drake, formerly like she, from far, far away New Echota, Georgia.

"Look, Mother, look, Eliza, look beyond those tall walnut trees. They're painting the columns on the new female seminary. Lucy's face broke into a promising smile.

CHAPTER
TWENTY-SIX
1847

Sixteen-year-old Lucy Drake sat shoulder to shoulder with Eliza Bushyhead as she cracked the whip over the back of the sorrel mare. The hack rolled down the slope toward Tahlequah, red dust swirling behind. "Did you ever think poor girls like us would be attending a seminary, Eliza?"

"It's a finishing school, Lucy. Do you think Miss Whitmore can put the finishing touches on us?" Eliza's laughter rippled behind them, startling a meadowlark on the fence post.

A sense of freedom surged in Lucy's heart as she pulled the reins with her kid-gloved hands and steered the horse past Chief John Ross's Rose Cottage mansion. She glanced at the half-mile-long driveway lined with pink roses.

Lucy recalled that only last week, the Chief housed 40 guests in the mansion. Tall Greek columns supported the wide portico with windows overlooking the extensive grounds and flower gardens. The greenhouse, stable, dairy, blacksmith shop, smokehouse, and cabins for over 40 slaves, half-circled behind the mansion among the hackberry, elm, and oak.

Neither Lucy nor Eliza, dragged through the poverty and misery of The Trail eight years earlier, could yet feel comfortable with such opulence, though Lucy did keep up her practice each week on Chief Ross's mahogany grand piano inside the parlor.

Lucy thought of the loving prayers of those who cared for them,

Reverend Worcester and his wife, Edmonda, who knelt twice daily, building up calluses on her knees, praying for her Cherokee girls.

She knew that even Reverend Worcester believed that had it not been for Widow Shining Star who'd taken them in, Lucy Drake would be in her grave from sorrow.

Through the years scars had crept over the edges of Lucy's grief. The stimulation of the seminary, the mixture of Cherokee girls, all the way from full-blood to one-sixteenth, the challenge of the Latin, Greek, philosophy, art, music, slowly turned Lucy and Eliza's minds from their orphaned status, and heavy losses.

Lucy's old friend of The Trail, Todd Wyeth, who harnessed and saddled horses at the livery, and threatened each week to return to Tennessee, chose not to continue his education beyond eighth grade.

Lucy's mind lingered on the memory of Todd and her mother on the trail. Caught on foot between Ft. Smith and Ft. Gibson in November. The People, stricken by pneumonia and typhus— huddled in the mud and the reeds. Saved from starvation a few more days when Todd had reached out with lightning speed to catch the muskrat.

And what about Jacob Bates at the male seminary in Tahlequah? A survivor, too, of the grave-marked overland trail, plodding in freezing winter alongside her father, Benjamin, and his father, Monroe.

Lucy slapped the reins and the mare turned onto Sequoia Street, leading toward Esther Shining Star's house. Lucy felt a sadness for Jacob; his father, noose around his neck, found swinging over a bluff on the Illinois the day after her own father's murder; Jacob's mother, now cooped up in the Nation's asylum in the southern part of Tahlequah, her husband's death, a weight too heavy for her already over-burdened soul.

Nevertheless, Jacob Bates demonstrated a courageous spirit in his shiny new boots, and broadcloth shirts, black eyes flashing at seminary girls, lips parted in a slow grin.

Lucy drew the hack up in front of widow Shining Star's dog

trot log house, cockscomb and petunias splashing color on both sides of the flagstone walk. Lucy stepped down, the skirt of her white chambray dress flapping in the hot September wind. "I wish I'd worn my chambray. I'm melting in the heat in this wool," Eliza said, leaping out. Her bonnet had fallen backwards revealing her hair coiled in a shiny bun.

"Just the answer to my prayers." Widow Shining Star held the railing and stepped down to greet the girls.

"Why, I just said to Yellow Cat, 'Time I get some company from my girls up on that fine hill and from that splendid school'." Widow Shining Star waddled, having gained considerable weight since the tragic deaths of Lucy's parents.

"My girls, come in and sit. You'll be pleased with my new violet horse hair sofa, and walnut rocking chair from Mr. George Murrell's Store down town. Come in and tell me about the girls up at the seminary."

Esther Shining Star's living-room reflected good taste: the fluted glass flower basket on her oak stand filled with zinnias and cockscombs from her own flower beds, a walnut shelf clock flashing its pendulum as it measured the time.

Mother Esther, as everyone called her, set the oval tray on the oak library table and poured tea into the china cups with the tiny pink roses splashing down their sides.

"Warms my heart, you girls taking the time to visit me. So much fuss and business around here, why, that new Male Seminary over yonder." She pointed northward out the window sporting wine drapes. Next, she placed her left hand over her breast as she bowed to hand tea to the seated girls who'd taken stock of her well-appointed room.

"You young ladies have the privilege of meeting any of those young gentlemen from the male seminary? She emphasized the word, "male," though she acted slightly embarrassed as if she knew she shouldn't have. Lucy realized that Mother Esther simply wanted to lighten their focus. Mother Esther believed there'd been too many long faces in the neighborhood the last five years. Eliza blushed as she lowered her head to stare at her blue serge skirt. "I don't have time for boys with my Latin and Greek, Mother Esther."

Lucy lifted her eyes directly upon Mother Esther's face. "And I'm busy memorizing passages from *Virgil*, Mother Esther," she replied, appreciating the light teasing.

"Took a bouquet of the last of my summer lilies over to your parents' graves yesterday, Lucy. Something beautiful about that cemetery overlooking the Illinois. That sweet grass, wind sweeping it." Mother Esther stood as if in a trance for a moment, reliving the event, knowing that it was important to talk about the deceased now and then.

"Put some flowers by Reverend Bushyhead's grave stone, too, Eliza. Folks around here revered your father. How we miss him. We do miss them all, but then, Lucy, tell me about the seminary." She seated herself in a rocker across from Lucy and Eliza.

Here it goes. Lucy didn't really want to talk about Jacob Bates's interest in her. Still, Mother Esther sat there, smiling, waiting.

Lucy hadn't even told Eliza about the poem she'd received from the tall male seminarian, showing off his writing abilities. Signed by the name, "Jacob Bates."

Yes, wanton Nature's dark-eyed child,
The jewel is for me—
The sweetest flower that gems the wild
Is the Rose of Cherokee.

For a moment, Lucy could see Jacob in her mind, tall as her father, broad-shouldered, smiling with those same dark eyes, eyebrows arched as he'd escorted her out on the portico at the opening social. Of course, under Principal Rebecca Whitmore's surveying eyes. Lucy realized it'd felt just fine, Jacob visiting with her on the portico, especially after so much loss, pain, separations and funerals. The years of stuffy little grade-school rooms, all the discomforts of sinking roots in a new land. Lucy realized her mind had wandered. She looked up.

"How can I ever thank you, Mother Esther, for all you've done? I couldn't have survived without you." She lowered her cup, noticing the roses on the saucer, then looked up at Mother Esther's brown eyes that carried traces of her own sorrows.

"I had to go on, Mother Esther. Eliza, also. Other girls at the seminary, orphaned too. Many traveled over The Trail as children, saw their fathers and mothers suffer and die . . . ."

"Were it not for our faith, we couldn't make it, Mother Esther," Eliza added. "Thank God for the funds from The Nation for our schooling." Lucy knew that Eliza appreciated the religion classes too, as she was every bit as faithful a Baptist as her famous father before her. "My mother often spoke of Reverend Bushyhead comforting The People along The Trail, Eliza. His prayers helped many, of that I'm convinced." Lucy's fingers rose to her chin.

Lucy had joined the Park Hill Mission southeast of Tahlequah, counting her blessings that she could study with Reverend Worcester, whom The People called 'The Messenger,' as he translated the *Gospel Messenger* and the Bible into Cherokee.

Lucy settled into the comfort of Mother Esther's living room, recognizing that it was good to renew old ties, walk the old streets. Stroll along Town Branch. Return greetings to the young men pouring out of that new seminary across. She wondered though, why did they have to arch their backs and strut so? Especially, that Jacob Bates who'd given her that poem? Jacob, only a boy when he'd struggled along the thousand-mile march with her father, Benjamin.

"One of those male seminarians is sweet on you, isn't he, Lucy?" Mother Esther dared to risk it, then glanced down at the roses in her carpet.

Lucy cleared her throat as she studied the pink rug-roses, then placed her teacup on the tray.

"It's this way, Mother Esther. Young gentleman going to escort me has to have standards. You know what Eliza and I endure up on the hill? Behind those porches and columns?" Lucy stuffed down the chuckles that pushed up in her throat, as she recalled the teasing she and Eliza endured after those male seminarians in their black coats finally left the social last week.

"You know, Mother Esther, the school schedule is enough to choke a horse. Miss Whitmore, Principal, that is, made us all memorize the philosophy and goals." Lucy cleared her throat to commence:

We the young ladies of the female seminary commit ourselves to become educated, self-disciplined and proficient, not only in the management of our homes, but in refinement and the art of diplomacy in order to properly meet others of high or low degree. Also show reverence to the Great Creator in order to ever richly, grow with our husbands, our children, and all others, especially ourselves.

"There." Lucy gasped for breath, her pointed shoe tapping one of the rug-roses.

Eliza stifled her giggles with an embroidered handkerchief. Lucy raised her chin, her laughter rose to the ceiling.

"Why, my dears, such a creed. Yes, choke a horse you say?" Mother Esther allowed herself a chuckle.

"Well, my daughters, it sounds stuffy but I can say this, it'll turn you both into fine ladies. Lucy, now I can't recall the name of that young gentleman who keeps asking about you."

Now Lucy had an opportunity to apply what she'd recited about diplomacy. "His name is Jacob Bates, Mother Esther. Wasn't it strange? The sheriff's deputy finding his father, Monroe, hanging from an oak over the cliffs of the Illinois River, day after they found my father murdered."

"Yes, my child. Tragic. More than strange," replied Mother Esther.

"Some people hint that Jacob's father committed suicide. Why would he do a thing like that?" Lucy rose to stand by the library table. "You know Jacob's not really an orphan. His mother, White Birch, survived the trek. Folks said she was tossed into the Mississippi River during the crossing. A survivor. Yes, Jacob's a survivor too." Lucy's voice hung, as she stared at the yellow hollyhock nodding at the window.

Lucy remembered her father telling how young Jacob, a superb swimmer, leaped into the raging waters to rescue a woman and an infant that fated day The People tried to cross the Mississippi.

"Well, anyway, when White Birch laid eyes on her husband Monroe's corpse, a suicide case, according to the Sheriff's report, her reasoning left her. An inmate, now, over at the asylum south of Tahlequah. Jacob visits her weekly." A lump crept up Lucy's throat as she reviewed such sorrowful events.

"And," said Eliza, "White Birch escaped once, wandering the streets in town carrying a tree-limb-club she'd picked up along the road, vowing vengeance upon the one who killed her husband.

"Yes, it was strange. Father considered Monroe Bates his friend," Lucy said. "Told me they were forced to build bridges together on The Trail, though I always sensed something amiss."

Lucy'd never admitted to anyone, not even Eliza, that she did not understand why that stalwart Jacob Bates, who'd been determined to get an education, even under difficult challenges, ended up calling a poor full-blood like herself a 'Cherokee Rose.'

CHAPTER
TWENTY-SEVEN

"I must memorize more scripture," murmured Lucy, as she pored over Psalm 107: "O give thanks to the Lord, for he is good . . .," in the spacious seminary dormitory room she shared with Eliza Bushyhead. "One must work hard to kill the *old nature* Reverend Worcester keeps talking about."

"Old nature does loom its ugly head," replied Eliza, rising from her desk where she'd grown weary of translating her Greek.

Both girls felt relief as the school year slid toward its closing. "Only six more weeks until we'll kick up our heels at graduation celebrations and the picnic by the river." Lucy turned to Eliza, smiling.

"I'm going to race through the sweet william, poke down the deviled eggs and sandwiches. Laugh and dance the May pole. Let down my hair. Breathe fresh air blowing off the Illinois. Pick a bunch of honeysuckle." Eliza tossed her *Virgil* text to the back of the desk.

"And I'll beat you in a canoe race, Eliza," Lucy said. "Only if Charles Walking Tall paddles the canoe for you," Eliza shot back.

Eliza stepped over to the wide window which, overlooked the spacious tree-studded lawn and Chief Ross's plantation. "You're correct about the old nature, Eliza. I struggle with it daily." Lucy turned towards Eliza who stared out the window. Lucy'd recognized an uneasiness rising in her breast lately. When the feeling became conscious and she named it, she didn't at first want to admit it.

She and Eliza had discussed it, the evidence in the weekly

issue of the student newspaper, *The Rosebud*, published by the girls themselves and sold for 10 cents a copy. At first, Lucy tried to reject the conclusion she'd come to, asking herself, could it really be? Class distinctions? Overtones of racism? Her irritation grew.

"Lucy, don't be too critical," Eliza'd said when Lucy pointed to the editorials emphasizing the "true woman" ideal. And the ideal seemed always to be someone white, very, very white, blue eyes, pale skin, blonde hair.

"Listen to this." Lucy grabbed the small paper on her chair and read the composition by a Victoria Rogers from one of the rich Old Settler families who'd migrated to Arkansas ten years before Lucy's family endured their forced journey.

"She peeped from her blue eyes and the crimson blush stole upon her cheeks.'"

Lucy turned. "How'd you like to see my blue eyes and crimson blush, Eliza? Do you see it? The crimson blush on my skin?"

Lucy hadn't realized how much anger she'd been repressing. And it was blue-eyed and yellow-haired Victoria Rogers who'd provoked most of it.

"Eliza, Lucy, you girls have a chance to see what *The Rosebud* published? My poem. My piece on "Beauty of the Soul". My piece on "The Power of Kindness?" Lucy tried to imitate Victoria's singsong voice.

"Don't you see how Victoria Rogers flaunts herself while Miss Whitmore and Miss Worcester dip their heads and look the other way? Are they blind?" Lucy searched her desk for an apple she'd wheedled from old black Dave, the cook.

"Would've served her right if the pond ice'd broken under her at the January skating," Eliza added.

* * *

Before the seminary year ended, measles struck the girls. Fever and sweat. Blotches. Thirst. Lucy and Eliza rolled in the hot bed in the stuffy room for two agonizing weeks.

Lucy recovered first. Eliza, though, still lay in bed, covers yanked to her chin. Lucy parted her hair, which had grown strag-

gly and lifeless from the fever. She brushed it, then coiled it up on
her head, though her arms trembled with weakness. She slipped
on her woolen skirt, blouse and jacket. Grabbing her slate and
books, she dragged off to classes, her mind foggy, her legs, like
rubber.

During the afternoon five-minute break, Lucy noticed how
Victoria Rogers kept sliding up to Miss Worcester, then bob over
to Miss Whitmore. The third time, Victoria had the gall to stare
straight at her and point her finger at her while whispering to
Miss Whitmore.

Lucy checked herself. "Handkerchief? Buttons all closed? Is
there a spot on my blouse? Did I drip egg-yolk or butter on my
front?" She felt the sweat breaking out on her forehead, she trembled
from weakness as she hunched in her desk.

"Lucy, my dear, it's your hair. I'm going to have to ask you to
return to your room and redo your hair. It doesn't become you,
sticking out the way it does," Miss Whitmore announced, her
mouth set in a straight line.

Lucy slunk off to her room. She yanked out the pins, grabbed
the hairbrush and pulled it through the tangled strands with the
broken ends. Though her arm ached, she gave it 20 extra pulls,
just to be sure. Why had the ends split and why did it insist on
standing up on top and at her forehead?

When Lucy returned to the classroom, there stood Victoria
Rogers, a know-it-all-look on her face as she translated a portion of
Greek. Victoria glanced at Lucy as she slunk to her seat. Victoria
halted her recitation to flash a look at Miss Whitmore.

"You may sit down, Miss Rogers. Your translation is accurate.
Well done." Miss Whitmore's dark eyes and stern face turned on
Lucy Drake's hair, which already had crawled from beneath its
pins.

"Miss Drake," Miss Whitmore said, staring over the top of her
textbook. "Miss Lucy Drake, please return to your room. Young
ladies have their standards here. You must arrange your hair again.
Please go back and redo your hair. Return to class promptly. I shall

call on you for your translation when you return." Miss Whitmore cleared her throat, her brows knit together.

Sickened by humiliation, Lucy raked the brush through her hair the third time as roommate Eliza raised herself from her pillow and giggled.

"Lucy, wet your hair. Part it in the middle. Plaster it down and . . ." Eliza fell back on her pillow, choking down her laughter.

Lucy wet her fever-ravaged hair, parted it severely, then braided it in two long braids.

"You mean like this?" Lucy's arms trembled from the strain and struggle.

"Yes, that's the way. Wad it up on your neck just like Miss Whitmore's."

Impish, Eliza Bushyhead fell back in her bed in hysterics. "I can't believe it, Lucy, you and your silky hair, having all this trouble. Oh," she rolled as she howled, "I'm glad it isn't me. Me with my frowzy hair and my name. Lucy, my name, *Miss Bushyhead*. Can you imagine?"

Every head turned as Miss Lucy Drake opened the classroom the second time, head regal, face long and drawn. She marched across the back of the room, then down the long side aisle, every neck turning to view her. A second Miss Whitmore walked the full length of the room, ugly knot of braided hair on her neck. Lucy marched across the front of the room with the astonished Miss Whitmore on her platform, holding her *Virgil* text.

Then brazen, Lucy Drake turned down the main aisle and strolled all the way back to her seat while the students gasped.

Miss Whitmore, comprehending the situation, smiled and dipped her head into her text. That was all. Then Lucy knew, Miss Whitmore, regal teacher, understood she'd been outdone. Victoria? Another matter.

* * *

A week later Lucy, while walking across the wide verandah, bumped into Victoria Rogers, who had written another article in *The Rosebud* that had irritated Lucy.

"Victoria, you were quite taken by those Osage young men who visited the seminary a few days ago, weren't you?" Victoria halted from her walk, long curls swinging at the sides of her face, stared at Lucy with her bachelor button blue eyes.

"What do you mean, Lucy, 'quite taken'?" Her mouth puckered.

"So you found them amusing? The Osage young men? Interesting, isn't it?" Lucy dared to goad.

"And," Lucy continued, lifting the newspaper to read: "their war dances were amusing . . . the lofty symmetrical forms and proud, free step of these sons of nature just from their wild hunting ground . . .'"

"Really, Victoria? You and your fair complexion? 'Their lofty symmetrical forms'?"

"I was merely reflecting my observations. It was not personal." Victoria lifted her chin, wanting to pass on by.

Lucy read, "'I found their war dances fascinating, those tall, dusky forms stomping and stooping around, making wailing sounds.' Victoria, would you like to demonstrate?" Lucy couldn't help herself.

Victoria, cheeks crimson with anger, drew her head back. Her shoulder nudged Lucy as she barged past. "Who are you to criticize me, Lucy Drake? You haven't had even one of your compositions published in The *Rosebud*."

Lucy knew it was intended as a put-down, but she turned to the porch railing to hold her sides, making sure that Miss Worcester or Miss Whitmore weren't coming up the steps.

Then Lucy recalled how last June, Victoria Roger's never-failing eye noted that she and Eliza and secretive Delilah Vann sneaked through the hedge row to Chief Ross's expansive apple orchard across the way. Never mind that the apples were only nubbins. The girls had gobbled them anyway.

Victoria had dutifully made her contact with Miss Whitmore.

When Lucy slipped to her door to answer the knock that evening, there'd stood Miss Whitmore, sly grin on her long face.

"Your medicine, Lucy." With a steady hand, she poured the nasty tasting castor oil into the waiting spoon.

"Open, Lucy. This is the green apple cure. You girls can't outdo me. Eliza, step forward."

Lucy could still taste the rancid castor oil.

"Their tall, dusky forms stomping and stooping around. Really?" Lucy snickered as she recognized how fair-skinned, Victorian Victoria's blood heated at the sight of the Osage dusky maleness.

"Even if I'd thought it, I'd never have written it," Lucy confided to Eliza.

CHAPTER TWENTY-EIGHT

Why did I invite Victoria? Lucy hadn't yet forgiven herself. Believing she'd goaded Victoria too much lately, and with the saturating emphasis on "Girls, you must be forgiving. 'Forgive us our trespasses as we forgive . . .'" Miss Worcester's voice lifted the phrase daily.

They had begged eggs from old black Dave in the kitchen. With the abundance of produce, old Dave always complied, besides, he enjoyed the girls' attentions.

"You girls going to call down Miss Worcester's wrath," he warned, sneaking the small basket of eggs to Lucy.

"Now you young ladies know Miss Worcester and Miss Whitmore don't allow no cooking in the rooms." But old black Dave was a willing accomplice. Lucy was confident that he considered it improper to disappoint two bright-eyed Cherokee girls like Miss Eliza and Miss Lucy.

* * *

A small group of sophomore girls frolicked along on their late afternoon walk to see the blossoming primroses, scattered here and there across the small prairie pasture.

Lucy turned a wagon wheel, then she noticed that the chaperone, Miss Tiller, a thin, single woman like Miss Worcester and Miss Whitmore, but 10 years older, bobbed along ahead.

Miss Tiller's head nodded forward, then dipped back like an old hen pecking at the gravel. Lucy decided she'd better compose herself and refrain from turning another wagon wheel and risk being labelled "aggressive and brazen" by Miss Charity Tiller.

To Lucy's left, Eliza bent and pulled up a generous handful of the wild onions surrounding her high-top shoes.

"Onions, onions. A party in our room," Eliza whispered, loud enough for Lucy to hear. Lucy glanced at Eliza and saw the mischief rise in her eyes.

The two girls dropped back, whispering their plans.

"Lucy, invite Nannie Holmes and Delilah Vann. And Lucy, let's beg Cook Dave for some fresh spring mushrooms and potatoes."

*   *   *

That night, after prayers and lights out, picnic time finally arrived.

Lucy slipped out through the wide door and slid silently down the hall. "Tap tap." Her knuckles rapped softly. "Time for our picnic."

Turning, she glided along the wall, staying in the shadows. But when she passed the stairwell, Victoria Rogers, in her Irish linen wrapper, ascended the staircase like a queen. The impulse. Even the Cherokee blood coursing through her veins should have warned her not to give in to impulse.

"Oh, Victoria, you startled me." Lucy whispered.

Now what? She thought. Better invite her, too. She already senses something's up. Appeal to Victoria's lighter side. Besides, Lucy thought, I need to make up for goading her. Been hard on Victoria lately. Yes, invite her.

"Victoria, a little party. In Eliza's and my room. Ten minutes. You come, too."

Victoria nodded and smiled, "Why, Lucy Drake. Imagine you inviting me. Why, thank you, dear." She dipped her forehead, slid through a shaft of moonlight by the stairs in her lurching saunter toward her door.

*   *   *

"Keep down the giggling," hissed Eliza. Mirth knocked at their ribs.

"Turn the lamp higher, Lucy," Eliza whispered to Lucy, the chief cook.

"Gonna blacken the pan. Who cares?" Eliza's giggles rolled out of her throat.

"Hand me the chopped mushrooms, Nannie." Purloined butter from the kitchen below sizzled as the mushrooms, begged from old Dave, slid in.

"Now the onions. Eliza, didya chop them?"

And, the smell. The lamp, blackening the bottom of the pan, did produce the required heat. The onions sizzled, their heavenly aroma circulating toward the ceiling.

"Eggs. Delilah, break the eggs." Lucy twirled the fork in her hand as their omelet bubbled and their mouths drooled.

"The window. We forgot to close the window," hissed Eliza, realizing that the odors could drift in the evening wind.

Nanny Holmes raced to pull down the massive sash.

"Lordy, lordy." Lucy laughed, as she turned the eggs.

Just when they had divided the golden omelet onto the saucers, appetites whetted by the onions, mushrooms, eggs and butter, and by the hilarious secretiveness of the party did Lucy remember, where is Victoria Rogers? I thought she said she would come.

There wasn't even time for the lump of dread to push up beyond Lucy's stomach when knuckle-rapping rattled the door.

"Lucy Drake. Eliza Bushyhead. Open this door."

Neither girl ever remembered Miss Worcester or Miss Whitmore having such long faces. Besides, thought Lucy, didn't they look old? Frowning that way, hair braided down their backs. And, weren't those flannel nightgowns ugly?

"Violations. Violations." Miss Whitmore clucked with her tongue. her long fingers pulled at her throat.

"And, Lucy and Eliza. Yes. You two are the responsible ones.

Delilah and Nannie, go at once to your rooms. Two demerits for each of you." Miss Worcester shook her head, her face drawn.

"Oh, Miss Whitmore . . ." Lucy attempted an apology. Her dark eyes followed the cracks in the floor at her feet.

"Miss Drake. And, Miss Bushyhead. Demerits. Full demerits. No week-end passes to Tahlequah. And, Lucy Drake, Miss Whitmore and I," Miss Worcester coughed, "have just been discussing how hard you've been on Victoria Rogers lately. Because Victoria has been so responsible this evening, we've decided to give her two bonus citizenship points."

* * *

Lucy and Eliza hunched and smoldered in their rooms, confined to translating from their Greek or pondering art history. "I'm going to yell a war-whoop when the picnic finally arrives," Lucy said, leaning back at her desk, odors from Chief John Ross's roses blowing in the window and making her dizzy.

"Jail, that's what it is. Ought to complain to the Board," Eliza replied, her hair hanging unbraided.

The seeds of resentment toward Victoria Rogers still lodged in her heart. Even though Lucy'd read the Apostle Paul in Romans about "the old nature and 'I do what I would not,'" still, it hung like a prune-pit caught in her throat.

It hadn't helped either when saucy Victoria Rogers returned from a frolic in Tahlequah and reported: "I strolled on the new gravel path along Town Branch with Mr. Jacob Bates from the *Male Seminary*."

Victoria dared stare Lucy straight in the eyes when she emphasized 'male'.

"You do know Mr. Jacob Bates, don't you, Lucy?" Victoria asked, mincing down the sidewalk past the walnut trees. Lucy had already told herself that nobody would be interested in a plain, full-blood like herself. Especially a poor one who'd been disciplined by Miss Whitmore and Miss Worcester.

CHAPTER
TWENTY-NINE

"Eliza, haven't you sewn your sash back on yet?" Lucy, who had managed to successfully tie the wide sash on her own white lawn, stepped over to the open window. "We don't want to hold up the wagons."

Lucy leaned out the window and surveyed the two flatbed wagons below. The chief steward, Dr. Elizur Butler and his wife, Martha, stood beneath a walnut tree wringing their hands as the two slaves, loaned for the day by Chief Ross, lifted the 10-gallon crocks of fried chicken and sliced ham up to the back of the first wagon. She noticed the girls clustering below, waiting Miss Worcester's instructions as to when to climb on board.

"Eliza, come on or I'm going on down without you." Lucy grabbed a white parasol, but, realizing she'd had troubles opening and closing it, decided to leave it behind. Besides, she thought, what does a full-blood like me need a parasol for, anyway?

When she and Eliza hurried out on the verandah, Lucy noticed Miss Worcester with her unbecoming little brown hat. Why doesn't she allow anyone to suggest another style?

Eliza and Lucy lifted their skirts and stepped up on the step stool black Leander provided. Lucy could tell by his broad smile that he'd assured himself that none of Miss Whitmore's or Miss Worcester's girls would have a mishap on his step stool while loading.

Lucy settled herself beside Eliza on one of the ladderback chairs, relieved to be on board at last. The draft horses snorted. Twenty-

five girls on each wagon, seated on the hard chairs swayed and
rocked, trying to control their giggles.

"Ooooooooh," the girls cried as the wagons lurched and the
horses drew them down the seminary hill eastward toward the
picnic spot on the banks of the Illinois.

"I remember last year, Ellen Adair and Elizabeth Ann Duncan
overturned in their canoes. I think they did it just so those male
seminary young men could dive in to rescue them," Eliza said,
clutching Lucy's arm.

"Even thinking of the canoes and the river and the copperheads coming out in the afternoon sun makes my heart beat faster,
Eliza," Lucy said.

"Potato salad. Slaw. Pickles and beets. Deviled eggs. Spinach
salad. Elizur, do you think we've enough baked ham?" Mrs. Butler's
voice drifted forward from the back of the wagon. Lucy turned to
glance, noticing Martha Butler twist her hands. "And the fried
chicken. Have to keep it cool in those 10-gallon crocks," she called
to her top-hatted husband beside her.

Elizur, shoulders swaying, muttered, "Yes, enough, Martha."

"All these giggling girls remind me of fresh wine poured in too
small a bottle," Martha said. "Listen to those girls fizz over."

And fizz over they did. End of the high-pressure year, the
supervisions, the commands, the "Yes, Miss Worcester. Yes, Miss
Whitmore. Yes, now I see." End of the mind-bursting calculus,
the throat-choking rhetoric, the tongue-twisting Greek, the mili-
tary-based physical education.

Backs straight, hair combed and curled, chins up, the girls
rode regally, some, like Miss Whitmore, with parasols up to protect their faces from the sun. Long frocks in yellows, white, cream
and light-blue. Sashes blowing in the wind. Hair ribbons tied
meticulously.

"Are you nervous about all those seminary young blades in
frock coats loping down the hill toward the river, Lucy?" Eliza
giggled.

Lucy straightened her shoulders and her mouth, afraid that

Eliza might let loose with a stanza of that poem Jacob'd sent her. "Yes, wanton Nature's dark-eyed child, / The jewel is for me— The sweetest flower that gems the wild / Is the Rose of Cherokee."

Lucy hated the way Eliza would howl and slap her thigh, a behavior frowned on by Miss Worcester.

Lucy looked ahead two rows at Victoria Rogers, recalling how Victoria kept on harping about her promenade along Town Branch with Mr. Jacob Bates of the male seminary. Lucy knew Jacob would be at the picnic. And Miss Worcester or Miss Tiller, one of the two, would be in charge of the games.

"I'll watch you, Lucy, so you don't get carried away. You do the same for me." Lucy could tell by Eliza's face that she'd decided to let up on the teasing. Chief Ross's slaves, Rufus and Leander, drew the great wagons up by the three spreading burr oaks that provided enough shade for 200 people. "Whoa. Whoa," they called in mellow voices.

The slaves held the reins in their white-gloved hands, silk stovepipe hats cocked on their heads, faces spread in smiles.

"Now you young ladies all take care stepping down."

Victoria Rogers tilted her parasol which matched her pink frock. She stepped down on the stool, hand anchored in Leander's, following Miss Worcester.

Lucy and Eliza stepped down next, though they would just as soon have jumped off the wagon bed in the back and galloped off toward the river.

The girls clustered nervously. If they giggled, they tried to stifle such outbreaks with their handkerchiefs.

"Lucy, there are some of Victoria's 'sons of nature, swarthy,'— what was the rest? Oh, yes, 'their stately symmetrical forms.'" Eliza pointed to the path on the right where a cluster of young male seminarians marched forward in their black frock coats.

The male seminary students descended, walking the entire two miles, trying to keep their black polished boots shiny, their black ties straightened—though they looked like they were choking in the starched broadcloth shirts, let alone the stylish frock coats. Lucy wondered if they'd all remember the instructions Reverend Woodward had probably given them on how to treat young ladies. Tensions mounted in the intoxicating spring air. Sweet william and dog-tooth violets tangled at their feet, blood surged eagerly through male and female bodies.

Lucy could feel perspiration trickle, as she gathered with the young women on the left, while the male seminarians clustered on the right. Chief John Ross stood before them, short, square, aging, his white mutton-chop whiskers contrasting with his ruddy skin.

"You are the shining stars of the Cherokee Nation. You are our life blood. You represent the best of our culture, you young men and women of the seminaries. Our Christian faith binds us together in one. Under the tutelage of your professors and principals, you have the finest modeling. Mount Holyoke awaits the young Cherokee sisters. Yale and Harvard await the gallant young men of the Nation . . . ." On and on droned Chief Ross. Lucy could tell by his voice and behavior that the Chief, bathed in southern aristocracy, was assured of his place in history.

"Now let us pray to Almighty God our Heavenly Father, giving thanks for the culmination of this school year, and for this bountiful food. Reverend Woodward." Chief Ross nodded to the tall, lean reverend from the male seminary, fresh from Yale.

Lucy glanced over at Reverend Doctor Elizur Butler and noticed his sad face. Why hadn't they called on Reverend Elizur? Especially, considering how he'd perspired trying to prevent a mishap, or leave a girl, a servant, or, worst of all, a crock of chicken behind.

Lucy's dark eyes took it in—Samantha High Moon swatting blue-tail flies that followed the horses, now buzzing over the picnic tables. Victoria Rogers, who didn't like long speeches or prayers, lifted her eyes across to the row of wide-shouldered young men in various attitudes of piety.

Eliza Bushyhead, hair crawling from beneath its pins, poked at it with her fingers.

Crocks of fried chicken, sliced smoked ham, dill pickles, sweet pickles, and red-pickled beets clustered on the tables.

"Oh, the deviled eggs," blurted Lucy. Lucy realized she shouldn't have said it out loud with Miss Worcester standing so close. Especially since the drastic ending of their "supper" a month ago. Manners. Restraint. Hold oneself back from the food, lest she bolt it, she said to herself.

The young male seminarians grinned and shifted their polished boots, sweat beads on their foreheads. Lucy wondered if Jacob would ask her to have lunch and sit with him on one of the blankets. She glanced downward so as not to appear forward.

"You may sit in circles on the blankets," Miss Charity Tiller called, nudged by Miss Worcester to give seating directions, as both she and Miss Whitmore's necks were busy turning, eyes searching for untoward moves from the "swarthy males". Lucy guessed Miss Whitmore wished that the clearing was wider and that stand of hazel bushes closer.

Then Hermann White Oak bent and bowed before Dora Fellers, a one-eighth-blood, thin, wispy, reddish strands loosened and catching in the wind. Miss Fellers blushed and nodded. Plates filled, they found their places on the blanket.

Ellen Adair stared at Joshua Chapin, the tallest and darkest of the full-blood males, until Joshua dislodged his feet and sidled up. "May I have the honor, Miss . . . ." until the maneuver of manners was completed and to Ellen's seeming satisfaction.

Then poet Jacob Bates, not six feet in front of Lucy, smiled, bent his arm at his waist and nodded, "Miss Drake," he greeted Lucy politely, then stepped a few feet closer to Victoria Roger's side where she seemed to be having troubles collapsing her pink parasol that matched her dress.

"Let me help, Miss Victoria. Yes, this way. There, these things have a way of fouling up sometimes." His hand brushed hers. "May I hold it for you? And, Miss Rogers," Jacob bowed, "may I have the pleasure of your company for lunch?"

Lucy saw Eliza stare at her and again was aware of perspiration on her brow. *What difference does it make? I don't have to put on airs like Victoria, and Eliza Bushyhead'll just have to close her mouth.* Lucy glanced over at Miss Tiller and noticed she seemed nervous.

*   *   *

Fifteen dozen deviled eggs. Three gallons of pickles. The layers of the mouth-watering fried chicken stacked in the towering crocks. The ham, the rolls and bread. The spinach salad and radishes. The potato salad. The pies, gooseberry, cherry, apple, peach, and blackberry, oozed their juices while Miss Charity swished away the flies with a willow branch.

Stocky half-blood Morris Sitting Turtle ran his thick hand over his hair which he'd attempted to slick back. Forcing himself to bow, it ended as a nod. "Miss Lucy Drake, may I introduce myself?" Though the blush didn't show through his copper skin, his shifting feet belied his nervousness.

So Miss Lucy Drake, in her white lawn with the wide white sash, knowing she'd hesitated too long in replying, and to avoid further bad manners, replied, "Why, thank you, Mr. Sitting Turtle. Yes, of course." Besides, she noticed Miss Whitmore was staring at her. "Never let a young man's height be a determining factor regarding character," Miss Whitmore'd announced in Feminine Hygiene class.

Lucy glanced to the left and saw Eliza sitting with Henry Hawk Wing on a blanket to the far side from Lucy and Morris, their backs against those hazel bushes that worried Miss Worcester so much.

*   *   *

Clouds billowed against the blue sky. The Illinois River murmured and rippled. Towering sycamores graced the bend in the river. A wind picked up, leaves shook and rattled as backdrop to young hearts. Backdrop for warm flowing blood, young tongues loosening to engage the opposite sex in dialogue with varying degrees of success.

"Games. Games," Miss Tiller announced, who seemed weary of her assigned duties. "Line up. Number off. There. That's it."

So the young men lined up in one line, young women in another, side by side with the males, facing southward, ready to play walk-a-mile. Elias Hog Shooter strolled down the young men's line, and Amanda Sweet Water, in her violet lawn, sashayed down the women's line. Nudging a walker out of place, she took the walker's place and stepped along with her new male partner.

Laughter. Giggles. Hilarity. Up the knoll, down into the meadow with the waxy mayapples. Along the fence where the Brown Swiss milk cows chewed their cud, lifted their heads and lowed. On and on they marched.

Lucy stepped along in the fresh air with Adam Going Wolf, then with Elias Hog Shooter. Next she had the fortune of keeping step with Jacob Bates. Warmth crept up her arm as his hand held hers.

"Lucy, you were sick with the measles, I hear."

"Yes, Jacob, very ill. I hope you never get the measles." Her feet kept pace with his, though the grass was thick and tall.

Lucy noticed Jacob grow quiet as if he were caught on some memory rolling through his mind. Then Lucy remembered her own father, Benjamin, tell of the night when measles broke out as they were camping by a river, how Jacob's father, Monroe Bates, struggled alongside Benjamin to rebuild the river bridge, the redneck scalawags had bombed in the night.

It had been Lucy's father who'd warned that the shamans shouldn't take children with measles into Long Man which was the Cherokee way. It'd been early fall and the water was too cold. How many had died? Lucy could still hear her father's sad voice as he'd told the tragic event.

Suddenly Lucy, was conscious of the swishing grasses at her ankles and aware of Jacob's silence. She understood, believing that his mind had caught on some memory. No one could predict when a survivor's mind would be snagged by the mention of one word, and for a space of time, drift away.

"Oh, where were we. Yes, Lucy, Miss Victoria told me all about it, and I'm very glad you recovered from the measles. Very glad."

Lucy couldn't think of a thing more to say. She wondered, did Victoria tell on Eliza and me? He obviously thinks I'm only half-civilized. Her self-doubt grew until Eliza, who was now "the tagger," touched her on the shoulder. Even though it was Jacob's hand she dropped, she felt relief.

Along towards four o'clock, after they'd played drop the hand-kerchief for a half-hour, Miss Tiller and both Miss Worcester and Miss Whitmore sagged in the high-back chairs under the oaks. They seemed relieved at last to get off their feet. Everyone knew it was "free time." Students, who wished, could go canoeing on the river, with Rufus and Leander supervising.

Couples were free to rest under the shade and grow in character from mannerly conversation, though in many cases the conversation seemed forced.

Laughter rose and caught in the wind. Victoria Rogers and Jacob Bates stood under a dogwood tree, Jacob's well-shaped-hands lifted a branch so that Victoria could pass underneath.

"Oh, you should have seen them, Eliza and that Lucy Drake. Honestly, Jacob, you'd have thought they had no manners at all. Stinking up the whole seminary with their dreadful cooking. Eggs must have been rotten. The nerve of those girls." Victoria held Jacob captive.

Lucy politely thanked Morris for his attentions, excused her-self to hunt for Eliza whom she'd last seen over by the stand of mayapples. Lucy found her working her way through a wild grape-vine, slapping her thigh in laughter as she held up the edge of her skirt to show Lucy the rip where she'd caught it on a thorn.

Their eyes met. Victoria's murmuring to Jacob drifted in the wind. Eliza bent double. "Runs us down to snag her man." Eliza straightened and caught herself as Miss Worcester turned her way.

"He'll see through her. Give him time. Probably already sorry he's hooked with her and doesn't know how to get away." Lucy giggled, but the old resentment nudged at her.

"Do you think he is 'one of those tall dusky forms stomping and stooping around, making wailing sounds'?" Eliza staggered sideways in her mirth.

Then it hit Lucy. Old times. Long ago, when she was eight years old on the Coosa. The elm sapling, six-inches thick. Lucy's eyes fell upon the sapling before her. Just tall enough. Limber, flexible.

"Eliza, old game when I was a child on the Coosa, come here. Reach the lower limb, Eliza. There help me hold the sapling down." They tussled as the young tree leaned toward them.

"Pull some more, Eliza, we almost have it." Lucy tugged. "Anyone looking? Miss Worcester, I mean?" Lucy smoothed her skirts under her and straddled the sapling. "Don't let loose, Eliza, until I tell you."

"Hurry, Lucy, I can't hold this elm much longer." Eliza stared at Lucy, anxiety reflected from her eyes.

"You can let loose now, Eliza. Let loose."

"Swish," went the sapling, swinging backwards toward its usual position with its giggling burden, skirt ballooning. The river rippled in the background.

Lucy Drake bounced and rocked like a baby robin on a willow branch.

"Oh, Lucy. Oh, Lucy, come down. Let me try. Or, can we do it together?" Eliza tugged at a limb to lower giggling Lucy.

Then it was Eliza's turn. Miss Tiller picked her way through some weeds, avoiding the nettles, to catch a glimpse of the proceedings causing such mirth. But she seemed unable to make up her mind just which part of the game was against the rules.

Lucy looked down from her perch noticing that the "tree game" involving herself and Eliza, and the half-dozen rowers in the canoes, were placing Miss Tiller under stress. She fluttered back to the bend in the river.

Next, Lucy held the sapling for Eliza, whose hair by now had escaped most of its pins. "Are you on, Eliza?"

"Let it fly, Lucy. You do it, I do it."

Lucy released her grip and Eliza soared even higher than she'd swung. The sapling teetered and bounced with howling Eliza. This time, they had onlookers. Victoria and Jacob Bates, who'd just come around the wide trunk of the ancient hackberry.

"Oh, Jacob. Mr. Monroe, look at Eliza. What fun. How on earth did you do it?"

Lucy, sensing time for caution, turned and began to pull the sapling earthward as Eliza leaped off.

"Oh, Lucy, let me try it. Let me try it." Victoria danced over, holding Jacob's hand.

Eliza stared into Lucy's wide-opened eyes, face expressionless as a lid of a Dutch oven. Lucy stared back as she tried to control her mouth and keep it in a straight line, her chin up.

Lucy felt her face twist. She had never seen Eliza Bushyhead so solemn-faced and old-maidish looking, standing like one of Chief Ross's stable slaves ready to obey Miss Victoria's bidding, or that of her handsome catch.

"You want to ride, Victoria?" Lucy hoped the honey didn't drip from her tongue and betray her.

"Oh, it is such fun, Victoria. Such fun. Mr. Bates can help us pull the sapling down. There, thank you, Mr. Bates." Eliza's face looked like the witch's in Hansel and Gretel when she bent to test the oven for two waifs.

Jacob's smile slid from his face, as he sensed something amiss. Lucy realized he was wondering about the relationship between the three of them. "Quickly," she said. "The quicker the better."

Victoria swept her hand beneath her skirt and seated herself on the drawn limb as if she were Lady Godiva mounting a steed to gallop down main street.

"That's it. Yes, Victoria," said Eliza. "Yes, you have your skirt properly folded under. No, Miss Worcester has no cause to complain."

The clear waters of the river behind them at the bend provided a mirror-like backdrop.

"Oh, Lucy. Oh, Eliza, let go now. Let go. I saw how wonderfully you bounced, Eliza. Such fun . . . .ooooohhhhhh."

So Lucy Drake and Eliza Bushyhead let go of the sapling and Victoria Rogers, lighter than either of them, sailed upwards, skirts flapping in the wind.

"Ooooooooooohhhhhhh . . . ." she howled. But, she didn't stop and rock in the tree top as Eliza and Lucy had done. Victoria Rogers took wing in her flapping pink dress as the sapling heaved her heavenward.

"Ohhhhhhhhh." Victoria's eyes widened in shock. Had it not been for the bend in the river, the water as backdrop, Victoria would have had that swarthy Jacob Bates stretch his handsome legs widely and reach out with his strong arms and catch her.

Instead, Miss Victoria sailed in the wind in the most perfect arc Lucy Drake'd ever in her life seen, then plopped into the Illinois River, pink skirts ballooning around her.

CHAPTER THIRTY

A school teacher, Eliza, that's what I'm going to be when I finish seminary," Lucy said.

"Me too, Lucy. A teacher in one of those little mountain schools, with a roomful of sober faced, full-blood children. But you, Lucy, you'll be married. How many times has Jacob Bates escorted you to Tahlequah? First to a play, then to the opera."

Lucy felt the warm rise of blood in her throat. The increased beat of her heart confirmed the feelings she felt for Jacob, his openness, his height and broad shoulders. The easy grin across a face of noble full-blood features.

Lucy admired his commitment and follow-through with whatever he decided to take on. Right now he seemed to be polishing himself to be a southern planter like Captain Lane, Chief John Ross, or Stand Watie.

Lucy wished her father were alive so that she could share her experiences with him. Her mother, too.

"When I'm with Jacob, it's always under the eye of chaperon Tiller bobbing her neck like an old hen. Her ears miss nothing," Lucy complained to Eliza. She even tried to discuss it with Miss Whitmore.

"Seminary rules are seminary rules, Miss Lucy. I'm certain Mr. Bates is a gentleman, nevertheless, all our girls court under supervision of a chaperone," Miss Whitmore had said. She drew on her gloves and picked up her parasol on her way to Tahlequah. Lucy'd heard that she had her own love, a Yale graduate and professor over at the male seminary.

Lucy's eyes brightened and her lips curved in a smile as she thought of Jacob taking her in his arms upon arriving back at the seminary. Miss Tiller had to skip up the stairs to her room for an emergency, leaving Jacob the opportunity to hold her beneath the candelabra by the door.

"Lucy, Lucy, you are my Cherokee Rose." He'd kissed her tenderly. "I didn't know his back would be so strong and his arms so firm and caring," Lucy whispered to herself afterwards. What is happening to me? she had wondered, the slow melting, the glow, the flame reaching upwards?

But there had been that matter at the picnic. Shame still hung at the edges of her heart as she remembered the sorry event, hilarious as it had been,—Miss Victoria sailing through the air and plopping into the river.

The screams, the race to the water's edge. Jacob, flinging off his coat, diving in to rescue Victoria.

The next week, the humiliating conference in Miss Whitmore's office, with Miss Worcester and Steward Butler present. She and Eliza had endured it. Now, Lucy and Eliza faced a session with Reverend Stableworth.

*   *   *

"Lucy and Eliza, not only will you beg Victoria's forgiveness, but you must make restitution. You're a Baptist, Eliza, your church may even require a public confession. The way they do it, isn't it?" Reverend Stableworth cleared his throat.

"Yes, it is," Eliza mumbled.

Lucy hung her head. I deserve it. I deserve it. The humiliation, the guilt. It's "the law at work within our members", the Apostle Paul wrote about. She sighed. "Reverend Stableworth, I've sinned grievously against one of our own seminarians," she confessed. "I am responsible for dumping Victoria into the river and, according to Miss Whitmore, placing her life in danger."

There, she'd said it. The words tumbled out like potatoes rolling out of the potato wagon.

"Sister Lucy," Reverend Stableworth said, "It is a noble thing for the soul, confession. Have you made restitution, sister Lucy?"

Lucy recalled that she had, in a way, at least as far as Victoria allowed. Even at that very moment when the three young men had dragged dripping Victoria out, Lucy and Eliza had tried not to howl, but rush to her side. She could still see herself.

"Oh, Victoria, Victoria. We didn't know. You couldn't hold on? It wasn't intentional. Forgive us, forgive us."

Victoria had glared and steamed, her yellow curls ruined, her expensive dress a soggy mess. After all, she probably enjoyed being buoyed up by the three muscular seminarians who'd plunged in and stretched her out, their voices frantic: "Are you all right, Miss Victoria?" Chief of whom was Jacob Bates.

"Restitution?" Lucy asked the reverend.

"Yes, sister Lucy. Restitution. It seems a worthy thing for you and Miss Eliza to do—that is, to earn money and refund the entire cost of Miss Victoria's ruined dress." He stroked one thin hand with the other.

"But Victoria purchased that dress in New Orleans on that trip down river from Fort Gibson. At least 45 dollars. Reverend Stableworth, where on earth would I or Eliza ever get 45 dollars?"

"There are two stores here in Park Hill, Colonel Murrell's and Chief Ross's," Reverend Stableworth clarified. "Approach them, perhaps they will take you on as clerks for the summer."

*   *   *

Lucy and Eliza stood behind store counters with aching feet the entire two months, saving every penny to reimburse Miss Rogers for her opulent pink dress. They begged Victoria's forgiveness and made restitution.

But after the confession with Reverend Stableworth, that very next Saturday, Jacob Bates knocked at the female seminary door and asked to see Miss Lucy Drake.

"You've been dating now for six months, Lucy. Jacob's going to propose one of these days. Are you prepared? Victoria Rogers is steaming. Simply steaming." Eliza chuckled and slapped her thigh, a behavior Miss Whitmore hadn't yet been able to erase.

*   *   *

The bay trotted up the hill. Jacob Bates's gloved hands held the reins, his shiny boots propped up on the front of the buckboard. Late summer wild roses reminded him of his Rose of Cherokee, Lucy, her pure silk hair, her delicate, cameo face, her smile, and yet, the seriousness in her eyes, and the way, when in doubt or surprise, she'd stare with those eyes and raise one eyebrow.

A wonder, isn't it, how neither of them had given in to despair? The terrible trek, the ordeals, the trauma of near starvation and indescribable poverty—yet, they were not bitter. And the doors to life were opening.

Jacob noted the goldenrod spreading along the roadsides, nodding in the wind. The approach of fall reminded him of the passing time and his last year in seminary. He pulled the buggy forward, tied the bay mare to the hitching post and glanced towards the second story window of the asylum.

Jacob couldn't remember how many of The People had become confused and lost their minds due to their sufferings on the trail. The indescribable indecencies. The infightings and the murders. The suicides. His own father's mysterious death by hanging over the river bluff on the same day Lucy's father, Benjamin Drake, had been murdered. Wonder if Mother'll even know me today?

Sadness crept upward at the dreary task of entering the asylum door—Mother's room, seeing her hunching there, almost unrecognizable. Her mind, a mishmash of varying bewilderment.

I want her to know. She'll be pleased I'm going to marry a full-blood. Yes, she'll be pleased.

*   *   *

"Mother," Jacob stepped into the small room with one window which she shared with an ancient woman who lay sleeping on her cot.

The hunched woman turned on her chair, filmy eyes and trembling head lifted, hair a shock of disheveled grey. "Jacob?" she croaked. "Jacob, is it you? Come, my lad, sit beside me. I've been watching the deer drink in the pool of the Coosa."

There were no deer and the Coosa was a 1000 miles away.

Jacob drew the bentwood chair closer to her, but before he seated himself, he leaned to kiss her cheek. *At least she recognizes me today.*

"I saw goldenrod opening along the roadsides today, Mother. When it opens fully, I'll bring you a bouquet."

"Goldenrod? Goldenrod. Tea, goldenrod tea, a tonic for . . ." her voice faded, and thin, long-nailed fingers lifted to her trembling chin.

"Mother, I've come to tell you good news." *How clear her mind is today. She even remembers goldenrod.*

"Yes, my son, what is it? News you say? Have they built a bridge across the Coosa? I always said it would ruin the crossing. Not there. Not there . . ."

"No, Mother. No. Not the Coosa." His heart ached at her disorientation.

"You must tell your father not to let them build . . ."

"Mother, the news I bring is about me." Jacob reached for her thin hand. He was thankful that she was clean. The shift encasing her emaciated body seemed recently laundered.

"Mother, I'm planning on asking a Cherokee maiden to marry me."

White Birch stared at her son with the glistening eyes and the lips parted in a smile.

"Marry? My little Jacob of the hickory and chestnut trees along the Coosa? Marry?" She turned her face, her filmy eyes widening.

"What is the name of this maiden?" She turned back to face Jacob, head shaking with palsy.

Today she's clear headed. Even asks a name without losing her thought. Jacob felt relief.

"Her name is Lucy, Mother. She's my Cherokee Rose. A fullblood, like me. A cultured woman. Attends the female seminary. Plays the piano over at Chief Ross's mansion, Mother. She's a young woman you'd like to know. I love her. Her name is Lucy Drake." At first, stillness reigned. The old woman said not a word. She turned a trembling head to gaze as out the window at the cloud slipping by as if her filmy eyes saw another world, a world and people, long ago.

Then she turned and tried to rise, weak as her legs were. Surprisingly, she heaved herself forward and fell across Jacob's shoulders, her fingers seeking to grasp and shake—her eyes, wild.

"No. No, no, no. No. Jacob, no! You cannot marry this girl. Lucy Drake? Lucy Drake? No, no, no."

Her nails dug. She pummeled his shoulders as her fragmented senses left her and her wail rose to the ceiling and out the window.

Two strong aides rushed into the dingy room and dragged the raving woman off the well-suited young man, now on the floor, protecting his eyes from her claws.

"You must go. You see she can't handle a visit today. Another day. You're her son, Jacob Bates, aren't you? You see, your visit's too upsetting, you'll have to go."

Like Mary in the gospel who "kept these things in her heart, pondering them," Jacob, too, pondered the event painfully. Why had it upset Mother so? Why the outrage? What was it? He concluded his poor mother's views made no difference in his plans. Nevertheless, he'd hoped she would have smiled, nodded and said something like: "Yes, Jacob, my son. Yes, I do remember her. That little Cherokee girl who came by riverboat with her mother, Abby. She was so brave. So brave, kiss her for me."

CHAPTER THIRTY-ONE

Two days later, a slow rain drizzled down as Jacob and Lucy sat in Reverend Stableworth of the Presbyterian Mission's office. The reverend in his black serge frock coat looked at the couple with pained eyes. Miss Whitmore sat beside Lucy in her navy suit with the high collar.

"My deepest sympathies, Jacob. She's with God now and out of her pain." Reverend Stableworth leaned toward the young man with the sorrowful face.

"I'm still in shock. I can't put the pieces together," Jacob said.

Lucy, in her mauve, tiered muslin dress and seated in the straight-backed chair, wiped tears at the corners of her eyes with her handkerchief. "Finding White Birch that way," she glanced at Jacob, "drowned in only two feet of ditch water."

"No one knows exactly how Mother escaped the asylum. Though Steward Crow Wing discovered a crowbar outside the main door, which had been in the kitchen to pry open a stuck cabinet door," Jacob shifted a leg.

"I first heard this loud pounding on the front door," Miss Whitmore said. "I grabbed my wrapper, lit a candle and hurried downstairs. When I opened the door, this woman, your mother, Jacob, knocked me down. Such strength she had. By the time I regained my footing and relit the candle, White Birch'd already rushed up the staircase.

"The poor woman pounded on all the doors she could on second floor, yelling, 'You can't marry her. He's your half-brother.

He's your half-brother.' Poor soul. Obviously completely out of her senses." Miss Whitmore wiped her tears.

"But the agonizing part of it is that it's the truth. Neither Lucy, nor I'd been told." Jacob glanced out of the window at the cold rain streaking the window pane.

"Father kept it from us all these years. But, may be he wasn't sure. I shall never forget, Lucy, the way your father looked at me when I almost drowned at the ferry boat accident on the Mississippi River. It was in his eyes. He was my father. Your father, *Benjamin*, was my father." Jacob covered his face with his hands as scenes of that fated day surfaced. He could hear the roar of the angry waters and feel the overwhelming fatigue. His head swirled in dizziness, a near-drowned Benjamin Drake whispered, "My son, my son, Absalom."

* * *

"Are you all right?" asked Reverend Stableworth, noting that Jacob had drifted away and was staring out the window into the rain. "Could I get you a glass of water, Jacob?"

"No, thank you, Reverend Stableworth. "Thank you. I drifted away momentarily, but I, I'm all right. Just tired. Where were we?"

"I was about to say that Reverend Butler sent his aide to get help from the asylum while we tried to bring White Birch downstairs at the seminary and calm her. Who would have thought a frail woman like that would have such strength?" Miss Whitmore shifted on her chair.

"Your mother shoved Miss Whitmore aside, Jacob, she fled into the darkness and rain," Lucy added.

"By the time Reverend Butler had the hack brought up and lanterns lit and started out, it must have been only 10 minutes— so sad. So very sad." Miss Whitmore wiped her tears.

"Reverend Butler had the driver turn down the road toward the asylum, thinking that White Birch, having made her announcement, had run out into the night and back to the home she knew." Lucy reached across to touch Jacob's hand.

"And even more soul-shaking, the announcement itself, 'you can't marry Lucy Drake. She's your half-sister.'"

Lucy and Jacob could only look deeply into each other's eyes, then lower them, as the feelings rose through their entire beings like floodwaters on the rivers they'd traveled in the past.

"Before I came here this morning, I checked it out with Chief Ross. He's in his seventies now. He knew everyone in the New Echota territory." Jacob cleared his throat. "He hesitated to talk about it. When I told him Mother was dead, he placed his hand on my shoulder and told me," Jacob said, holding back tears.

"Chief Ross said they were of the same Blue clan, Benjamin, your father, and White Birch, his first love. Handsome and beautiful and so young. Marriage within the same clan was forbidden," Lucy said, wiping her eyes with her handkerchief.

"Chief Ross told of the angry family and the young lover, Benjamin, turned aside, who soon married Lucy's mother, Abby, dead now for at least eight years," Jacob said.

"It's true, Jacob. Why didn't I ever see it?" Lucy said.

"My mother married Monroe Bates of the Wolf clan. I was born eight months later." Jacob cleared his throat.

"It would not have happened in these days," Lucy said, turning to look again at her half-brother, wide shouldered, masculine jaw, fine hands.

"No, Lucy, today, it would not have happened. Old clan laws are no longer followed by most Cherokee people." Jacob shoved his white handkerchief into his breast pocket.

They had to open new parts of themselves, Jacob and Lucy, for all those feelings, bereavement and sorrow, the avalanche of the half-buried agonies of the Trail of Tears endured by them both. Challenged now to reshape a love they'd shared, they silently vowed to seek new patterns of meaning for the words, "brother," "sister."

"No, we will never marry," they said to each other, "but it's a comfort to know at least we have a bit of family."

CHAPTER THIRTY-TWO

1861

The full-bloods and the half-bloods, who lived in the fertile little valleys by the rivers and in the thick oak woods, spoke of Lucy as "the loving woman among us".

How could it be? Educated, cultured, a delicate-featured lady, whispered about as "the one who used to play Chief John Ross's great piano".

"My little seven-year-old Rising Fawn nearly died from pneumonia. Though the shaman tried, she only crept closer to death. Then Miss Lucy came. Never left her side for two days." Red Bird Cutler smiled as she looked at Sun Shine Moses.

"My boy, Running Wolf, brings his books home and reads to me. He says, 'Miss Lucy said, Miss Lucy said . . .'" Sun Shine Moses's eyes reflected her pride.

"Miss Lucy says she's at home in one side of Trotting Wolf Wilson's and his wife Ground Hog Mother's dog trot cabin," Red Bird added.

"Miss Lucy's a member of one of those churches way over on Park Hill, but she sits with us at the Baptist meetings. Have you ever heard her sing?" Sun Shine threw a braid back over her shoulder.

On and on, the neighbors north of Tahlequah shared among themselves the virtues of a teacher like Miss Lucy Drake, who lived among them.

"I forgot to tell you," Red Bird said to Sun Shine after services in the log church. "After little Rising Star could sit up and I could nurse her back to health, Miss Lucy got on that pony of hers and rode off up the hill." She cleared her throat. Tears came to her eyes as she remembered. "That afternoon I looked up and there was Miss Lucy, her bed piled on a travois behind that pony. Brought it for Rising Fawn. Would have it no other way. I know she slept on the floor for three months."

* * *

The years rolled by as Lucy Drake and Eliza Bushyhead leaned over the heads of the backwoods children, leading them through their Cherokee and English grammar, spelling, arithmetic and geography.

Today Lucy, having dismissed her 27 pupils, stood on the porch of Split Fork School. No sooner had she seated herself on the log step in the April sunshine than someone slid through the buck brush—her old comrade from The Trail, Todd Wyeth.

"Lucy, I wondered if you'd still be here." Todd strode forward silently, comfortable in his loose-fitting ticking trousers, calfskin miner's boots, turbaned head, and long black hair framing his smiling face.

"Todd, I'm delighted you've come." A tremor of old remembrances, old pains and sorrows stirred Lucy's heart. A vision flashed in her mind of a half-frozen little boy on a pad of mud in a slough reaching into frigid water to grab a muskrat. Her mother, Abby, near death with cholera.

Lucy jumped up and raced down the sandy path, arms outstretched she embraced the smiling full-blood who smelled of cedar-berries, walnut leaves and leather.

"Todd, Todd, how are Yellow Wing and the twin boys?"

"Fine, Lucy, fine. They send their regards. Yellow Wing is expecting another baby come July." Todd grinned across gleaming teeth.

"Ran into your brother Jacob yesterday in Tahlequah at the

livery. Colonel Murrell's made a gentleman out of him over at that grand place. I asked Jacob to ride out here and meet us today."

Memories clustered in Lucy's mind of her hours at Colonel Murrell's opulent mansion down the hill from Rose Cottage, the numerous receptions, celebrations, accompanied by Eliza, Victoria, and other classmates. Twice, the Colonel had asked her to honor them by playing his piano for the hushed audience.

Lucy thought of how long it'd been since she'd ridden out of these woods and back to the high society of Park Hill. Give me time, school over in another week.

"Teaching here next year, Lucy?" Todd seated himself beside her, stretching his long legs, scratched boots encasing his narrow feet.

"Oh yes. How can I leave the children? I'll stay, unless war breaks out and prevents it, Todd. So much confusion. North. South. Our people on both sides. Chief Ross and his indecision about it."

Worry pushed at Lucy's mind. She was glad for the opportunity to share her worries with Todd and half-brother Jacob when he arrived. How long had it been, anyway, she wondered, since she'd seen him? And when on earth was Jacob ever getting married?

Gravel rolled and the sounds of parting brush indicated someone riding down the trail. The spirited Morgan snorted and picked his way through the cedars carrying the man in his thirties, as always, dressed impeccably. Emblem of the Knights of the Golden Circle, announcing Southern loyalties, pinned on a wide lapel of his well-tailored riding coat. Jacob Bates reached with his long fingers to lift his wide brimmed planter's hat.

"Lucy. Glad you're here too, Todd. So much is happening, we need to talk about it. May not have many more opportunities to get together."

He tied the black horse to a twisted redbud, strode over to Lucy, bent and brushed her cheek with his lips. She rose smiling, reached out her slender arms and encircled his neck to return the kiss.

Lucy, too, needed to discuss the times with someone close to her, someone who lived in the heart of The Nation. "I worry about the two of you," Lucy said as she reached out to break a blade of bluestem that'd sprouted and spread at the porch step.

"What will happen to our young men, you both?" Lucy didn't finish the rest of her thought, How could I stand losing either of you, a brother by blood, a brother by virtue of bonding on the trail?

"I've joined the Keetoowahs, Jacob. You know my nature— keep the old Cherokee ways, the traditions. And," Todd added, his voice tightening, "the Keetoowahs take a stand against slavery. If there's a war, I'll go with the Union forces." Sadness slid over his wide, brown eyes.

"You at least are honest, Todd, I understand it." Jacob looked Todd straight in the face. "Even Chief Ross is torn. Says our treaty rests with the United States government and our alliance is better with the Union than with the Confederacy." Jacob's eyebrows tightened. "But," he added, "Chief Ross himself is a slave owner. Complicated, isn't it?"

"The worst news is that Arkansas seceded from the Union a few days ago," Lucy said. She'd hated to read the fateful news in The *Cherokee Advocate.*

"Even more serious," Jacob added, "is the fact that the United States had Colonel Emory remove the Union troops from Fort Smith. Left us no federal protection here in Indian Territory. We're divided with both pro-slave and anti-slave people. That's you, Todd, and me, isn't it? I hold no grudges. But that's the way it is." Jacob locked his fingers together. "And the facts were, the Keetoowahs supported, at least as of now, Chief Ross, because he said 'Union alliance helps us keep our land'."

"What about Stand Watie? He's been Ross's enemy for decades? Fled to Fort Gibson after those terrible murders which Ross denied knowing about." Todd looked at Jacob for an answer.

"Watie's been commissioned a colonel by General McCulloch of the Confederate Armies. He's rounding up Cherokee troops right now. Our Nation's abandoned by the North. Would you believe that after a long discussion with General Pike, both Stand Watie and Chief Ross, old enemies, colluded? Grabbed the Confederate flag and held it up together, officially joining the Indian Nation with the South?" Jacob looked at Todd in silence at the grave situation. He picked up a mauve-colored pebble and toyed with it, sensing Todd's sadness over the threats of having to leave his family. "And you, Lucy, could you still stay and teach in these hills if war breaks out?" Jacob tossed the pebble.

"All I can foresee is tornness. I thought such agonies were long over. Hearts and souls ripped from bodies—the clouds of war are here now," Jacob said, turning to face Lucy.

Lucy looked up at both of her beloved men. One, wearing the crossed pins of the anti-slavery Keetoowahs, the other, the order of Southern aristocracy, the emblem of the Knights of the Golden Circle, sworn to preserve the Confederacy and slavery.

"Strange, how we never talked about slavery at the seminary." Lucy's eyes, filled with love, studied Jacob's face. He's so like my father.

"Couldn't afford to." Jacob lowered his pained eyes. "Even Reverend Worcester and the missionaries, they all avoided the topic. We have almost 2,000 Negro slaves in the Cherokee Nation. Rich planters, mansions, you know, Lucy. You still play that big piano up at Rose Cottage?" Lucy noticed how carefully Jacob looked at her, concerned with her safety as he was.

"And," added Todd, shifting his narrow boot. "The fact is most of the Nation is not made up of aristocratic southern planters. Most Cherokees are full-bloods, or half-bloods. Small farmers. Hunters. Living in log houses back here, Lucy, where you and Eliza teach."

Lucy knew he was correct. It had seemed that the small percentage of light skinned, highly educated ones who imported New England teachers, had set a course. Now that course met unalterable obstacles.

"One of the reasons the seminaries closed," Lucy added, "it

wasn't the kind of educational focus most of the Cherokee youth needed. Eliza and I always knew we were in a New England finishing school, however westward it was."

She felt a sadness and loss at the memories of the white-columned seminary and their disciplined, mind-stretching days. She even missed Miss Whitmore and Miss Worcester, both well-married now and mothers.

"It had to happen. If there is a civil war, something new, more suited will emerge." Lucy stood, graceful in her light-blue gingham, the wind caught her skirt, blowing it back against her legs. Lucy paused, then turned to Jacob. "What ever happened to Victoria Rogers?" She smiled, remembering her flight through the air, heaved by the sapling.

"Victoria? Why, Lucy, Victoria married Phenias Johnson, a rich planter down on the Red River. Has five children. One a year. She's violently angry at her husband and threatens to leave for the city." Jacob grinned, remembering the day he'd ruined his best serge suit plunging into the Illinois to save Victoria. He turned to face Lucy, and braved a smile.

Lucy knew that Jacob worried about her, alone with the old Indian couple in the woods, invading guerrilla bands sneaking in to raid and plunder.

"Lucy, what do you learn here among the people of these woods?" Jacob leaned on the post holding the porch roof.

"Oh, every day something new. Do you know how to stop an owl hooting outside your window keeping you awake at night?" Her dark eyes gleamed.

"No, how do you stop an owl from disturbing your sleep?"

"Well, Little Fawn says there's no need to get upset or create a commotion. Just tie a knot in the left-hand-corner of the bed sheet and the owl will go away."

"Wisdom of the backwoods." Jacob laughed and Todd joined in.

"I love it so, being here. The children have an innocence and a deep wisdom. When I told Charles Walking Horse about my leg cramps last week, he gave me the solution. "Why, Miss Lucy. Just reach out and turn your shoes upside down alongside the bed and the cramps will go away.'" Lucy chuckled. "See, there are many benefits, as well as the beautiful woods in their seasons.

"And Todd, for you—Mother Green Corn Smith told me you can tell if your new unborn is to be a girl or boy. Simply tie a cork on a string and hold it in front of Yellow Wing's belly. If the cork goes around in a circle, it'll be a girl. If it swings back and forth, she'll have a boy."

They laughed, all travelers of bygone days. But the traces of The Trail were there in their minds and hearts, on their very bodies. It accounted for the sudden solemnity that slid over their faces. Their silence from time to time. They knew they would always be bound together by their sufferings of the Trail. And now, would there be more?

When Lucy glanced up at Todd, she saw him as a boy in rags, starving. She could hear him. "Don't worry, Lucy, Private Greenway says tomorrow the General will pay us for our stolen land and belongings. Tomorrow, Lucy, your mother will have her money in payment for all her things left behind."

Lucy felt herself drift back in time as she looked westward through the stand of redbud and oak. Refugees. Fort Gibson. Hope in their hearts. No payment for their new Echota lands. Mother Abby near death. A jarring wagon ride into Tahlequah. A kindly soldier Greenway bidding her good bye.

*   *   *

After Lucy's 'brothers' bid her good bye that spring day, the storms of war rolled toward the Indian Nation.

In less than a month, Union forces invaded the Cherokee Nation, sweeping up Chief Ross, his wife, Mary, and their small children, dragging them northward to abolitionist Kansas where they were held hostage.

"But in spite of the Southern alliance, I've always been for the Union," Ross maintained.

Whisked off then to his wife Mary's home in Philadelphia,

Ross journeyed to Washington where he spent the Civil War years in dialogue with President Lincoln, the Congress, the Commissioners of Indian Affairs. One thing in mind. Always, "What is it I need to do to maintain our beloved Cherokee Nation?"

"Perhaps it is," whispered President Lincoln, "one mark of a great man."

*   *   *

Guerrilla raids ripped the Cherokee Nation. Quick, demeaning, burning raids by Union scavengers, who galloped into the Nation, burning, raping, killing. Then, they turned northward or eastward, awaiting engagements in larger battles.

Finally, a greater rip, as John Drew and a regiment of Cherokee Mounted Rifles, all anti-slavery full-bloods, vowed revenge against the Union raiders.

Yelling their blood-chilling war whoops, they galloped through the night toward Pea Ridge, Arkansas, Todd Wyeth among them, once the little lad of the Trail of Tears.

But when avenging General Stand Watie and his Confederate troops descended from the south upon Park Hill, all the remembrances of John Ross's threats against the Treaty Signers surged in his heart, inflaming his brain.

"There it stands. Chief Ross's Rose Cottage. Burn the killer of the innocents' mansion, the slave holder and traitor in Washington," General Watie said, though he himself was a slave holder.

*   *   *

Those who stayed behind turned their eyes upward toward the Park Hill ridge as their voices mingled, "Don't remember ever seeing such a fire. Flames from hell leaping, burning, jumping from building to building. And chief Ross's mansion, too."

Aristocratic Cherokee women of one-eighth-blood, one-sixteenth-blood wept and threw together their silks, their silver and jewels. Commanding their slaves, they fled for Texas and Arkansas.

Then avengers, red hot with fury at Confederate Watie's attack, swished through in counter attack. The hodgepodge Union bushwhackers set fire to Tahlequah.

Tired old Esther Shining Star lifted herself from her rocker when she heard the gunfire. Wild bullets struck her lamp, spilling the oil. Flames leaped.

In horror Mother Esther looked on, mother to over 400 homeless refugees of The Trail. Her heart failed and her body slumped to the floor, consumed by the flames.

*   *   *

A scattering of full-bloods hunched in the hills, Lucy Drake among them. Ever vigilant, ever watchful for the sudden thrust of the rifle of a Union avenger or outlaw Rebel raider.

The wind howled through the burnt and crumbling nation of the Cherokees.

CHAPTER THIRTY-THREE

A man in his mid-40s shifted his wide shoulders as the fine sorrel mare picked her way down a rocky ravine.

His mind wandered as he thought of how much he'd missed the woods, the streams, rivers and towering trees. He thrust his angular chin upward, as his grey-green eyes sought the sun. "Be in Tahlequah tonight, Beauty," he spoke to the mare, nudging her in the ribs with his heel as she lowered her head for the steep incline.

Andrew Greenway, trader with the Osage, northeast of the junction of the Little and Big Arkansas, knew he'd be riding into dangerous territory. Nevertheless, he realized that the successful businessman is the one who gets there first.

"See if there can be any early contact with the Cherokee agents or chiefs," he'd told his partner, Mosley, before he rode off south-eastward toward the Cherokee Nation.

Selling his share of the trading post on the Walnut to his partner, Edward Mosley, seemed a good idea. He planned on opening a new one to cash in on the Osage trade at the junction of the Big and Little Arkansas in Kansas.

Besides, Andrew realized that now the war between the states was over, he could visit the government offices in the Cherokee Nation, if anything was still standing. He wondered what would be out at Fort Gibson since his early days there, and how migrations from the Nation on westward to the junction of the Arkansas Rivers were moving along.

As he leaned in, dodging a low limb from time to time, remembrances of his days with the Cherokee emigrants flooded his mind. Glad too, that his six years with the army were over before the terrible war.

And news was that the Great Chief John Ross had died and was buried near Park Hill on the Illinois. Tahlequah had burned and now lay in shambles. The Cherokee Nation torn. The new Chief Downing, interested in reopening the seminaries.

He thought of the Cherokee woman with the delicate Madonna face, Abby Drake, and that she'd had a daughter. A little girl about eight or nine, a fine-boned child who'd taken on the role of an adult.

The horse stumbled as Andrew Greenway remembered The People enduring so much suffering with such little complaint. Sometimes, he could still hear their prayers and hymns, even though he hadn't become a member of any church, Andrew considered himself a believer in his own way. He'd told his business partner that he needed to settle down and find the right wife.

Surrounded by the thickening woods, he breathed in the spice of the sassafras, the sharp odors of the oak and hickory, the sweetness of the walnut as he brushed their leaves.

He planned on a full dinner, come evening, at a hotel in Tahlequah where, no doubt, there would be Cherokee maidens, that is, if there was a hotel still standing.

*　*　*

On Spring Branch, a few miles down the trail toward Tahlequah and the Illinois, old Trotting Wolf Wilson and his faithful wife, Ground Hog Mother, sat on the breezeway of their cabin facing southward toward the meadow and their grazing cows.

"Where's Miss Lucy?" Trotting Wolf turned to Ground Hog Mother in the split-willow rocker.

"Why she got an early start hoeing the melons and corn down by the branch." Ground Hog Mother smiled at her husband, rose and strode into the cabin to pick up her knitting, her red calico "tear dress" catching in the wind.

* * *

Lucy Drake, barefooted in the soft earth she'd turned with her hoe, felt her own life-blood flow through her.

A good day. A summer without serious mishap. They were among the few, she and the Wilsons, who'd clung to their homes in the woods while the war had raged on.

The wind caught wisps of her hair and her muslin dress flapped around her shapely legs as she dragged the hoe back and forth. She smiled as she looked 200 feet beyond at Spring Branch murmuring along. Lucy knew he'd be sitting there, little eight-year-old Charles Walking Horse.

"Miss Lucy, I watch that big old bass every day of the summer. Gonna catch him when my arms get long enough," he'd often told her.

* * *

Down by the rippling creek sat the boy, Charles. Half-hidden in the shade of the spreading poke, purple with berries. He waited, eyes focused upon the deep pool at his bare feet. In time, the fish would lift itself in the blue-green pool.

And little Charles knew if he were quiet enough and still enough, the doe and fawn might come down in the shade of the willows beyond for a drink.

But he knew also that in another half-hour, old king snake would slide out of the shadows to warm himself on the wide cottonwood that'd fallen across the creek, providing a sturdy bridge.

Old king snake. At least five feet long, grey with yellow-and-orange-and-black spots. And old king snake would sun himself for an hour or so until his blood heated too much, then lift his head and begin his slow slide down the log to the shade of the roots still partially buried in the reddish earth.

The child waited. The day was good. The earth sweet and mellow. Catbird called. The hawk soared. Charles didn't have to tell himself to watch out for copperheads or rattlesnakes. He'd learned to be vigilant.

Glancing up, he saw his beloved teacher, Miss Lucy, hoeing the corn and melons. He loved Miss Lucy but he dreaded leaving this enchanting outdoors for the seclusion of the schoolroom, Miss Lucy or no Miss Lucy.

When the crows rose up, cawing from the tops of the black locust eastward, little Charles knew someone, or something was approaching. Miss Lucy, caught in her hoeing and her thoughts, seemed unaware.

The child hunched and waited, his brown eyes focused across the wide creek. At first, he thought it was a deer, but then, he saw that it was a man creeping through toward the path. When Charles saw the point of the rifle he wanted to yell and warn Miss Lucy.

Indian blood told him, "Be silent. Wait." Besides, Charles knew that he was within rifle range and his life might be in danger. Wait.

Then he noticed two more ragtag Union bushwhackers loping behind the staggering man ahead.

The child's heart picked up its beat. "Miss Lucy," he rasped in a hoarse whisper. But the wind, against him, caught his words, sweeping them away.

*   *   *

Renegade Hagley Lutes, first of the three, pushed through the elderberries by Spring Branch and the old fallen log. He swiped a dirty hand across his stubbly face.

"Well now, Harley," he called out, turning a dirty-scarved neck, "We got us a Cherokee beaut up ahead. Shhhhhhh." He lifted a filthy finger to his cracked lips, cautioning the two bumbling followers, eyes shiny with lust for what their eyes at last beheld, a lone Cherokee woman, slender one at that. Cabin in the background. Nobody in sight.

"Oh, Rufus," rasped the short one, "you see that skirt again them legs?"

"Shut up and be quiet. Want to wake the dead? Hurry on behind Hagley and get across the creek on that log, or you too drunk?"

Little Charles Walking Horse worried as he noticed Miss Lucy hadn't seemed to notice the intruders but kept on scraping with her hoe. His heart palpitated.

He watched as renegade Hagley's feet sought purchase on the long root of the fallen cottonwood, eyes on the woman in the field. "Get across this branch, Rufus, you and Heavener come at her from opposite sides." Hagley lifted the point of his rifle.

It seemed to little Charles that the whole world stopped turning. It seemed as if the wind halted, that the water didn't ripple and surge below—that the trees didn't sweep limbs and leaves together in the wind.

Then it was as if the world froze in silence and old king snake crawled out of the knothole at the fattest part of the dead cottonwood, just after the third renegade planted his wide boot on the tree trunk.

Tipping and tottering in their intoxicated states, the vagabond trio teetered along the log, grinning through face-stubble. Their heaving chests betrayed hearts beating wildly, blood surging with lust and the fevers of anticipated cabin-raiding.

Still the hoeing woman hadn't noticed. Charles wondered why Miss Lucy didn't drop her hoe and run for the rifle above the fireplace. It seemed as if the events taking place before his eyes were caught in heavy molasses.

When the third rank-smelling bushwhacker staggered about four feet along the log, all three trying to balance themselves to keep from falling, little Charles knew it was time.

He leaped from his perch. "Rattlesnake. Rattlesnake. You men know there's a big rattlesnake on the log?"

The renegades' faces broke into masks of fear. Eyes widened in terror. "Oh my God." Hagley Lutes hollered, alcohol fumes drifting down on little Charles below.

And old kingsnake himself participated. Lazy, sluggish and fat, he lifted his neck and wide head before he'd surge himself off the log.

"Look, see that whopper rattlesnake. Shoot, Hagley." Rufus,

Hagley's mate in stealth and raiding, pointed at the snake, the other arm flapped to keep balance.

Hagley cursed. "Hold still." There was a blast from the rifle, but the bullet sang wide to the side.

While the stooges staggered in fear, little Charles raced up and grabbed one of the outcropping roots of the log. His heave rocked it just enough to cause the renegades to lose their footing and all three plunged into the yellow-and-green bass's hole beneath.

By now Miss Lucy'd had time to size up the happenings, drop her hoe and race into the cabin for the gun.

"Are you all right, Charles?" She stood at the edge of the creek at the butt of the fallen tree, rifle pointed at the dripping renegades.

"The first one of you that steps up out of that creek gets a hole in his head." Miss Lucy Drake lifted the rifle barrel. She pulled the trigger, aiming above their heads, to show them she meant business. The gun didn't fire.

But Lucy Drake surprised herself. She never knew where those words she'd said even came from. A female seminary graduate saying such things?

But then, once she'd helped dump an annoying girl in the river, hadn't she?

They'd saved themselves from harm and a raid, she and little Charles. Before Miss Lucy or Charles could turn around, a wide-shouldered, middle-aged man in smart riding clothes rode through the stand of elderberry.

"I've got a good bead on them, lady. They're not going to be causing you any more trouble now." Greenway held his rifle steady, pointing.

Lucy looked up at the stranger and yet? No. Not so strange, she thought. Where have I seen him before?

"We're all right, sir. But we'd better get these men tied up and under guard. You going on into Tahlequah?" asked Lucy, like an old gunslinger used to such events.

Greenway stared at the lithe woman, muslin skirt framing her slender body and noticed the delicate features and her fine skin.

"Yes, I'm riding on in to town. I'll get these bushwhackers tied up. Get them into Tahlequah and whisk them off to Federal Prison at Fort Gibson." *Where have I seen that woman before?* Andrew Greenway lifted a hand to his chin.

Lucy wouldn't have the raiders shot. She didn't believe in killing, though she would have attempted again to fire over their heads had they lurched at her. But Charles Walking Horse let her know that she wasn't a genuine gunslinger when he said, "Miss Lucy, did you know that rifle you got in your hands ain't got any bullets in it?"

After Greenway'd tied the vagabonds' hands with their own belts, then roping all three together with his cattle-rope, he reached up to tip his hat.

"Well, Ma'am . . ."

Lucy stared at him as he said, "Perhaps, we'll meet again under more pleasant circumstances." *What was throwing him off guard?* She realized she was staring. "Sir, you couldn't be?" She lifted a perfectly-formed hand to her face, a wisp of black silk dislodged and blew around her forehead. "You didn't escort emigrant Cherokees in the Trail of Tears days, did you?"

He turned. The smell of leather and spicy woods drifted from him. The sorrel mare snorted impatiently.

"Why, yes, I did. Escorted several groups from Fort Smith. Met the riverboats there. First one, people got on keelboats behind a little steamer called the *Velocipede*. Never forget it. Little Cherokee girl, a boy named Todd and the girl's wounded mother."

"Sir, your name couldn't be Andrew Greenway, could it? And do you know about paw paws?"

CHAPTER THIRTY-FOUR

Six hanging oil lamps with red-tinted shades plus the candle in the middle of each of the tables cast a mellow light for dining at the Red Cedar, the only hotel not completely burned during the war.

Lucy, in her burgundy dress with the tiered skirt, high neck and covered buttons, sat opposite Andrew Greenway. A simple gold bracelet on her wrist emphasized modesty in appointments and good taste.

Andrew tried not to stare at Lucy as she raised her chin, back erect, and looked into his eyes, unable to hide the feelings that crept over her face.

"I remember the last time I saw you, Andrew." Her voice faltered as her hand reached for a water tumbler.

"Not in the army any longer, Lucy. Just plain old 'trader Andrew.'" His smile revealed gleaming white teeth contrasting against his tanned skin. His grey-green eyes reflected the gold of the candle-light, as he smiled at the charming Lucy Drake across from him at the cloth-covered table.

"Mr. Greenway, as I was saying the last time I saw you, Mother and I'd stepped out of the wagon in the middle of a muddy street here in Tahlequah." For a moment, Lucy could still feel the coldness of the November wind, their half-frozen feet and hands, clutching the rags that hung on their bony frames. Dumped in a strange land, penniless. Memory traces made a collage in her brain—the sicknesses, the deaths, the murders and the suicides. Brutal soldiers and kind soldiers, like Andrew Greenway. Above all, the grind-ing gut contending with starvation.

Lucy caught herself, realizing that this was not the time to indulge in the memory of her past sufferings.

"You were very kind to Mother and me, and to Todd Wyeth, the little boy who joined us on *The Smelter* on the Mississippi."

A young Cherokee waiter in a frock coat, white shirt and black tie, white towel folded over his left arm approached their table.

"Trout for the lady." He placed the gilt-edged china plate in front of Lucy.

"And, your order, sir." He placed the plate weighted heavily with a well-aged steak in front of Andrew.

"More burgundy, sir?"

"Thank you, yes." The waiter poured from a crystal carafe into the wine glass. "One of the hardest things I ever had to do was to leave you, Lucy, with your mother and friends in the middle of the street. I was a soldier under orders and had to return to Fort Gibson, assigned to a campaign to prevent a Cheyenne uprising."

"Mother hadn't yet recovered from her head injury. I had to take charge." Lucy's mind caught memories of their 1839 arrival. The lonely disembarking from the wagons in muddy, cold streets. Widow Shining Star's loving care. Benjamin collapsing at the door. A new girl's seminary rising on a hill.

* * *

Andrew allowed Lucy time to emerge from her memory. He'd no-ticed it before, how these survivors sometimes drifted away. She lifted her eyes, then smiled at him.

"May I order you some sherry, Lucy?"

"No, thank you, perhaps some coffee later." Lucy noticed his well-manicured nails and his fine hands. Her eyes lingered on the suit, an excellent wool set off by the silk cravat. The grey at his temples gave him a distinguished look. She smiled again, lifting her fork to take another bite of the succulent trout.

"Tell me about you, Andrew. You must have been very young then." She sipped from the crystal tumbler.

"Actually I was. Seventeen, though I was tall. Thin as a rail, too. Signed up for the army and lied about my age. I was supposed to be 18." Andrew grinned.

"You were from an eastern state?"

"Kentucky. Pa and Ma were poor hill farmers. When bad years struck, I headed out on my own. Signed up and was assigned to help with the Cherokee removal."

Lucy saw his eyes lower, recognizing that he must have felt the pain, too, at those words, *Cherokee removal.*

"Colonel Greenway, will you and the lady be having dessert?" The waiter added the title, considering Andrew's elegant attire.

Lucy ordered the apple dumpling with rum-sauce, recommended by Andrew. Where is this leading? She noticed how warm she felt. No, alive, like when she used to dance down the verandah of the seminary, laughing with Eliza.

* * *

Three weeks later, after their fourth dinner together, Andrew guided Lucy down the old walking trail along Spring Branch. Memories of school days and times crowded Lucy's mind. Victoria Rogers. Her half-brother, Jacob Bates. Miss Whitmore, Miss Worcester and the girls. The gazebo ahead had survived the war, though the framework was almost completely covered by the wisteria.

They stood listening to the murmur of the clear water of Town Branch, Andrew in his frock coat and elegant cravat, placed his hand around her waist. Lucy allowed herself to feel his strength and warmth.

Then Andrew turned, leaned down and kissed her gently on the lips.

CHAPTER THIRTY-FIVE

Lucy glanced outside the south window of Eliza Bushyhead's log-walled room, assuring herself that Brindle, her riding horse, was content, grazing under the shagbark hickory.

"I couldn't believe, Eliza, that after all this time I'd be so confused."

Eliza, 35-year-old Blue Vale schoolteacher, who shared the four-room log house with Eli and Rachel Foxkiller, poured another cup of sassafras tea for her friend who sat in her only rocking chair.

"I knew you'd marry some day, Lucy. Men always stop in their tracks to turn and look at you. But me, with my hair? my awkwardness? Well, wait and see, wait and see, I tell myself. Besides, my life's full here, teaching the children."

Lucy turned to Eliza, recognizing that she needed her input. Not necessarily advice, but at least, a listening ear. "Andrew has only been here six weeks. How can a person know such a thing in six weeks?" Lucy paused, hand at her chin.

"Six weeks? Yes, time is important, but what does your heart say, Lucy?"

"Eliza, how do people know they're in love? Or if it is only a dream, a passing thing? And at my age, too."

"It's bursting out all over you, Lucy. You can't hide it anymore than the honeysuckle bush outside can hide from the bees. He's a good man, Andrew Greenway. Name of one of the Apostles, isn't it?"

"That's part of the problem, Eliza. You know your father was a minister. Andrew's not a church member. I never dreamed I'd think of marrying a man who wasn't committed to the church. Yet, Eliza, I'm drawn to Andrew. I feel at peace in his presence. I talked with Reverend Mock about it."

Lucy leaned back on the violet cushion, rocking silently on the braided rug beneath the rocker.

"What did Reverend Mock have to say, Lucy? I doubt very much if he forbade it."

"No, no such counsel. He asked me if I believed in my heart that Andrew was a good man. I said 'how could I doubt it, after the Trail of Tears?'" Lucy glanced through the window to see if her horse was still content outside.

"That was a long time ago, Lucy. A long time ago. People change. The war. Everyone uprooted now—So many young men who didn't return from the battlefields."

Lucy noticed Eliza's voice fading. "Andrew wants to settle in a place called Wichita Town, a little crossroads place at the junction of two rivers. Plains Indians and buffalo beyond. Osage people southward and the Wichitas, imported from Texas during the war."

"Yes, it'd be a change, Lucy. A new town, new settlers, new after-war growth. Always a school opening up somewhere. Educated woman like you could easily get teaching jobs."

"I'd be a full-blood in the white man's world. Did you forget?" Lucy felt a heaviness slide down over her breast. "You really think, away from the Nation, they'd hire a full-blood like me? Greek, Latin, music or no Greek, Latin and music." Lucy looked down at the braided rug.

"I believe you could start your own girls' seminary, Lucy. But, aren't you sidestepping the real issue?" Eliza smiled.

"Well, Eliza, anyway Reverend Mock asked me if I believed that verse in First Corinthians: 'For the unbelieving husband is sanctified by the wife, and the unbelieving wife is sanctified by the husband'."

"But you said earlier, that Andrew had his own faith, that he wasn't really an unbeliever. And Lucy, I hope you said, 'yes, I know and believe that verse.'" Eliza looked steadily at Lucy.

"I thanked Reverend Mock and went home to ponder the words and to pray about it," Lucy said.

Eliza walked over and placed a hand on each of Lucy's shoulders, then she lifted one hand to stroke her silky hair done up in a French roll. "I see the goodness in Andrew these few weeks, Eliza. It frightens me, though. We've been through enough troubles in the white man's world. Why should I invite more? We struggle here after the war, but times will get better. If I leave for Wichita, I'd be away from you. Besides, all those strangers." Lucy rose from the rocker.

"Well, I can tell that when Andrew looks at you, Lucy, there's no question in my mind how he feels about you. Those long eyelashes and those grey-green eyes."

At the mention of Andrew's eyes, Lucy felt a warmth creep up her neck. She realized she couldn't restrain a smile.

"See, even when I talk of him, Lucy, you beam like Magdalene seeing Jesus. Besides, I'm partial to lean-faced men with cleft chins."

Lucy looked at Eliza, allowing the silence for a moment.

Eliza turned to stare out the window past the red hollyhocks, the valley and creek beyond. "He'll take you away from the Nation. To Kansas—out on the plains with the Osage and Wichitas. Lucy, how will you be able to live without these hills and trees?" Eliza bit her lip.

Lucy glanced at Eliza, who'd turned from the window; she realized she must allow Eliza to share her pain too, the pain of separation. "You would have to come and visit us often, Eliza. Riverboat part of the way, stagecoach the rest. You'd have to come often. May be in a few years there'll be a train."

Then it dawned on Lucy that by such a statement she saw herself settled with trader Andrew Greenway of the sweeping grasslands and never-ending plains in that place they called *Kansas*. "He's a trader. Rather well off. Selling his post to a partner in

Towanda. Andrew says he much prefers relocating at the junction
of the Arkansas Rivers. Be a city there, some day, he says.'"

"Then you'll be a city lady, Lucy. I can tell he's a man who
likes style. Certainly wears his suits well. If you're not going to
turn and stare at him sauntering down the sidewalk in Tahlequah,
Lucy, I will." Eliza cleared her throat and laughed.

Lucy reached out to put her arm around Eliza's waist, drawing
closer to her old friend.

"He'll build you a Victorian house, leaded glass, chandeliers,
sweeping staircase. Want me to come up and design you a new silk
dress?" Eliza beamed.

They laughed together. Then they cried on each other's shoulders as the thoughts of the pain of parting took root. They had
suffered through the war years. Who hadn't received the fated news?
"Killed is such-and-such a battle?" Eliza's two cousins—Lucy's
friend, Todd Wyeth, shot at the battle of Pea Ridge.

They realized that the flow of life couldn't be stopped, that it
brought partings and new beginnings, such as Lucy's brother, Jacob,
now a lawyer down in Fort Smith.

* * *

That afternoon Lucy and Eliza rode their horses over to the old
seminary building southeast of Tahlequah, past the rubble of Chief
Ross's once magnificent Rose Cottage.

They stretched themselves to reach up through the weeds and
scrape away grime with their fingers and peek into the gloomy
building.

"Why, it's still loaded with military machinery, guns and . . . ."
Lucy said.

"Yes, it was used as a storage for the Confederacy during the
Civil War. What a shame." Eliza leaned closer to see if she could
see the grand staircase.

"It's as if one can still hear their voices, the singing, the translations from *Virgil*, the prayers . . . ." Lucy's voice faded.

"And Victoria Rogers's 'swarthy masculine forms' article in the *Rosebud*," Eliza added, nostalgia heavy in her voice. At the mention of Victoria Rogers, Lucy and Eliza elbowed each other, then rolled in the weeds and grass and howled as in old times.

CHAPTER
THIRTY-SIX

Lucy Greenway wondered if the tall windswept prairie grass stretched on forever. Wind caught wisps of her hair which had worked loose from under her broad-brimmed hat. The spring wagon rocked lightly as Andrew guided the black team he'd purchased in Tahlequah for the journey.

"I've never seen the ocean, but it must look like this." Lucy's fingers closed around Andrew's arm. She felt the hard muscle of his upper arm and was reassured.

Andrew turned his smiling eyes upon her face.

"And Lucy, my dove, it seems to never end."

Three ring-necked pheasants swooped from the four-foot grasses sweeping up and outward, circling toward the ever-stretching horizon.

Lucy could feel the sense of freedom surge through her.

"Andrew," she said, "I was Lucy of The Trail, Lucy of the female seminary, Lucy the schoolteacher in her crowded little school. Now, my darling, I am Mrs. Andrew J. Greenway."

Andrew guided the dashing team down an incline and across a shallow dry creek. "And I like the last the best of all, Lucy. Lucy, *my* wife."

"I'd feel lonely, Andrew, the wind, the endless grass, if I weren't here with you." Her fingers tightened as she gathered strength from his presence. She glanced up at his tanned angular face under the shadow of his hat-brim.

"Alone. Yes, the prairie makes one feel alone. Even lonely. But I will never be lonely either, Lucy, not with you by my side."

Andrew slapped the reins as the team trudged up an incline. He shifted the reins to one hand, encircling her waist with his free arm.

Lucy realized that her fears and indecision had blown away like fluff from the milkweed pods scattered through the prairie grass.

Gone were the anxiety-laden dreams that had so recently engulfed her at night. Dreams of twisting trees, black-limbed, reaching, grasping over dark waters. Long Man surging out of control. Now swirling, now boiling. The People crying in pain and grief.

Lucy'd rolled on her goose feather pillow, drenched with sweat. Long Man had stretched himself across the land providing a way for The People. His currents whipped at her dress, she felt her feet slipping into the vortex of the Tennessee River whirlpool.

Then Lucy felt her body flying, soaring like the night hawk, but she never fell. Suddenly the eyes of her spirit opened and she heard The People singing, "O have you not heard of that beautiful stream . . ."

Lucy clutched her fingers around Andrew's strong arm, assured that God was with her. There will be more rivers, she knew, and there was always *The Beautiful Stream* flowing inside, guiding her on to the new frontiers.

* * *

Lucy reached up to draw the brim of her hat down to keep the afternoon sun out of her eyes. She caught a glimpse of Andrew dipping his head so he could scan her face. Her heart warmed at the admiration in his look. "Isn't it a thing to ponder, Andrew, the turnings of one's life? Just when one believes things are all figured out something new slides in?"

"Me? You talking about me? I slid in?" Andrew chuckled.

"Yes, Andrew. You slid into my life. Just when I thought I'd go on teaching forever. I loved those children, they needed me and I needed them. Those frightful war years." Her voice caught.

"There'll be need of a fine teacher like you, Lucy, in Wichita Town. In time. You'll see. Fine schools. Another seminary. May be two. But then—," Andrew drew her close again. "You'll be a little mother first—our children, you know."

Lucy felt the surge of emotion rise in her heart.

"Children? Yes, Andrew, I do love children, but, a baby? Andrew you know my age, I'm 35."

"And my dove, I'm 43. I'd say we are the proper ages to be parents, wouldn't you agree?"

Andrew drew the wagon under the shade of a lone elm hanging over the rim of a small ravine. In the distance, a herd of antelope grazed serenely. White wisps of clouds drifted lazily. They stepped down out of the springwagon to stretch their legs, then sit for awhile in the shade of the lonely elm.

"Be near El Dorado near evening. More trees along the rivers, Lucy. Valleys with willows. We'll set up our tent and build a fire. Anxious for another of your campfire meals."

"But my prairie chicken rolled in the fire last night." Lucy chuckled.

"That's because I was teasing you. Kissing you, and I let the spit stick burn at one end. I raked it out. delicious. Fresh and delicious."

"Tonight, Andrew, I'll make sassafras tea and we'll watch the full moon rise over the hills. What do they call them? Flint Hills?"

"Yes, Flint Hills. But first, we must go swimming in the Walnut." He cleared his throat, grinning, teasing her.

"Well, Andrew, that too. But . . ." she didn't finish, overcome with love for her husband. They stood, arms around each other, both knowing the wide embrace of the endless prairie and the bowing grasses. Though Andrew towered a foot above her head, Lucy threw her arms around his neck, entangling her fingers in the mane of greying hair. She inhaled the saltiness of his body and smells of leather. She kissed him as they held one another in the sighing afternoon wind.

That evening in the little glen by the Walnut, they listened to the night sounds together.

"Whippoorwills, Andrew. What do you think they say to each other?"

"Why, my dear, they say, 'I love you, I love you, I love you,' don't you think?"

Later, they feasted on the two-pound bass Andrew'd harpooned in the bend of the river and the golden fried potatoes in the little iron skillet. The sounds rose about them, a night hawk, the cicadas, the murmuring of the river over the shallows, the soughing wind in the willow above.

Andrew, sitting on a fallen tree trunk after his supper, pulled at his boots. "Toes never feel so good as when they come out of boots and socks and sink into the buffalo grass like this."

He stood, stripping his broadcloth side-buttoned shirt over his head, chest bared in the moonlight and the balmy breeze.

Lucy's eyes followed his fluid movements, the lithe easy motions of his arms and muscles. He had repeated to her many times, "You are so beautiful." But Andrew had his own beauty. His leanness. His fine long legs, his broad back and the chest where her sorrows disappeared when he drew her cheek to it.

Andrew continued disrobing. "Come my dove." Come. He reached out his arm, angular hand beckoning her touch. His white feet entered the water. On the far side of the river, an erect white shaft of a sycamore root lifted in the shallows.

Lucy let her dress fall from her shoulders. She couldn't control the trembling in her legs. Her eyes filled with mist, her breath caught as she entered the river. Tongues of clear water lapped at their thighs. Then they swam in the cool blue pool at the river bend, the moon turning their embracing bodies to silver.

CHAPTER
THIRTY-SEVEN

The morning seemed unduly steamy and the air heavy and close. "What happened to the breeze? I thought in Kansas the wind always blows." Lucy tossed her wide-brimmed hat behind the wagon seat. Already, her hair was dampened by perspiration. Reaching up with one hand, she brushed back a straying wisp.

"It's going to storm. Wanted to reach my post near Towanda by noon. Those clouds get any closer, we're going to have to pull under a cliff or a stand of trees, if we can find any, while the storm moves over." Andrew turned his face upwards to study the clouds.

Lucy had seen many storms. Never did she forget the pounding cold rain on the Mississippi Long Man. Saved by the Above Being that day. For a moment, the scene flashed before her, the whippings of the keelboat grounded on a sand bar and loaded with wanderers, cold water sloshing over the deck.

Old slave woman named Black Bee struggling with a seedy corporal over a bottle half-filled with bad whisky—crashing through the rail then both of them sailed out into the dark waters. Their cries, caught up in the wailing wind. Now that same wail in the wind. Lucy felt a shiver run down her spine.

Within minutes, morning light dimmed as if a huge hand pulled a shade of boiling black clouds across the vaulted sky.

"Don't like the looks of those clouds." Andrew looked southwesterly and noted a small herd of antelope bouncing across the prairie, obviously seeking the shelter of a ravine or a cluster of shrubs. The wind whipped loose folds of Andrew's broadcloth shirt around the small of his back.

Then, the ear-splitting crack of lightning followed by the earth-jarring thunder. The team snorted and pawed at the grass beneath their feet as if unsure of the hands that held their reins.

"Try to make it to that ledge. Dry ravine ahead to the left. Towanda not more than three or four miles over those flint hills. Wait until the storm passes before we start that climb. Giddyup!" Andrew slapped the reins, voice drifting in the wind.

Without warning, the hail descended. Bruising, moth-ball-sized hail—stinging, pounding, pinging.

"Gee!" Andrew flicked the whip and urged the team to a gallop as the light wagon rocked toward the right and the white outcropping cliff.

"Isn't it dangerous to get down into a ravine with a storm coming, the water?" Lucy had seen storms before, but this was her first Kansas prairie storm. The howling wind and blowing rain tore at her body and soaked her dress. Hail pelted with fury.

"Get under the seat, Lucy. Under the seat." Andrew called. "Draw that canvas over your head. Gee, gee." He stood to guide the team under the outcropping of shale and dwarfed hackberry and wild plum.

By now, the prairie grasses stretched flat, waving, whipping. There was scarcely any light at all as the cold rains roared and water eddied in the ditch below.

Lucy watched Andrew, knowing that his narrowed eyes focused up the gully, taking note of the increasing rivulet. They were not in immediate danger on the ledge, but the rock they stood on rose only three feet above the rocky stream-bed.

Andrew's team reared at an extraordinarily close crack of lightning, which split a scraggly elm not more than 100 yards away. With the pounding rain and the howl of the wind, conversation was impossible. Ten minutes passed. Twenty minutes, twenty-five.

Then the rain stopped. Stopped as if a raging out-of-control steam engine had rocked across the prairie, the caboose, a purplish cloud rolling dizzily ahead of the westerly winds.

From somewhere, a meadowlark emerged, sailing to a lower

branch of a shuddering prairie sunflower that hadn't completely flattened in the winds.

The sun, diffused by the rising mist over the prairie, sent out extravagant beams like ladders leading to heaven.

The horses, knowing the storm had passed, neighed and nodded to each other as Andrew climbed back on the wagon-seat.

"How sweet it smells, the grasses, the fresh rain." Lucy glanced up the little ravine, noting the rolling gravel and pebbles gaining speed ahead of the rising water. "Come my darling-drenched-bride. You Cherokees take great pride in your immersions in Long Man don't you? Well, this time, Long Man came at us from above." His teeth gleamed through his tanned face, his pectorals swelling the wet shirt which chilled his skin.

"Haw." Andrew slapped the reins and they were again on their way up the slope out of the rocky ravine as the sounds of roaring water descended from the west down the creek-bed.

"Come, my darling-little-wet-hen." He laughed. She laughed.

"Oh, Andrew. We had a wonderful bath again this morning but it won't take long for our clothes to dry when the wind comes up again, will it?"

*   *   *

In another hour, they rode over the last outcropping of flint on the hill.

"Towanda up ahead." Andrew pointed to the half-dozen shabby buildings hunched on the prairie, softened by the rising mist now heated to sweltering by the sun. Steam rose from the heating ground. "And over there, whoa. Whoa." He pulled the reins, halting the horses abruptly.

"Andrew, what's wrong? Why did you stop?" Lucy saw the uncertainty on his face.

"Thought for a minute we were lost. No, that's Towanda—Osage Indian encampment in the hollow below to the right. But . . ."

Lucy clasped his right biceps, feeling the slight quivering. She noticed the blush at his cheek-bones, the heightening light in his eyes. "What is it, Andrew?"

"It should be over there. Over there socked between those scrubby prairie elms." The horses snorted again and started to move.

"Whoa." Andrew pulled the reins, bewildered.

Lucy strained her eyes but she could see nothing but three scrubby trees and an oblong blackened spot in the prairie grass. "Why, Andrew, I believe there's been a fire. May be the lightning . . ."

He slapped the reins across the horses' rumps. "Giddyup." The wheels whirled through the bluestem, the ox eye daisies, the towering sunflowers. "Giddyup."

Lucy stared at his face, which seemed feverish now.

When he'd pulled the team to a stop and hurled himself over the wagon-box, he stared with disbelief at the charred rubble and fire-scorched trees. "Raiders. Outlaws burned the station. Where's Mosley?"

Lucy recalled hearing him talk of his trader partner, Edward. How Edward Mosley had been a compatible partner. Slow, but steady. Every week, he counted the cash and entered it in the ledger. Then he'd ride down the slope to Towanda to deposit it in their separate accounts at the bank.

Andrew'd figured with the bank account and the sale of the Post building and business, they'd both have a more than comfortable bank roll. Certainly enough for that clapboard house in Wichita Town and a hefty amount towards a ferry to take people across the Arkansas.

Lucy saw the grave first. Only a soft spot in the burnt prairie grass. And the makeshift broken slab where someone had scratched the name, "Edward Mosley".

Lucy moved closer to Andrew and placed her warm arm around his waist. She listened to the heavy disappointment in his voice as he said, "Now, my dove, I can't sell a burned-down trading post. There goes the extra 1200 dollars Mosley and I were counting on." The wind started again, Lucy's blue skirt flapped around her legs. "Andrew, why? Who could've done it?"

"It's not unusual out here. Outlaw bands. Could be Indians angry over the government moving them off their lands. I understand that. But I believe this is the work of scalawags from over Wichita Town way."

Lucy watched Andrew stride over to the rough spot in the grass and the slab-of-a-marker. Taking off his hat, he knelt before his trader companion's shabby grave marker.

Lucy, without a sound, eased herself down by his side, a stand of black-eyed Susans nodding at her knee. She took his big hand, bowed her head to pray silently with him. She was not at all a stranger to death and to graves.

Why, Andrew's hand is cold. Is he chilling? Lucy stared at his face, now pale and lips turning blue.

Lucy could see the disappointment and fury in Andrew's eyes as he guided the trotting horses down the muddy street of Towanda Town. Three mangy hounds yelped behind them as mud flew from horses' hooves and wagon wheels.

"Whoa." Andrew leaped out, cheeks flushed. His long fingers tied the team to a cedar hitching post in front of the little native-stone bank.

"Come, my dear. All's not lost. I have an account here. Elias Ramer'll apprise me of the situation."

As they pushed open the heavy oak door, Elias Ramer, behind a wrought-iron grill at the counter, looked up, his handle-bar mustache emphasizing his dour look. "Greenway. About time you got back to these parts. Bad news, I'm afraid. You been up on the hill yet?" Ramer's voice trailed as he cleared his throat, sad eyes focused upon Andrew, then shifting to Lucy.

Lucy could see it in his face, he, rolling it through his mind: "Cherokee. Andrew Greenway's married an Indian woman."

"The Post. Elias, what happened?" Andrew leaned on the ledge by the iron grill.

"Bunch of raiders rode through here a month ago. Sheriff Potter said it might be a gang led by someone named Jesse James. Rode on eastward raiding and robbing. Shooting up the works. Real outlaw gangs over there in Missouri. Ought to stay out of Kansas."

"Mosley. They kill Mosley?" Andrew straightened.

"Sheriff said he must have resisted best he could. But since he'd been down to the bank the day before to withdraw his account of 1,100 dollars, I'd have put up a fight too." Banker Elias cleared his throat, glancing back over his shoulder to Lucy.

Lucy stepped to the counter, her hand grasping Andrew's. I wonder if Andrew is ill? She felt his hand, noticing how hot it was.

"My account, Elias, is it secure?"

"Oh, yes, Mr. Greenway. Secure." Banker Elias's face broke into a grin.

"We here in Towanda not gonna let a robber gang bust up our bank and take depositor's money. Nope." He turned to spit a brown streak toward a brass spittoon.

"Clerk Conway there, he's a better shot than Sheriff Potter. Got a Colt strapped on him now and keeps two shotguns under the desk. Nope. Robbers not going to find it easy at this bank." He lifted his craggy head which tilted on a thin, wrinkled neck.

"Mr. Greenway, you all right? You look feverish—you got a lot of color in your cheeks."

Andrew straightened his shoulders, tipped back his wide-brimmed hat. Perspiration soaked through his shirt under his arms. He realized he was chilling. He looked down at Lucy, and noticed the worry in her eyes.

"Meet my wife, Mr. Ramer. From the Cherokee Nation in Oklahoma. Mrs. Lucy Greenway, seminary graduate and a schoolteacher." Andrew's chin lifted and his feverish eyes reflected love and pride.

"Why, how do you do, Mrs. Greenway," Elias said without a smile. Lucy concluded by his voice and look that he didn't believe in whites marrying Indians, full-bloods at that. She wished she'd had her shawl to draw around her shoulders, summer or not.

"My account's secure then? 1,200 dollars?" Andrew asked.

"Secure, Mr. Greenway. Secure."

"Going to rebuild the Post on the hill?" Ramer's face creased as he tugged at his sleeve.

Andrew turned to place his arm behind Lucy and draw her closer.

"No, Mr. Ramer. Lucy and I plan to settle in Wichita Town over on the Arkansas Rivers. Whole city's going to burst right out of the prairie grass there. You'll see."

"Sorry to hear that. Figured it, especially with the Post burned and the Osage moving over that direction anyway. Besides, all those hunters bringing in those buffalo hides. Right on the Chisholm Trail, too. Good location. Sad to see you go." He seemed to be trying to hide his disappointment.

"Mrs. Sapler still take in roomers across the street?"

Andrew pointed to the two-story unpainted house across the dusty path.

"Hotel now, Mr. Greenway. Didn't you and your woman see the sign? *Hotel Towanda*. Puts out a good spread for her roomers too. Better get yourselves registered before evening. Cowboys on the trail be in here come dusk. Dance in the saloon tonight and the Osage having a pow-wow on the Walnut. Lots of excitement."

Banker Elias stared at Lucy as if he doubted lodging would be available for her at Mertice's. "You play the pi-anna, Mrs. Greenway? Hoover Conklin surely needs someone to play the pi-anna for the dance at the saloon tonight. Other girl run off with a cowboy."

"Mrs. Greenway plays classical music on the piano, Mr. Ramer, hardly anything suitable for the dance tonight." Andrew lowered his head. In spite of the fever, his eyes shone with pride.

Lucy smiled up at him, trying to cover the worry behind her smile.

"Yes, well, Mr. Ramer, thank you for attending to my business. Edward's too. A terrible loss. Come, Lucy."

She grabbed his hand tightly as he headed toward the door. He wobbled slightly and a cough ripped up his throat.

CHAPTER
THIRTY-EIGHT

Andrew had lain for two days in the hot little second-story bedroom in Mertice Sapler's hotel. "I'll be better come morning. You'll see." Andrew's voice rasped heavily. Lucy held the water glass for him but he only sipped a few swallows. She worried because last night, he couldn't seem to eat the chicken soup Mertice Sapler fixed for him.

"You must drink more water, Andrew." Lucy held one hand behind his perspiring head as she held the pressed-glass tumbler to his lips again. A tremor ran up Lucy's spine as she noticed how his fever raged. A heavy wheeze rattled his chest, he struggled to breathe.

"Better tomorrow, Lucy. The team. Where's the team? Bring them around. Get my pants on, we'll head to . . ."

Lucy could see that Andrew was delirious. To make matters worse, Mertice Stapler'd told her yesterday, "No, they ain't no doctor here in Towanda now for two years. Doctor Skilltow was drunk most of the time anyway. Since the business was slim, he moved on westward."

Lucy raked her mind. She wondered if she could slip down to the livery, hire a horse and ride over to El Dorado, eastward. Or, would it be better to leave Andrew in Mrs. Stapler's care while she galloped across the prairie toward Wichita on the river?

"How can I leave Andrew, thrashing and drenched?" she whispered to herself. She decided she'd better strip off his wet gown and get him into a dry one. Pulling gently at the gown to remove it, she reached for the cloth and wash-basin and began to bathe him with lukewarm water. The rattle in his breathing worried her.

She lifted out his shirts and three pairs of pressed trousers from his trunk. There it was, another nightgown. Whipping it out, she shook it. Fine summer linen. Well made. Get him in this. Her mind raced as she performed the nursing duties while a determination born of months of uncertainties and sufferings rose within.

"Why, Mrs. Greenway," Mertice Stapler said, head bobbing up the stair landing. "Do you think you might send for Doctor Monarez? He's a Mexican. But, he sure did get that big-headed baby down Beulah Pilfer's chute, spite of what her husband said."

Lucy wondered why Mertice had to emphasize that the doctor was Mexican. She decided she didn't have time to think about what Mertice thought of her, a full-blood married to a white man.

Lucy took Mertice's suggestion. Send for Doctor Monarez, Mexican or not, in El Dorado. Hire the oldest stable boy at the livery.

"Be back with the doctor come evening, Ma'am," Matt Hawkler, the stable boy, yelled back. She could tell the boy was glad for the business. Matt, elbows akimbo, galloped off toward El Dorado.

*　*　*

When Andrew finally dozed off in a deep sleep and Lucy had adjusted the windows so that a breeze would cool the room, but not blow directly on Andrew, she took time to freshen herself.

She opened her trunk and selected clean undergarments then pulled out her violet calico with the white lace bodice. Andrew liked it. When he opened his eyes, the sight would perhaps cheer him up. Get the doctor here soon as possible.

What more can I do? Lucy poured lukewarm water from the pitcher with the pink hibiscus on the side into the huge matching bowl. Wringing out the washcloth, she bathed her face, her neck, her arms.

"Don't panic," she whispered to herself. She looked at Andrew, wide-shouldered. Muscles. Radiated health, didn't he?

She thought of their embracing on the buffalo grass by the

Walnut. No, she wouldn't allow fear to cloud her mind and con-
fuse her. She'd keep a clear head. Besides, the doctor would be
here come evening. Matt promised.

* * *

Shadows lengthened and the late summer evening grew languid
and sticky. Still, the boy hadn't returned. Lucy rose from the bedroom rocker, descended the pine steps. She opened the screen door,
shaking the flies loose, and stepped out onto the porch.

The three hounds that had followed her and Andrew as they
rolled into Towanda, lay under a sumac bush at the edge of the
yard, yellow eyes focused on her, long tongues lapping and dripping. Worry settled like the malaise of the dusty evening. Dog
days. Andrew—could it be pneumonia? He, so strong and youth-
ful?

Lucy recognized Andrew had had his own sufferings. He'd
been through tough times as a child, nearly starving in his Kentucky backwoods home, glad for a turnip when he was a child.
The toll of escorting refugees on The Trail bore on him. Years in
the Army. No telling what he'd suffered there, diseases, that is.

Lucy fretted. Where on earth was that stable boy? She walked
to the edge of the dusty street, lifted her hand to shade her eyes as
she stared eastward across the hills.

"Ought to be riding in, Matt and the doctor, any time, Mrs.
Greenway, anytime," Mertice encouraged, though her face reflected
a certain smugness about the fee she'd earn from such an extended
stay.

Mertice'd stepped out from her kitchen to catch any breeze
away from her cookstove where her beans and ham-hocks boiled
for the guests' supper, rolls baking in the oven beneath.

But the boy didn't return.

"Should I send someone after him? May be he got lost?"

"Ain't going to get lost riding to El Dorado. He knows the
way. Doctor probably pulling out a baby out east of town. Them
farmers' wives over there insist on pouring out howling ones each
year." Mertice wiped her brow with the back of her hand. "Snake-

bite," she continued, "could be someone snakebit. Them country children get into everything. Ought to stay out of them gypsum gullies. Rattlesnake territory. One bite enough to send you to perdition."

Lucy wished Mrs. Stapler would close her mouth. She didn't need that kind of encouragement. "I must go in, Mrs. Stapler. Let's try the chicken broth again. I'm going up to Andrew."

Lucy never quite knew how she managed to nurse Andrew through the night. Delirious, he twisted and thrashed about. When she could keep him back on his pillow, she tried to sing to him as she bathed his brow with the washcloth.

O seek that beautiful stream Its waters so free are flowing for thee. O seek that beautiful stream.

By noon, the next day Matt returned, the nag plodding along. Seeing him approach, Lucy leaned over the porch-rail by the sagging morning glories. "Where is the doctor?" She clutched her throat. "Why, Mrs. Greenway," the boy who'd slid off the horse, dug his toe in the dust. "I waited all night on Doctor Monarez's porch. Slept on the porch swing. He didn't come. Neighbor woman said he rode off east over them hills. Country woman trying to have twins over there and they ain't coming out right. At least, that's what his house woman said."

Lucy could see the boy wasn't lying and that he was sleepy, tired, and thirsty.

"Oh, God," she whispered. "Mercy. Mercy. Andrew dying of pneumonia upstairs. Merciful God above, help me."

She pulled a 50-cent piece out of her pocket and handed it to the fourteen-year-old boy. "Thank you, Matt. At least you tried." Lucy turned to Mertice Stapler. "Oh, my God. What am I to do?"

"You ever tried a *witch doctor?*" Mertice stared at Lucy with her grey eyes, feet spread apart.

Lucy straightened. Mertice's words checked her racing thoughts. "There is a shaman around? A Holy Man?" Could it be?

"If you could make it down to the river where them Osage are squatting, you might come up with a Witch Doctor. Folks told me about old man Trotting Wolf. Viola Heavener swears he cured her Lizzie of the whooping cough with his dancing and smoke and chants."

Lucy's mind whirled. Back, back, along the trail between the blessed chestnut trees of New Echota long, long ago. The chants, the Holy Men. The miraculous healings. The wading into Long Man for healings. No. It couldn't be.

"Matt, here's a quarter." She dug in her pocket for the coin. "I need the horse."

Lucy realized there was no time to hurry to the livery for another one. "Tell the liveryman, I'll pay when I return." Off Lucy galloped, violet skirts flapping in the wind, wisps of hair dislodging.

*   *   *

Holy Man Trotting Wolf was old. "Ninety-seven summers," he mumbled in reply to Lucy's inquiry.

"Cherokee? Yes, I'm Cherokee." His voice wobbled and cracked. "Married an Osage woman. Lived with the Osage 40 years." He spoke with ancient rhythms, his voice wavering in the wind. He studied the well-dressed Cherokee woman who'd galloped right into the Osage camp, startling everyone.

"Oh, blessed relief. God is hearing my prayers," Lucy mumbled out loud to the ancient shaman who leaned on a crooked hickory stick. He was dressed in canvas pants with overhanging buckskin shirt, his white hair parted in the middle. Two long braids framed his walnut-colored face, wrinkled as last winter's apple.

"Do you have his beads?"

"No, my husband doesn't wear beads. He's a white man." The old ways—Cherokee men wear jewelry, not the women.

"Do you have his scarf? The shaman's voice wavered in the wind, his burning eyes focused on Lucy.

Fear clutched at her breast. Why hadn't she thought about it? The shaman always needed the sick person's beads or scarf, or . . . "All I have is my husband's coin purse."

"That'll do." The Holy man squatted by the trunk of the walnut tree at the edge of the river. Eyes closed, his wrinkled hands mauled the leather-pouch to sense the life and presence of his patient.

He nodded and muttered a sentence of an ancient prayer while Lucy told herself, stay out of his way, don't spoil it, give him time. She remembered how it was of old. First the shaman needed time to sense, to know, to prepare spiritually.

The Holy Man turned to the bent crone to his left, his wife, Tall Cedar. "My tobacco and flint."

With these items in his hands, before the small pile of dried grass and broken twigs, he struck the flint stones. Smoke rose, and a tiny orange flame leaped up.

Again, ancient words and phrases and noddings of his craggy head. He tossed a pinch of tobacco into the flames. "It is good. It is very good. The winds take it up and it circles toward Towanda where he lies."

*   *   *

At last, Lucy had him in the room with the prostrate man whose chest heaved for air. The shaman had dawdled so long at the door to perch a buzzard feather above the ledge while he bowed and mumbled, "I am going to leave you on watch here. Now you will also be the finder for me of all good things."

Lucy wanted to scream, "Do something now! Hurry."

But the Ancient One took his time, palsied arms and hands trembling over Andrew's drenched form as his hands searched over his body, six inches above the sweaty nightgown. He mumbled. He prayed.

Lucy tried to remember. To stop a cough—what was it? In the old days? Pray to the Great Blue Being Above? "O Lord Jesus Christ," she prayed silently, "give the Ancient One your power. Heal Andrew."

Now the Ancient One tottered and rocked in a small circle in the room, mumbling, praying to unseen powers.

Lucy remembered more. For colic, in the old days, they prayed to Ni Ta we he u, the Great Above Being. "O God, help us," she muttered audibly.

For a moment, doubt and shame gripped her. Her fingers clutched her throat. Blasphemy? Devilish? Dragging this shaman into this bedroom? "Lord, have mercy."

Back in the woods east of Tahlequah, where she taught in her little school, many of the ministers in the Indian churches were not only preachers of the Word, but shamans as well; still applying the ancient healing medicines, formulas and prayers.

O God. If it is sin, forgive me.

Lucy stared at the Holy Man who'd squatted on the floor, obviously in a trance, head thrown back, mouth open, eyes focused somewhere beyond the visible world. His body jerked as if convulsed.

"Strip off his gown," mumbled the shaman.

Lucy tugged downward from Andrew's shoulders.

The shaman stood up, surprisingly with strength, not needing his cane. Reaching for his deer-skin bag on the bentwood chair, his fingers searched and dug. Two herbs. One treasured and preserved from the easterly homelands, Boneset. The other, inner bark of the willow. Holy man Trotting Wolf looked at Lucy, herbs in hand. "I must have hot water to make a brew." He coughed.

"Hot water for tea, Mrs. Stapler. Hot water, oh, please bring hot water." Lucy called down the stairwell.

In a moment, Mertice waddled up the stairs, nostrils pinched at what she considered offensive, the smoky odors of the wrinkled old Witch Doctor murmuring devilish prayers before her. But Lucy noticed how Mertice cooperated and concluded she'd observed this before. After all, she'd mentioned it to Lucy, even if she seemed to resent the *Indian*, dancing and mumbling in her room.

The shaman poured the scalding water into the sacred gourd attached by a thong to his side. He scattered the willow powder on the steamy water and swirled the gourd while still praying. He bent his head, opened his mouth and blew over the steamy water three times.

"A bathing cloth." The shaman glanced at Lucy while one arm waved at unseen beings.

Lucy handed him one of the washcloths on the rail of the washstand.

The Holy Man began to drag the wet, steaming cloth across the surfaces of Andrew's body until he'd bathed his entire body. His voice cracked and trembled. Tears streamed down the deep furrows of his dark-walnut cheeks. He gasped for air.

"Hold his head." Lucy lifted Andrew's head while the shaman poured the remaining liquid between Andrew's lips. Then, he repeated the entire procedure with the precious Boneset-leaf tea.

Lucy realized there'd be no waddling to the river or plunge into the cold waters. Not here. Andrew was too ill.

Abruptly, the ancient one gathered his draw-string bag, picked up his crooked cane with his knobby fingers. It seemed as if the drenching sweat from Andrew's prostrate body now transferred itself to the Ancient One's trembling body.

Down the steps he hobbled to retrieve his holy buzzard feather lodged there for the blessings of all. Lucy knew he'd be back in seven days. Seven, a holy number, allowing time for healing.

CHAPTER
THIRTY-NINE

Two days after the shaman's dances, prayers, teas and washings, a weary Lucy Greenway looked out of Mertice Stapler's upstairs window. She clutched her throat and her eyes brightened. Below by the yard gate, Doctor Monarez tied his dusty horse to the hitching rack. He leaned forward, wobbling up Mertice Stapler's steps to the porch, his face etched with evident weariness from the challenges of frontier doctoring.

Lucy raced down the steps and out on the porch. "Thank God, you arrived."

The bedraggled man clutched a worn medical bag, looked up into Lucy's face. "You the lady with the sick husband?"

"Yes. I'm Lucy Greenway. It's my husband Andrew. Doctor, thank God above, he's doing better."

Doctor Monarez sagged on the bent wood chair by Andrew's bed, eyes and mind absorbing the situation.

Lucy stood by the doctor, listening, waiting. The fatigued doctor threw back the sheet covering Andrew, who'd just awakened from a deep sleep. He placed his gigantic ear, black hairs curling from his ear cavity, against Andrew's broad chest.

"Hummmm. Hummmm." He lifted his shaggy head, turning blood-shot eyes to the Cherokee woman at his side, awaiting his bidding. "Crisis is past. He's resting. Heartbeat steady. Weak, but steady. Whatever you've done, you've brought him through. I could prescribe some calomel, but it would do little good now. Opium would only slow down the heart beat, same with bleeding."

"Oh, blessed God above," Lucy whispered. "He will live?"

"Oh, yes. Had pneumonia before." The doctor tapped Andrew's chest with two dark, flat fingers with torn nails, leaning his head forward. "Keep that basin handy. He's going to be spitting up handfuls of phlegm. Give him whiskey and honey five times a day." The doctor straightened his slumped shoulders. Lucy caught the drift of whisky on his breath.

"Yes. Not his first attack. Susceptible to lung ailments. Have to watch him. A veteran, isn't he? Lots of veterans come down with lung ailments." Doctor Monarez closed his worn bag.

"Oh, thank you, Lord God above," whispered Lucy.

*   *   *

And then, according to the ancient ways, the shaman returned seven days after his first visit to see if his potions, prayers, chants and washings, plus favors gained from the blessed buzzard feather, had been of avail.

He beamed at the patient, sitting up, fever now gone, slurping the hot broth Lucy spooned into his wide mouth.

Andrew grinned. "Whatever you did, Doctor Shaman Trotting Wolf, you see the results. Thought I was a goner. Couple days more of bed rest and Lucy and I are going to climb back on that spring wagon and rock on over to Wichita Town. Show her the land, the rivers. Sink down some roots. Give Lucy a chance to pick up a wheelbarrow of buffalo dung for her cook stove." Andrew laughed.

He cleared his throat, wiping his mouth with the napkin Mertice had remembered to supply for the ailing man. But of course Mertice, standing by, beaming, took credit too.

"Don't forget, Mr. Greenway, I was the one who suggested it," but Mertice didn't mention her resentment at the dirty Witch Doctor who stank up her house.

*   *   *

As the spring wagon rocked through the tall bluestem and prairie flowers, Lucy asked herself, why have I come to this windswept place? Where on earth are the trees? The wind. How can anyone endure the howling and the twisting of such wind? What would Eliza Bushyhead think of this endless prairie?

She thought of her school, her beloved children. And, the church. Scattered throughout the woods around Tahlequah, the little Indian churches, the singing, the prayers, the close knit fellowship. The majesty of the services of the Moravians at the Seminary. The Presbyterians and Congregationalists and Baptists at Park Hill, where they rebuilt after the war. The sound of the pump organs, the crescendo of pianos, especially Chief Ross's massive imported grand.

The memories of Chief Ross spoke of a world long gone. How long, now, had that noble Chief of the Cherokees lain in his grave by the Illinois?

A refrain from Bach circled through her mind and soul: "Jesus, Priceless Treasure, gift beyond measure." She thought of the steeples and church towers rising up into the blue skies of Tahlequah. Where on earth was a church in this windswept country? What have I left behind? she wondered, as her fingers toyed at her throat.

Andrew's voice brought her out of her reverie. "Whoa." He pulled back the reins, halting the team on the rise overlooking the valley of the Arkansas.

"There she is. Spread out like the garden of Eden." His arm swept in an arc as if to measure the immeasurable expanse of grassland extending westward until it met the white cloud bank on the horizon.

Lucy stared in silence as she wrapped both hands around Andrew's left arm. The aromatic winds circled their heads. High above three eagles soared, then dropped to survey the glistening waters of the river, lined with willows and towering cottonwoods.

"Andrew. Why, it's beautiful. Don't move. Let our eyes soak it up for awhile."

They both knew that the moment required silence. Lucy felt a friendliness in the wind, loneliness too, but now they basked in its friendliness. A spicy sweetness spread by the waving grasses ascended from the earth. Though it was only a few minutes, it seemed an eternity. Andrew threw back his wide brimmed hat, turned his now leaner face to his radiant wife, placing his arm around her waist. "Yes, my dove. Drink it in. It is like an endless purity, isn't it? The waving grass, the glistening water, the never ending skies— an endless purity."

Lucy's dark eyes focused upon the black and brown mass which seemed to rise in waves and ripples, way, way beyond the Arkansas River, westward where the blazing sun pierced the clouds with its rays. "Andrew, that moving. Looks like velvet, black and brown velvet. Animals?"

"Yes, my dove. Animals. You're looking at a herd of several thousand buffalo moving across the prairie. Reason it looks so beautiful close to the rivers is that the buffalo graze the bluestem, keeping it mowed like a lawn."

He had spoken of 'endless purity' of the grassy plain, but, already the air of the 'endless purity' had been split by arguing voices of traders, cowboy cursings, carpenter tools, ripping and pounding. The purity, smudged by the dust of the driven cattle and trailmasters and the hordes of buffalo hunters beyond the river. Already, the rude upshot of buildings sullied a portion of the waving grasslands right at the fork of those rivers.

As they rolled in closer, the onslaught met them: the putrifying smells of buffalo hides drying in the sun, the souring mash of the brewery, the manure piles at the stables, the filth heaved out open windows and back doors, the swarming flies and the ripening odors from the leaning privies.

Andrew slapped the reins. "Giddyup, got to get this bride down into Wichita Town and get her settled." His eyes swept the junction of the rivers. "That's where I'm going to have my ferry-boat service," he pointed, "right there, below the fork of the rivers. You'll have to hold the sacks for the cash coming in from that ferryboat, Lucy." He grinned, anticipation lighting his eyes. He had cash enough to finance it, but he and Lucy would have to rent until he built up enough cash to start a clapboard house. Had his Towanda Post not burned, of course, it would have been different.

"Be a bridge there soon, though. Ferry service won't last long. And then, the longhorns coming up the Chisholm trail from Texas, fording the river, the cowboys, chuckwagons and trading wagons all paying toll to cross and stay dry." Andrew beamed. Lucy could sense the life-blood flowing through his body and her love for him warming his soul.

"Need a son or two to help with it all, Lucy."

Her fingers tightened on his arm, the sweetness of his sun-dried shirt rising to her nose.

"Besides you, Andrew, are you aware that I don't know a soul in that town sprouting up down there?" The cupid's bow of her upper lip set in solemnity and resolve.

* * *

Three months now, they'd lived at the cavernous, though gloomy Durfee's Trading Post at the mouth of the Little Arkansas, Lucy's belly swelling with her pregnancy.

Andrew hadn't been able to contain himself when he discovered her secret. He grabbed her, whirled her around. Dancing. Clapping, hooting until Agnes Mead, wife of Wichita's most prestigious trader, and Catherine Greiffenstein, wife of Wichita's second most prestigious trader, coupled their hands and danced in a circle on the wide planks with them.

They'd welcomed Lucy with open arms, these women. Lucy soon understood they were both used to the rude and surprising outcroppings of life on the frontier, the disappointments, the shocks, the fun-loving wholesomeness, the virility dripping everywhere.

"Being with child proper way to be, Lucy Greenway," beamed Agnes Mead in her swishing green taffeta skirt, reddish hair swept up and held in place by opulent pearl-studded combs as if she believed in displaying her wealth. Lucy's eyes surveyed Agnes's amethyst brooch, the garish diamond ring, and three-strand string of pearls her big-bellied husband had purchased for her on his trading travels.

"You'll like this Wichita Town life, every day, something different. Why only yesterday, a dozen milk cows from across the Little Arkansas waded across, lumbered into the garden back of the post, ate up most of the beans before the stable boy and that Mexican liveryman, Manuel Rodriguez, nearly died of heat prostration getting them out."

"And," Catherine added, "there it was in the paper next morning, 'The profanity provoking predators, the innocent-eyed cows are preying in the fenceless gardens.'"

Lucy leaned on the window ledge, thankful for a breeze catching her neck. She could not deny the sadness that slid over her heart like a cloud over the sun.

"Don't you fret, Lucy Greenway. Your man'll do just fine on that trader's circuit. Better get yourself a couple of tow sacks to hold the money when Andrew gets back with my Bill's trader wagon." Catherine giggled and rims of flesh beneath her fine-clothed body shook.

Without delay, traders Mead and Greiffenstein had loaded the oversized trader wagons for the trails, coffee, flour, sugar, pots and pans, tobacco, bolts of cloth, spices, knives, axes, and shovels. "Scatter the Indians southward, gotta take the goods to them. It works. It works well. Be back with a load of tanned hides and a sack of cash from the land transactions. Money burning the fingers of those Indians."

So, off rumbled Andrew and colleague Gifford Dotson, another newcomer, seeking a fortune in Indian country.

"It is all so new. I'll have to keep myself busy. I told Andrew to let me help in the trading rooms downstairs. It helps pass the time waiting on the customers," Lucy said, as she smiled at her new friends.

Lucy's proficiency in several Indian languages and dialects enabled her to make more sales.

But only a few Indians straggled in, Osage, Wichitas, and an occasional Plains Indian from beyond the rivers, displaying their perfectly tanned hides. The United States government again entered into a treaty with both the Wichitas and the Osage, securing their lands for the settlers. These changes left the Indians with heads spinning from the infighting, the lawsuits, government proclamations, and the eventual fated moving of the Wichitas from their homelands to Indian Territory southward.

*   *   *

"The Wichitas failed miserably at their attempts at farming. Floods, grasshoppers, drought. New treaty. Moving them southward. That's what you hear, moving them southward," Andrew had explained.

Lucy stepped to the spacious window overlooking the one main street of Wichita Town, two dusty paths with prairie grass between the paths traversed by three mangy hounds.

The Wichitas' heart rending wailing's, like that of the Trail of Tears, rose into the wind, circled over the banks of the two rivers and lost itself in the prairie winds.

Lucy watched the wagons packed with the Osage and the Wichitas rock southward past the spot where Andrew had already put down his stakes marking the site of his ferry. The wagonmasters cracked whips as the mules entered the waters at the shallows. The half-submerged wheels carried the dispossessed to new lands selected by their governing officials in whom they'd put their trust.

A few Osage, blankets over their shoulders, waded into the river, refusing to climb in the wagons and ride. When Lucy pondered it, it came to her. Her father, Benjamin Drake, had been one of the walkers, forced to stagger over a thousand miles. She shuddered as she remembered the skeletal man stretched out at the threshold of Esther Shining Star's Tahlequah home that day so long ago.

The next day, Lucy picked up a copy of the *Vidette*. She read: "The air was filled with the cries of the old people, especially the women, who lamented over the graves of their children, which they were about to leave forever by proceeding to the new reservation."

Lucy felt the child within her move. She stifled a sob as visions of torn earth and quickly wrapped bodies of Indian children were lovingly laid into the ground along the shores of great rivers, while their mothers were forced to stagger onwards, hearts overflowing with sorrow, toward unknown lands.

Lucy knew that some day it would be over. Stealing the homeland from beneath The People. The lands would be taken, secured by the United States government from coast to coast. Native homelands disappeared faster than a child could pour sand down a badger hole.

"Government calls it 'Manifest destiny', Lucy," explained Andrew. "Westward expansion. The emigrants never cease to come. New railroad be shooting through here next year, now that the Osage are leaving. You'll see. Shoot its way all the way to the Pacific Ocean."

Lucy noted the sadness, too, in Andrew's voice. Was it really manifest destiny? Was it the will of God? Was it his destiny for the white folks to steal the lands from The People?

Then Lucy thought of the schools, the Moravians and the Presbyterians, the Baptists and the Methodists. Which ones had been underwritten by the American Board of Missions? Actually paid by the United States government to 'educate the savages' in order to make it easier to take their lands by 'integrating' them into the great and wonderful ways of the white people, though they would not even be citizens. And, if that didn't work, manifest destiny called for forced removal. How could it be? She felt the stabbing of doubt. The church. Accomplice? She'd like to go over it with Reverend Worcester, a liberal Baptist, 'The Messenger,' he'd been called by The People. But, neither he nor Reverend Mock ever spoke out against slavery or the United States government funding the 'education of savages.'

Then Lucy realized that 'the church,' grounded on this earth, was a human institution, but its center was somewhere else. In God. In the blessed Christ. Yes. This is the way it is in this world, "this present age', with its 'principalities and powers', spoken of by St. Paul, she thought.

Lucy Greenway was hungry for the church. Her tongue loosened as if ready to sing 'Come Thou Fount of Every Blessing.' Sing it in the moaning, slow style of the Cherokees. Sing it to the melodious humming of the pump-organ. When on earth would her fingers touch piano keys again? Where were the churches of Wichita Town? Questions kept rising within her.

Just as Lucy resolved to discuss church and religion with Agnes Mead and Catherine Greiffenstein when she saw them again, she was startled by the yelping of a pack of dogs racing down the main street, accompanied by the wild howling of children.

Lucy rushed to the open window, poked her head out just as a cloud of dust settled around her face and hair.

Below her, three gangly boys, bare footed, dirty faced, torn breeches flapping around their ankles, whooped.

One, the tallest with the hair like a poorly bound sheaf of wheat, threw back his head, opened his mouth and hooted his curses into the air. "Whoopeeee. Whoooopeee." Then he spied Lucy leaning out the window. "Up there. Up there." He directed the attention of his howling comrades to the "Indian squaw," leaning out the window. "Lookit this here? Lookit this here?"

The boys howled and stomped in the dust. For them, it had been a good day. No sooner had the last weary Osage dragged himself across the river than they'd scattered to the bluff and Indian burial grounds. Here they pawed and dug, fighting each other for scraps of pottery. "Moccasins. Old rotten moccasins," panted the middle-sized boy with the freckled nose.

"Silver earrings. Earrings," howled another. Then, the surge of their blood and animal lust as their eyes laid hold of the real discovery.

The ruffian raised the stick with its tottering burden.

Lucy Greenway stared straight at the eyeless sockets of a skull hoisted on a cottonwood stick, thrust up in her face as the boys bent and howled.

The second, a sweaty, fat boy with missing teeth, raised an even longer cottonwood stick toward the shocked woman staring at them.

"Lookit this here, Indian squaw. Lookit. This here one still got hair on it. Har, har, har."

Lucy started to whisper, "Oh my God, when will Andrew come home?" but she sagged to the pine boards beneath her, before she could utter the words.

CHAPTER FORTY

"Reasonable cash flow," Andrew concluded, leaning against the kitchen doorway of the new five-room clapboard house at the southern end of Wichita Town. "But the ferry'll be put out of business soon as Greiffenstein gets the new bridge built over the river there at Douglas next year. I want in on that venture. Plan to review it with him today."

Lucy wondered if Andrew was aware of how striking he looked in his new tan tube trousers and brown frock coat and single breasted waistcoat, with the rolled collar that matched his trousers. Andrew had tied his light-brown silk cravat the neck of his stiff high collar shirt with the pearl studs. His greying hair, barbered according to the new fashion, fell to one side and to the collar at the back, covering his well-shaped and close-fitting ears.

Lucy felt the love well up within her. *How I love him. Look what he's done in such a short time.*

With that young Frenchman, Jacques Fouquet, operating the ferry boat, and Andrew free to focus his energies in several enterprising ways, they had been able to draw up the plans for the house and build it within three months after Andrew returned from the Texas trading route.

Andrew had to take out a loan from Phenias Johnson, the loan officer at the Woodman's Bank. The 11 percent interest on the 800 dollars worried Lucy, who liked to keep her bills paid, her ledgers accurate. There had been enough pressure and change upon their arrival at this bursting Wichita Town, with its throngs of yelping cowboys and the never ending clouds of choking dust at cattle drive time.

But the best, of course, was little Alonzo, their half-blood son.

"Why, of course he's Cherokee. Lineage runs on the mother's side. You know that, Andrew," she'd teased as Andrew clasped his fine hands behind his back and leaned on to the newborn's face while the baby howled his greetings. "The son you wanted, Mr. Greenway," maid Ramona said. Her gathered wine skirt and tightly braided black hair, pinned in a fashionable Spanish style, set off her aquiline profile as she took the new son, clasping him to her bosom, cooing.

The name, Alonzo, Italian though it was, suited the happy little child well. He looked Italian with his radiant skin of the half-blood and dark eyes of his mother. Named after Alonzo Gambino, a half-blood friend of Jacob Monroe's back at the male seminary, whose father was an Italian immigrant. Lucy always liked the name. Sounded Cherokee, the rhythms. Alonzo, like the sighing of the wind in chestnuts on the Hiwassee, long ago.

"Be a Harvard professor someday," Catherine Greiffenstein said, casting her eyes on the infant for the first time.

That was something that had worried Lucy, the schools. How on earth does one educate children decently in a wild west cattle town? She and Andrew planned to give serious attention to that.

*   *   *

They both knew it was the proper thing to do, mingle with the townfolk at the Fourth of July picnic on the river west of Main, in the grove of cottonwoods and river willows, despite sand burs in your stockings and clinging to one's pants and skirt's. Grit in your shoes and slippers. Blue flies zinging at your forehead, dust whirling. Horse manure everywhere. Nevertheless, "Dress your best, Lucy. My wife is the most charming woman in Wichita Town," Andrew urged, clasping her and throwing her in a Virginia reel whirl.

She selected the pale pink muslin with the eight-yard skirt over hoops. Andrew had brought back the material on the trading venture last year, imported from Mexico. Though she was perfectly capable of making her own clothes, Andrew had insisted that seamstress Becky Coolridge, down at the lower end of Main, cut the fabric, fit and style it for her.

Lucy turned before the dark oak bureau mirror as the seven graduated flounces swished at her turn. The wide ties of the white satin bow at the right side of her small waist swept downwards to within a foot of the hem of the last tier. Lucy's small feet were encased in black leather shoes with one-inch heels.

Changed her hair style, too. Though Andrew always said it made no difference how she fixed her hair. "It always looks blooming beautiful," he reassured her.

For the picnic, she parted it in the middle. Not a streak of grey, pure black silk. She pushed it toward the temples, giving a fuller look. No plastered down spinster Charity Tiller of the seminary look. Ivory combs embedded in the thick strands at the back allowed two ebony coils to spill over her shoulders, left and right.

The dress's tight-fitting bodice thrust her breasts upwards, the high round collar encircled her throat. "Proper for a Christian woman," Lucy said, as Andrew drew up behind her kissing her on the neck.

*   *   *

Merchants and business people hosted the celebration by the river in the July heat, including "Dutch" Greiffenstein, Doc Lewellen, store owner, Lon Kertzler of the barber shop, G. M. Weeks of the lumber yard, W. C. Woodman of the bank and others, whose names Lucy had difficulty recalling, since stores and trading shops were sprouting up through the dust quicker than she had been able to keep count.

Seventeen buildings had hunched here when she and Andrew drove down into the valley. Look at it now. Hundred seventy-five, last count, folks said. Never mind the stench in the wind from the tannery on the river, with its unending supply of green buffalo hides. Lucy hoped today, at least, the wind would blow from the west, or northwest, sparing their noses.

Folks were grateful that the merchants had thought enough of the picnickers to provide them with wooden folding chairs and benches, spread in circles through the short grey-green buffalo grass and the drifting sand. To the right, by the cottonwoods, spread the long tables, heavy with crocks full of potato salad, pickles and cold puddings. Cool moisture dripped in rings around their sides.

"Sure glad the meat comes fresh from the spit and the fire," Lucy said, remembering the stench of the rotten buffalo meat across the river where even the buzzards grew discouraged trying to keep up.

They sat, Lucy and Andrew in their best. Andrew had donned his brown frock coat and brown top hat. He yawned and sighed, sinking into one of the chairs, handsome legs stretched out before him as raucous sounds of the revelers swept over them. "Get up to 95 today," Andrew said, shutting one eye, tipping back his hat as he squinted at the blazing sun.

Lucy, seated by Agnes Mead on her left, was thankful that they'd decided to pay Ramona to sit with Alonzo, sparing the infant the sting of the flies, the dirt and dust up his nose and down his throat as well as the ear-splitting yelps and beatings of the drums of the band of Arapahos, dancing for an audience on the right riverbank.

"Barbecued buffalo," hollered the greasy-aproned cooks bending over the earthen pit where the glowing coals vied with the sun radiating heat.

Buffalo. The word saddened Lucy. How long? The merciless slaughtering for miles on each side of the river—how long? For what? Dollar for a hide? Three dollars? Ride out there any day in the summer, hides spread in a four-mile square drying in the sun. Buffalo carcasses exploding in the heat. Bones blanching, grinning through the spaces between the hides.

But Lucy realized by now that was how the Greiffensteins and the Meads got rich, by the buffalo hide trade. Thousands of hunters, with their huge trading wagons packed with hides, rolled into Wichita daily. The Hayes and Brothers Purchasers poked out the cash for the hides, then the traders packed their oversized wagons in and headed for Leavenworth. Hundred twenty-five thousand dollars from one single trip.

"Got prairie chicken, too. Roasted prairie chicken," the cooks shouted, looking up. One, a Mexican with a huge down-turned mustache, glanced over at the strikingly beautiful Cherokee woman in the pink tiered dress and the ebony hair sweeping over her shoulders on either side.

Just as she glanced at the portly cook, melting in the heat and his sweat, he caught her eye, lifted a half-roasted prairie chicken on a yard-long fork, the legs dangling, neck twisting. Winking at her, he called: "Madam, how'd you like your chicken done? Or, druther have a slab of this yellow catfish?" He beamed as he returned to forking, basting and prodding.

"Another thing," she had told Andrew. "With those 20-foot seines, they're dragging the fish out of the rivers in such abundance, soon there will be none."

All one had to do was to look at the barbecue. Take your pick of roasting fish, black cat, yellow cat, white bass, carp, perch. "Old man Hollingston and his boys haul out a wagon load a day. Sell the good fish for a nickel a pound, the odd varieties for three cents at the corner of Market," Andrew'd replied. It saddened Lucy. The waste. Couldn't they see? It didn't take a brainy person to see, once more farmers settled in around the rivers, ripping open the grass with their plows, the rivers would soon slow, fill with sand and silt, choking the fish. Why, in time, probably be able to walk across the river, most anywhere.

But Lucy Drake Greenway had seen it before, agonized over it before, back in places with beautiful sounding names like New Echota, the Coosa, the Tennessee or the Hiwassee.

"Hired them Mexicans to do the barbecue. Brought in the carcasses from west of the river yesterday morning. I said they ought to have had an ice house to keep them in overnight," Doctor Allen murmured. He had seated himself beside Andrew, sporting one of those new bowler hats and a brown cravat to match.

"Terrible to have an outbreak of food poisoning." The doctor coughed and spat in the dust.

But, Andrew Greenway didn't have a queasy stomach. Not with his stint in the army. Not since the Trail of Tears.

Lucy, who had remembered it would be proper as well as a good thing to wear a straw bonnet, shifted the brim as she glanced up at her husband.

"Reminds me of a picnic on the Illinois River, long ago. I was a young seminary student then. What a difference." Her voice faced as she recalled the event on the verdant grass among the oaks and sycamores. The bashful, handsome young men, desiring to win the affections of some Cherokee maid. Jacob Bates, her half-brother. How splendid he'd looked that day, ebony hair parted in the middle, tipping his black top hat, bending his arm at the waist of his frock coat as he greeted her. Victoria Rogers too. Yes. Where was Victoria? Was she still pouring out babies for her planter husband? Wonder if she and Andrew would ever take a carriage down to the Red River someday? Thoughts took hold of her.

"Let me. Let me," cried a small boy, reaching up for the limb of a small willow to her left. Two chubby cheeked boys were attempting to pull down a lower limb in order to climb up and ride on the sapling.

Lucy smiled, as visions emerged of Victoria in her lavish pink dress, astraddle an elm sapling years ago taking flight in a perfect arc, only to alight in the Illinois.

Worked the rest of the summer in Chief Ross's store to pay for it. The wages of sin, she thought.

And, sin? Did anyone talk of sin around here? In spite of the town ordinance against carrying guns, shoot-'em-ups were not at all uncommon. Sunday? The sabbath? No liquor served on the sabbath? Who believed that?

Even at this picnic, everyone knew what sloshed around in the assortment of jars and jugs, let alone flasks slipped from pocket to mouth behind a tree trunk to fortify oneself for a spirited picnic.

And the brassy ear-splitting sounds of that band hunched in a semi-circle on the porch roof across the New York Store. Would the off-beat, the off key music never stop? Would it always fracture the ear drums, day and night? Lots of citizens wondered about that.

Wichita Town, Wichita Town. Lucy smiled amidst the hub-bub of it all. Guess I'll have to write a song about Wichita Town someday, she mused.

Then Agnes Mead clasped Lucy's arm with a white-gloved hand. "Why, I do declare. Well, I'll swan. Would you believe the nerve?"

Catherine Greiffenstein, leaned forward in her tight-fitting dress of blue Chambray gauze, a dress much better suited for a more slender woman than she. The plume on her small hat, cocked to one side, shook as she swung her heavy jaw in disbelief.

Lucy shifted her eyes towards the two sweating women Catherine pointed at.

"That one's named Ida Mae Roost," whispered Catherine, eyes rolling. Ida Mae carried a light blue parasol that matched her new style dress of matching blue, flat over the front with the fullness drawn back over a pouf formed by several frills of horsehair cushion. "Bustle," they called it. Though the skirt reached the ground in front, a small train dragged in the dust after her. Around the bustle swagged a wide band of wine colored cording with heavy fringes.

"That other woman, shorter and stouter's named Vina Napp," Catherine rasped behind her hand. Vina stepped along with a definite hip-walk in a more traditional, but showy street dress of green silk, green plisse over the silk gown and matching bonnet, faced in pink.

"How did they ever get across?" Catherine's gloved hand reached her mouth in shock. "The nerve."

"Probably came across on the ferry. Could have had a boat of their own. Doesn't take much effort to row across the Arkansas, does it?" Lucy stared at Matilda. "Actually, now the spring rains are over, most folks could wade across it, if they weren't too afraid

of the quicksand." Lucy wondered why Catherine was so astonished, but as the two strikingly attractive, well-dressed women
sauntered closer, she could see the bright red painted lips and
rouged cheek bones.

"From Delano. Across the river." Catherine gasped. "Devilish
town. Regular Sodom, Delano. God ought to smite it off the face
of the earth. Those women live above Rowdy Joe Lowe's Saloon
over there. God forbid." Catherine fanned herself.

Then Lucy had a flashback to when she was an eight-year-old
child and first saw painted-faced ladies of the night slipping into
the Cherokee camp, wending their way through the men, beckoning the young ones.

Lucy knew of the dreaded diseases, the pustules and sores outcropping on lips, and young men's eyes popping out of their heads.
Lucy realized she should have known it would be here, too. She
already knew Wichita Town was not all sweetness and purity of
fresh waters and prairie grasses, wind and white cloud. Now, these
ladies of the night risked the scorn and rebuke of proper matrons
like Catherine and Agnes.

Andrew, stretching his long legs, extending his toes in his
leather boots, glanced up at Ida Mae Roost as she peeked from
beneath the fringe of her blue parasol at his face and took note of
his dark sandpaper jaw. She closed her eyes as she nodded her
head, as if she realized he'd noticed her, a well-suited man with a
golden chain across his wescott.

Lucy didn't cringe. She pitied such women. She knew that
behind the street finery beat the sorrowing heart. These were poor
girls from the hinterlands. From the southern hills. From some
windswept sod house, where the root basket and wheat-grain-sack
collapsed in emptiness. They had been turned out to keep the rest
from starving. These girls flocked to Wichita Town with its wild
exuberance and opportunities for hope. It offered them its brassy
band, its dust and mud streets, cowboys in leather chaps with the
hair still on them, wearing sweaty, widebrimmed hats, holsters,
sagging from the iron weight of pistols, dragging at their hips.

And, oiled-haired businessmen, too, sporting smart suits from the New York Store.

May be Ida Mae and Vina would be invited to sit by a sweating cowboy, or ranch hand, or even perhaps a clerk at the bank, or merchant or a businessman. Their mouths already watering at the thought of roasted partridge or a slab of smoked white bass from the river. Men folk crossing the river to Delano Town to visit Rowdy Joe's tavern. No doubt at all.

Hadn't everybody heard, "everything goes in Wichita"? But even better, There is no gambling device known to the world that is not in full operation over in Delano Town." In Rowdy Joe's Saloon. And, the girls in the rooms above. Hadn't they heard?

* * *

Episcopalian Father John Hilton strolled through the crowd wearing an old top hat, frayed clerical collar and a black morning coat, which hung lower on the left back side than the right. His white sideburns and mustache indicated a man in his fifties. His worn morning coat and baggy pants indicated a man of scarce means.

Lucy recognized Father Hilton. "I've been wanting to talk to him about helping out in the Sunday school. All these children in Wichita. We need churches and Sunday schools," she had said to Andrew several times.

Lucy's hunger for the church, for the readings from the Gospels, the hymns, the sermons and the benedictions gripped her in a holy longing.

"In time," Catherine chimed in. "In time. You ought to see what kind of a church Father Hilton holds services in, down at the end of Waco. Stick-and-wattle. No more than seven-foot high. Buffalo skins pitched on the roof and dirt on top of that. Mercy, mercy. Enough to scare the very angels away."

Lucy had seen the hunching, stick-and-wattle building and the only way she could recognize that Christians actually worshipped there was when she and Andrew had driven by in the buggy,when Father Hilton and a short Mexican were sweating in the scalding sun trying to attach a cross, made of crooked cotton-wood sticks, to the top.

Lucy's reverie was interrupted by a comment Catherine then made. "Presbyterian minister in town, Lucy. You folks down in Tahlequah and the Indian Nation had Presbyterians, didn't you? Or, Congregationalists? Or were all those Indians Baptists?"

"Presbyterians, yes. Oh, yes. My mother was baptized. It seems so long ago." Lucy's voice faded as a wistful look spread over her face. "I belonged to the Presbyterian Church. Park Hill Presbyterian Church." Old memories pushed through her mind, tears welled in her dark eyes. Memories. A lost world? The church burned in the terrible war. Was her church letter still in her trunk?

"I hear his name is Reverend Boggs. We'll have a church rising up over Wichita Town soon, Mrs. Greenway. You'll see. Be needing someone to play the pump organ or a piano. Wouldn't that be something? A piano?" Catherine's eyes widened as she smiled.

Lucy smiled, not noticing her fingers actually moved at the mention of the word piano. She saw it again, she heard the reverberating sounds from the great instrument on the rich rug in Chief Ross's mansion, the strains of Bach's "Jesu, Priceless Treasure".

*   *   *

Above the shrieks of children chasing hoops with sticks, murmuring rose from the Cheyenne, Sioux, Wichita, Waco, Osage. Cowpokes whooped as the brass band blared. A fat cook stood in the clearing to announce: "Barbecue ready. Step up. Step up. Buffalo, fish, partridge. Fat or lean."

Andrew stood, stretched his shoulders and placed his hat back on his greying hair. "Lucy, my dear, may I have the honor of your presence at this banquet?" He bowed, then tipped his hat. They laughed. Lucy's tiered pink gown fluffed and swayed in the breeze.

"Of course, my dear—." But. Before she could finish, she nearly fell over. Who on earth was that tall lady in a spanking new style bustle dress of yellow silk, trimmed with swags of braid, saucy turban hat with white feather bobbing above her yellow hair, done in a French roll?

And the tall, lean man in a fawn-colored morning coat, brown tube trousers and matching satin waistcoat and cravat? He sported a studded walking cane and light-colored gloves too.

Who on earth?

"Why," said Agnes Mead, "Lucy, have you met the Johnsons yet? Phenias Johnson from down on the Red and his wife, Victoria? Five sons. Can you believe it, and still, a waist like hers? He's one of the new bankers in town."

Would the wonders never cease in Wichita Town? "So our paths cross again, here by the Arkansas," whispered Lucy. Yellow-haired Victoria Rogers Johnson a banker's wife? That ought to suit her just fine.

"Andrew, let's step to the board. I'm ravenous." Lucy's fingers wrapped around his arm, a new challenge lighting her eye.

CHAPTER
FORTY-ONE

"Why, Lucy Drake. Imagine," Victoria's eyes flickered and flashed over every inch of Lucy's hair, her bodice, her dress, as if she were evaluating the cost, the quality, the taste.

"Yes, Victoria. We meet again. Looks like God plans for us to be city ladies, doesn't it?" She knew it sounded silly after she'd said it, but she struggled to be cordial.

"Lady? Yes. I told Phenias it might not be possible for me to live here in Wichita, Kansas, but he assured me that this'll soon be a prestigious city, and I could actually get my dresses from New York at the New York Store. Imagine." Victoria covered her mouth with a yellow-gloved hand, picked up her fork, plunging it into the smoked breast of partridge on her plate.

Lucy'd had the consideration and brains to inquire about the five sons and that'd ended in a prolonged monologue about the rowdy little boys, Eldon, Orval, Jerel, Curtiss and Emmit. What disgusted Lucy was the way Victoria, a Cherokee seminary graduate, denied her Indian heritage. Besides, she'd never once inquired about her son, little Alonzo.

"Lucy, you're full-blood. I know you noticed how fair Phenias's and my boys are. White. Yellow-haired like me."

Victoria still considers herself a stripe above full-bloods like me. She turns her back on her own Indianness, Lucy thought. Next, she noticed Victoria's eyes widen and how she twisted her neck to stare at two muscular, bronzed Sioux young bloods, sauntering down the middle of the dusty street, wearing only buck skin breeches on account of the heat and baring swarthy biceps and pectorals. Victoria had written about such 'male swarthiness' in her school paper, long ago. It seemed clear to Lucy that Victoria married Phenias both for money and for his Anglo paleness. One way to leave the Indian behind is to merge with the Caucasian race. Presidents from Thomas Jefferson down to Johnson had believed that, hadn't they?

Guilt stabbed Lucy for judging Victoria when she too, had fallen in love and married Anglo Andrew. And, Lucy wondered Victoria, no doubt, had inherited money. The sale of their cotton lands on the Red allowed Phenias a heavy investment in the Woodman Bank. 'Loan Officer,' ran the advertisement in *The Vidette*.

Then, as they struggled to visit, two newsworthy items nearly made Lucy Greenway topple off the picnic bench, and she hadn't had time yet even to fork up a taste of the barbecued buffalo.

Phenias Johnson straightened his narrow shoulders in the fawn-colored morning coat, his thinning hair rising awkwardly in the wind. "Mr. Greenway," he'd said, "think you made the right move, taking out a loan, putting a mortgage on that 80 acres of river bottom land. Now's the time to build or add on before the price of lumber keeps on rising."

Lucy hadn't known about that. Married now for two years, she was discovering this part of Andrew, his judgments, made without her knowledge. Realizing his love for her, she held back her words. Later, they would talk. So far, they had only paid a dollar-and-a-quarter per acre for the 80 across from where their small five-room house rose up facing the Arkansas. But, Lucy guessed, by now with the boom, the land would be worth considerably more. Yet, mortgaged? Why hadn't Andrew told her? Not the Cherokee way. Not at all.

At first, only murmuring two tables down westward near the river bank. "This meat taste all right to you?" A hollow chested, well-suited clerk from the M'Knight Wines and Liquors on Main, dared to inquire of his neighbor, who wolfed down a generous well-roasted portion.

"Smoke from the barbecue," grumbled a bleary-eyed cowpoke,

"smoke from the barbecue." He forked in a blackened chunk, grease dripping down his stubbly chin.

Down eastward at another table, Lucy heard the words: "Children, stop forking the meat, it doesn't taste right. Put down your forks," a matronly mother said, breast buttons near bursting from her full bosom. "Ezra, don't you think the buffalo meat tastes funny?"

Groans. Curses. Rumbling rose from table to table. To the left, five angry cowboys lurched upward, heaving the table, the heaped plates scattered. Lucy scanned the scene in dismay.

"Buffalo meat's spoiled. Rotten." Curses caught in the air.

Andrew, who had finally forked up a portion, held his grinding jaw. His eyes stared at Lucy. Then, he turned, hawked, and spat the half chewed morsel to the sand and bruised buffalo grass below. "They're right, Lucy. Folks, the meat's tainted. Don't eat another bite."

Andrew had forked meat on many excursions and cookouts from soldiering, from trading campouts, from cowpoke chuck wagon stops. He was an authority.

"Phenias. Merciful God, save us. Phenias, will we die?" shrieked Victoria as she stood up. Lucy's head swirled and her stomach rolled, though she had only lifted a sliver to her mouth, occupied as she'd been with the prolonged and one-sided conversation with Victoria. But, it came back. A wave of nausea. Her eyes closed as she slumped off the chair like a sack of flour sliding from wall to floor. Her nostrils open to the smells and eyes to the sight of the starving People, crowded around barrels recklessly pried open, knives gouging in, retrieving the rotten pork sent by Colonel Arbuckle, on the over land trek from Fort Smith so long ago.

*   *   *

"Buffalo meat spoiled. Heave it in the river." Fist fights broke out between the sweat-drenched cooks, slick with grease from the cookfires, and the cowpunchers in denim vests over cotton pullover shirts and cowhide chaps.

Unrepeatable curses filled the air. Words, Agnes Mead and Catherine Greiffenstein rarely heard, except on chance outbreaks like that day. Lucy lay in the dust, her fabulous tiered dress flapping in the wind and sand. Andrew reached out to the table behind him, grabbing Doctor Allen's arm.

"Heave the buffalo meat in the river," yelled the crowd of the cowpokes, tipping and tossing their 10-gallon hats above a blackheaded young Osage, faces flushed from nips at the liquor jugs. They all roared as they heaved the tables of buffalo shoulder, haunch and tongue.

Respectable ladies grabbed their skirts, those without bustle trains having an easier time, as they minced and shrieked for the safety of the wooden sidewalk across the street from the melee. Water splashed as chunks of the rotten meat hit the river. Wild youth, intoxicated by the frenzied outbreak, grabbed the crocks of potato salad and lemonade. Slops splashed picnickers and revelers, as broken crock portions ricocheted through the air, followed by gobs of potato salad and slaw. Roasted buffalo legs bobbed, circled, then caught in the current before they were swept downward toward the ferry.

Ida Mae Roost and Vina Napp looked on in dismay, their luncheon and business prospects obviously ruined as broad shouldered, grinning cowboys in expensive Stetsons with rattlesnake skin bands, who'd been enjoying their company, leaped to join the fray.

"Too spoiled even for the carp," called one gangling cowpuncher, red bandanna flopping beneath a pointed chin.

But Lucy Drake Greenway, her worried husband leaning over her as Dr. Allen checked her over, missed out on the particulars of the picnic disaster. She awakened from her faint in time to hear Dr. Allen tell Andrew something she'd wanted to keep secret another whole month.

"Why, Mr. Greenway. Believe Mrs. Greenway is in the family way."

CHAPTER
FORTY-TWO

Andrew grinned as he held little Jeannette, almost two by now.

"Andrew, she takes after you." Lucy held out the child's little fingers. "Look at the nails. You have handsome hands, these are tiny repeats of yours."

She stood on tiptoe to kiss his cheek. She wore her new pale blue, tightly-fitted basque, hooked up the back. Two children now, and her waist, still small.

"Still the prettiest woman in Wichita," Andrew murmured in her ear as he kissed her neck. "It's the Cherokee blood, Lucy."

The new 10-room house on south Main sat squarely on its stone foundation like a satisfied Dutch queen, surveying a windmill on the flatlands. The expansive new two-story front, added on to the small five-room rectangle, making the shape of a "t", sported an opulent parlor, large enough for celebrations and gatherings of business friends and colleagues interested in building Wichita Town.

Ramona now served as both cook-assistant to Lucy and nurse-maid to the two children. Alonzo, going on four, needed less supervision, but Jeannette reminded Andrew of a Cherokee child let loose in the woods after being cooped up in a cabin for the winter. Here. There. Under the Duncan Phyfe mahogany sofa, with lyre ends, retrieving her rag doll, eyes sparkling, cooing the doll's name, "Dotty, Dotty."

The kitchen sported a new, wide cast-iron cooking stove. "Look at the size of that oven and the reservoir," Ramona beamed. And the kitchen windows, tall and wide, four of them.

"Get a good cross wind in here to take out the heat," Andrew bragged.

Wide walnut moldings from wood imported from Emporia. Four fireplaces—all with marble facings and mantles shipped upriver from Fort Smith. The dining room, walnut Duncan Phyfe there too. Table long enough to set for 24 people, though now collapsed for eight. China cabinet rising up on the east green brocaded wall, mirrors reflecting the pale greens and ivory of china, the blue and opalescence of expensive glassware. The cabinet, purchased at H. Bolte Furniture Parlor, which also advertised 'a full line of undertaker's goods'.

"We don't have to do everything all at once, Andrew," Lucy had cautioned him with her usual reserve. Like a team they were, not mismatched, but he more daring, willing to risk. Andrew tried to understand her caution. Her past. But, now, look how the good things rolled in? Douglas Avenue and Main Street, bustling.

Drawbacks too. The dust. Wagon loads and piles of cattle and horse dung. The flies. The stifling dust and heat when the Texas cowpokes drove thousands of longhorns on the Chisholm to Abilene. "But, it was good for the ferryboat business, wasn't it?" Andrew asked. Trailmasters, drovers with wallets well-stuffed with greenbacks, chuck wagons and service wagons all beckoned the ferryboat across to the southwestern side. But now business was practically dead. And the cattle? Andrew knew Wichita patrons agreed, "Need the drovers' money, let them drive their herds right through town." They all jealously panted for business, like stray hounds salivating at a lone rabbit.

Andrew knew from newspaper reports that upriver 14 miles, Park City officers and businessmen also vied for the reckless spending of the cowboys and drovers.

*   *   *

The next Wednesday, a bright July morning, Andrew stopped at the lumber yard where owner Weeks spouted off about the cattle drives and impending changes.

"Mr. Greenway," Weeks said. "You depend on the drives and

the drovers for your ferry business. Did you know Abilene town officials had decided that they wouldn't allow that any more cattle coming up the Chisholm from Wichita to Abilene?"

"Well, I read something about it in the *Vidette*," Andrew, who'd hadn't yet taken time to consider it seriously, replied. "Well, it's serious, Mr. Greenway, and we merchants may have to do something about it," Weeks's brow creased.

"Those drovers like Wichita night life, I wouldn't worry too much," Andrew said.

"Guess you didn't know that Park City officials maneuvered Indian Agent Shanklyn to get the railway to build a cutoff from the Chisholm Trail to Park City, loop the cattle northwestward toward Ellsworth. Load them in cattle cars there." Weeks spat in the dust. "We'll be left stranded." Andrew frowned.

"Yep. Rowdy Joe's Saloon and Vina Napp, Ida Mae Roost and the other girls were left high and dry. Your ferryboat tied to the bank." Weeks slapped a fly.

"Let's organize a posse to ride toward Texas and stop the cattle train and drovers." Andrew dug his shoe-toe in the dust and stared at Weeks. "Don't know if we could halt them at this late date," Weeks said. "I hear they're already loping northwesterly toward Ellsworth. Bypass Wichita."

"You hear what Major Shanklin did?" merchant Niles English, who had joined them, asked. "He rolled off with wagons to meet the cattle drovers near the Red River, wagons loaded with liquor, eats and goods to bribe the drovers. Yep, I bet he promised heavenly bliss in Park City, once they bypass Wichita."

* * *

Down on the Red River, Shanklin and his grinning scouts stopped near the Lawrence ranch on the Cowskin. From that point, they removed the marking stakes that pointed the drovers and their longhorn cattle train toward the wide streets of Wichita and Rowdy Joe's Saloon, among the numerous others in Delano.

Nervous cowpokes jerked up the old markers and hammered new sign posts pointing toward Park City and Ellsworth into the hard ground. "Leave them Wichita folks high and dry," Shanklin vowed.

A cowpoke on the Lawrence ranch, understanding what was happening to his business friends in Wichita, sneaked off on his pinto to spread the word about Shanklin's dastardly actions.

*　*　*

"It'll ruin my ferryboat season," Andrew groaned. Visions of payments on the mortgage soon due with that loan officer Phenias Johnson at the Woodman Bank, flashed into Andrew's mind.

"Hafta ride out and stop them," yelled merchant Niles English.

"Count me in", hollered Mike Meagher.

"Strap on my six-shooters, we'll halt the mangy rascals," J. M. Steele hawked, accompanied by frowning Jim Mead.

Off they rode, joined by the Jack-of-all-trades, Andrew Greenway. Galloping across small ditches in the prairie grass, they followed the Chisholm Trail, leading down to the Lawrence ranch near Clearwater.

They rode hard through the night until their mounts were exhausted.

"Camp here rest of the night. Get a little shut-eye. Ought to be seein' the first of the herds coming past in a few hours," English said, spreading a blanket over his saddle for a pillow.

"Sure don't want to miss them," Andrew said, bones aching from the long ride. Just as the sun cast a pinkness in the eastern sky, old Shanklin galloped through the sand, bluestem, and helter-skelter buffalo bones, ahead of a drove of bellowing longhorns, cow pokes behind, on their early jog to Park City.

"You the Wichita delegation?" Shanklin grinned, riding up to Andrew, gloating in his slick maneuvering.

"We got a bunch here that's going to stop you, Shanklin," Andrew said, holding the bridle of his horse.

"You guys too late. This cattle train on the way to Ellsworth through Park City. Better grazing. Don't have to have cattle breaking legs and necks trying to cross the Cowskin or the Arkansas."

Shanklin spat a glob of tobacco juice and wiped his mouth with the back of his hand.

"Probably right. We're too late," said Niles English standing near Andrew. "Poor season for businessmen in Wichita this year." Andrew understood, knowing Niles, too, owed money at Woodman's bank.

"Don't give up," Andrew rasped in a low voice as he mounted his horse. "Follow me. Shanklin doesn't have the last word. We'll talk to the drovers and cowpokes ourselves."

So they galloped onward another two miles, Andrew and the four horsemen, feeling like school urchins trying to manipulate their teacher into postponing an arithmetic test.

Over a grassy hill they loped, longhorns and cowpokes behind, drovers riding in the distance. Andrew's heart picked up its beat. "May be we're not too late," he said to himself.

Jim Mead dared ride straight in front of the train of longhorns snorting in the cool morning air. His mount reared. "Halt. Halt. We've got news for you." Mead waved his hat.

Drover Wily Pritchard, riding up on a black stallion, scowled as though he was ready to brush horseflies from his cheek.

"Halt the train. Whoa, whoa," Andrew yelled, nudging his roan forward.

"Shanklin's given you bad advice," Jim Mead called. "Old trail over the Arkansas to Wichita is the better one. You ought to know we've been treating the drovers and cowpokes right in Delano and Wichita." Andrew, sizing up the situation, wondered: Are we too late? Would they be overrun by the stampeding longhorns?

"You'll miss paradise," called Mike Meger. Andrew knew he was referring to the good times the cowboys seemed to have with ladies like Vina and Ida Mae, all the music, drinking and reveling in Delano in the late hours of the night.

Andrew was convinced that Drover Pritchard knew the five meant business, since they dared to ride right into a moving cattle train and risk getting shot.

"We've been told all the grass is burnt over there toward the

Arkansas. Besides, might have cattle breaking their necks crossing the rivers," Pritchard replied.

Just then, old Shanklin who'd smugly assured himself he'd had the business bagged for Ellsworth and Park City, rode closer to the cluster from Wichita. Then, turning, he called to the cow-pokes behind him. "Old trail is closed. Ride east toward Wichita, you going to get lost. Cattle break their necks. Follow me. Be in Park City come evening." But Shanklin seemed worried as the Wichita five honed in closer to the drovers.

They leaned in to tell the drovers the glories of Wichita and Delano. Hats rose into the air accompanied by "Hurrah, hurrah," and, "Well, don't that beat all, in Delano? All night long, too?"

Andrew grinned as Jim Mead rode closer to share the names of certain ladies and passed greenbacks and promises of libations for thirsty throats, come evening.

Pleased to try and alter the course of the train so his business could succeed, Andrew felt pangs of guilt as he heard the names passed on to the leering cow pokes, Ida Mae Roost and Vina Napp. "I won't tell Lucy about this," he muttered. Jim Mead continued. "Girls there have races from Rowdy Joe's to the river, no clothes on, either." Mead snickered and said, "You cowpokes can bet on em, which one reaches the river first."

Waves of laughter and hoots of abandon rolled down the line of rowdy cowpokes. Drover Prichard gave a wave and command. The great herd began to move again, turning, this time toward Wichita, leaving Major Shanklin and his men forlorn on the prairie with winds whipping their bandannas, outdone by the Wichita mavericks and ladies with names like Ida Mae Roost and Vina Napp.

Andrew Greenway and his colleagues disappeared over the prairie like a coyote scurrying to his den before daybreak.

"They'll be at my ferry before I get there," he murmured, grin on his face.

*   *   *

The dusty cattle rumbled onward, fording the river just below the ferry. Only one calf broke its neck while attempting to leap up the river bank. Grinning Jim Mead happily forked over 15 dollars to the drovers in payment for the unfortunate calf.

And, the Delano bands lined up and sounds of clarinet and trumpet and drum resounded over the sand dunes of the Arkansas River. Then, Ida Mae Roost and Vina Napp sallied out on the porch to lean over the railing at Rowdy Joe's Saloon, watching the lusty cowboys, hooting, cursing, hollering, as they rode into paradise, visible only now and then through the rolling dust.

CHAPTER
FORTY-THREE

Late afternoon, the 11,000 longhorns bellowed into Wichita and the money rolled in. Andrew tied his horse to the hitching post by the river and scurried to the ferry to lend a shoulder to his Frenchman, Jacques Fouquet. Their backs strained and ached as they poled the ferry back and forth with its loads of riotous drovers and cowpokes on pawing mounts, asking, "Where is Rowdy Joe's?"

By the time the brassy sun slid into a cloud bank westward, Andrew's pocket bulged with greenbacks and silver coins. Spreading the cash out on the desk in his ferry shack by the river, he counted. "Seven hundred dollars. All in one afternoon. Enough for the payment on the Woodman loan." He congratulated himself.

Leaning back in the second-hand oak chair, he glanced out over the rippling waters as the shadows from the west bank lengthened. He thought of Lucy. Lucy, Lucy, petite Lucy. Soul of an angel. Whatever her past sufferings, they had not left her soured and bitter. The children, Alonzo—handsome, inquisitive mind. Jeanette—eyes of an Egyptian beauty, same reserve and grace as Lucy. Handsome children, half-bloods. Take them back to Tahlequah next summer. Visit the Nation, acquaint them with Lucy's heritage.

Andrew, eyeing his pile of cash, felt a ripple of exuberance warm him as he thought of the handsome suit he'd buy for Alonzo tomorrow and the finest dresses for Lucy and Jeanette at the New York Store.

And, if the river didn't lower and the drovers kept riding up, cash enough for a grand piano for Lucy.

*   *   *

While Andrew ferried the drovers, Lucy, back home, had a visitor from the Woodman Bank. Loan officer, to be exact. Mr. Phenias Johnson, sporting oval wire-rimmed glasses on his thin nose, coughing, cleared his throat and asked for "Mr. Greenway."

"You have papers for Mr. Greenway?" Lucy dared to inquire.

"Mrs. Greenway, I regret to inform you that the payment on your property loan is now three weeks overdue and a rather high interest penalty will be charged." Mr. Johnson looked down his thin nose. He left his paper and card, requesting that Mr. Greenway report to the loan officer of the bank next day.

The thing Lucy hated most about it was not Andrew's oversight, he'd have the money, she hadn't doubted that. But, she had to wonder—did Phenias Johnson tell Victoria about the oversight?

"That's just like full-bloods. Irresponsible. Lazy. Never collect, once you loan them money." She could hear Victoria's shrill voice. A stab of guilt hit her as she realized she was making a judgment against Victoria. "Forgive me, Lord," she prayed silently.

*   *   *

That night, Lucy waited with Alonzo and Jeanette at the table, set with four plates sporting tiny rose buds, squat pale blue tumblers in front.

"Mama, why doesn't Papa come?" they cried.

"Your father's had a very busy day, children. All those wild cattle galloping across the river ford and tumbling through the streets. He's very, very busy. Let's eat. Ramona, bring on the meatloaf and limas, let's get the children started with their supper."

That afternoon, the children had stood on the porch, glowing with excitement as the thousands of bellowing cattle lurched at the west riverbank, tossed their heads, raised their tails, horning each other into the shallows, swimming now and then, until they reached the eastern bank, heaving themselves upwards, blowing, belching, lowing. Merchants stood by grinning in anticipation of cash. Stragglers and shoppers fled from the streets to doorways to save their hides from the stampede.

Boiling clouds of lung-choking dust billowed and drifted in the wind. "Ramona, close all the windows," Lucy called, as she raced to slam the doors shut. "Mercy, mercy. We'll have to clean this house from top to bottom when it settles.

"Children, come in off the porch. Too much dust." And, she was concerned, the children inhaling the billowing clouds. She worried, too, about Andrew and his lungs, his propensity for pneumonia, breathing the heavy dust.

Before she went back indoors, Lucy overheard the street talk.

"Tomorrow the dung wagons," Tajo, a short Mexican in a ragged sombrero, yelled as he walked up, Main in front of the Greenway house, scurrying to stay ahead of a longhorn, tilting its horn at the straggler.

"And the gut wagon after that," replied Gustel Steiner, a stout German woman who worked at Pertice Lone's laundry, catching up with him.

* * *

A part of Andrew broke loose when the last of the cattle drovers' horses leaped off the ferryboat. A part that nudged him down the pulsing Main Street, light in his eye. It was the noise of it. The pandemonium. The circus-like frenzy. Not three rings, but six, seven, a dozen. Saloon doors flailed open, braced back for crowds of thirsty revelers who'd soon spill out onto the board walks.

Ida Mae and Vina and 13 other *ladies* slipped on their best dresses for social occasions such as this.

Circus-like noises, too. Brass bands whooped it up, hackers yelling and cursing. The ladies, now on the streets, laughed and called. Dogs yelped, drovers cracked whips, while here and there pistols shot recklessly into the air, accompanied by blood-curdling yells. The hollering cow-pokes strutted, many with bowie knives swinging, or a brace of Navy revolvers sagging over the hips, swinging to the jangling of spurs with bells on their heavy cavalry boots below stinking rawhide breeches with the hair still on them.

"Just for a half-hour or so. Tired as I am. A little drink for old time's sake." A part of Andrew did miss soldierly comradeship. After all, didn't he have a life of the roving plainsman, the reckless gambling soldier, the tongue-in-cheek mischievous life of the trader long before he was tied down in a marriage?

Weren't they all supporting the ballooning new Wichita, the cowpokes at the bar-rails, the bartenders, hands covered with beer-foam, slinging the mugs down the planks, weaving through the crowds, shoulders groaning from twenty mugs on a tray? The hard liquor too, glistening in crystal bottles, orange, amber, clear, spilling out into the crystal jiggers.

Yellow lamplight cast even more friendly air as the celebration took form. Here a group, there a group, trail masters shouldered through the noisy crowds, fresh from the barber shops where they'd splurged 75 cents for a shave and bath—hair oiled and perfumed by macasar oil, beards trimmed. Suit merchants peeked through saloon windows to size up the crowds while they anticipated reducing their stocks next morning.

Then, one of the Wichita policemen, Wyatt Earp, who doubled as a gaming room operator, come night, tilted his sandpaper chin and yelled, "Gambling. Poker and keno here. In here. Gather in. Get the gaming started."

Lanky cowboys leaned and shoved. Chairs overturned as they fought for the best seats. The ladies grew bolder, circling around, placing hot palms on broad shoulders.

"You can play keno and drink, too. Girls," yelled Wyatt, "keep the drinks coming in."

Andrew, hearing it all, followed in, seating himself where the yellow light shone on his playing card and tokens. Win a little surplus for Lucy. Buy her a surprise souvenir to remember the good fortune of the day, he thought. He cleared his throat that had grown hoarse from straining and the dust. Win enough, see if I can find that piano, tomorrow.

*   *   *

Lucy didn't hear Andrew when he first entered the bedroom. She remembered hearing the clock downstairs strike two, minutes ago. Guess she'd dozed off again.

Andrew slid in beside her.

"Oh, Andrew. I worried about you. Where have you been?" Lucy sat up.

"We'll talk about it in the morning, my love. In the morning." His throat, raspy.

How tired his voice sounds, she thought. Yes. In the morning. Andrew was a good man. He had a straining day. Back-breaking work, poling that ferry. They'd count and deposit the money in the morning, Lucy agreed.

"He is my love," she reminded herself, but, a part of Lucy Greenway worried about his silence. Just where had Andrew been? What delayed him so? She lay down, reaching for one of those angular, well-shaped hands she loved to clasp, now blistered and callused from the ferry pole. It throbbed warmly, yielding with love to her hand.

* * *

The mouth-watering smells of bacon frying downstairs met Andrew's nostrils as he awakened. Rousing himself, he was aware that his throat was sore and that he was feverish. "Feel like a ragged, worn-out hound," he breathed to himself as he reached for the pitcher to pour water into the bowl and begin his shave.

Lucy, glowing in a red calico dress with tight bodice, kissed him as he strolled into the kitchen. After the breakfast of Ramona's hot biscuits, the eggs, sunny-side-up, as he liked them, and the crisp bacon, all washed down by black chicory-laced coffee, Andrew stood up. He walked to the side bedroom which he used as his office, seated himself on a swivel chair, elbow on the desk, head in hand.

"You're worn out, Andrew. The long ride yesterday. You should have seen the children, how they danced and laughed at the cattle rumbling up that riverbank, lurching down the street."

She reached for his blistered palm, "Ramona, look for the salve, have to do something about Andrew's broken blisters."

Lucy could sense Andrew was struggling as if he wanted to talk, but had trouble beginning.

"Andrew, the bank." Lucy began. "I mean, Victoria's husband, Phenias Johnson, the loan officer at Woodman's, paid me a visit yesterday."

She handed him the note from Johnson.

"You already know about this. Cash now to take care of it today, Andrew."

Realizing that he might be ill or too fatigued to bother, she offered to go down town for him. "My darling, I can take care of the loan payment. You'll need to give me the amount."

Andrew's green-grey eyes were red and blood-streaked. His throat on fire and perspiration beaded on his forehead.

"Lucy. Lucy." He lifted his hand. "Lucy, I'm ashamed to tell you this. Guess I got a little carried away last night. Carried away." He looked out the window as the wind caught the lower branches of the cottonwood they had planted. Andrew sagged as if he felt an emptiness inside, even greater than the expanse of bluestem sweeping eastward.

It hit her like a stone dropped in a clothespin bag around the waist. The money? Where had he been? Had it been enough? But, the ferry scarcely halted yesterday, back and forth, back and forth. Fouquet, gasping for breath. Cattle drovers shelling out the fee. What happened?

Then, she knew.

"Lucy. I got in late last night. Didn't want to waken you. Got carried away in the Keno Corner Gaming Room last night. Don't know what came over me. Tired. A drink or two. It all seemed so easy. Gambled a lot in the army. Pastime for cowboys on the plains. For the traders, too." His voice was a whisper. His fever mounted.

"You lost the money?" Lucy wished she hadn't asked. He could make it up. The drovers were still cursing and stomping at the river bank. Today. Tomorrow. Why, she could pole the ferry herself. She knew about bridges, or no bridges, fords, the wiles of Long Man. "Seven hundred dollars. Vanished like that." He snapped his fingers. Andrew leaned back, his broad shoulders covered by the fresh-laundered broadcloth shirt Lucy herself ironed for him, smelling of the sweetness of grass and sunshine.

"Ahead, first couple of hours. Then, something changed. No matter how I played, I was on the down hill drag." His voice faded.

Lucy knew he felt shamed like a scolded hound dog. She'd not make it worse. The day was early. They both could hear the bellowing cattle still crossing the river. The run wasn't over. More money to be made. Put on her straw hat and get out there herself and pole the ferry with Fouquet. Put Andrew to bed upstairs. After all, he didn't gamble every day. Hurry the money over to Victoria's gloating husband by evening, or at the very latest, in the morning.

Lucy felt his head. "Andrew, you've got a fever. The trail ride in the night. Sleeping on the ground. The strain of the poling and . . .," Lucy caught herself. "I'm putting you back to bed."

"I'll work awhile with Jacques, Lucy. If I see it's too much, I'll come in at ten o'clock. Give it a try."

Before she could contradict him and whisk him upstairs to bed, Jacques Fouquet stepped into the room, his little French beret, which he wore summer or winter, in his hands. He bowed politely.

"Mr. Greenway. Mrs. Greenway," He nodded again, politely, "Forgive me for barging in, but I knew you'd want to know, sir."

"Want to know? Know what?" Lucy's heart missed a beat.

"Mr. Greenway, the ferry's hung up on a sandbar. Water's too low. Drovers, cowpokes, chuck wagons, whole business, all going to have to make it across the shallows. That ferry's not going to move until we have rain. And, I mean a considerable rain."

And the cash, gambled away in one fleeting night. The note past due, interest doubling daily. Lucy could already see Victoria's gloating face.

CHAPTER FORTY-FOUR

Lucy flicked the whip over the rump of the draft-horse team as the wagon rolled through the tall bluestem, west of the Arkansas.

"Oh, Mama, isn't it fun?" Alonzo, eyes bursting with pride at his mother's driving skill, chuckled and clasped his sister Jeanette's hand.

The children rocked and laughed, both with straw hats firmly tied under their chins.

"Papa will miss us, won't he, Mama? He will be all right. Ramona will take good care of him?"

"Yes, Alonzo. He is in good hands." Lucy flicked the reins as the boxwagon lurched. Large box, strong horses. If she was going to sell buffalo bones at Hayes and Brothers, she'd bring in a toppling load. Five dollars a ton for heads and ribs. Shins and shoulder blades, 10 dollars a ton. Horns, 30 dollars a set. Ship them off to Philadelphia to the fertilizer factories. Horns for the umbrellas, fans, and pipes. Lucy decided three trips out on the wind swept bluestem prairie and she'd have Mr. Phenias Johnson's payment.

* * *

"Don't do it, Lucy. I'll find some way. We can sell something," Andrew had cautioned. Then his face had wrenched in pain as he moved his leg on the firm mattress. "I'll try to be like you, Lucy, take this added flailing of life without grumbling and complaint. Shouldn't have happened, breaking a leg."

Lucy knew that the guilt over his gambling losses was enough to keep his spirit groaning for another week. He'd rushed out, in spite of his sore throat and fever and Lucy's worry, to help Jacques pole the ferry off the sandbar, if they could manage it. Tie it up on the eastern bank by the landing. Secure it until the rains came.

When they'd reached the ferry in the little skiff, they had been greeted by Ramona's 10-year-old, Miguel, waving a happy "hello".

"I waded out part way, Mr. Greenway. Had to swim about 10 feet to get here." He beamed in the pride of his achievement.

Andrew hadn't minded. Who could keep the boys out of the river? Folks worried about quicksand, but that was up where the rivers joined just below Rowdy Joe's Saloon.

Andrew and Fouquet had struggled. They poled. They perspired. Andrew's head had begun to swirl in circles. He knew he was ill and would have to go home to bed.

"We'll make it, Mr. Greenway. Push, Jaques, push." Miguel had even grabbed a pole to help.

They dislodged the ferry and it zigzagged in the shallow water toward the eastern shore. But when it was about six feet from the bank, Miguel, wanting to show his prowess, leaped into the water, attempting to wade and jump to shore. He miscalculated the weight and speed of the ferry. Andrew saw that the boat was in danger of smashing the lad against the landing.

"Miguel, out of the way." Andrew threw down his pole, leaping in ahead of the zigzagging ferry.

Fortunately, he was able to grab Miguel by the britches and heave him up on the sand out of the way, but before he could get his own leg up out of the water, the boat hit with a sickening crunch.

"Bad break, Andrew Greenway. Bad break. Mrs. Greenway, more plaster," Doctor Allen ordered while he placed a splint on the throbbing leg, struggling in the heat to smear on the plaster. "Going to be laid up at least three months, break like that," he told Andrew.

*   *   *

"Your father'll be fine." Lucy assured the children. She left the *Vidette* on the stand by his bed along with a copy of *Pilgrim's Progress* and Mrs. Stowe's *Uncle Tom's Cabin*. Ramona had promised Andrew an appetizing lunch of buffalo roast, onions heaped around it, mashed potatoes and gravy, and for a vegetable, the tasty green beans.

Lucy surveyed the opening plains beyond the river. The sweet aroma of the grasses invigorated her. The touch of the morning winds cooled her brow. It even refreshes one's spirit, she thought. Blue, blue, blue skies and drifting white clouds. Lucy felt free and clean from the dust, the manure, the upshot houses and privies, the rowdy saloons, the street garbage, boxes, bags and trash and stinking-rot-smell of drying buffalo skins along the board walks. Clean. Free.

She knew too, that pain lurked here on the prairie, the pain Indians felt at the buffalo slaughter. The crest-fallen Plains People, shoved onward, the very fabric of their lives torn from beneath them. Bones, the tokens of the pain, now lay hidden by the four-foot bluestem and wild flowers. Lucy knew, if she listened, she could hear the sorrow in the wind.

"Will we see some Pawnee Indians, Mama?" Asked Alonzo, black eyes shiny with anticipation.

"It is possible, my son. Possible." Lucy didn't think they'd have any trouble with Plains Indians. Not now, since the government built the forts westward and sent out the militia to corral them. Pain stabbed at her heart as old memories crowded in. Memories of land stealing, the lies of government officials, the ignored treaties. For a few minutes, she saw herself on the Coosa River back near New Echota. How was it now, New Echota? The Academy? The Supreme Court building? The churches? Burned? Torn down? Who lived there now? Would their own house still be standing? The longings flooded her soul like the sudden burst of mid-morning wind. It was as if their howling carried ancient voices of the great chiefs, Chief Tecumseh, Chief Hicks, Chief Ridge, Chief Ross. Could their stentorian voices still be circling in the wind? "The Mother of the Nation has forsaken you because all her bones are being broken through the grinding." Words as moving as the great Hebrew prophets, Isaiah and Jeremiah. The wind sighed, catching the brim of her sunbonnet. Lucy knew that somehow it was all mysteriously connected, the past, the present. The pains and the joys. The suffering and the healing. Long ago, The People understood that the Above Beings wove all the strands together, for they, great weavers of the universe, knew everything. They loved The People . Lucy realized she was caught in the prelude to prayer and worship. Oh, when will there be a congregation of Christians in Wichita, she pondered.

No, I'm not a Plains Indian, she thought. Lucy realized that Indianness was woven through every warp and woof of her being. When I get back from bone loading, I will talk to Andrew about taking the children down to the Nation. I'll show them where we worshipped, she thought. Her heart picked up a beat. Someone said that a new Presbyterian minister was in town planning meetings in that new Eagle Block. Could it be?

Bones at last, white as sepulchers. Black-eyed Susans poked their heads through eyes of skulls. Clumps of milkweed in purple bloom nodded in the wind as if to shake off the sulfur butterflies.

"Mama, Mama, throw it in the wagon." Little Jeanette, her white pinafore catching in the wind, her Egyptian eyes wide in excitement, handed a rib to Lucy.

The pain seared through Lucy's chest. The bones. The death of the buffalo, their livelihood, now shoved westward. The faces of the Cheyenne, the Sioux, the Pawnee, corralled, the United States government handing out rancid allotments.

Lucy bent over, her orange calico dress billowing. She heaved the bleached buffalo head, surprised at the weight of the skull. "Plunk. Plunk. Rattle." The bones hit the wagon floor and sides.

"Oh, Mama, isn't this fun?" Alonzo raced to grab a huge shoulder bone, not realizing he'd need help to get it in the wagon.

Bleached bones flew and bounced on the wagon floor. Little Jeanette hollered and tottered in the heavy bluestem chasing a swallowtail butterfly. "Mama, isn't he beautiful?"

"Yes, child, so beautiful." Lucy's back ached. She stopped, wiped perspiration from her brow with the back of her arm. Beautiful. All of it beautiful. Except the bones. Lucy acknowledged she was a child of the *Trail of Tears,* who knew of bleached bones and graves, and mud and roiling waters, of cholera and dead things. But, life was like this prairie, wasn't it? In spite of the *Trail,* in spite of the starvation, the death, the wailing at the burials, always, always, the new and beautiful rose up through it all, like the clump of yellow coreopsis at her feet. Her mind drifted.

Then her eye caught the purple cornflower nodding between a blanched leg-bone and a rib. Life and death. Who could unravel the mystery of it? Who was that Old Testament prophet who wrote: "thigh bone connected to the hip bone . . ."?

By noon, the wagon was more than half full. Lucy took out one of the two-gallon jugs, poured the water into a pail to water her horses who had stood so patiently in the sun.

"Now we'll eat, children. A picnic."

They sat down in the shade of the wagon, unwrapping the brown-crusted bread Ramona had baked. Lucy cut three large slices of yellow cheese. "Don't want to take ham sandwiches out on the prairie on a scorching day like this. Remember the Fourth of July Picnic?" Ramona had said. Who in these parts could ever forget the picnic? "Could take smoked fish or beef, but that'd make the children too thirsty," added Ramona.

They wolfed down the salted and peppered hard-boiled eggs, even more delicious eaten in the fresh outdoors. Big bites of Lucy's famous juicy dill pickles followed. "We ought to do it more, Mama." Little Alonzo beamed.

"Tomorrow. Tomorrow, my children. We'll make at least three trips out here."

Lucy kept her eye to the western sky now and then. Dry period, but one never knew just when a prairie storm might sweep up threateningly, like it did when she was a bride and first rolled across Kansas prairies. The hail. The drenching rain. Lightning and thunder crashes, and Andrew's near fatal illness.

*   *   *

Jeanette and Alonzo, straw hats askew, held to the edges of the wagon seat, beaming, as their mother eased the horses down the slope into the sandy, near-dry Arkansas.

"Giddyup, ho there." Lucy slapped the reins, but the horses picked their way carefully. The bone wagon rattled and lurched at first, then settled into an easy swinging roll into the shallows. "Giddyup." Lucy, glad for a safe crossing, halted the team. "Children, run on down home now. Papa's waiting for you. He'll be so glad to hear your stories. I'll be there soon as I dump these bones at Hayes."

The children slid down out of the high wagon, bare feet flying as they hit the dust, scurrying toward home, Papa, Ramona, and supper.

Fortunately, there was only one other wagon unloading, and nearly finished when Lucy drove up. Nab McGuire, in charge of bone unloading, looked up at Lucy.

"Why, Mrs. Greenway. Fancy seeing you drive in. Well, yes, Mr. Greenway is laid up, ain't he? Too bad about him breaking his leg. Pull right up, I'll get Wapi and Vito right on your load."

The Arapaho lad and the Italian teenager took over, heaving the bones by the brick wall. Three piles, heads and ribs, shoulderblades and shins, and, to Lucy's delight three perfect sets of buffalo horns.

Lucy helped herself to a drink from the dipper by the pump, then sat on a cottonwood stump in the shade of the quick growing tree-of-paradise which'd shot up by the wall.

She wiped her brow. Hot now. Evening air heavy. She knew her dress was drenched in the back. She wiped the perspiration from her forehead with her arm.

"Why, Mrs. Greenway, you got a right good supplement here to the ferry, seeing it's grounded this dry spell.

Looks like with them horns, good sets, all three, and them other bones it's going to come out at 95 dollars."

"Ninety-five-dollars?" Lucy smiled, pleased.

"I'll have a load in here tomorrow and day after, if it doesn't rain, Mr. McGuire." She pocketed the bills, tired but happy. A good day. A fine day with the children on the prairie. She hoped Andrew would understand just what it meant to her and the children, spending the day on the prairie. Even more important than the money. Lucy, in spite of the tiredness, felt lighter already.

But then, a vision of Victoria and her loan officer husband, Phenias, crossed her mind. She cleared her throat, one hand in a dress pocket holding the bills. "I'll have enough money to stave off any foreclosure on our house by the end of the week." Fatigued as she was, she felt the smile spread across her face.

After dropping the wagon and team at the livery, she picked her way down the board sidewalk, southward towards home.

* * *

Late afternoon strollers on their way to the saloon or general store wended their away around trash and crates stacked near Schackley's Saloon. Two well-dressed women were approaching. The older one with the closed parasol, which she used as a walking cane as she waddled up town towards Lucy Greenway, nodded her head, mumbling to the younger one.

Then it hit Lucy, how she must look, hair, wet from sweat, hanging out from under her sunbonnet, which itself was bent out of shape by the whipping afternoon winds. Sweat staining her dress front and back. Feet in work brogues, she only wore in the garden and now, two well-dressed women approaching. " Victoria Johnson and her mother-in-law, Ophelia Johnson? Is it?" she whispered to herself.

She recognized them. The old lady in a walking costume of purple velvet plisse over pale blue silk. A black velvet bonnet, faced with violet ribbon, lifted her head, nodding and teetering, as she picked her way up town through the trash on the walk. Lucy could see Victoria in a sweeping white, worked muslin dress over a fashionable hoop-skirt, pointing and chatting like a magpie. Out for an evening stroll, maybe dinner at The Occidental, thought Lucy.

What should I do? Thoughts circled. Turn, go back? Cross the street and dash into the hardware?

There they were, Victoria, lifting her powdered chin, her bright blue eyes, cold as a chunk from Tobler's ice-house. The old lady thumped with her parasol.

Lucy had to face them, face streaked with the dust and sand of the river bank. Dress spotted and drenched, bonnet sagging over one eye. I smell of horses, too.

Thump, thump, went the old lady's parasol-cane.

"Good evening, Victoria and Mrs. Johnson? Mrs. Ophelia Johnson from Fort Smith, isn't it?" Her voice hadn't failed as she spoke first.

"Why, Lucy, imagine." Victoria eyed Lucy up and down, as if glad she had confronted her in compromised attire. "Mother Johnson, this is Lucy Drake, who used to live in the woods with the full-bloods north of Tahlequah."

Lucy looked right at Victoria's cold eyes, glazed in 'better-than-you' triumph. No "Mrs. Greenway". No "This is school teacher Mrs. Lucy Greenway." "And," Victoria continued, goading, "I do believe Mr. Johnson paid a second business visit to your husband today. He runs the ferry, doesn't he?"

She knows we're behind on the loan. Phenias told her, Lucy thought to herself, raising one hand to tilt back the bent sunbonnet brim.

The old lady clutched Victoria's arm with her purple gloved hand, eyes watery, mouth set in a down-turned half-circle, glaring at the full-blood Indian woman in a sorry dress, who dared approach her on this sidewalk. Lucy could do nothing about her face, stained and dirty. The couple stared at her dress. Victoria had always grumbled about careless full-bloods. She used to say, "Can't make a silk purse out of a sow's ear." Lucy stood still until she realized that someone had to step back so that they could pass on the narrow board walk. Victoria stared ahead. The old woman pounded with her closed umbrella on the left edge of the sidewalk.

Lucy realized it meant, "Over there. We're not moving for a

dirty full-blood Indian woman. Step off the walk."

It was only a moment, the terrible humiliation of it, but it seemed an eternity. Time stood still and in only a second as the degradation upon her people by the hand of whites, seized her. And, Victoria, one-sixteenth Cherokee, and a female seminary graduate, too.

What shall I do? Shall I refuse to budge? Lucy seemed caught in molasses.

"If thine enemy hunger, feed him . . .and whosoever shall compel thee to go a mile, go with him twain." The words of Jesus in St. Matthew coursed through her soul. Could she even move her feet? A hound dog raced by in the dusty street, unaware of the spiritual and psychological warfare between the two opulently dressed Wichita ladies and a badly soiled, small Cherokee woman.

Lucy Greenway, who once stretched forth her delicate hands to give a concert on the nine-foot grand at the Murrell plantation at Tahlequah for the seminary social, stepped off the rough boards. Her weary feet sank near the pile of stinking horse manure as the flies circled her feet. "Go with him twain. Go with him twain."

She had done it. Lucy Greenway didn't look back at banker Phenias Johnson's proud wife, in her fitted muslin, nor at the stony-faced old woman, thumping along with her cane, grumbling about Wichita Town and the dirty Indians.

CHAPTER FORTY-FIVE

After her bath that night and once the children were sound asleep from the exhausting day, Lucy reclined, back against a fluffy goosedown pillow beside Andrew, propped up by his pillow, feet outstretched, protecting his leg. She tried to hide the blisters on her hand from his eyes.

Andrew, amazed at Lucy's strength and will, smiled, though the guilt of his gambling sins still lingered. He knew Lucy didn't want him to feel shamefaced and hang-dog. Another thing, he thought, she never seems to judge others or say unkind things about them. He leaned to kiss her cheek, now touched by her rosiness from the exposure to sun and wind.

"It was invigorating. So refreshing. I'd forgotten how it could be out there. Nothing, but endless grasses waving in the wind. Blue skies. Floating clouds. I wish the flowers could have lasted until Jeanette brought them to you." Lucy returned his kiss, then grabbed his hand.

The grandfather clock, downstairs, struck nine and the full moon cast a silver light into the bedroom from the east window. Through both wide-open windows, a refreshing breeze blew over the smiling couple.

"You had a caller today, Lucy. Too bad you weren't here."

"Really?" Who could it be? New neighbor? Catherine Greiffenstein hadn't been down since they enlarged the house. "Was it Agnes Mead?"

"A soulful-looking man named Wilburforce Boggs."

Andrew smiled, spilling out the name. "Heavy name. Got to

back up and gather speed to keep your tongue from tangling when
you say it. Presbyterian minister. I knew you'd like to have been
here. Some ideas about starting a congregation."

At last. A minister. Presbyterian? Methodist? Moravian? What
matter. The gospel. The precious "good news", The People had
responded to with eagerness back in Tennessee and Georgia. The
solemn services at the seminary. The august Reverend Bushyhead.
Oh, where was Eliza? Thoughts rolled through Lucy's head as the
memories engulfed her, her dark eyes staring out the western window.

"Why, Andrew. Too bad I wasn't here. What did he have to
say?" She turned, looking into his grey-green eyes.

"Well, he said he'd heard from the Greiffensteins that there
was a full-blood Cherokee woman living in this dusty outpost who
was a Christian. Presbyterian, to boot. Heard that you were a female seminary graduate."

Andrew smiled, tightening his hold on her blistered palm.

The words 'female seminary graduate' seemed unreal. She had
a fleeting vision of herself and Eliza standing, shoving back the
weeds and elderberries, looking through the spider-webbed windows of the closed seminary, floors sagging from heavy Civil War
artillery. A world long gone, with its stimulation of the intellect
through Greek classics, philosophy, art, music, religion.

And her world now? This burgeoning upheaval of stones and
boards splitting the air with the riotous cries of Wichita Town.
The Indian whoops, drunken yells of the cow-pokes and reveling
in the all-night saloons? Ida Mae and Vina and Rowdy Joe. Buffalo hides and bones. The lumbering, bellowing longhorns stampeding in the streets. Skulls of the dead thrust on crude sticks in
her face. A dried-up river. Wind, wind, wind, lonesome wind.
Lucy felt tears creep to the corners of her eyes and course down her
cheeks.

"Didn't he ask you about the church? Andrew, did he say anything to you?"

An uneasiness crept over Andrew at these words.

"Yes, he asked me about my religion. Wanted to know if I'd been baptized. Courteous. No intrusions. Like I said, he was a soulful-looking man, not at all given to pushiness."

"What'd you tell him?"

"Why, I said I'd been raised in Kentucky hills by country Baptists, but that I never joined the church. Not that I don't believe, Lucy. You know that. My blessed mother was a praying woman, a fine Christian."

Lucy knew that. She sensed it, Andrew's belief. In spite of his disastrous evening at Keno Corner, she wouldn't have married him had she not discovered that he was indeed, an honorable man. A good man. Just look how he treats the children and Jacques. Businessmen of the town look up to Andrew Greenway. Yes. She wouldn't be pushy either. Town council talking about naming a new street after him. Think of it. "Greenway Avenue." She smiled.

They settled down on the goosedown pillows, turning out the lamp as they drifted off to sleep—Lucy, a new glowing in her heart. A church? In Wichita? At last. Will it have a piano or organ? Will they have me, a full-blood, as a member? The thoughts came as her tired body eased into sleep.

* * *

It was even more fun next day out on the prairie. Only their laughter, their dancing and abandon in the wind kept them from being overcome by loneliness in the vastness of the sea of grass and billowing clouds in a sky dotted now and then by eagles, meadowlarks, and pheasants. They howled too, when they stepped too close to a prairie chicken's nest and had to contend with the feisty little mother hen, feigning a broken wing, as she clucked and stretched herself to drag them away from her nest.

The wonder of it. The extravagance of love between mother and children. Lucy stopped to look at them. Alonzo, beaming and staggering, arms clasped around an extra-long blanched rib. Jeanette, hopping, dashing here and there after a black-and-yellow swallowtail butterfly, dislodged from the heavy clump of orange butterfly-bush.

"Wouldn't Papa like it? Being here. I wish he could come out here with us," said Alonzo, lifting his smiling face to his mother, who studied a massive skull twenty feet away.

"Oh, he promised, children. Last night. I made him promise to come with us. When his leg heals. All the way out to the Ninnescah River. He promised."

Lucy kept her eye on the bank of clouds that'd clustered on the far western horizon. Weren't there when we came out here. Storm can whip up almost without notice. She glanced down, glad that today was cooler.

"Thud. Bang. Whop." The bones rose in a heap in the wagon, as the patient horses grazed and snorted.

"Mama, look, horses. Riders." Alonzo, dropping a jaw-bone still laden with ivory teeth, pointed southwesterly.

Lucy straightened, her blue calico and white apron whipping around her legs. She shielded her eyes with her hand and stared where Alonzo pointed.

A surge raced through her heart. Riders. Plains Indians. Comanche? Cheyenne? Pawnee? Friendly and helpful? Threatening, kidnappers of children and women? Lucy knew that the time was not yet past when wagon trains or small parties could be ambushed by unfriendly Indians.

"Children, come here." They tottered toward her in the thick, foot-binding grasses as grasshoppers flew. Lucy reached out, clasping their hands, one on each side of her. The very thing Andrew'd feared, she thought, as she remembered his hesitating to let them come today.

"Oh, Mama, fun. Fun. Indians on horses, riding right up to us." Jeanette danced in glee.

"Will they stop, Mama?" Alonzo was less sure. Some of Mother's Indian stories were filled with caution. There had been wars between the settlers and the Plains Indians—spear thrusting, arrow piercing. Wagon-loads of folks corralled on the trail, robbed, burned, scalped.

But Alonzo was used to Indians in Wichita Town. He played

with the silent and dark-skinned children at the celebrations, dancing in the streets, the Arapaho, Pawnee, Cheyenne. Here and there,
a sad-faced Osage who had wandered back to old homelands. Lucy
hoped the three riders would turn, ride off in the distance, yet,
without hesitation, the horses and riders loped toward them. One
held either a long stick or a spear lifted in the air. What now? Lucy
considered it all seriously.

They could feel the thump of hooves and now hear murmuring in a language the children didn't understand.

The pinto stumbled in a gopher hole, regained his stride, the
rider threw back his head and howled in laughter.

Jeanette tightened her grasp on her mother's two fingers, poking her two right fingers into her mouth.

Lucy realized she must show no fear. After all, she thought,
I'm an old hand with Indians, back east, on The Trail, in Wichita
at the trading post. She could figure out almost any Indian language if they gave her a few minutes. Smile. Remember to smile,
she said to herself as she began to pray silently.

Two of the brown horses reared, snorting, as their riders brought
them to an abrupt halt. The third galloped beside his friends,
then, leaning forward, yanked the reins of the pinto.

All three plainsmen stared at the lone woman in blue calico
and matching sunbonnet, and at the two handsome children, a
boy and his little sister.

Lucy couldn't even measure the time. They stared at each other.
Should she speak first? The eagle feathers in their hair, the bared
torsos, arms ringed with feather bracelets. Belts of feathers circling
their waists above antelope-skin breeches. She dared to risk.

"Hello, a good day to you." She spoke in her best Cherokee,
attempting a smile.

The three grunted words, then looked at each other.

"Mother. Why don't they smile?" Alonzo tugged on his mother's
arm, as the tallest one thrust the spear with the dangling feathers
near the top into the prairie grass.

"Hush, child. Hush. We must wait."

All three riders dismounted, striding leisurely toward the trio on the vast prairie. Lucy's rented team lifted ears, snorting at the strangeness of the newcomers, the smells, their horses.

"Cherokee. Cherokee squaw." The tallest rider, stood before Lucy and Alonzo. Lucy caught the smells of strange oils rubbed on their skins. Alonzo noticed they were darker skinned than his mother. The striding Cheyenne stared with unmoving face at the mother and children. "Little girl. Young enough yet to be a Cheyenne," the tall Cheyenne uttered, eagle feather in his hair. Lucy realized that he understood he was standing before an Indian woman who had married a white man as he obviously noticed the children were half-blood.

"May be the little one and the boy, too, too long in the white man's world." The powerful Cheyenne drew up his chin.

"Cherokee. Yes, we're Cherokee." Lucy wanted to say more, like, "we're picking up bones." But that was obvious, wasn't it? Bones, sacred to plains Indians. Lucy stared, her Indian nature telling her what was racing through the stalwart Cheyenne's mind. She tightened her grip on Jeanette's hand, prepared to fight if she had to. She could conk a tall man with a heavy rib bone, if it was required.

The tall Indian's face changed, his eyes lightened, as if he had moved through some inner turmoil. "Help squaw and children." Obviously, the leader of the three, he dug the shorter hawk-nosed one on the left with his elbow. Then he elbowed the lithe, younger one on his right with the eagle feather stuck at a saucy angle in his hair.

Lucy exhaled, but still on guard. They are going to help us, she concluded. Her heart lessened its pounding.

The bones flew. Heaving the giant white skulls, they arched their backs. Leg bones and ribs flew.

"Horns for mask, wear to dance," smiled the hawk-nosed one, muscles glistening through the oil on his skin. He tossed the elegant horns into the wagon.

When the hawk-nosed Indian found a skull with well-preserved horns, he paused. Straightening, he lifted them upwards toward the sun which cast motes through the skull eyes. He turned three times, mumbling, eyes half-closed.

"Mama, what . . ." Alonzo started to ask.

"He's praying, my son. Praying." Lucy knew the Cheyenne plainsman was offering prayers to The Great Ones Above in behalf of the buffalo, their past, their terrible and incomprehensible slaughter—praying for their return. Tears streaming from his eyes, the tall Cheyenne walked over and laid the skull and horns at Alonzo's feet.

Yes, thought Lucy. Yes, it is holy. This is sacred ground for these people. We should apologize for violating it. She started to speak.

"The buffalo," the hawk-nosed one pointed to the wagonload of blanched bones, "they still live, they feed you?" The tears streamed.

"Yes," said Lucy, her cheeks wet also. For these few minutes, she relived the depths of Indianness—felt the overwhelming grounding of spirit beyond self, beyond the six gathered humans dwarfed on the prairie. She, too, prayed that the buffalo would return, but in her heart, there was an ache, as she realized it would not be.

On and on, they labored, heaving bones as the sun climbed toward midday. Soon the three Cheyenne warriors' faces split into broad smiles.

"Little fawn beautiful child." He referred to Jeannette, whose world had widened. Lucy knew the child couldn't wait to tell Papa.

"Son, like my son." The leader straightened, belt of feathers fluttering in the breeze, as he pointed to Alonzo.

"How many children do you have?" asked Lucy, glad that they had made the decision to befriend them.

"Two boys. Two girls." He cast his eyes to the horizon as if he saw them tumbling over the prairie, or as if he had a vision of them, lodged far off by a winding prairie river, waiting his return.

When the bones reached the bottom of the wagon-seat, their

helpers stopped, bowed and smiled, then leaped on their steeds.

"Good bye, little mother," they chorused in Cheyenne, "good bye, little Real People." And they were gone.

"Mama, are they coming back?" Alonzo stared at the vanishing riders.

"No, child, they are leaving. Wave good-bye."

* * *

All three stood quietly absorbing the events of the last minutes. Lucy felt the longing in her heart for the quiet dignity of her people on the Coosa, the culture of New Echota, back in Georgia before the White Man destroyed it. Tears clustered in her eyes at the remembrances. She stood still while savoring the experience. Then, she turned to the happy children. "Come, children. We can climb on now, we'll ride to the edge of the Cowskin and find a cottonwood. We'll have a picnic in the shade. Won't Papa be pleased to see us home early?"

"Look, Mama, oh, look," bubbled Jeanette, her white pinafore ballooning as she tottered toward a yellow moth-mullein plant. Beside it gleamed the dazzling white shin bone. "Oh, Mama, I'm going to bring this one yet."

Lucy turned as the child, not more than 40 feet away, leaned down, laughing as she tugged at the glistening bone in the bright sunlight.

A chorus of crickets, grasshoppers and minute grass creatures chirped and sang among the rattling blades of the tall grasses. "Oh, Mama, look." Just as Jeanette bent to lift the bone, another one, thick at the middle, greyish-brown markings on its back, primeval flat head, rose up with lightning speed. She tried to lift the bone, but the weight of the heavy rattlesnake, body writhing, fangs still anchored in her flesh, pulled her to the grass. Her screams rose in the wind.

Lucy leaped. How could it be? No. No. No. Not this. Not after such bliss on the prairie and Cheyenne friendship. No. The universe echoed her scream. With lightning speed, she found strength to strike the rattler a dislodging blow with a rib bone.

Grasping the child, she turned to the wagon. "Alonzo, get on the seat. Oh, my God. Oh, my God."

What should she do? Her mind circled for answers, as the child, fainting from pain, lay back in her lap.

"Oh, merciful God above. Oh, blessed Jesus Christ. Mother Mary." Lucy prayed. "Oh, Above Beings of my grandfather and grandmother and the great Chiefs. Help me. Help me, help me."

Lucy scanned the horizon with eagle eyes. Were the Cheyenne riders yet in sight? Could she still call to them? They would know what to do. What was it? How did they do it in the old times? No Cherokee ever died from the bite of a moccasin, a copperhead, or a timber rattler back in Tennessee and Georgia.

The Shamans, the Holy Priests. They knew what to do.

Realizing that she must do something, as the poison already was rushing up the child's arm, the purple swelling pulsing.

Cut the arm. Yes. Lucy grabbed a fragment of rib-bone and sliced with its razor edge, making an "x" on the tiny arm.

Oh, Merciful God. Yes. There. She bent over, placing her mouth over the unconscious child's terrible wound and began to suck and spit the bitter venom.

Realizing that this was all she could do now, she bound the wound loosely from a cloth torn from her skirt. It would swell more.

"Giddyup, giddyup, Alonzo, hold on. Mother must hurry. Hold on to Jeanette." The child lay across Alonzo's legs, head in Lucy's lap. But the wagon was heavy, the horses only draft horses, the grasses tall. "Oh, my God. Deliver us from this evil," she prayed. Then, Lucy Drake Greenway comprehended the meaning of Rachel in the Bible, weeping for her children. She could not even think of the rest of the verse: "the children that were not."

CHAPTER
FORTY-SIX

Five months later, Lucy in black mourning voile, black mushroom hat with veil, Andrew, broad shoulders draped in his black frock coat, and Alonzo, in his round-coat and short navy trousers, sat on the plank stretched between two nail kegs in the large upstairs hall of the new brick Eagle Block building.

"Remember now thy creator . . ."

Reverend Wilburforce Bogg's voice, well modulated and with a southern edge, echoed in the cavernous room, dimly lit by the insufficiency of the three kerosene lanterns.

Lucy wanted to be here at these meetings. Reverend Boggs had made his intentions quite clear. Time for a church in Wichita. Consider these meetings the launching. "Everything has a beginning."

Lucy wondered if she could be present, emerging from her grief. Fully present. Glancing at the flickering light of the lantern, her mind was transported two miles eastward.

What does it look like in the moonlight, the little lonely mound? Jeanette's resting place. Home for her body until the earth splits—her spirit with God.

In her mind, she could see the grey stone with the etched words:

"Little voice forever stilled."

Ramona had raced for Doctor Allen when they lumbered in with the stricken child. Lucy had already known it was too late.

Andrew hadn't smiled once since that day. It was as if the pains of his life, his childhood poverty, his agonies in his service during The Trail days, his months on the western plains, his own search for meaning as a father and husband, congealed in the hour of the child's death, into one concentrated moment of pain. And they, all three, were still enshrouded by that hour. The hour of grief.

For Alonzo's sake, Lucy pushed her soul, shoved her body with its lead-weight arms and legs through the days and weeks. She could not stand the sight of the *Vidette* with the day of the week and the year plastered across the top. "Stop. Stop the world," her grief called, but the words raced to the corners of the universe. No one answered. She asked herself, is such silence the voice of God?

The meetings. Even Andrew agreed. The meetings might lighten their grief, though they all still felt raw, naked at public exposure.

Lucy had liked Reverend Wilburforce Boggs in spite of the lumbering name. He reminded her of pictures in her old art books back at the seminary. Paintings by El Greco, the elongated, bony bodies, stretched and off-center amidst the backdrop agonies of life. Reverend Bogg's face, itself, pure El Greco, including his olive-cast skin, set off by the bushy black beard, heavier on one side than the other.

The eyes, darker than Lucy's, stared over the prominent nose and mustache with the absorbing look of St. Peter fresh glimpsing his Master walking on the water toward the boat. A face of passion, earthly and unearthly.

He took a few steps back and forth behind the pulpit—more of a foreward lope, head thrust ahead of his shoulders. Long, thin legs encased in baggy black tubes, bending and leaning as if struggling to carry the soul and heart reflected in the lopsided face, nodding above.

A man suited for the cloth. A man suited for Wichita, Kansas. A man, like the very Jesus himself, acquainted with grief and sorrow.

"For everything, there is a season . . .A time to weep, and a time to laugh; a time to mourn . . . ."

The preacher lifted his chin; dim lantern light cast an ungainly shadow, which highlighted the disproportionate face, where
the soulful, dark eyes surveyed the congregation.

Congregation? How many? 18? 20? Lucy hadn't counted. In
front of her sat Catherine and Dutch Greiffenstein, dressed in the
latest fashions available at the New York Store. Already, folks spoke
of 'Bill' as the father of Wichita. Portly 'Bill' perspired as he leaned
forward to catch the words.

To the side sat the Frenchman, Jacques Fouquet, who'd been
able to pay for a fresh hair cut and shave and sported a brown suit,
polished boots grinning beneath pant legs.

Lucy didn't recognize the people behind Fouquet, though she
had seen them over at Hayes and Brothers store. And Enis Copeland
and his thin wife, Eulonda, with the rolled orange hair, sporting a
blue turban hat with white feather, sat beside Fouquet. Lucy had
noticed Mrs. Copeland had a good voice as they sang, "When I
Survey the Wondrous Cross." They needed an organ or piano,
though, thought Lucy. Oh, when on this earth of pain had she last
thought of sheet music, hymnals, the rising notes of minuets,
marches, hymns, concertos?

Edward and Margaret Peck from the country. Eighty acres
south of Wichita, Margaret leaning forward with her sunburnt,
lined face and faded hat. The two daughters, Anna and Mary,
sporting their first 'store bought' dresses, both violet chambray,
tight at the bodice and neck.

Carpenter Roland Bowes, who had helped build their house,
bobbed in late with Samuel Dunbar. To the right, a towering William Gill, who clerked at the W. A. Thomas and Company Grocery House on Main Street, nodded as he slept.

To Andrew's and her surprise, who should enter just before
the opening hymn, but opulent-bellied and dandy-suited Rowdy
Joe Lowe, from the saloon in Delano across the river. Lucy knew
Rowdy Joe had nearly lost his life recently in a shooting, the events
still being sorted out. Rowdy Joe could profit from the reading
and Reverend Wilburforce's undulating words, she thought.

But whose was the soprano voice, shrill falsetto with uneven vibrato? Lucy thought to herself. I'd forgotten how off-key Victoria used to sing. How could she forget that voice? She looked over left for a glimpse. There sat Mr. and Mrs. Phenias Johnson. Victoria, dressed in a tiered blue silk with a mantilla, trimmed with dark lace thrown over her shoulders, saucy small bonnet with a cluster of roses on her yellow hair. Phenias sported a pearl-grey vest with rolled collar and diamond stick pin, face long, eyes shifting as if he felt out of place or knew too much about the indebtedness of those about him.

I'm surprised. Thought Victoria would surely wait for those Episcopalians to get their church built, Lucy thought. But, that tacky little buffalo skin-and-dirt covered hogan they called a church, with its crooked cotton wood stick-of-a-cross had turned elegant Victoria off, she concluded.

Just when Reverend Boggs was getting ready to call out the number for another hymn, a medium-sized young woman, garbed in what once seemed to be a silk dress of opalescent hue, a dress that had obviously had its former extravagant trimmings removed, slid through the door. Her head was encased in an old style bonnet, which hid her face and did not at all match the altered dress. With lowered eyes, her body, though full bosomed and comely, slunk on the back bench in the space by the door.

William Gill and Roland Bowes turned and stared at the newcomer. Lucy only got a glimpse as the woman slid in on the newly sawed plank.

"Ida Mae Roost?" Lucy asked. Yes, it was. Ida Mae, from above Rowdy Joe's Saloon, whom she had seen the day of the picnic, dressed in her best afternoon promenade clothes. Obviously, Ida Mae wanted to be unrecognized. She grasped a hymnal with trembling hands, lifted an unpainted face.

Victoria Rogers Johnson dug Phenias's ribs with a sharp elbow, her mouth turned down.

Lucy knew, however, that El Greco, from her seminary art book, would want to paint a face and figure like Ida Mae Roost's, just as he painted the Penitent Magdalene long ago. And paint the startled Wilburforce Boggs, whose red and sensual lips, under surveillance of an iron-disciplined will, rejoiced to see another possible member of the new Presbyterian church.

Their voices bounced off the wooden walls after the service, folks greeting each other, some highly motivated, envisioning the new congregation. In back, the silent woman, who trembled holding her hymnal and who reached up to pull her poke bonnet even further over her face, turned, wistfully, to go.

Lucy, seeing Ida Mae, head bowed, exiting the doorway alone, stepped briskly forward.

"Miss Roost. Miss Roost. We met once in the post office." Lucy didn't mention the Fourth-of-July picnic. She offered her gloved hand.

Ida Mae halted, turning with head still bowed. "Yes. Yes. Mrs. Lucy Greenway. I do remember. You were so kind." Her voice was faint, as if her spirit fought to enable her to stand and visit. "It was when I told you of my Uncle Jeremiah's death, out in the sod shanty by the Willow-Wallow." Ida Mae lifted her eyes to Lucy's face.

"I remember, Ida Mae, and I was so sorry. I do hope your aunt is adjusting to the bereavement."

"I know about your sorrow, Mrs. Greenway." A tear coursed down Ida Mae's pale cheek. "I know what it is to bury your baby."

Ida Mae's suffered great losses, too. Dear Lord. Lucy clasped her handkerchief.

"I'm glad you came, Ida Mae, stop over for a cup of tea when you can." What more can I say? Sorrow and grief nibbled at the edges of Lucy's heart, yet she saw suffering in Ida Mae's eyes, suffering that awaited the touch from another human soul.

Lucy didn't even bother more than a cursory glance, noticing Victoria and Phenias Johnson's scorn at her forward moves in addressing a Wichita Town soiled dove, and thus, in their eyes, soiling herself.

CHAPTER FORTY-SEVEN

"You should apply for the teaching position, Lucy. No other applicant can do what you could." Andrew's warm voice encouraged Lucy as she turned from the parlor window to look at Andrew, white shirt open at the collar, arm sprawled over the back of his leather chair.

"Yes. I think of it, Andrew, teaching again. With Ramona here with Alonzo, perhaps it would be all right. Sometimes, I think about my education and wonder if I'm wasting it." Lucy turned to stand behind Andrew's chair and ran her fingers gently through his heavy, greying hair.

"I don't know where they'd find an applicant who could teach so many subjects, Lucy, Latin, music, art, geometry, calculus. Guess, they'd not be interested in the Greek, though."

Lucy listened to her husband's encouraging words. "But Andrew. I'm not a white woman. You forget that. You know when I go into the stores here, most of the clerks wait on Negroes before they will wait on a full-blood like me, don't you?" Lucy clarified the painful situation, even though she thought Andrew already understood.

But the very next day, sun shining brightly, new green leaves rattling in the elms, Lucy climbed into the shiny new buggy to head for Mr. Bill Grieffenstein's opulent mansion to begin interviews with board members for the teaching position. "Good-bye, Andrew," she called back at her beaming husband at the gate.

*   *   *

More than a trace of anxiety pushed at Lucy's heart as she sat in Mr. Greiffenstein's walnut-paneled office, back straight on the chair, modest hat anchored appropriately on her well-combed hair.

Opulent-bellied Bill Greiffenstein shifted his weight in the oak desk chair.

"Well, Lucy, I mean, Mrs. Greenway, you do have a fine background. Ten years? You have that much experience?"

Mr. Greiffenstein couldn't help but take an extra peek at the charming woman so handsomely dressed, sitting before him.

Lucy could see that Mr. Greiffenstein was caught in a to-and-fro wondering about her, a full-blood applying for the position, even if she was Andrew's wife. He stood, stared out the window facing the street as if he had to shift a few things around in his mind, the changing times, the scarcity of teachers. Then he sat back in his chair, tilted back and asked more questions, his big eyes twinkling, half-grin at his sensuous mouth.

*   *   *

When Lucy stepped back into her buggy, she smiled to herself, glad that the interview with Mr. Greiffenstein had been successful.

"Get up, Dover." She slapped the reins as the buggy rolled on down Waco toward board member Wilus Hogenworth's two-story house. She realized that her anxiety had lessened considerably. With affirmations from such an important Wichita figure as Mr. Greiffenstein, new courage swelled in her heart.

"Only two more board members to call on," she whispered to herself. She pulled her buggy in front of the two-story clapboard house with the centered front door and the four windows, upstairs and down, staring at her.

"Why, come in, Mrs. Greenway. Yes, I remember you. We've crossed on your husband's ferryboat."

Edith Hogenworth wrung her hands in front of her. Lucy, noticing, was aware—She's not quite sure what to do with me.

Lucy stood in the vestibule while Edith scanned her hat and

face, her tiered lawn dress, light tan with dark-brown trim.

"Mrs. Hogenworth, I'd like to see Mr. Hogenworth. I understand that he is a school board member. I'm applying for the teaching position." Lucy smiled. At least, they let me inside the front door, she thought, the smell of furniture polish engulfing her.

"Come into the parlor, Mrs. Greenway. I'll tell Mr. Hogenworth you're here." The smile left Edith's face.

Lucy sat on the pale green upholstered chair with the walnut arms by the stark window. In a moment, a round-shouldered, balding man entered through the double doors of the room.

Lucy stood and extended her hand. "Mr. Hogenworth, we've met before at the Johnsons' this past March—the charity drive for orphans."

Wilus shook hands with Lucy. She realized his eyes surveyed her, up and down. Lucy reached up to check her hat.

"Do be seated, Mrs. Greenway. Yes. The school. Applying for the job, Edith says." He cleared his throat.

Lucy could do nothing about his stare other than endure it. She saw Mr. Hogenworth lift one eyebrow.

"Why, yes. Mrs. Greenway, we have two boys of our own in the school. Twelve and 13 years old. Not exactly the easiest boys to manage. I guess you knew the scholars ran Titus Block, last year's teacher, clear off the school ground."

A silence hung for a moment. Lucy realized she would have to present herself as one who could take charge as well as instruct.

"I had instruction in pedagogy from Miss Worcester, a Mount Holyoke professor." Lucy doubted if they'd have another applicant who could say that. "Mr. Hogenworth, I do believe I'm qualified. May I tell you of my background?"

"Why, yes, that's what I need to hear." Hogenworth leaned forward with his austere face. "Tell me what studies you have had."

"I'm a female seminary graduate, Mr. Hogenworth. I received a classical education in the capital of the Cherokee Nation at Tahlequah."

Lucy enumerated the long list of subjects, including Latin,

mathematics, logic, music, and art.

"We need a teacher who knows how to teach arithmetic. My boys are behind in that subject. Could you teach algebra?"

Lucy saw his face recompose itself as he probably realized he had been smiling too much before an Indian woman.

"Mr. Hogenworth, I can teach calculus and algebra as well as ordinary mathematics." She placed one gloved hand into the palm of the other, tried to smile pleasantly as she felt hope rise in her heart.

For a moment, she thought of her and Andrew's discussion the evening before. "I have small children Andrew, may be I should wait."

Andrew had replied: "Lucy, get started. Alonzo'll be in school another year. I want you to be his teacher. No one in Wichita is as qualified as you."

Lucy glanced up at Mr. Hogenworth as the silence hung.

He rose from his chair, put a closed fist to his mouth and stared out the window at Lucy's black horse and spanking new buggy. He turned to face her. Lucy rose.

"Mrs. Greenway, have you met the other board members?"

"I've called on Mr. Greiffenstein, Mr. Meeks, Mr. Hayes, and now my visit here with you. I have only to interview with Mr. Phenias Johnson, loan officer at the bank." Believe I'm making some progress, Lucy thought.

"Well, thank you, Mrs. Greenway for coming by. Yes. Well, we have only one more applicant, Mr. Levi Ledbetter, but I dare say, he's not nearly as qualified as you. Yes. Well, thank you. Yes. I can present your name to the board at our meeting next week."

*   *   *

Lucy guided her horse and buggy into the lane leading to the carriage house besides Phenias and Victoria Johnson's 12-room house, set back on an expansive lawn.

She tied her horse to the hitching post, then followed the brick walk that led around to the steps and wide verandah. She turned the handle of the door bell, then brushed the elm seeds from the folds of her skirt.

A black woman, dressed in a black dress, white apron and cap, opened the door.

"Yes Ma'am?" said the stout woman, staring at her.

"Good afternoon. I'm Lucy Greenway. I'm here to consult with Mr. Johnson." Again, Lucy's left hand sought the comfort of the palm of her right hand. She had told herself in the buggy, "this will be the hardest interview."

"Why, Indians have to go to the back door," said the maid, her broad face reflecting a more than moderate amount of understanding as she faced the full-blood before her.

For a moment, Lucy was stunned. At Victoria's house? In a flash, she realized she shouldn't have been. She had waited at the New York Store while Mr. George Gettes, one of the clerks, waited on four others, all who'd entered the store after her. She knew the signs on privy doors behind every downtown building read, "Niggers and Indians Keep Out."

I was naive to believe it'd be different here at the Johnsons', she thought. Hurt pushed at her heart as the betrayal gouged. Somehow, I'd expected more. Lucy lowered her head. Her heart continued to pound. Why did I come here?

The house was large and it seemed like a 10 mile walk to Lucy, as she picked her way to the back door which opened, following her knock, by black maid Olivia.

"Yes Ma'am. You follow me, Mrs. Greenway. This way to the parlor. I'll tell Mr. Johnson you're here."

Lucy sat on the wine-colored sofa wondering where Victoria was. Carnations. A bouquet of carnations in a cut-glass vase graced the walnut and marble table. She hadn't thought of it, but the Johnsons must have their own greenhouse. All was quiet, except the ticking of the cherry grandfather clock, its pendulum swinging as if to measure the silence.

The maid leaned in, "It'll be quiet in here this afternoon. Miss

Victoria had her carriage driver take her and the boys uptown to the New York Store," she added.

"Why, Lucy Greenway!" Phenias, in his grey waistcoat and black cravat, hair slicked forward over the balding front, strode into the room.

Lucy stood, extending her hand. "Mr. Johnson, good afternoon. I'm here to apply for the opening at the school." Lucy felt her face warm as her smile spread.

"I see. Have a seat, Mrs. Greenway." His eyes half-closed. "The teaching position, you say?"

For a few minutes, Lucy answered Phenias's questions. She had already concluded that he didn't at all consider Victoria a Cherokee, with her light skin, blue eyes and blonde hair, regardless of her education in the Cherokee Nation with her.

Lucy didn't want to think he was stalling.

"Why, uh, Mrs. Greenway, or, may I say, Lucy—considering my relationship with you folks already?" He cleared his throat.

He inquired about the studies she had had at the seminary.

"Those are important subjects. Yes. Latin, mathematics, you say?" Phenias glanced down at the flowers in the rug, then glanced back at her. "Could you teach some music, Mrs. Greenway?"

"Yes, Mr. Johnson. I sing and play the piano. Perhaps, Victoria has already told you, I gave concerts at Chief Ross's Rose Cottage and at the Murrell mansion at Park Hill. Of course, that was before the war." Lucy realized she shouldn't appear to overrate herself, but, he did ask, didn't he?

*   *   *

Lucy hummed to herself on the drive home. She recognized it had been good, getting out like this. Why, it was a review of her life. Answering questions they asked. And, she felt a secureness, too, about how she had answered their questions.

Hadn't they all agreed to support her? After all, didn't they all say there was only one other applicant and, Mr. Mock had leaked it that he had no education beyond the eighth grade, but was a 'smart' man?

* * *

Two weeks passed. The school board held its Tuesday meeting hiring session. Lucy hadn't heard a word.

"Just wait, my dove. You'll see." But Lucy wondered if Andrew wasn't blind to reality, loving her so fully as he did.

Next morning, there it was in the *Vidette*.

"Wichita's school board, under the leadership of Mr. J. M. Meeks, reported that they have come to a conclusion regarding a teacher for next year.

"We all came to the conclusion, considering our town and our students, that Mr. Levi Ledbetter was the right applicant for the scholars," reported Mr. Meeks. "*The Vidette* offers its congratulations to Mr. Ledbetter. The board reported there was only one other applicant, a person who wasn't an American citizen."

Lucy plopped on a kitchen chair. "Andrew, I didn't get the job." Her sigh was more of a gasp.

Andrew walked across the kitchen to stand by her. Lifting the paper from her hands, he encircled her in his arms and lifted her to an upright position facing him. His arms tightened.

"Lucy, Lucy, my love. You mustn't worry. May be it's better this way." He rocked her in his strong arms.

"Andrew, I shouldn't have even applied." She could smell his bay rum shave lotion.

She let him hold her for awhile, allowing the comfort of his arms to overcome her disappointment. "Do you think it was the Johnsons who pulled the rug out from under me? Victoria? Couldn't stand me getting ahead of her?"

"Well, since you asked, Lucy, yes. It must have been the influence of Victoria and Phenias. I ran into Phenias on the walk outside the bank. He didn't want to look me in the eyes. I forced him to by insisting on a chat.

"'You'll be making a decision on a teacher, soon, won't you?' I asked.

"'Yes, of course,' Johnson added. Then he said, "Victoria and I have five sons. Mrs. Johnson believes the town can't accept a full-blood, Mr. Greenway, let alone a *woman* trying to handle all those rowdy boys. I think you understand what I mean.' Then, Johnson simply left me standing there and walked into the bank. But, to be honest with you, I figured the rest of the board would out-vote Phenias."

"Andrew, Phenias is the bank loan officer. Probably all those board members, except Mr. Greiffenstein, acquired loans through Phenias Johnson."

Lucy hoped Andrew didn't hear her sob. She buried her head into his chest as the hurt seared her like the demeaning insults, jabs and indignities hurled at them on The Trail years ago.

CHAPTER FORTY-EIGHT

"Just as soon as we finish with the church," Andrew said, "we'll start on a room for your school."

Lucy looked into Andrew's grey-green eyes, eyes she had first known as kindly eyes when she was an eight-year-old on The Trail. "I, I don't know, Andrew. You mean here? Here in our home?"

"Why not? Big enough house, plenty of room upstairs. Finest teacher this side of the Mississippi. I can add on another wing, if it is necessary."

The more they thought about it, the more it seemed the right thing to do, a finishing school for Indian girls of the area.

"I could give back some of what I gained, couldn't I, Andrew? It is a good idea." Lucy's heart leaped at Andrew's suggestion. "Let's wait before we do any house-remodeling until after the church is built. The Lord's work comes first."

Andrew agreed. She knew he recognized that she had always put the church first. She also knew that Andrew would do his best to help. Besides, she knew, there was a part of him that really did like that odd-looking Reverend Boggs, in spite of his name. Spunk. That's what it was. Andrew liked men who showed spunk.

As Lucy rode along the dusty street towards the church building site by the river, she couldn't help singing. My life is worthwhile. I have something to give back. I'll teach again. I'll help full-blood girls, Osage, Waco, Creek—give back some of the wonderful lessons from Miss Worcester and Miss Whitmore at the seminary so long ago. Why hadn't I thought of it before?

Lucy also thought it a good idea, Andrew discussing with those

powerful and rich men, Mr. Greiffenstein and Mr. Mead, about
providing scholarship money for the poor Indian girls. "After all,"
said Andrew, "didn't they make their money from the Indian trade?
Give them a chance to give something back."

* * *

"Haw," she called, as she drew her new buggy up to the left of the
elm sapling that had struggled to root itself in the sandy soil.
Tying her horse to the sapling, after she dismounted, Lucy joined
in the excitement of the people scurrying to put the roof on the
new church. Anticipation of the opening day flowed through her.
She lifted the cloth from the corner of her basket to check her pies.

Lucy looked again at the skeletal frame of the First Presbyterian Church rising into the prairie air at the southeast corner of
Second and Wichita. The volunteer crew heaved and nailed the
studding and rafters.

"Nail her tight so's no prairie winds'll take her down," commanded William Gill, climbing to the roof peak. Roland Bowes
unloaded cedar shingles. "Get these started tomorrow before the
wind comes up. Morning is better." He coughed and spat dust.
Lucy noted the smell of fish in the air drifting from the rivers, a
freshness too, of the westerly winds sweeping over the awakening
grasses of the prairie. She and Elda Gill spread the make-shift table
with a cloth. Soon, she knew, it would be covered with cakes and
pies, big jug of lemonade weighing it down. She hoped the flies
wouldn't be too big a bother, since it was early in the season.

They all knew that the weather could change in minutes into
a late spring snowstorm, a whipping, drenching rain. Or, the sun
could come out in a cloudless sky and blast them with early heat.
Tornado season, too.

Jacques Fouquet and Andrew Greenway rode up in a spring
wagon to the 50-by-25 foot frame building, to help lay the wide
pine flooring.

Lucy liked seeing her Andrew grinning so, his cheeks highlighted by a blush due to his morning drive in the wind. And, she
thought, Where did he get all that lumber? But, wasn't Andrew

always surprising her? Does our bank account allow cash for that big a load of floor planking? But it was for the House of the Lord, wasn't it? They could discuss it later. "We won't even wait for the ceiling, once they get those shingles on the roof and the floor is in, we can go ahead and hold services." Reverend Wilburforce Boggs nodded and beamed, his ruddy face sweaty, beard in tangles, holy light in his sad eyes, as his wife, Ellen, looked on in pride.

Margaret Peck and her two daughters, Anna and Mary, as plainly garbed as their names, rolled through the pack of hounds and strewn manure in their spring wagon with baskets of sandwiches and jugs of lemonade for the workers. Lucy stepped up to greet the arriving women, glad that she and Ramona'd spent the evening before baking rolls, two chocolate cakes, and pies—three gooseberry, four cherry and two apple, for the hungry workers.

"Except the Lord build," exhorted Reverend Wilburforce with the urgency of an Old Testament Prophet. "Except the Lord build . . ."

Just then 10-year-old Jareth Bowes sidled up to Lucy as she tasted the lemonade to see if it was sweet enough. "That sure was a lucky thing, wasn't it, Mrs. Greenway?" Lucy reached for a tin cup to offer the boy a drink. "What was a lucky thing, Jareth?"

"Why, Mrs. Greenway, surprised you didn't know. That Frenchman with the funny hat told me Mr. Greenway sure was lucky in the poker game last night at The Buckhorn, winning all that money. Two hundred and fifty dollars. Think of it." The boy smiled proudly up at "Miss Lucy."

Lucy felt dizzy, but only for a moment. At least, it's going for the church floor. Yes. The church floor, she thought, steadying herself. "Oh, Andrew, Andrew, and how much I love you," she whispered, as she glanced over to see him sweating, his strong arm pounding the nails into the heavy floor planking. Right now, she decided to tuck Jareth's surprising news underneath somewhere. Discuss it with Andrew at a proper time. The right time, she concluded to herself.

*   *   *

In two more weeks, the sturdy frame church stood proudly near the Arkansas River in its spanking coat of white paint. Five windows on each side, admitting the light of the prairie on the west, and jutting framework and stone of buildings on the east. Front door thrust open in a hearty welcome. The smells of spicy cedar, sweet pine and sourness of raw oak, mingled.

Reverend Wilburforce's face seemed even more lopsided this day, like that of Nehemiah surveying the rebuilt Jerusalem walls, yet apprehensive about the future. The day required solemnity. Delighted with the new church poking into the skyline, it'd be unchristian to gloat. Charter Member day. And, he planned to read from Jeremiah: *I know, O Lord, that the way of man is not in himself, that it is not in man who walks to direct his steps.* So far, there were 13 of them, planning to make statements of their faith, or in the case of two, baptism and reception into the church.

Reverend Wilburforce twisted in his uncertainty about Mrs. Victoria Rogers Johnson and husband, Phenias, who planned to be among the candidates—Victoria's church letter of transfer in hand, same as that of Lucy Greenway, the Cherokee woman. Victoria had failed to give notice that she too, once was numbered among the Cherokees, back in the Nation.

Reverend Boggs clutched his worn leather-covered Bible with his oversized hands, knuckles scarred from scrapings during the roofing of the building. His black hair, caught in the March wind, brushed back roughly with one hand, accented his prophet-Jeremiah-look.

Lucy wondered what Reverend Boggs's thoughts were about this town. The wildness, the rawness, the newness, rupturing the prairie, scouring the riverbanks. Granite and brick buildings rising up; the stately Eagle Block building, the mud and manure of the wide streets, the blood of the slaughterhouse, the effluvia of the tannery leaking into the river. The towering Mead mansion. Dozens of small cottonwood log or clapboard shacks, hastily nailed together, with leaning back-yard privies, drainage seeping toward the rivers. The opulent Greiffenstein mansion, looming up in a grove of cottonwood and willow on Jefferson. The new Douglas Avenue bridge that funneled the lowing, rumbling longhorns straight into the middle of the town in cattle drive season. The rattle of the Cannon Ball stagecoach rolling in from Pratt, bringing the entrepreneur with carpet bag, the spectacled, hopeful merchant-to-be. The forlorn sod-house prairie girl, broken by exertions of body and soul for existence on the lonely prairie, who had given up, willing to risk seeking her fortune above a saloon. The wailing's of the steam engines on the new steel tracks of the Wichita and South Western. Coyotes howling at a full moon as if they were reminding one of the sins of David, as well as one's own. Ear-splitting yelps of a pack of yellow hounds tumbling through the dusty streets. And the firm and solid oak planking beneath the churchgoer's feet Andrew had provided. But, Lucy concluded, the Reverend didn't know about that yet. The gunshots, cursing and howls of late-night drunks, yet uncorralled by Wyatt Earp and his deputies. The everlasting blaring of the brass band on the balcony across from the New York Store. The swish of skirt and flash of leg and breast, and the giggles of Ida Mae Roost and Vina Napp and their business sisters, kept in employ by hundreds of cowboys, drovers and businessmen passing through, and the local male residents, secret partakers in sin, most with names Reverend Boggs did not yet know. The hooting and piercing yells of the crowds of men, young and old, shaven and unshaven, in broadcloth and worsted, in canvas ticking and rawhide, bathed and unbathed, placing their bets on which one of Rowdy Joe's girls could race the fastest, naked, to the Arkansas River.

Saloons. Saloons. The smells of wine and sour beer. Of fine bourbon and Scotch, mixed with the heavy wild-blood odors of the heaps of partridge, pheasant, rabbit, and deer carcasses—some awaiting shipment to eastern cities, others to be butchered for the salivating restaurant crowds, forks and knives in hand.

Spurs on ragged boots below rawhide breeches of the cursing cowboys, brace of Navy pistols swagging at their hips. Strollers on board sidewalks in latest style fine suits purchased at Hayes and Brothers. The widow McCarty and her steamy laundry, and outlaw son, Billy the Kid. The signs posted: "Everything goes in Wichita. Leave your revolvers at police headquarters and get a check. Carrying concealed weapons strictly forbidden." Signs largely ignored, because only part of the influx of humanity could read English. Mexicans, salty cattlemen and ranchers in Texas sombreros and leather leggings, velvet jackets with bright buttons.

Variety Theatre, sporting nightly exhibitions, called *A Scarcity*. Scarcity of clothing worn by female performers. A "Free and Easy."

Full-blood Cherokee, Sioux, Cheyenne, Wichita, Waco and Osage, in various styles of dress.

* * *

Lucy looked down at her bosom and lap, draped in the finest navy voile. She reached up to check the small navy hat on top of her upswept hair, cluster of violets at the crown and brim. She crossed her ankles and clutched the arm of her dashing husband, Andrew, and smiled at Alonzo with the dark silk hair that wanted to curl in the wind. Her fine hands clothed in navy gloves, clasped her husband's arm tenderly while Andrew purred as if he had no doubt but that she, Lucy Drake Greenway, was the most beautiful woman in Wichita. They didn't call it a 'town' anymore, since it was incorporated.

Then Lucy closed her eyes and prayed silently on such a joyful day, the day of her homecoming to a church in Wichita, Kansas— at last.

CHAPTER
FORTY-NINE

Lucy was glad she'd been able to rescue her church letter from her trunk upstairs in her bedroom. Pastor Boggs planned to read it today, confirming her Christian status. She braced her back, clasping Andrew's warm palm. Why were they waiting? Why didn't Reverend Wilburforce begin the service?

Finally, the soulful minister stepped down off the platform, leaned over in a whispered consultation with Agnes Mead.

Lucy overheard double-chinned Agnes whisper hoarsely. "Oh, no, Rebecca Sowers won't be able to come today, her children have the chicken pox."

Stranded, and Reverend Wilburforce ecstatic over the ornate pump organ on the right side of the platform with its red carpet foot pedals and ivory keys. Founding day. Charter members. Water for the baptisms. Church letters in hand. Candidates instructed and present. Ready to begin the service and no one to play the organ donated by Rowdy Joe, himself. Lucy and Andrew focused their eyes on Reverend Boggs.

He cleared his throat. His black worsted frock coat, shiny at the elbows. "Ahemm. My dear brothers and sisters, we have a bit of a problem this morning." His head tilted. "By some miracle, we are blessed with a new organ for our sanctuary. Mrs. Rebecca Sowers had agreed to play the hymns for the service today, however, Sister Mead informed me that Sister Sowers will not be able to attend."

Folks shifted, glancing at each other. They waited.

"I'm sure that in a crowd like this on this Sabbath morning, there is one person whom God is touching who will be able to fill in for Sister Sowers. One person. Kindly lift your hand."

Reverend Boggs's sad eyes lowered, blinked, then opened, giving him the appearance of the pitiful man left stranded at the edge of Siloam's pool when the waters were miraculously troubled. "The Lord is calling. Who can assist in the Lord's worship this day?"

Reverend Boggs surveyed the small congregation. Rustling and murmuring rose up as they reflected, reviewing their talents.

Lucy saw the preacher glance at Mary Peck in her country plainness. She remembered hearing Mary play 'Santa Lucia' on her zither, once. Would that qualify her? She concluded it would not.

Ellen Boggs told her that she'd once played 'Old Black Joe' at a school contest and won the white ribbon. Lucy noticed Ellen lower her head.

Lucy had heard that carpenter Roland Bowes, with his big hands and red arthritic knuckles, sometimes played 'Will the Circle Be Unbroken' on his Aunt Evangeline's organ. She noticed the carpenter stare at the wall.

Then Lucy glanced over to the left where sat Victoria Rogers Johnson, dressed in white silk with a pale blue shoulder shawl and matching bonnet sporting calla lilies. Victoria twisted as if she wished she could rise to the occasion, but, Lucy recalled, Victoria never did learn to read notes.

Then came the words, 'Sister Greenway. I do believe you have a piano now in your home. Yes. How the Lord provides. Sister Lucy, would you honor us and help us start the service?' Reverend Bogg's sad eyes implored, "You can't say 'no' to God."

Lucy felt her heart pick up its beat. Her breath caught short. She tightened her grasp on Andrew's hand, her eyes riveted to his. Her eyes told him, "I really don't want to do it. It's too public and too soon. The prejudices against my people." For a moment, the vision of Victoria and her mother-in-law, Ophelia, forcing her off the walk, flashed before her.

Only last week in the tacky little post office in the grocery store, she had been pushed aside. Three of them in the lobby. She had stepped to the window, "Mr. Kellogg, a penny stamp, please." But before she could get the penny out of her purse, the raking, hurtful words.

"Why, Milo Kellogg. You're not gonna wait on a full-blood Indian before us white ladies, are you? Ellie and me been back here writing our cards on the bench." Bessie Mae Trump's face ballooned red and the coarse, poorly groomed hair curled on her thick neck as she elbowed Lucy with a fat arm.

"These Choctaw Indians are dark, aren't they, Milo? Pushy too. How come Constable Earp don't shove these wild Indians back to Oklahoma and Texas? Niggers moving in over east of Main. What is the town coming to?"

Lucy had turned, stepped aside, but not without overwhelming humiliation piercing her heart.

"Never get in a pissing contest with a skunk, you'll lose every time," her father once told her. So she decided to absorb the pain like the blessed Jesus absorbed the pain of the nails through his hands.

Lucy had wanted to reply to coarse Bessie Mae who had shoved her aside. Clarify that she was not a Choctaw. Cherokee. Cherokee, of the civilized tribes. Female seminary graduate. Student of French, philosophy, Greek, art, music . . . She knew that being full-blood in Wichita on that day was to be considered as low as a yellow hound, wandering sideways down the dusty street.

Lucy Greenway didn't want to be so public today. But, Andrew returned the handclasp and smiled with his captivating eyes of love. Do it, Lucy, my darling, for the Lord and for me, his look told her.

Lucy stood, catching glimpses of the blue-, black-, brown-, violet-, pink-, and white-clothed people, all staring at her. One, the one in white with the calla lilies on her expensive hat sitting by a banker and five sons, all elegantly dressed, stared with cold blue eyes, lips turned down.

Lucy wanted to sit back down, but that would make a scene.

On the platform, she pulled back the red plush stool, smoothed her skirt, drew it up. Yes. There was a hymnal on the rack. She removed her gloves and reached for the stops, arranging them for the best modulations and harmonies for hymn tunes. "Lord help me," she prayed. Could she keep pushing the pedals, the bellows wheezing as her fingers followed the notes?

"Praise God. See how the Lord provides." Reverend Boggs beamed, even though his shirt collar was sweaty and his cravat askew. "Praise God. Sister Lucy, let us sing number 216, 'Walk in the Light'."

Oh, thought Lucy, a good hymn, theologically sound: 'Walk in the light, so shalt thou know, the fellowship of love'. Two sharps. Easy. Four-four time. Her feet, encased in fine leather shoes with inch heels, bent at the ankles to begin pumping. Her delicate fingers stretched out before the ivories. The harmony rose up.

Easy. Yes, I can coordinate it all, the pumping, the pressing the keys. Not at all like the piano, but . . .

And they sang. Hearty Wichita Town singing. Strong male bass, vibrating tenor. Mary Peck's alto and Esther Gill's sharp soprano. Up and down like a child romping up and down the sandhills along the river: 'Walk in the Light, . . .the beautiful light of God'.

Lucy Greenway on the plush-covered stool, her arms stretching over the keys and her black eyes riveted to the notes in the hymnal didn't have time to notice. One person did not sing. Not at all. The one dressed in opulent white silk with the blue shawl and calla lilies on her hat.

Actually, Lucy was surprised at how easy the hymns had been to play, though she would have preferred to play something a bit more sophisticated, such as Bach's 'Jesu, Priceless Treasure'.

She even thought, momentarily, how nice it would be if Reverend Boggs had chosen 'O Have You Not Heard of That Beautiful Stream?' Such a soul-moving hymn. Besides, she and many of the others were certainly acquainted with streams. 'Rivers', in fact.

As the organ's blended murmurs rose, visions of rivers flowed through her mind: the Coosa, the Hiwassee, the Tennessee, the wide Ohio, the threatening Mississippi, the Arkansas, the Illinois by the seminary, long ago.

Reverend Boggs is proving himself today, she thought, playing the last verse of the hymn. His monotone voice held the last note far too long.

Next, Reverend Boggs announced his text: "For other foundation can no man lay than that is laid, which is Jesus Christ," pointing out the firm foundation for his church.

Then Lucy had clustered with the other charter member candidates before Reverend Boggs at the pulpit. She noticed he had their church letters on top of his Bible and ritual manual. Her letter there on top, from the old Park Hill Presbyterian Church back in the Cherokee Nation that had burned during the terrible war.

Reverend Boggs beamed, seeming certain that this church would grow and prosper. Lucy glanced over her shoulder and could see platinum-headed Andrew in his fine frock coat and blue cravat, smiling at her with pride, as she stood alongside Victoria and Phenias Johnson, and 11 others.

Reverend Boggs began. "Dear friends, today is a blessed and happy day, the day we receive our charter members . . ."

Thoughts gripped Lucy's mind. What is wrong with Victoria? Her face. Flushed as if she's angry. Lucy looked up to face Reverend Boggs who turned to the membership confession page of his handbook. She noticed Phenias attempting to calm Victoria by a subtle whisper, but Victoria elbowed Phenias in the side.

Then it seemed to Lucy as if the floor split open beneath her feet and the earth below that. The words echoed though her heart and soul.

"Reverend Boggs," scolded Victoria Rogers Johnson. Lines furrowed her brow, her chin trembled.

A terrible hush swept over the congregation.

"Reverend Boggs, do you actually think that I am going to join a church that puts full-blood Indians in places of such prominence?" Her voice trembled with jealousy and rage.

Me. She means me. Oh, Victoria, how could you, Lucy thought, tears crowding at the corners of her eyes. She simply can't stand it, Reverend Boggs asking me to play the organ this morning.

Reverend Boggs's face fell, then his head shook as if he had palsy. Before he could think about what to do, Victoria turned, her icy blue eyes flashing scorn, ignoring the bewildered folks on the benches behind her. Then, as if she had forgotten something, she turned back to face the trembling preacher.

"And, give me back my church letter." Victoria's gloved-hand clawed the air.

Taken off guard, Reverend Boggs searched under his Bible for the letter. Dropped it. But, before he could retrieve it from the floor, Victoria swept down like a pelican gulping a fish and raked it up. "Come on, Phenias. Come on, boys. We'll have to wait for those Episcopalians."

Elegant Victoria huffed out and down the dusty path to their waiting carriage, she and her milk-toast husband and trailing sons.

CHAPTER FIFTY

On Thursday morning, just after Andrew had kissed her and left for his new position at the Mead Trading Company, Lucy decided to put in a couple of hours of practice on the grand piano in the spacious parlor bay window. She smiled, realizing that it was mysterious how she got the piano which appeared a few days after Andrew's disastrous gambling night, following the cattle drive.

The ivories felt smooth and as silky as the keys on Chief Ross's great grand at Rose Cottage. A melancholy mood slipped over her as she played from memory, a Stephen Foster piece, 'Way Down Upon the Suwannee River'.

The song made her think of her childhood home back in Georgia on the beautiful Coosa, the sweeping chestnut trees, the sparkling waters and her dear mother Abby's voice.

Pausing for a moment, she glanced out the right side of the bay window, noticing a girl who she concluded, must be about 14—an Indian girl. Could be Creek, or Osage.

The girl's sackcloth dress hung ungainly, her face smudged with stains. From the tannery on the river, thought Lucy. A shame how Bilcock Ruster hires those native girls for a few pennies. The girl stared at Lucy's window, as if caught up in a dream.

Lucy rose and walked out on the veranda as pity for her rose in her heart. "My school. Yes. I must start a female seminary here. Oh, dear God, yes."

Lucy stepped down on the flagstone walk and approached the dirty urchin who still had not smiled.

"Good morning, Miss. Can I help you? Did you want something?"

The girl's eyes fell to her dirty bare feet beneath the frazzled hem of her dress. Lucy could see by the streaks on her cheeks that she had been crying.

"What is your name, Miss?" She waited, knowing the girl was overpowered by her appearance, the house, the flowers in the yard, all impossibly out of reach for such as she.

The waif lifted her head, gave it a toss to shake the black tangles out of her eyes. "My name is Blue Star. You're Mrs. Andrew Greenway, aren't you?" she asked, faintly.

"Yes, Blue Star, I am. What a pretty name. My Cherokee name I used as a child was My Home. Lucy lifted the gate-latch. "Wouldn't you like to come and sit on the verandah with me and visit?"

"Oh, Missie Greenway, could I?" The child-girl staggered, as if the wind would brush her into the lilac bush.

Lucy guided the thin girl with the haunted look up the walk. "Sit here, Blue Star," she pointed to one of the lawn chairs on the porch as she selected the one opposite it. "What brings you past my house?"

"I live down past the river southward, Mother and I, in a house she put together with scraps and boards she found. We both work at the tannery." Her voice faltered. She tried to hide her dirty feet beneath her skirt. "I stopped when I heard the music. You play that piano, Mrs. Greenway?" Blue Star leaned so that she could see the grand piano inside the bay window.

"Why, yes, I do, my child. I used to live in the Cherokee Nation back in Georgia. It was there I learned to play the piano at the mission. A wonderful school. But, that was long ago."

Blue Star looked up at Lucy with wistful eyes, eyes filled with nameless longings. Lucy could see the girl was caught on the edge of the gulf that separated the poverty-stricken and the uneducated from herself. Lucy realized that this very experience was the confirmation that she needed to open her school.

They visited. Lucy offered Blue Star a cold glass of tea, then one of the sugar cookies Ramona had baked yesterday afternoon. Then she asked, "Have you ever attended school, Blue Star?"

"Oh, no, Missie Greenway. Us full-bloods got no chance here. That little school uptown is for regular citizens. We Indians ain't citizens of the country, you know."

Old pains seized Lucy. She remembered the rejections, humiliations, impoverishment of being torn from her own home. Lucy reached across, clasping the girl's lye-scarred hand.

"What would you say if I told you that I'm opening a school for girls like you. Would you come?"

Blue Star lifted her dark eyes. "Oh, but, I couldn't. Mother and I only earn enough for a little bread. She even traps for our meat and fishes from the river. No. She needs the money. We couldn't pay . . ."

"No, my child. I'm not asking for your money. Suppose there was a fund to take care of the cost. It can be arranged. Would you come? Do you know other girls who would come?"

"Oh, Missie Greenway. Could it be? Me? Go to school? Do you think I could learn music? Play the piano?"

"Well, Blue Star, we would certainly give it a try."

Before the short encounter ended that morning, Blue Star gave Lucy the names of five other Indian girls who, like she, scrounged like stray dogs, foraging for food to keep body and soul together. Lucy had her confirmation—there would be at least six or eight girls, come fall. "I must tell Andrew to have Mr. Hayes look for student desks. The large bedroom upstairs would hold six or eight with plenty of room. Yes."

*　*　*

Three weeks later, the temperature rose to near 100 degrees. A languid air hovered over the town. Those tilling gardens moved slowly and with little hope, wondering when the rain would come. The few wagons that rolled down the streets whipped up clouds of heavy dust, which settled, giving the trees an olive drabness. Merchants tapped their fingers beside their cash registers, weary of waiting for customers.

With cattle drives tapering off, the merchants knew that they had to cater to the farmers as well as the townsfolk. Dogs yipped, chasing a few rabbits who'd managed to find some wilted green. Today, not even a cloud in the sky. By noon, it would be brassy with burning heat waves dancing off bricks, cement, and roofs.

Upriver, by the confluence of the Little Arkansas and the Arkansas, a 10-year-old boy, Jerel, middle child of Phenias and Victoria Rogers Johnson, stumbled out on the elongated river sandbar which had grown daily. A small flock of white egrets flapped their wings, rose and scattered in a sky spotted with wisps of clouds.

The boy picked up some white-and-purplish river stones and tossed them at the egrets but missed. He moseyed along as if he considered the whole day boring, the sun too hot. He sought to break the boredom by playing near the water. He knelt out on the edge of the sandbar to see if he could imitate the Indians, lie still and then, almost miraculously, sweep up a fish with his hands.

"Don't go out on any sandbar in the river alone," his parents had cautioned him. But his friend, Billy Shackley, was laid up with a high fever, in bed now for three days.

"No, Billy's still pretty sick, Jerel. He's not going to be able to play with you for some time. Tell your mother I sent for Doctor Allen." Billy's mother had shut her door. "You'll just have to play alone, Jerel."

The boy, on the sandbar, found a stone, shoved it through the sand playing locomotive, losing himself in his play. In the distance, the freight train wailed crossing the bridge, loaded with cattle and farm products on its way southeast. The boy made chugging sounds along with the wailing train.

Mercifully, a few clouds rose in the west, spread and grew large enough to edge over the burning sun, now and then creating a shade.

Few people were out on this morning. Jerel decided he would play about an hour, then it would be time to scramble out of the riverbed and scurry for home. Dinner time. He would have to listen to his mother scold about the sand in his clothes.

*   *   *

Southward on Main Street, Lucy Greenway had spent 30 minutes this morning writing, of all things, a letter to Eliza Bushyhead, underlining, "Please come for a visit."

She grabbed her straw hat with the wide brim and bright orange band, bow in the back. Stepped down her sidewalk and up the street. Lucy hoped the pack of mongrel hounds wouldn't sally around a corner, lope up the street and nip her heels. She thought of the girl, Blue Star, and the excitement about her school filled her heart.

Lucy mailed her letter at the post office, then decided she would take the path over to the park by the confluence of the rivers. Memories of the Fourth of July picnic made her smile to herself. Sit there by the river under those Russian olives someone had planted and cool off. Be a breeze there.

Just as she seated herself on the picnic table bench, she heard the cry—a fearful cry of: "Help, help."

Leaping up, Lucy raced up the sand-dune, past a pile of boards and driftwood left by a flood months before. Peering down into the wide channel, she could see the water circling, wending its way downstream around the sandbars. Pigeons and sand cranes rose up from the banks and circled westward.

Then she saw the child.

"Help me! Help me!" The cry sounded desperate.

Lucy leaped down the bank, her shoes filling with sand. Then she recognized the struggling boy at the end of the sandbar. Victoria Johnson's third son, Jerel, stretched flat, legs sinking in the sand, water seeping up around him. The sand, bubbling strangely.

"Hold on, I'm coming," Lucy called. She hopped across some rocks to the sandbar, then circled northward, turned and raced out on the elongated edge where the boy was struggling.

Quicksand. "Oh, God, no, no."

The child's feet had sunken in so easily, besides, the spring-fed waters bubbling up from somewhere deep below, actually made the sand-water-boil-and-bubble cool. Very cool.

A stench rose from the brackish run-off waters, mixing with the bubbling spring water from below. Lucy was almost to the child. "Don't move," she called. "Jerel, stop struggling. Don't move."

Lucy knew that every twitch of muscle only embedded an arm, a foot, a leg, deeper into the quicksand. "I'm almost there."

Lucy kneeled and started crawling on her hands and knees on the gravel, skirt of her orange calico catching and bunching beneath her. Her dark eyes opened wide with dread.

Four feet more. Reaching out, Lucy was able to get a firm clasp of Jerel's left arm. "Hold on, Jerel, hold on. I've got your arm. Stop struggling while I pull you back."

Lucy heaved. She prayed and groaned. But, in her efforts she failed to notice how her own knees chilled in the seeping spring waters below, or how the boiling, softly shifting wet sands crept up her calico-clothed legs. Lucy let go of the boy's arm in order to keep her right elbow and shoulder from sinking. She knew that the thing to do in quicksand was to spread yourself, arms straight out from the body. But, as she struggled to flatten herself and reach again for the boy, she realized that it was nearly impossible. Reach out with an arm, go down on the opposite side.

"Lord God above," she mumbled. "Lord God, give me strength. Don't let this boy disappear right before my eyes."

"Help!" The boy got a glimpse of his helper, stretched out in her orange dress. "Help me, Lucy."

It didn't matter to him that this was 'that pushy full-blood Cherokee woman' who had allowed herself to be pushed to prominence in the church and that his mother definitely didn't like her and encouraged him never to play with 'dirty full-bloods', and, of course, that included Alonzo, though he was only half-blood.

Then Lucy Greenway remembered something. She had once observed a cow caught in the quicksand on the Ninescah when she and Andrew took a drive out on the prairie last spring.

Farmer Steckley and a crew of cowboys found a willow pole

and inserted it beneath her sinking body, allowing air to enter, breaking the vacuum.

Lucy spied a crooked willow stick left by a long ago current. By straining and tugging, she was able to back out of the sand-lolly that sought to entrap her, then rush to pick up the sturdy but crooked stick.

"Jerel, stop moving. Just hold still." She tried to comfort him. "I'm going to stick this pole under your legs and try to release them. I can reach you and I'll grab ahold of you."

But the concern mounted as she saw that the boy was now embedded completely up to his armpits and slowly sinking.

Though her own feet and legs disappeared to above her knees, she pried. No avail.

All at once Lucy's feet and knees sank deeper, deeper. Then fear rose to her throat as she realized the deathly threat of the shifting watery sands and their treacheries. Lucy Drake Greenway feared for her life. The boy, lighter, still maintained a survival position, though, now brackish water was seeping on top of the sand beneath his cheeks.

"Oh, Lord God," Lucy cried. "Somebody help us."

Her life flashed before her. Towering chestnuts and a little girl and her smiling Indian mother on the Coosa. The stinking, crowded conditions of the concentration camp by the river. The packed keelboats and the treacheries of the river at the whirlpool on the Tennessee.

She saw an old black woman named Black Bee smiling at her. A woman whose mixture of faith in the Christian God and in witchcraft propelled her up threatening rivers.

"Old Long Man you Cherokees talk about, going to get you," she smiled and her thick throat rumbled.

Lucy saw the face of her half-brother, Jacob Bates, smiling at her, handing her a poem, 'The Rose of Cherokee'. Chief Ross smiled at her. Principal Chief Ross extending his arm toward the piano bench and the nine-foot grand.

She heard the singing from Park Hill churches and Reverend

Worcester reading the Bible, turning his turbaned head to smile and nod.

A man named, what was his name? Why, it is my dear, dear father, Benjamin. Look at his loving face. Such light in his eyes. He looks for mother and Aunt Rachel and Grandmother Drake. He smiles and beckons me.

Lucy's mother, Abby's, face rose before her, on her deathbed, smiling, praying for her little girl of the Trail of Tears.

A steamboat with a strange name, *Velocipede*, chugging up the Arkansas, loomed before her eyes. A beggarly pack of starving wanderers on foot, seeking a homeland, came into focus. She heard the wailing of The People of the Trail of Tears.

A smiling young soldier named Andrew Greenway looked down upon her childish face, teetering before him alongside a boy named Todd. He handed her a blanket and some corn.

Long Man. *Long Man*. It is *Long Man of the People who has the last say*. Lucy knew Long Man contended with her, now, sucking at her feet, encasing her legs in the slow moving, sinking sand. Long Man, mocking and laughing at her.

The female seminary loomed into focus, and the girls—Eliza's face reflecting friendship and love. Victoria Roger's tightly-drawn face.

Warmth flooded her soul as a man named Andrew held her in his arms. Then he fell. Sickness. Dread. Long Man again reaching for her, for Andrew.

Lucy Drake Greenway knew she was in battle for the life of Victoria's little boy, and in the same battle for her own.

Suddenly, a part of her spirit broke loose. She could hear herself singing that hymn.

O have you not heard of that beautiful stream
That flows through our Father's land.
Its waters gleam bright in the heavenly light,
And ripple o'er golden sand.
O seek that beautiful stream . . . .

Oh yes. They all were singing the hymn. Mother Abby, Ben-

jamin, Aunt Rachel, Grandmother Priscilla, Chief Ross, Eliza . . .
could it be that the Above Beings were there, behind them, in that
light?

And Lucy knew she was singing of the beautiful stream with
them all, as suddenly, her body shifted to the left and the swirling
sand gurgled at her armpits. The child ahead of her with the terrified, glazed eyes, inhaled as the first lapping of sand and water
entered his mouth.

CHAPTER
FIFTY-ONE

Upriver by Rowdy Joe's Saloon, Ida Mae Roost, known at the saloon as "Miss Tinsel," stepped out on the boardwalk to hightail it over the bridge to get the mail for herself and Vina Napp.

She had combed her reddish hair in an upswept roll to keep her neck cool. Her green street dress, once her best, given to her by drover Colonel Likens on his way to Abilene, flopped around her shapely legs in the breeze.

What is that hollering all about? Her eyes flashed toward the river bank.

She thought of her job at Rowdy Joe's, of her recent drop-in to the meetings Reverend Boggs held in The Eagle Building. She thought of the kindness of that Indian woman, Lucy Greenway, who had asked her to come up on her shady porch two months ago for a cup of tea and had invited her back to services, though she had not gone back.

"I believe I'm gonna' start looking for me another job. Wait on tables? Plenty of restaurants. Probably, none of those high-falutin' ladies in those big houses would hire me." Ida Mae mumbled to herself, as lonely people often do.

"Oh, my God. Doesn't anybody hear us?" The desperate cry rose over the riverbank, punctuated by three crows, sweeping past Ida Mae, cawing raucously.

Startled out of her reveries, Ida Mae leaped up the sand dune to the river's edge. She froze at the sight a 100-feet before her. Two people, a woman and a small boy, the boy almost completely un-der the water and sand, and an Indian woman, wallowing around, obviously trying to save the boy and now herself. Doomed. They looked doomed.

"Hold on. I'm coming."

Ida Mae spied a four-foot-long wide board, caught in an old drift.

The sand gave way beneath her feet as she descended. She rolled, still clutching the board, landing on rough gravel at the bottom in a half-foot of water.

"I'm almost there. I'm almost there. Stop struggling.

Quicksand. Quicksand. Oh, my God." Ida Mae's heart froze in fear. Lucy saw Ida Mae racing toward her, her heart leaping in encouragement. "Ida Mae, I've got a hold on the boy's arm. If I go down, I'll go down holding up this boy. Try to save him first."

Ida Mae plopped her board on the sand bar, the front end sinking three inches into the sand and boiling water.

"Oh, it's Mrs. Lucy Greenway. Why, Mrs. Greenway, you just stop moving, now. Old Ida Mae's gonna' get you both out. I got a calf out of the quicksand once out on the Willow-Wallow."

Ida Mae struggled and stretched trying to reach the boy first, but Lucy was there ahead of her and the boy in front of Lucy.

"I'm going under. Help." The boy, now crazed with terror, turned to flash a glazed look at Lucy.

With a desperate lurch, arms, legs, torso, heaving herself as much as possible, Lucy managed to get her arm around the boy's neck, and lift his chin.

"I've got you, Jerel. We're going to get you out. You'll see."

But Lucy didn't believe her own words.

* * *

Since it was noon hour, Phenias Johnson pulled down the shades in the bank as Mr. Woodman locked the front door. He decided to take a stroll over to the Empire House, sit at a white-cloth-covered table for an opulent lunch of quail or smoked bass.

What is that sound coming from over the river bank?

Phenias turned his head. Stopped to listen. He shifted his feet, shod in fine polished shoes, around a pile of dog dung, his pearl-grey morning coattail flapping in the wind. Not another bunch of Rowdy Joe's girls racing to the river, is it? Disgusting. He strolled on down the board sidewalk passing three Osage young blades, bare torsos shining in the sunlight.

Again, the piercing sounds. A fight?

Phenias decided to stroll over to the riverbank and see for himself.

Then he saw. "God above." Phenias prayed. "I can't believe what I'm seeing. Jerel? In spite of what I said to him about going into the river? Jerel. Oh, my God."

Phenias stumbled, fell and rolled down the sandy bank, landing in the water muddied by Ida Mae, moments before.

Repulsion rushed from his belly to his throat when he saw one of Rowdy Joe's women trying to shove a rude board under the boy. But, was it Jerel? The sand and mud-covered boy no longer made any sounds, his head fell back, eyes glazed in exhaustion, no longer able to move a muscle.

And, who was that dark-skinned woman floundering ahead of Ida Mae? Lucy Greenway? Could it be? Wallowing like that?

Then Phenias emerged from his shock. "That's right, ladies . . . " Dear God, I just called them ladies, prostitute Ida Mae and full-blood Lucy Greenway, who'd allowed herself to be pushed to prominence a few Sundays ago, "ladies?"

"That's right. Try to lie flat and shove the board under him." Phenias crawled out on the sand bar, his grey-and-black-striped pant knees sinking in the muck. Hair on his neck rose as he realized he was placing his own life in jeopardy.

"Stay back, Mr. Johnson. Stay back. Ida Mae and I have it under control."

At last they heard a sucking and release of air. Lucy had poked the willow pole under Jerel again, while Ida Mae on her board, lifted the boy. He moved a half-foot upwards, head now out of the quicksand and water. "Merciful God." Lucy breathed.

By the time, Constable Wyatt Earp slid down the riverbank, getting the back of his pants full of sand, Ida Mae had the unconscious boy, grasping him under his armpits, laying him on her board. But Ida Mae herself was sinking up to her hips.

"You can get me out later. Later. Take the boy." She screamed to anybody, Lucy, Phenias, Constable Earp. Anybody.

"Oh, God, look at Mrs. Greenway, she's about to go under," screamed Ida Mae. "Grab her."

Phenias, his own body, now six inches down in the quicksand and water, reached out. His hand searched for Lucy's left arm.

"I've got you, Mrs. Greenway. Stop struggling."

Custer Terpinstep, who worked in the brewery, and Oliver Snow, descended the riverbank and loped out on the sand bar.

And the men, Wyatt Earp, Custer, Oliver and Phenias Johnson all flailed and panted. At last, they dragged Ida Mae Roost back and up, out of the sand and water grave.

Wyatt Earp shoved the men aside. "I've got ahold of Mrs. Greenway. This is Mrs. Greenway, ain't it?" It was hard to tell, as Lucy was completely covered, face, arms, dress, entire body with the silt and sand and river muck.

And the two, along with the little boy who awoke and began crying when he saw his father, lay prostrate on the gravel bar. They had saved the boy. And, they saved each other. Well, toward the last, they did have the help of the men. And the help of God.

Lucy coughed, fell forward in exhaustion and vomited, sand and water she had swallowed gushing out.

"Old Long Man didn't get me." Lucy teetered, falling back to the gravel. Ordeal over, Lucy Greenway was assured with an unfathomable knowing that there was another stream. She had touched it, felt it flow over her soul. The beautiful stream.

Chills shook and convulsed Lucy's wet, thin body.

CHAPTER
FIFTY-TWO

How is it that I'm here striding along with Father on this strange road? The last I thought about it, weren't we, Mother and I, on the *Maybelle,* chugging along up the Tennessee? Packed like cord wood, but, all of us knowing that Unelanohe, Maker of All Things, had never left us.

What did it matter, on the Tennessee, or ambling through Kentucky with Father? Crowds of The People were here, too. Marching, swaying, singing . . .what were they singing?

Lucy's father, Benjamin, smiled down at her as she strode briskly along in her white doeskin dress. How soft, against her skin. How warm his hand. And his smiling face, still young, burnished at the high cheek bones. Delicate bones beneath the skin. Yes. Cherokee people were beautiful. Lucy smiled because she knew he loved her.

"Father, I know Mother is waiting for us up ahead. Just beyond the clump of willow, between the cattails in the ditch and the willows. You'll see . . ."

* * *

Lucy's feverish mind traversed the course, the trail of The People, where over 4,000 died along the way. She did not understand it, skipping along with her father, when, just minutes before, she had sat plastered against the rail on the keelboat, smoke from the steamboat ahead billowing over them.

But, who knew the ways of Unelanohe? Who knew the mysteries of the Three Beings, who perpetually communed in love?

* * *

"She's in a feverish sleep," whispered Doctor Allen, reaching out to feel Lucy's pulse, her flesh, hot, burning, his nurse, Alice Hodge, standing by his side.

Andrew didn't want to break out sobbing in front of the doctor and in front of Alonzo, who stood in the doorway, his silky hair, parted on the side, combed immaculately. "She will awaken, won't she? Lucy will wake up again? asked Andrew"

"If she awakens, we must not exhaust her with too much talking. A little. That's all. I must insist. I'll leave Nurse Hodge here to attend her until . . ."

Doctor Allen did not finish the sentence. But, already Andrew knew, and he believed Alonzo knew too. It was in the doctor's eyes.

"You know, Andrew, she's full-blood Cherokee. These full-bloods don't handle pneumonia well at all. No resistance. The exhaustion from rescuing that lad, and the cold spring waters. She was in the water too long."

Andrew hated that newspaper, the *Vidette*. He was glad Lucy'd not seen it, too sick. He couldn't disturb her with it.

Lucy Greenway, a full-blood Cherokee and wife of trader Andrew Greenway of this city, distinguished herself by her bold rescue of Mr. and Mrs. Phenias Johnson's son, Jerel, last Wednesday. While playing in the river, the boy became bogged in quicksand, eventually sinking in up to his mouth.

Mrs. Greenway, hearing his cries, quite heroically rushed to his rescue. We do report, also, that she was aided by one of Wichita's soiled doves, Ida Mae Roost, who lives above Rowdy Joe's Saloon in Delano . . .

It has been mentioned to this reporter that Mrs. Greenway has come down, since the rescue, with a fever . . .

Andrew knew Lucy would have heartache over those words, "soiled dove".

"Andrew, I wouldn't have made it without the help of Ida Mae. God sent her at the right time. How is she?" Lucy's words still rang in his ears.

Yes. How was Ida Mae? Does anyone care? Lucy is right. People shouldn't write such ugly things.

Andrew recognized that women like Ida Mae were paid by some of the well-dressed businessmen and bankers of Wichita. And, Lucy mentioned several times, "Remember, Andrew? Ida Mae slipped into the meeting above the Eagle Block building when Reverend Boggs first held meetings. I believe her heart is good. She is searching. You'll see."

* * *

Reverend Wilburforce Boggs, his shock of wild hair raked down in back, black-suited, black tie slightly askew, made his fifth visit next day.

"There is no hope, is there, Andrew?" He reached out with his oversized hand, clasping Andrew's.

Andrew, too choked to reply, turned his burning eyes and sorrowing face toward him. His silence was his answer. He tightened his grip around Alonzo's waist, the child, he knew, absorbing the grief in his own pain-filled breast.

"Is Mother going to die?" Alonzo was bold, looking the preacher straight in the eyes.

"Doctor Allen says she has a few hours, my son. A few hours. Alonzo, Andrew, would you like us to kneel while we pray?"

"Yes," whispered Andrew. "But before we do, Reverend Boggs, I want to show you something. It fell out of Lucy's Bible. I want you to read it."

Andrew handed a small yellowed paper, edges torn, to the minister.

Reverend Wilburforce adjusted the small paper, focusing his eyes. "For the unbelieving husband is sanctified by the wife, and the unbelieving wife is sanctified by the husband . . ."

"Yes." Reverend Boggs cleared his throat, his hand trembling.

"It tells you how much she loved me," said Andrew, tears coursing down his tanned cheeks. "Everyone who knew Lucy, knew she was a godly woman. She never pushed me, or argued with me about my faith. It was as if she had an abiding faith that I, some-day . . ." Andrew sobbed.

"Yes, my friend, Andrew. Yes. A great love, from a great heart . . ." Reverend Bogg's face glistened with his own tears. "It's in your heart, Andrew, your faith. When this passes, this hour, you must come and we will talk about your baptism."

They knelt, Andrew, arm around Alonzo, before the opulent Duncan Phyfe sofa with the lyre ends. The lace curtains across from the sofa drifted out like angel's wings, the bouquet of white mock-orange in the opalescent vase on the stand blessed the air with heavy incense. They prayed.

*   *   *

By three o'clock that afternoon, Doctor Allen realized it was time for him to take complete charge, for the family was too grief-stricken. He cleared his throat, stepped forward and placed his arm around Andrew, who stood tall, draped in his best pearl-grey frock coat, white collar around his fine neck, pearl-grey immacu-late cravat, as Doctor Allen began to lead them through such an hour.

Andrew already felt the mantle of such hour falling over his spirit as if something holy enshrouded him.

"Alonzo, my son, we must listen carefully to Doctor Allen and nurse Hodge."

The spacious living room below was crowded by now. Ramona Rodriguez, in her best black voile, ushered them in, seating them with a sweep of her hand. She did not have to caution silence.

Victoria Rogers Johnson and Phenias sat at the left end of the sofa alongside Agnes Mead and Catherine Greiffenstein, both of whom wore expensive dresses of simple cut, glitter of jewels absent for the occasion.

Victoria Johnson's face was puffy from pain and weeping. The Peck sisters, who had brought a huge split-hickory basket of sand-wiches and canned foods from their garden, sat draped in their

best summer chambray, faces set in the pious reflections appropriate for the hour of death.

Eliza Bushyhead had arrived the day before on the train. She
sat erect in a dress of violet summer muslin with a worked collar,
her troublesome hair in a modest upswept coil anchored by combs,
tears in her eyes. Her soul, reflected on her face.

The handsome full blood, attorney Jacob Bates, sat beside Eliza.
He lowered his head as if he were thinking of some old poem.
Jacob, clothed in an expensive blue frock coat suit, crossed one
long leg over another, polished black boots gleaming beneath his
tube trousers.

Andrew could faintly hear the words he kept whispering: "Why
did I wait so long to come to see Lucy?"

The cherry grandfather clock struck four, just as Doctor Allen
came to the top of the oak stairs. "Mr. Greenway, yes, bring the
boy, Alonzo . . ."

The words fell like night air, laden with midnight fog, onto
their souls. "You may come now. Only a few minutes. Moments,
really."

Father and son wept by the bedside of the sleeping woman,
two shiny coils of black hair slipping past the face with classic
features. Wiping his eyes with a white linen handkerchief, Andrew
took Lucy's hand in his.

"Lucy, my love . . ." his voice faltered. He reached for Alonzo's
hand. "My son . . .Cherokee. She loves you so. And, she loved her
people. I must take you back to visit her homeland. You're Cherokee, too, Alonzo."

Lucy opened her eyes, her face highlighted by the rosy color at
her cheekbones, due to the fever.

"Why, my darlings. Andrew. Alonzo," she whispered. She tried
to reach out to embrace and kiss them, but strength failed.

Leaning forward, they in turn kissed her as if they wanted to
pass to her an eternal love, but human hearts, Andrew knew, could
not rise to such task. Nevertheless, they gave her the love of son

and husband, the love of this earth, touched by the love from above.

Doctor Allen stood at the door as they came, one by one, up the stairs in the hour when a human soul enters the valley of the shadow, awaiting the journey beyond.

* * *

"Eliza, oh, Eliza," Lucy again opened her eyes in amazement.

At first, Eliza could not speak because of her weeping. Collecting herself, she bent over and kissed Lucy's burning cheek. "Lucy, Lucy, my old seminary pal. Lucy." She held the hot hand lovingly.

"You and I were children of The Trail, weren't we, Eliza? And, we survived. We survived. Eliza, do you hear the singing?"

"Oh, yes, Lucy. The singing. The Cherokee people have always been a singing people. Yes. I hear the singing." Eliza realized there would be no purpose in disagreeing with Lucy at this hour.

"It is about a stream, isn't it? Could it be the Coosa?" Lucy's eyes seemed to clear.

"Yes." Eliza felt her heart breaking. "Yes, it surely must be . . ." She could not finish. Before she could say more, Doctor Allen gently lifted her arm to usher her out of the room.

* * *

Last of all, Victoria.

Doctor Allen, who knew, as did the neighbors of the town, of Mrs. Johnson's steady animosity toward Lucy Greenway, folded his arms and looked at her with a stony face.

"No, Mrs. Johnson. I won't permit it."

"I beg you. I beg you." Victoria broke into uncontrollable weeping. "Oh, I have sinned against this woman. She is an angel of God. She was a seminary student with me in Tahlequah. We are—Cherokee together. You cannot let her die with this guilt on my heart."

Phenias stood to hold Victoria, otherwise she would have fallen.

"Let her go in, Doctor Allen. Let her have a moment."

Yielding to Andrew, Doctor Allen permitted it. "Not more

than one minute. Do you hear me, Mrs. Johnson, not more than one minute."

Nurse Hodge led Victoria into the wide room with the pink curtains and pink spread where Lucy lay, black coils framing her youthful-looking face as if she'd lain down for a short nap. She looked as if she were dreaming peacefully, perhaps of the Hiwassee, the Coosa, or the Illinois.

Lucy opened her eyes, taking a few seconds to focus. She tried to reach out with her hand, but her arm fell to her side.

"Why, Victoria Rogers. Why, dear Victoria. Come here." She smiled.

Victoria's face twisted as if her heart wrenched and shredded like a stick of cane poked into the sorghum mill. Hot tears flowed.

"Oh, Lucy, Lucy, forgive me, forgive me, forgive me . . ."

"Why, Victoria. Don't grieve so." Lucy moved her fingers, faintly pressing Victoria's hand. "I love you, and you are forgiven. How is Jerel? He is such a fine boy. You must raise him in the church. And, he and Alonzo must play . . ." but, her eyes closed as she drifted away in a deep sleep.

* * *

"That's all now. You all should go," said Doctor Allen, not recognizing his own fatigue, determined to fulfill the duties of the doctor at the deathbed.

But, there was a scraping, as hard heels hit the porch boards. A woman in black silk, tightly fitted at the neck, black hat on her red hair, netted veil over her face; a comely lady who stepped up to the door and gently rapped.

Andrew, face etched by suffering, looked through the window, recognizing Ida Mae, waiting.

Andrew opened the door. "Why, Miss Roost." The grieving friends and brother stood back against wall and furniture as the stranger walked in, head bowed. Doctor Allen, recognizing her, spoke boldly to the "soiled dove".

"I can't allow this. You must go." He stared at Ida Mae in his disbelief.

The woman surprised them all by going down on her knees, beseeching, gloved hands clasped, imploring.

"Let me only look upon her face once more. It was when we struggled together that I realized what unselfish love was like. Lucy placed the boy before herself. She would have even died trying to save him as well as me."

The sounds of the weeping woman would have turned hearts of stone.

"Please, a moment, please." Andrew's eyes pleaded.

And so, Ida Mae Roost was permitted to kneel before the dying Cherokee woman, the woman of The Trail of Tears.

Lucy, opening her eyes briefly, recognized Ida Mae, touched her hand and smiled.

CHAPTER
FIFTY-THREE

Andrew guided the smartly matched team as he drove toward Waco
Street for his appointment with Reverend Boggs at the First Presbyterian Church. Alonzo, in a new brown suit that perfectly
matched his eyes, leaned back on the leather seat beside him. Andrew glanced down at the boy and wondered: How can I guide
him through this grief?

Songs of the mockingbirds and cardinals drifted in the cool
breeze blowing over the river. Sweetness drifted from clover fields
westward, and lingered in the air. Road dust muffled the horses'
clopping feet as the buggy rolled by a stone wall, softened by
cascading honeysuckle.

* * *

Alonzo was caught in his own reverie, his grief assuaged as he remembered that now there were two stones on the grassy hillside,
eastward.

How the prairie grasses swept in fresh sweetness between the
pine trees there. Not so lonely, now, Mother and little Jeanette.
Could it be, as they lie side by side—like the Eternal Ones who
constantly visit with each other in loving voices as Mother de-
scribed it?

When Papa kissed Mother that last time, just what was that
river or stream she mentioned? He knew his mother loved and
often spoke of those rivers, the Coosa, the Hiwassee, the Tennessee, with an uplifted face and a far-off look in her eyes as if she were
hearing their rippling waters. Alonzo wished she would have had
strength to sing it for him one more time, that day. A song, he

sensed, even in his tender years, that had life-sustaining power, 'O have you not heard of that beautiful stream'?

* * *

Andrew Greenway, too, was thinking of the stream, remembering how Lucy always said, "It flows for everyone, Andrew, everyone."

Its waters so free are flowing for thee.

"Yes," Andrew whispered to himself, as he reached for Alonzo's warm hand. "Let's sing it, son, Mother's song."

And so they sang, father and son in the bright morning light; meadowlarks perched on a trumpet vine by the wayside, joined their rising voices.

Its waters gleam bright in the heavenly light, . . .

O seek that beautiful stream . . . .

Andrew's grief eased for a moment, as he remembered school-teacher Eliza Bushyhead's parting words after they buried Lucy, and covered her grave with the white daisies they all had gathered. She had been Lucy's life-long friend, hadn't she? "Alonzo, your mother's friend, Eliza, remember her words? 'I'm coming to Wichita, Andrew and Alonzo, coming to Wichita to start Lucy's school.'"

"Miss Eliza will be a fine teacher, won't she, Papa? Alonzo tipped back his black-ribboned hat and smiled up at his father's shaven jaw.

"Yes, Alonzo, a fine teacher. Your mother would approve. He slapped the reins, encouraging the horses across a wooden culvert.

"Why, son, I've gone ahead and ordered new schoolroom desks from Mr. Hayes. And, Alonzo, don't you think Mother's grand piano will fit perfectly in that big bay window in that upstairs classroom?"

"Yes, Papa, I think it will be perfect." Alonzo smiled.